Windswept

ANN MACELA

PRESS®

Medallion Press, Inc.
Printed in USA

<u>4 ANGELS</u>

Francie and Clay are two strong characters. The author brings them to life with her depiction of their growing relationship. Francie doesn't believe what Clay is telling her, and it becomes a fun-filled struggle for him to convince her. She is a great heroine—one this reader thoroughly enjoyed. She shows signs of stubbornness and vulnerability. Clay is a man who takes it for granted that his soul mate will fall into his arms. He is shocked by Francie's reaction, and at times, his responses to her are quite humorous. This couple was great together, and the chemistry was just right. Not only does the author give us a lead couple to love, the people surrounding them are winners too, from Daria to Tamara. They all add to the richness of the story. Run, don't walk to get your copy of DO YOU BELIEVE IN MAGIC? It is a fun and fast read—perfect for the beach or in your favorite spot for reading!

— *Susan T, Fallen Angel Reviews*

"DO YOU BELIEVE IN MAGIC? is a light romance, a good choice with which to while away an afternoon."

— *Lisa Baca, Romance Reviews Today*

DEDICATION:

To my late parents who always told me I
could do anything I set my heart and mind
to—and who said, "Of course, you're going
to Rice." I wish they were here to read
Windswept.

Published 2008 by Medallion Press, Inc.

The MEDALLION PRESS LOGO
is a registered tradmark of Medallion Press, Inc.

Printed in the United States of America
Typeset in Adobe Caslon Pro

10 9 8 7 6 5 4 3 2 1
First Edition

ACKNOWLEDGEMENTS:

First and foremost, I wish to thank Helen Mason, my friend since we were four years old, and her late mother, Frances Marrs D'Albergo, my "second" mother. When I told Helen my plan for *Windswept*, she suggested we visit St. Francisville, Louisiana, where her mother had visited many years ago, and research the plantations there. Helen also found Mary Maude's name. I could not have written the book without her astute observations.

Many thanks:

To the city and plantations of St. Francisville for preserving the past and to their docents and guides for answering all my many questions. They are the models for my fictional St. Gregoryville. And especially to Mary, my friend and a native of St. Francisville, who suggested the itinerary and gave me so much valuable information.

To the History Department of Rice University, where I discovered Southern history and learned how to write.

To my critique partners for their careful readings and wonderful suggestions. To the members of Windy City Romance Writers and RWAOnline for their help and support. And especially to JoAnn Ross and her Writers Group for their friendship and encouragement.

continued ►

To the RWA chapters who were kind enough to choose *Windswept* to reach the finals in their contests in the Single Title Contemporary category in 2004: San Diego Spring into Romance, Northwest Houston Lone Star Writing Competition, Northeast Indiana Opening Gambit, Mid-America Romance Authors (Kansas City) Fiction from the Heartland, and West Houston's Emily.

And especially to my husband Paul, for his love and support. I couldn't do any of this without him. Besides, he helps me with "research."

Windswept

ANN MACELA

Chapter ONE

The Journal of Mary Maude Davis Jamison
Windswept Plantation
St. Gregoryville, Louisiana
June 1, 1830
A warm summer day with no rain

My name is Mary Maude Davis Jamison and this is my journal, a present from my beloved husband, Edgar. He tells me it is customary for plantation masters and mistresses to keep written accounts of the events occurring on their property. I am looking forward to recording my life so our children and grandchildren will know of us and our perfect love.

I shall begin by describing myself and Edgar.

I am nineteen years old and have been married to Edgar John Jamison since April 1, 1830. I am slender, of medium height, with black hair and blue eyes. I have never considered myself to be pretty—never, that is, until Edgar taught me how to see myself through his eyes.

Edgar is a tall, handsome man, twenty-eight years of age with dark brown hair and hazel eyes. The blade of his nose has a small hook, but instead of detracting from his beauty, it only enhances his attractiveness—at least to me.

The first time I met him at a party in Mobile, I was struck by the elegance of his posture, the width of his shoulders, and most especially by his gentlemanly demeanor. He is already a man of substance and property, but there is a playful aspect to his nature I didn't expect as he was quite serious to begin with. He now laughs easily and often, even at my puny attempts at humor. I doubt I will ever meet a more pleasant and easy-to-get-along-with individual. Thank goodness he is not like those arrogant, overbearing men so prevalent in society.

As I have come to know Edgar, I have realized he is a truly kind man, solicitous of my well-being and my feelings, with never a harsh word. Neither does he have, as I have noticed in other men, the imperious attitude that assumes a woman has the intellectual capacity of a grain of rice and must be controlled by her "lord and master" in every endeavor.

We spend hours simply talking with each other, conversing at length on all sorts of subjects. He speaks very well and has plans for political service. He is not put off at all by my education—or by my opinions, even though Mama often told me gentlemen did not like ladies who talked about such manly matters as politics. Well, it is her and Papa's fault I have them since they educated Belle and me just as they did our brothers Rob and Harry.

At my parents' home in Mobile, Edgar courted me as if I were a princess, and he quickly drove thoughts of any other suitors completely from my mind. Our honeymoon to New Orleans was like being in heaven. I should probably not write such a thought in this journal, but my memories of the glories of the marriage bed and his introduction to it still make me deliriously giddy. I love him so much. I foresee many days of utter happiness stretching ahead of us into eternity. Growing old with this man will be such a pleasure.

———◆———

Present Day
Houston, Texas
Friday, May 4

"Tell me, Dr. Browning. Why should I hand over the Windswept papers to you?"

"Because, Mr. Jamison, I'm the best person for the job and because I had an agreement with your grandfather." Barrett Browning put all the confidence, sincerity, and honesty she had into her words and tone, but she couldn't help gazing warily at the man sitting behind the large ebony-and-teakwood desk across which papers, files, and pens marched in ordered precision. She wondered if he could see her tension.

E. Davis Jamison looked like a mid-thirties, taller, harder version of his grandfather—much harder. While Edgar Preston Jamison's soft greenish-brown eyes held a roguish glint, Davis's were hazel granite, and the glint was suspicious. While Edgar had the appearance of a benign elderly bald eagle with bushy white brows and silver hair, Davis personified the alert, vigilant bird in his prime, a black eagle if there was such a beast, with straight black brows, straight black mustache, and black hair combed—how else?—straight back. To complete the family, and avian, resemblance, Davis had inherited Edgar's slightly hooked nose—a direct bequest from Edgar John Jamison, family progenitor and Windswept's first master.

Davis did have the same soft, deep, Southern drawl of his grandfather, but the grandson had made his into a voice of command. Barrett simply understood that when the man spoke he did not need to raise his volume to be heard—or obeyed. Neither did he need his six-foot-plus height or his charcoal gray power suit to command. Authority radiated from him in waves.

She could handle the type. She was used to dealing with large, overbearing men—even those whose voice and glance sent little shivers up her back. Her reaction must come from the importance of the situation. Now, if he would only come to the decision she needed. He wasn't going to be easy to convince; she could tell from his posture and his hooded stare. He didn't appear to be actively hostile, but he wasn't going to let anybody put something over on him either.

She wasn't trying to do anything of the sort, of course, but, as she waited for Davis Jamison's reply, she couldn't help thinking, and not for the first time, how sorry she was Edgar had passed away in early April. The old man's lawyer had reported his death to her, per his deathbed instructions. She had gone to the funeral in Louisiana, but, not wanting to intrude on the family's grief, had not introduced herself there. After all, she'd met only a couple of Edgar's relatives in passing, and a funeral was not the time to be pushy. Instead she had waited until later in the month to ask Davis for an appointment to discuss the plantation papers.

The man had proved difficult to pin down. He seemed to be on the go a great deal, either traveling on business or over in Louisiana tending to the estate. She had persevered, however, and now here she sat, in a downtown office building in Houston on the first Friday morning in May, hoping to make the same agreement, a contract that could make or break her career, with another Jamison.

Davis had accepted her condolences and then sprung his question with no preliminary chit-chat. She could not read the thoughts in his half-closed eyes as he listened to her answer and studied her for a long moment. He leaned back in his big, black leather chair, tented his fingers under his mustache, and said in his soft, deep voice, "Tell me about this agreement."

Edgar had not told her much about this particular grandson, but she had researched him carefully after finding out Davis was the executor of the estate. His venture capital firm, Jamison Investments, was known for its integrity and trustworthiness, as well as its ability to make global deals without any information leaking to the press before the formal announcement. Jamison moved quickly, quietly, and successfully in financing new companies and bringing existing companies to rewarding partnerships. At the same time, he was reported to be a shrewd judge of projects and their proponents—and an expert negotiator. All right, appeal to his instincts and show him the profit.

"Your grandfather and I were collaborating on a history project using the records from your family home, Windswept Plantation," she explained. "I believe you and I can be of mutual assistance to one another if we finish the project. Had he mentioned it at all to you?"

Davis nodded affirmatively but said nothing.

"It's rare to find complete plantation records especially in an area occupied by the Federal Army during the Civil War, and even more so when the place is prone to hurricane and flood damage. Your grandfather said your family was blessed with a roof that stood up to storms and ancestors who stood up to Yankees and who couldn't even throw a newspaper clipping away." She couldn't help smiling at the remembrance.

Davis did not respond. His stare reminded her of the ones she received from students who did not want to volunteer an answer to a question. If he thought he could rattle her with such a tactic, he was mistaken.

"He wanted me to work with him to inventory the papers," she continued, "to look at them with an eye to their historical value, to see if enough data existed to put together a family or plantation history. In return, I could use the information I found to write academic articles about life at Windswept or other subjects that came to light from the research. We would discuss my writing a book or books, possibly the family history, after we had assessed the records. I was to spend this summer with him at Windswept to catalog the collection.

"My personal goal in this project is to produce scholarly, well-documented work. Any article would be in a professional journal or any book from a reputable academic publishing house. Your grandfather and I discussed our plans in a number of letters. These are copies of our correspondence and will give you a more complete idea of our plans." She rose to hand him a file folder, then resumed her seat.

Barrett forced herself to remain silent and wait while Davis looked at the letters. It was not the time to run off at the mouth as her brothers often accused her of doing. Besides, she wanted to see how he liked being on the receiving end of the silent treatment.

She used the opportunity to glance around for the first time since she walked into his office on an upper floor in the building. Up to now, she had concentrated her gaze on him and it was something of a relief to break eye contact. Except for the colorful abstract art on the walls, the office was what she had expected for the CEO of an investment firm: furniture made from rich woods; darker reds and blues in the upholstery and carpet; and a view to the north stretching so far, it seemed you could see all the way to Dallas. The place even smelled rich: a blend of leather and furniture polish and something else she couldn't quite pinpoint. But it caused her to shiver again. Resolutely clamping down on her reaction, she turned back to him and watched him read.

After reading the first three letters, he riffled through the remainder. Closing the folder, he leaned back and said in his low drawl, "My grandfather did mention the project to me before he died. Let me ask you a question about the papers themselves. What value do you think is in them?"

Ah, she was correct, he was interested in profit. The problem was, her definition of profit would not be the same as his. All she could do, however, was make her case.

"Value? Monetarily, I don't know." She shrugged. "Piecemeal, probably little unless Abraham Lincoln or Jefferson Davis or some other famous person wrote or signed a letter. I have no idea what the going rate among signature collectors would be. Some institutions may be willing to purchase the collection, but to receive the best price, you need to know the content before putting it on the market. To take a tax deduction for a donation of the papers, well, again, you need to know the content."

She stopped, but he asked no follow-up question.

He didn't look bored, thank goodness, so she continued . . . with her definition of profit. "Historically, the records are priceless. From what Mr. Jamison told and showed me, they are, for all practical purposes, complete from the time the first Jamison inherited the property to the present day. The pictures one hundred and seventy years of records could draw, the new light they could shed, the understandings they could lead to, in all branches of history—political, economic, social and cultural, local, and national—are incalculable."

"Aren't you being extremely optimistic?" Davis asked with a skeptical lift of one dark eyebrow.

Barrett shook her head. "No, sir, I don't believe I am. When I visited your grandfather over the past school year, and especially when I spent some of Christmas vacation with him, we started the work. I read part of Edgar John Jamison's journal from the eighteen thirties. That book alone holds numerous commentaries on political and economic events as well as recording the day-to-day plantation activities."

She had to smile with joy as she remembered reading some of the correspondence. "And the letters between his wife Mary Maude and her family were absolutely wonderful, full of long descriptive passages about everything from the children's schooling to slave activities to local gossip. I see no reason to think the remainder of the papers won't be just as rich. Or richer." The recollection of the wealth of information in just those few letters made her almost giddy, and she stopped talking so she didn't babble.

"What's in this for you?"

Well. His question brought her back to earth with a thump. She couldn't, wouldn't, tell him *all* of what was in it for her. How much did he already know, she wondered, and what exactly? What was he seeing when he looked at her? Damn, she was having trouble reading this man. She was beginning to feel like she was back in grad school, taking her oral comprehensive examination with profs who wouldn't indicate what they thought of her answers. She'd give him the expurgated version.

"First, the chance to write real history, to contribute to our understanding of how people, especially women, lived at the time, what they thought about, their hopes and fears, how they were affected by major events like wars, depressions, and minor things in everyday life." Barrett knew she sounded idealistic and more than a little pompous, but she was being truthful; she loved delving into the lives of real people.

"Second, quite frankly, promotion to associate professor and tenure. Research and publications are the path to success and a permanent appointment as defined in the academic world." She wasn't about to discuss what—or who—else was involved in her promotion, so she changed the subject under the guise of answering his question. "No money was changing hands here, Mr. Jamison. I wasn't paying your grandfather and he wasn't paying me. I look at this as pure research and part of my job as a historian."

"What's in it for me?"

She counted off her points on her fingers. "First, the opportunity to contribute to the historical record, to help us understand the past. Windswept and its inhabitants played an important role in Louisiana and Southern history in general. Its story should be told.

"Second, completing the inventory with a professional appraisal is also a way to find out what's in your family's records. I know who to call for help in the event we find some information of more than usual historical interest outside my field of expertise."

She realized she had gone into teacher mode, enumerating points just as if she were lecturing, but it was too late to stop now. "Third, I can help determine the appropriate place for the papers if you choose to donate them to an institution such as a library or archives. If you wish to sell them, then you will have the catalog records to secure the best price. No matter what you decide for a permanent disposition, I do recommend you place them where they'll be open to scholarly investigation."

She couldn't help grinning at her next point. "And fourth, if you're looking for adulation, there are numerous historians and archivists who would be happy and willing to grovel at your feet for access to the papers."

"Are you one of them?" He returned her grin with the smallest of smiles.

She drew herself up and looked him straight in those hard, appraising eyes. "No, sir. I don't grovel."

Davis just bet she didn't. He smiled to himself, but was careful not to let his amusement show. The determined tilt of her firm chin told him she wouldn't beg, but he would also wager she could wear you down with any number of cogent arguments until you agreed with her point of view. She'd tick them off with all her fingers and some of her toes to make him listen.

When he'd agreed to the meeting, he hadn't known exactly what to expect. During his last days, Granddaddy had told him about the bequest of the family records solely to him, and the will explicitly instructed him not to leave them with the house but to take immediate personal possession. When he'd tried to talk to the old man about the collection and his plans for it, however, Edgar had said only, "Protect the records. You'll understand later." Of the professor, he hadn't said much beyond, "She's the one for the job and she knows what to do. Talk to her." And he'd grinned when he'd said it—the same grin he used when about to trounce his grandsons at chess. Then he'd changed the subject and refused to discuss the matter further.

Davis remembered the professor as the woman he'd noticed at the cemetery during his grandfather's funeral. He'd wondered who she was, but she disappeared before he had the opportunity to introduce himself. She hadn't come by the house afterward.

Professor E.B. Browning. She'd shaken his hand with a firm grip when she introduced herself as Barrett Browning, and she'd looked him over with big, intelligent, dark blue eyes. He wondered if he met her standards.

Professor Browning met his, at least in physical appearance. Her features were regular, with a small nose and a slightly wide mouth to balance her large eyes. When she smiled and especially when she talked about her work, she seemed to glow from within. Her prim outfit, a conservative navy business suit with a knee-length skirt and a white silk blouse, contrasted wildly with her unruly dark brown hair. It was a veritable riot of generous curls, silken tangles calling to a man's hands. Five-four or five-five, if he measured correctly, probably twenty-eight to thirty years old. She had trim ankles and small feet. The rest of her was slim but not straight. In fact, she curved enticingly.

Her looks and intelligence, her response to his questions, and those eyes made him want to know her better. But he suppressed his interest behind a façade of polite inquiry.

He reminded himself she was here because of Windswept and those damn plantation records. Just one more problem, as if he didn't have enough to do, running his own business, making sure the estate was settled, and dealing with the family, both close and extended. He'd planned to contact her in the future, but she'd called and asked for an immediate appointment.

He had agreed to the meeting mainly to get some answers, especially to the question of his grandfather's motives for the bequest to him solely, but he couldn't bring himself to ask her about Edgar's purpose. To do so would place him in the disadvantageous position of her knowing he didn't have all the facts—a location he never inhabited in a negotiation.

And this discussion was definitely a negotiation. He realized he had gone into his usual stance when being introduced to a new project: Listen and watch. Give away nothing. Say as little as possible. People often let slip important details when they were trying to fill silences. In this particular instance, he occupied the high ground, however, since he was asking the questions.

Curious to see how she'd like the next one, he said, "Are you going to try to prove a thesis with this research? For example, the downtrodden nature of women's lives and how beset they were by men and the system? Or another feminist polemic?" He kept his tone bland, but he watched her reaction.

She returned a look revealing several of her thoughts at once: speculation about his reason for those particular questions, exasperation at them, and determination to convince him. Davis was correct about that chin of hers. She wanted the access Edgar had agreed to, but she wasn't going to beg. He thought he saw her clench and unclench her jaw before answering, but her voice was mild and reasonable.

"If you read the correspondence, you'll see your grandfather and I went over what I might find and how I would use it several times. We had a great deal of fun discussing in writing and in person what I would do and how I would do it." She paused and gave a little shrug. "I will miss our talks and his letters very much." Her sorrow at losing his grandfather showed through for a moment, then she returned to her point.

"My goal is to find out what happened on and to Windswept and its inhabitants and how they fit into their times. No more, no less. This is very basic, very personal history. Any interpretations or conclusions I come to will be from the material, as free from cant and bias and preconceived notions as I can make them."

She skewered him with a direct blue gaze. "Now, I can't prove otherwise to you until I do the work, except by referring you to my published articles, my peers and colleagues, and my major professors, but I must tell you, my conclusions will be my own. I will not be pushed into anyone else's thesis, including yours. I respect it's the history of your family, but I won't white-wash or embellish it." She raised her stubborn chin. "Mr. Jamison respected my professional integrity. I hope you will also. I'm passionate about my work but dispassionate in doing it."

And what else are you passionate about, Davis asked himself. He might like to have the answer to that question, and his body twitched in response. He ignored both his mental and physical reactions. "That's acceptable."

Her lips firmed for a second, then she looked at him rather anxiously. "May I ask where the records are now? I hope you didn't leave them unprotected at Windswept."

"As we speak, they are being delivered to my home here in Houston."

"Oh, good." Barrett almost slumped with relief.

For some reason, she felt immensely better knowing the papers were in Houston and not back in Louisiana. Certainly it was because coming down here from the Dallas-Ft. Worth area would be easier than the long drive to the plantation. Assuming, of course, he'd honor the deal.

Despite the vulnerability it revealed, she could think of nothing to do but be straightforward and hope for a similar response from him. She'd been answering his questions; it was time he answered some of hers. She leaned forward but kept her hands loose on the chair armrests hoping her nervousness wouldn't show. "May I ask if you have decided what to do with them? May I have the access your grandfather agreed to?"

He subjected her to another long look without words. She had to fight not to move, not to at least to clench her fists, not to elaborate on her question, especially not to think of how much of her life depended on his next words.

"Honestly, I don't know what I'm going to do with them," he answered finally. "Dealing with the various bequests has taken more time than I realized."

"Yes, I understand," Barrett said to fill time while her brain whirled. She was discouraged by his statement, but hoped she still had a chance. He hadn't answered her second question, so she tried again. "I know I don't have any right to ask this, but I'm under a time crunch. Would it be possible for you to come to a conclusion fairly soon? You can always make final disposition of them later. But in my case, the school year will be over in three weeks, and if I'm not going to be working on Windswept, I need to arrange other research projects. I'll be happy to work under any schedule you set up."

He nodded and murmured, "Let me review your correspondence and get back to you."

His words were a clear dismissal. She bit her tongue to keep from pleading and pulled a pen and her card from her purse. She quickly jotted phone numbers on the card and rose to hand it to him across the desk. "My office number is on the front. The first number on the back is my home in Grand Prairie. The second is where I'll be after five tonight and until noon on Sunday, if you have any questions." She tried to smile encouragingly and convey at the same time the underlying message to make up his mind *quickly*.

"Fine." He rose and came around the desk to shake her hand. "It was a pleasure meeting you, Dr. Browning. My grandfather told me you brought him a great deal of joy over the past year, and I'm grateful for that."

He smiled when he said it. With her hand in his,

Barrett looked up at his face and felt a tremor run up her arm and down her body as if a great seismic upheaval had just shaken her foundations. His stone covering had crumbled and another Davis Jamison shone through—a thoroughly charming, extremely attractive man. His eyes even softened and she could see gold flecks in them. He looked more like his grandfather than ever.

"Thank you," she managed to say through the lump suddenly forming in her throat, "it was a pleasure meeting you too. I will miss him."

"I will also." He ushered her out of his office and walked her to the reception area.

"Thank you for your time," she said.

"Thank you for your explanation of the situation," he answered.

She walked across the broad expanse of deep blue carpet and opened the outer door. She could feel his gaze on her, and she couldn't help turning back to him. Their eyes locked and she felt the impact in her bones. She froze for the barest second before she forced herself to blink and break the contact. She could not muster a smile or a word, only a nod, and she somehow made her feet take her out the door. As it closed behind her, she almost fled down the corridor.

Once in the fortunately empty elevator, Barrett

let herself release some of her tension by shaking her fists in the air. She satisfied her need to scream with a closed-mouth "Mmmmmmmgh!"

She felt like she'd just run from one end of campus to the other in the middle of a Texas summer heat wave, only to be bowled over by a blue norther roaring out of the Panhandle. What an imposing, intimidating, challenging man to deal with. A shiver ran down her back, and she shook herself. What a difficult, gorgeous, *hard* man.

He was a hell of a negotiator. Look at how he had asked all the questions, let her ramble on, and given her no real clue to his own opinion.

So, where did the visit leave her?

She'd blown it; her career was over.

Her one chance to plumb unbelievably rich historical sources, to make career strides swiftly, to get out from under the grasping, obnoxious fingers and vindictive nature of Horace Glover, and she'd slammed right into the impervious smooth marble of Davis Jamison. He wasn't going to honor his grandfather's agreement. He didn't give a flip about his family history, much less history in general.

He didn't have the time to think about the papers. What was there to think about? What time did he need to give to the project? All he had to do was turn her loose and go away. He wasn't his grandfather, who could supply hours of family tales, legends, and relationships. She and Edgar had already put a family tree together. She didn't need Davis for that kind of information. All she needed was access, but he didn't want to be bothered, either with the papers or her.

What was she, who always had planned out her life, every step of her career, going to do now? She had been relying too much on the plantation research project to even consider other possibilities. She needed to have at least one paper ready to submit to a professional journal by the end of the summer, and she didn't have a clue what to study if she didn't have Windswept.

She had to keep her goal in mind: an associate professorship with tenure, a permanent position at her university. Then she wouldn't have to worry about looking for another place, another college, and could concentrate on what she loved to do: teaching, research, and writing. But first, department promotion rules required she publish at least two more articles; the informal grapevine, however, claimed a book contract would clinch the deal. And she only had a couple of years to do it. Windswept could have given her all that and more. Assuming she could conquer department politics, especially those involving Full Professor Glover.

She had two tasks now. First, convince Davis

Jamison of the worth of and need for the inventory. She'd send him a persuasive, comprehensive letter delineating all the reasons why he should give her immediate access to the papers. She'd talk to some archivist friends for more reasons not to let old records deteriorate. Call on a couple of her former professors to bolster her arguments. Just knock his socks off with the need to settle it now. If he had so much to do, she could reduce his workload by handling the matter for him.

Second, come up with another research topic, another plan, just to be on the safe side.

"You can do it," she muttered to herself. "Let it percolate in your brain for a while. Think about it all the way back to Grand Prairie and you'll have ideas coming out of your head. And you have friends to be with tonight and a party tomorrow to get your mind off your troubles."

The doors opened. She threw her shoulders back, pulled her jacket straight and strode off the elevator, head high.

———◆◆◆———

Feeling a jolt of awareness to the soles of his boots from their brief locking of eyes, Davis watched the door close behind Barrett. He regretted for a moment she lived so far away. His first impression had been correct; he would have enjoyed her company on a personal basis.

And the reaction he'd seen in her eyes told him she was not immune to the attraction either.

She would certainly be a contrast to his usual companions, fashionable trust-fund society types or driven women in corporate careers. The former had never worked a day in their lives and read few books of any consequence—or few books, period. The latter read the *Wall Street Journal*, *Business Week*, and *Forbes*.

All of them were useful for socializing, for maintaining an appearance, even for some relaxation—all he wanted from any woman these days. Most of them were not interested in or capable of carrying on a complicated conversation about anything other than their main pursuits. The good professor, he was sure, could converse on a number of subjects and would probably talk his ear off in the process.

He shook his head. He didn't have the time to daydream about what wouldn't be. He had just returned from a trip, first to Washington, then to Louisiana. He had work to do.

Intent on plowing through the pile of accumulated papers, phone messages, and e-mail, Davis returned to his office, taking off his coat on the way. When he sat down, however, he picked up her file folder first and turned to the pages at the back where Barrett had included her curriculum vitae.

Her full name was Elizabeth Barrett Browning. No wonder she went by Barrett—probably had been teased all her life about having the name of the poet. He did not care for his own first name, but he was named after his grandfather, so what could he do except go by his middle one as she did?

She had done her undergraduate work at Rice University and received her masters and doctorate from the University of Virginia. Currently she was an assistant professor for women's studies at the University of Texas at Grand Prairie. He noted her degrees, honors, and publications. She certainly appeared to have the qualifications to work on the Windswept papers, but then Granddaddy wouldn't have picked her if she hadn't.

He sat back and rubbed his right forefinger along his mustache. Suppose he agreed to his grandfather's deal. She'd have to work in his home. He didn't like the idea of a stranger being there when he was absent, even with his household staff present. He liked even less sharing his space with said stranger. The house—to be exact, his office there—had become a welcome retreat, a place where he could think and plan without interruptions, without pressure, without . . . distractions.

If she came, she'd be a distraction, all right. A big one, both to his work efficiency and, to be honest, to his libido, if her parting look was any example.

What about the job she would be doing? Would he have the time to supervise her? Would he need to? Could he trust her to do the work alone? He didn't know. After all, Edgar would have been right there with her all the time. Could he trust her with his family history?

Could he trust her, period?

He'd trusted a woman before, and look what it got him—a kick in the face.

He also distinctly remembered the words of his grandfather during their last visit together. "You're the protector of the family now, Davis," the old man had stated. "I know you're not the oldest of the cousins, but you're the one with the most sense. The one I could always count on in a pinch. That's why I'm leaving our real heritage, the papers, to you. They tell our story. As for the rest of the family, some of them bear watching, and some need a helping hand from time to time."

The task of protecting the family was his true inheritance, he realized, and shook his head. It was not going to be easy. Some members of the extended group were fractious at best, bellicose at worst. Some required frequent attention, others were perfectly happy to maintain contact through annual Christmas cards. But making sure they were all safe was his job now, and not an unknown responsibility, thanks to his own father's early death. "All right, Granddaddy," he murmured to himself, "I'll do my best."

As for the Windswept papers . . . He looked at the work stacked on his desk, then at his crowded calendar. Pending deals demanded his immediate attention. He needed to go to Washington and New York soon. He really didn't have the time to bother with the family history at the moment. Or with the good professor. The papers would keep. They'd sat there for all those years; they could continue to sit. It wasn't like they were going anywhere.

He'd let her know his decision tomorrow; he owed her at least a quick resolution to the question. With a vague feeling he was missing some vital point, he put her card in the folder, closed it and added it to the stack to take home. Then he rolled up his sleeves, picked up the first set of files on his left and dug in.

Chapter
TWO

"Davis, I want to know what you did with the Windswept papers."

The harsh, angry voice coming from the doorway spun Davis around in his chair, and he half rose before he recognized his intruder. Lloyd Walker, his cousin.

"I'm sorry," his usually unflappable executive assistant said from behind Lloyd. "I couldn't stop him."

"It's all right, Peggy." He sighed and felt his mouth flatten. He'd managed to avoid Lloyd at the funeral and afterward, but he knew he couldn't do it forever. Something must be important to have brought him all the way from Louisiana.

Davis looked at his watch; he'd only managed to get in two hours of work. He hoped he could get rid of Lloyd quickly. "Come on in," he said.

He looked his cousin over as the man stopped in the doorway to glare, a tactic Lloyd had learned from his father. The stance and the expression were meant to be imposing or menacing, and Thomas Walker had the bulk to make them so, but Lloyd just could not carry it off. He came across more as a seething tea-kettle than a powerful steam engine.

He didn't look good for someone only two years older than Davis. Lloyd was beginning to put soft, pudgy weight on his medium-height frame; his hair was already thinning and showing a bit of gray in the brown; and his beady, light blue eyes stared out through metal-rimmed eyeglasses with smudges on them. His tan suit was rumpled and his tie hung loosely around his neck. He certainly didn't resemble the prosperous lawyer-and-businessman image he usually projected.

Davis had long thought Lloyd to be officious and self-righteous. He had tried to order Davis and the other kids around as if it were his right as the older cousin. Almost every time they were thrown together by family considerations, they fought—physically as boys, verbally as men.

He knew Lloyd resented his success in these bat-tles and in his business and especially in the favoritism Edgar showed toward him. Lloyd had considered him-self to be the appropriate executor of their grandfather's estate and foremost guardian of the Jamison fam-ily name, and hadn't been happy when he discovered Edgar had named Davis to the executor's post. In fact, Lloyd had stormed out of the house after the reading of

Edgar's will. Now here he was in Houston.

"What do you want, Lloyd?" Davis asked as he leaned back and threw his pen on top of the business plan he had been studying.

"I want to know what you're doing about the Windswept records, of course. I told Granddaddy they should remain in Louisiana and be properly cared for. I need to go through them." Lloyd stalked over to the desk but didn't sit, clearly attempting to loom over his cousin.

"Oh, sit down. You know you can't intimidate me," Davis ordered, disgusted by Lloyd's bullying tactics. And about those damn papers again. He was wasting more time on those old records than he had to spare. "Why in hell do you want to look at the papers?"

Lloyd sat down and glared across the desk. "Because *things* in those papers could hurt the family if they got out."

"Things? That's a precise definition, isn't it? Besides, what could there possibly be in the old collection to cause any harm now?"

"My mother told me so after she found out you were taking them away. She said Grandmama had told her the terrible tales and falsehoods in them would ruin the family's standing in the community if they became common knowledge."

Davis regarded his cousin sourly. He knew both Lloyd's mother—Cecilia, his own father's sister—and his late grandmother well. Both women were adamant about protecting the family's reputation and place in society against slights or slurs, real or imagined. Edgar himself hadn't given a damn what other people said or thought, and he'd put up with his wife's obsession by ignoring it. But Grandmama had passed on her predilections to her daughter and she to her son.

Davis could understand how Lloyd might have the wind up his ass from his mother's doomsayer prognostications. Lloyd was still getting a lot of mileage out of the family connections, living as he did in St. Gregoryville, the nearest town to the old plantation. His law practice and business interests served some of the most socially and politically conservative elite in the state, the type of people who asked, "Who's your family and what's their status?" first and centered their impressions, their business, and their social activities on the response. If you weren't from the "right people," you didn't stand a chance with them—unless, of course, you had something they wanted. And once they got it, they dropped you as quickly as possible.

"What 'terrible tales' specifically?" he asked. "What did Aunt Cecilia tell you? Did we have horse thieves or embezzlers or murderers in the family way back when? And if we did, so what? What possible harm could come to us now?"

"Mama wouldn't tell me."

"Wouldn't or couldn't? Does she have any real facts behind her statements?"

Lloyd hesitated. Davis could almost see the wheels turning as the man tried to decide what to tell him. Whatever his cousin said, it would not be the whole truth.

"She wouldn't tell me," Lloyd finally said. "She said it was too awful for her 'sensibilities' to even think about. Who knows? What if one of our ancestors stole something and their descendants sued? We could lose the property we have left. It's bad enough Grand-daddy left the plantation house and grounds and so much money for maintenance to the state. Hellfire, Davis, we could lose more if what's in those papers comes to light."

Lloyd was getting red in the face, a sure sign he was winding up for a blow-out of an argument. Davis shook his head and hoped the man wasn't too far gone to listen to reason. "I doubt it very much, and what do you mean, we 'lost' the house? The building is an al-batross to us, since none of us want to live there. Now, the state Parks Department will have a new gem for its collection, and the new tourist attraction will create jobs for the community.

"And you didn't come out of this empty-handed, either. Granddaddy left you some prime land. As for the papers, Edgar left them to me and me alone, to do with as I please. You do remember, don't you, his will was explicit in that regard?"

Lloyd grew sullen. "Why you? You never showed any interest in them before."

"Neither did you."

"I might have, but you know good and well Granddaddy wouldn't let anybody see them. After Grandmama died, he buried himself in those boxes. Unhealthy, living in the past that way. But we're in the present, and I still say a family member should be the one to go through those papers, and I'm the one."

"No, Lloyd, you're not. I've just been conferring about the papers with the history professor Edgar was working with. We need a competent professional to assess what we have, and then we need to make them available to scholars. Windswept is part of our country's history and it deserves to have its story told. It's what Granddaddy wanted." An idea began to form in Davis's mind as he realized what he'd just told his cousin. He needed to think it through, preferably without Lloyd's complaints.

"You been talking to the snippy young woman

Edgar was enamored with?" he snarled. "I met her. She didn't impress me at all. I don't think she has enough experience to take on such a task. Let me get someone from Louisiana State or Tulane."

"I'm going to take care of the records according to Granddaddy's wishes. Knowing you, you won't like whatever I do with them, but they're going to get the care and consideration they deserve, and if we find some 'awful' ancestral shenanigans, so be it. The family can take it."

"You're just like Granddaddy," Lloyd accused. His face growing redder, he rose and leaned over the desk. When he took a gulp of air, he looked distinctly like one of those fish who puff themselves up to frighten predators away. "Neither of you has ever given a damn about the family's reputation, but it means something to the rest of us, especially those of us still in Louisiana. I'm not going to let you broadcast family secrets all over creation. I'm going to stop you somehow and protect our family heritage myself."

"Lloyd," Davis said, dropping his voice into the lower register that usually warned Lloyd to shut up.

It didn't work this time, however, because the man was too far gone. "You listen here," his cousin said, waggling his finger at Davis, "I will get those papers."

Davis swallowed the angry words on the tip of his

tongue. Arguing did no good with Lloyd. It never had and never would. "We'll let you know what the professionals find. Now, get out of here. I have work to do." He rose and advanced toward the smaller man, ready to usher his cousin out of his office by whatever force necessary.

Lloyd must have recognized his intent because he retreated, still spouting threats about stopping Davis and gaining control of the papers.

When he was sure Lloyd had vacated his premises, Davis returned to his desk, but spun around in his chair to look out the window at the distant horizon. He pensively rubbed his right forefinger along his lip under the mustache.

Damn. He no longer had a choice. He had to settle this mess with the papers or Lloyd would make a pest of himself and soon the entire family would be in an uproar. While he sincerely doubted any nefarious, hitherto unknown, reputation-killing deeds lurked in the letters and journals, the only way he could convince Lloyd and Aunt Cecilia of it would be for someone to go through them.

And that person would not be his cousin—which meant he'd have to deal with Barrett Browning.

He inwardly chuckled as he remembered what he'd said to Lloyd about Windswept deserving to have its story told. She had made a better argument than he realized. She'd convinced him and he hadn't even known it until the words came out of his mouth.

He had only needed the little push of Lloyd's paranoia to make dealing with the papers seem like the most logical, indeed the only, course of action. But not unless he could allow her access and still monitor the situation. Make sure Lloyd stayed away while he himself was on hand to answer any of the professor's questions about the family. Be there to nip any problems in the bud. Guarantee the protection of the family, whatever she found.

He thought the idea through. The scheme should work, he decided, and he would accomplish three objectives: take care of the Windswept records the way Granddaddy wanted, get Lloyd out of his hair and, finally, get to know Barrett Browning better.

He chuckled again. Damn, if she didn't have him thinking in terms of lists, like she did. Smiling, he turned back to the business plan on the desk.

In the hallway outside the Jamison Investment offices, Lloyd fumed as he punched the elevator button. The trip had been a waste of time, and his own wife correctly predicting Davis's reaction did not make the results any easier to swallow. He had never been able to win an argument with Davis. His fists clenched in frustration.

Davis always asked the questions he didn't have the answers for. For example, the question of his mother having the facts to support her statement. Truth be told, he wasn't sure if she did, but he'd pretended he knew to appear on top of the situation.

If he had to guess, he'd say his mama didn't have direct proof. She was recalling old stories she had heard long ago from *her* grandmother, Grandmama's mother, Mary Elizabeth Jamison. Why she'd never mentioned the tales before now—hell, who knew? Somebody must have said something to her at the funeral to trigger the recollection. When Lloyd had talked to her after the movers showed up the day before yesterday to load the boxes of papers, she had been adamant, almost hysterical, about his obtaining the records and stopping the female historian from looking at them. He had tried to pry out more facts, but his mother liked being the keeper of secrets, and she would not give him details or name her sources.

Whatever the secrets might be, she had frightened him with her tales of impending doom. What a mess. His business investments were doing poorly, and he needed every one of his connections. A blow to his reputation and standing in the community would undermine his clients' confidence in him and could hurt him badly. He couldn't afford to take chances.

Edgar's leaving him little actual cash didn't help his outlook either. The bottom land was good, but nobody was buying at the moment, so he couldn't sell it quickly for an infusion of cash. He had almost reached the limit of his credit resources, and the bank wouldn't be in a hurry to loan him more. Especially once they took a look at his books. Damn Joe Blinford for dying and leaving all the accounts screwed up!

He certainly wasn't going to a member of the family for a loan. The only one with ready money was Davis, and Lloyd would be damned and cooking in hell before he asked that particular cousin for help. Davis would only make him grovel and then refuse him in the nasty way he had—or, worse, give it to him, putting him under his thumb forever.

As far as the bequest of the Windswept papers was concerned, he had talked to Edgar's lawyer, ancient Mr. Jules Beauregard, before he went to see Davis, and the old geezer had informed him in no uncertain terms that the will was unbreakable. If Lloyd wanted to try, it would cost him dearly. Taking the estate to court was out of the question.

After a day's thought and review of his financial

situation, he'd decided he couldn't risk hurtful news. He had to get his hands on those papers, no matter what. So he had tried bluster. He should have known better. The tactic had never worked on Davis. For sure not since his little shrimp of a cousin had grown taller and heavier and able to beat the crap out of him.

Hellfire and damnation. He had to do something. He stormed out of the elevator and headed for his car. It was a long drive back to Louisiana. He'd surely think of a solution to his problem by the time he got there.

Chapter

THREE

The Journal of Mary Maude Davis Jamison
Windswept Plantation, June 15, 1830
A warm summer day, rain this morning,
steamy this afternoon

Goodness, I meant to write sooner in my journal, but it has been all I can do to record the weather and significant occurrences. I must relate the tale of our plantation.

We are now living at Windswept, which Edgar inherited last year from James Wade, his mother's widowed and childless brother. The plantation of 1000 acres straddles the Wayward Bayou leading into the Mississippi River near St. Gregoryville, Louisiana. I am told the plantation gets its name from nearly being swept away by a tremendous storm.

James Wade immigrated here from Virginia in the late 1790s, having obtained a land grant for 400 acres from the Spanish, who owned the area at the time.

He brought his wife Emily, their four children and 50 Negroes—I can't imagine how difficult the journey must have been. He built the house and proceeded to work the land—some indigo at first, then cotton. By 1825, he had amassed another 600 acres and 50 more Negroes. Tragically, his wife and children did not live to celebrate his success. Emily and three of the children died from yellow fever and the last son perished in a carriage accident just five years ago. Wanting to keep the property within the family, James bequeathed the plantation and all his property to my Edgar.

Like many of the houses are in this area, the house is a raised wooden, two-story cottage, with a wide gallery stretching across the front and around its left side. James built the house and other buildings from cypress and blue poplar stands growing on the property. Surrounding buildings include the kitchen, laundry, milk house, smokehouse, and a commissary for storing food supplies.

After the first cash crops, James planted an avenue of oak trees along the road leading to the house. These are growing well, and within my lifetime, I believe, we will have a marvelous, leaf-shaded alley bringing visitors to our front door.

Visitors enter our house through a reception hall on its right side; a curving stair rises to a balcony and hall for access to the four upper-story dormered bed-rooms. Throughout the first floor, tall windows let in light and help to circulate the air.

Pocket doors lead from the hall into a large double parlor across the front of the house. These absolutely charming rooms are filled with graceful furniture and marble fireplaces. James and Emily were well known for their generous hospitality and entertained numerous dignitaries and notable persons here.

Another set of double doors from the front parlor brings you into the dining room, which can also be reached from the entrance hall. It overlooks the back garden and is within easy access of the kitchen.

When I first walked into the parlors and dining room, I could feel the love and comradeship James and Emily had known in their lives. The rooms welcome visitors and put them instantly at ease. Emily deco-rated them in warm colors and placed the furniture in comfortable arrangements that practically beg you to tarry a while and enjoy the company.

Emily, bless her soul, had exquisite taste when it came to the house, but she was not interested in flower gardens, and what few exist are in some disarray from James's neglect. The vegetable plots and orchards could also use some attention. Thanks to my mother's tutelage, I am an avid gardener and look forward to establishing my own mark on the grounds with new gardens and some greenhouses. I see no reason why we cannot enjoy the variety of fruits and vegetables available in the larger cities. How much better they will taste knowing we raised them ourselves!

But back to my description of the house. Behind the second parlor is the master bedroom with a massive mahogany bedstead and equally massive armoire. A one-story addition to the house, reached either from the bedroom or through a door from the side gallery, holds Edgar's small study.

My husband (Oh! How using that term still thrills me!) is already talking about adding on to the house, on the other side of the entry hall, most probably a larger bedroom for us and a music room. I would love to have a piano again.

I certainly could not ask for a better, more commodious, more welcoming house in which to begin our life together. The furniture is elegant, but comfortable, and the colors on the walls and in the draperies and upholstery are bright, but soothing. Indeed, it's so much more than many newlyweds have. There is ample room for, dare I hope, a family, and I look forward to growing old with Edgar in this house.

No, it's more than a house, it's a home. Our home. James and Emily left us a wonderful heritage. I only hope we will prove worthy of it.

———————◆◆◆———————

Present Day
Saturday, May 5

Late Saturday afternoon, Barrett drove her Honda along winding Memorial Drive. Posh neighborhoods lay to her right and left, she knew, but they were hidden by the thick woods and bushes, not to mention the high fences lining the road.

"Be cool, be cool. It will be good news or he wouldn't have called you," she said out loud in the hope she could calm herself down. "He wouldn't want to reject you in person. He's hard, but he's not cruel."

She hoped, she prayed. Maybe she'd jumped too fast to the conclusion of doom like her brothers always accused her of doing. What exactly had he said during their phone conversation?

Davis had called right at the end of the birthday party for the eight-year-old daughter of Barrett's best friend—since the seventh grade—with whom she was staying. She had extricated herself from the jumble of presents, wrapping paper, cake, and shrieking little girls and picked up the extension in another room.

"I have a proposition for you relating to the Windswept papers, Dr. Browning," he had stated, his deep drawling voice making her heart race. She'd practically leaped through the phone lines when he asked, "Would it be possible for you to come out to my house to talk about it?"

He'd told her he was on a tight schedule and to come right away, so she hadn't stopped to change from her jeans. When she turned off Memorial and onto residential streets and looked at the commodious houses around her, she hoped she hadn't made a mistake by not putting on more business-like clothing.

"Don't worry," she fussed at herself. "If he wants you, it doesn't matter what you're wearing." She paused, frowning.

"Whatever." She shook her head and felt the curls bounce. "The Windswept papers are what's important."

She glanced at her scribbled directions again and prepared to turn left. Within minutes, she pulled to a stop, and apprehension about her attire returned.

Davis Jamison lived in a contemporary, glass-and-steel, two-story house tucked in a piney cul-de-sac reached by a bridge over a small bayou. Encouraged by Houston's semi-tropical climate, tall pine and oak trees and dense ligustrum bushes completely cut it off visually from its neighbors. A rich, dark green carpet of

St. Augustine grass surrounded the house, and flower beds sported azalea bushes and clumps of gold and red day lilies. Crape myrtles lined the far edge of a parking area from which a driveway continued around the side of the house.

Barrett looked around when she climbed out of her car. She didn't feel at all like she was surrounded by a big city. She could hear mockingbirds chattering and smell the new-mown grass as she climbed the three wide steps leading under a glass-roofed overhang to the front door. She rang the bell.

An Hispanic gentleman in his late fifties or early sixties answered the door and she identified herself. "Please come in," he said and ushered her through a foyer into a large, sun-lit living room. "Please, have a seat, and I'll tell Mr. Jamison you're here."

Barrett thanked him and when he left, she turned in a complete circle to take in her surroundings. The interior of the house matched its exterior in contemporary starkness. The entry foyer was two stories high from its black granite floor to the top of its vaulted glass ceiling. A living room stretched away to the right of the front door and a dining room to the left, each two steps down from the foyer. Their ceilings were also high, just below the arc of the vault. The dining room was separated from the entry by what appeared to be a free-standing set of panels of intricately carved dark wood, but there was no barrier to the living room.

A wide staircase rose at the back of the foyer. A long balcony looked down on the entry and the dining room, and she could see the tops of doors, so rooms must open off the gallery. What few solid walls existed were a glossy white. The remaining ones were all shaded glass.

The living room in which she stood was probably larger than the entire lower floor of her condo. The long, charcoal gray leather sofa, black metal-and-leather Eames chairs, and white-marble-topped coffee table at the far end all had clean, uncluttered lines. Another grouping around a clear glass cube was made up of dark blue—what were those chairs with the curved chrome legs and curving seats and backs called?—Barcelona chairs, that was it.

Thick, pale gray rugs delineated the seating areas, and the glossy, dark reddish-wood flooring offered contrast to the furniture. Between the panes of glass at the far end of the room, an expanse of black marble rose to the ceiling. Above the fireplace at the marble's base hung a long abstract painting. Its bright swathes of red, purple, blue, and yellow brought splashes of color to the room, but the effect was more like an assault on her vision than a counterpoint to the green outside. A couple of abstract silver-and-bronze sculptures stood on pedestals next to the front glass wall.

Although the air conditioning was set to a comfortable temperature, she couldn't help but shiver. She sniffed and caught whiffs of both furniture polish and glass cleaner. Despite the sunshine, the colors in the painting, and the greenery outside, the room felt austere and somewhat bleak, as if nobody lived in it. No family pictures or little personal mementos cluttered the side or coffee tables, no flowers added gaiety, no cooking smells overrode the scent of furniture polish, no soft throw pillows blurred the sharp lines. Even the leather couch seemed to have an edge.

Maybe the main, or only, purpose of the room was to entertain. She could easily imagine a glittering crowd of the wealthy and famous gathered here. Not exactly her kind of people, but certainly the type Davis Jamison might invite—those with the money to invest in high finance deals. She vaguely remembered reading about his party-going-and-giving activities in her research. She wondered if he had decorated the room or had a designer do it. What did the décor say about the owner?

No, not a topic to think about at the moment.

Thanks to the glass walls, if she ignored the furniture, she could pretend she was outside. Through the glass on the side of the room opposite the front of the house, she saw a patio and pool between another wing of the building. More St. Augustine stretched from the far end of the pool to a low wall. On the other side of the wall the land appeared to drop away. She assumed Buffalo Bayou or one of its tributaries was at the bottom of the drop.

Feeling distinctly out of place in her jeans, she sat gingerly on the edge of one of the Barcelona chairs and gazed out at the pool. The patio was a welcome contrast to the interior. Nothing abstract or hard-edged out there. Riotous red, white, and blue petunias overflowed large terra cotta planters, and pink roses and yellow hibiscus bloomed next to the windows. A jaunty blue-and-green umbrella rose over patio furniture with deep cushions covered in the same colors. The cheery space seemed to be inviting her to stretch out on a lounge or take a dip in the sparkling blue water. She definitely preferred the exterior to the chilly interior.

She heard voices and rose to meet her host as he and the other man entered the room.

"Dr. Browning," Davis said, advancing, hand outstretched, a smile on his face. "I'm glad you could make it. Thank you for coming so promptly."

"Thank you for inviting me." Marveling again at the difference a smile made, she shook his hand and immediately felt a rush of heat. Heat that seemed to follow his eyes as he looked her up and down. Oh, why hadn't she taken the time to change clothes? She released his hand as quickly as possible.

"Shall I bring coffee or iced tea to your office, sir?" the Hispanic man said.

"Would you like something to drink, Dr. Browning?" Davis asked.

"No, thank you. I've had so much ice cream and cake I couldn't hold another thing." And she was probably on a severe sugar high. *Calm down. Don't make a fool of yourself. And don't babble.*

"Oh, that's right, you mentioned a birthday party when I called." He didn't take his eyes off her as he said, "Nothing for us, then, thank you, Gonzales."

Barrett refused to let herself fidget under his gaze. He appeared pleased to see her, but his eyes had a calculating look—and a glint she couldn't quite identify. She reminded herself he was known for making multi-layered plans and she needed to keep her wits about her. She knew negotiating tactics dictated she wait for him to bring up the subject of their meeting so she wouldn't be forced into the role of supplicant. Tired of his silence games, however, she decided to come right to the point. "Have you come to a decision about the Windswept collection, Mr. Jamison?"

"Possibly," he drawled, then flashed her another smile. He turned and headed for the foyer. "Come with me."

She shook her head to clear it from the effects his voice's velvet rumble and the Edgar-like roguish sparkle in his eyes, and followed him out. What was going on here? What was he up to? She felt a bit relieved when she took note of his khaki pants and navy knit shirt—and slim hips and broad shoulders. At least he was dressed casually and she didn't have to face the power suit on top of everything else.

They walked down the front hall, past the stairway on the left and a wall of more glass on the right, through another door and into another hall. Barrett realized they had essentially walked around the pool into the wing she had seen from the living room.

"I transact business from my home from time to time," Davis explained. "This part of the house consists of my office, an assistant's office, and a conference room. This is the conference room." He opened a door and turned on the light.

Barrett walked into a large room and stopped in her tracks. A long conference table split the room down the middle, but she barely noticed it because lined up on all the available wall space and even in front of the windows were boxes and trunks: cardboard, wooden, and metal, of varying sizes, piled five or six high and two or three deep. There had to be at least three hundred, probably more, containers in the room. In the far corner squatted two wooden barrels as well. The scent of old paper and dust permeated her lungs. It smelled wonderful.

"Are these what I think they are?" she gasped.

"The Windswept records? Yes, they are."

"Oh, my." She felt her excitement growing as she walked around the room, noting the years marked on the labels: 1833, 1897, 1943, 1880, 1859, 1920, and more. So much more. She ran her hands over an 1833 carton, then shoved them into her back pockets to keep from opening it just to have a glimpse of the contents. She didn't have permission yet.

Oh, please, let me have them, she pleaded silently to whatever higher entity might be listening. He wouldn't have asked you here if he wasn't going to give you access, she reassured herself. She turned back to find him studying her again with a penetrating gaze and a give-nothing-away expression. Damn, what was the man thinking?

Davis watched her roam, saw how she reached out to touch a box here and there before putting her hands behind her. He was glad he had told her to come immediately because she looked just fine in old worn jeans and a Rice University T-shirt. Good legs, longer than they had appeared in her suit. Nice butt. Excellent breasts, thrust forward as they were by her posture. Her unruly chocolate-brown curls still rioted—and still called for a man's taming hands.

His grandfather had enjoyed his friendship with this woman, he concluded after reading their correspondence file. Edgar showed more enthusiasm and energy in his letters to her than was evident in his family communications. Barrett was probably the reason the old man had lived longer than his doctors predicted. "This is someone you need to know better," he suddenly remembered Edgar telling him during those last days.

Davis intended to take his grandfather's advice. He did not question why his plan felt so right, but it was the same feeling he had when working on the best investments he had ever made. He didn't believe in intuition exactly, but had learned to trust himself and the hunch.

And under any circumstances, Lloyd wouldn't get his hands on the papers.

"Come into my office and let's discuss my proposition," he said. He suppressed his smile at the look on her face; if it were any indication of her feelings, he might have to drag her out of the room with wild horses. "It's okay. The records will still be here."

Barrett took a very deep breath. The nearness to her goal and the musty smell of old papers were making her almost lightheaded. She pulled her hands out of her pockets and clasped them in front of her. "Sorry. My fingers are itching. It's torture to be in the same room with them. And there's so much more here than I expected. I saw only about forty or fifty boxes at the plantation." She followed him out of the room. "Where were the rest?"

"I think you saw only the records from 1830 to about 1870. The remaining records were in three other rooms and the attic. This is the secretarial office," he said as they passed through an outer office with a desk and computer. A photocopier/laser printer/fax resided in the corner and a table and chairs stood next to the full-length windows overlooking the pool.

They walked through the door in the far wall and into Davis's office. "Please, take a seat." He gestured her to a chairs-and-sofa group on the right side of the room next to the windows.

She looked around as she moved to the sofa. The office was masculine in tone and furniture and, like its secretarial counterpart, also overlooked the pool. In contrast to the living room, someone definitely lived here. A couple of sports trophies, a number of family photographs, and the mixture of books and small items on the shelves lining the left wall between the offices proved it.

Against the wall opposite the windows was an entertainment center with television, radio, and sound system. Round and square pillows and a knitted afghan in vibrant blues, greens, and reds decorated the navy couch. On the paneled wall behind the desk hung a small abstract painting and a couple of diplomas. His mahogany desk, like the one in his downtown office, was neat, its furnishings and files marching in straight lines up the side and across the top of the glassy surface.

He sat on a chair across the coffee table from her and picked up a folder lying on the table. She recognized it as the file she had given him and mentally crossed her fingers. She still couldn't tell if he had decided in her favor.

"I read your correspondence. You and my grandfather clearly enjoyed the research and each other," Davis said and watched her curls bounce as she nodded in reply. He thumbed through the file and put it back on the table. "Then I came home and here were all those boxes. Like you, I hadn't realized there were so many. As I poked around in them, it struck me rather forcibly that I do not want to turn over family records to just anybody and certainly not without knowing what's in them first."

In fact, he'd been surprised—no, astounded—at the depth of emotion he'd felt reading letters written by his great-great-great grandfather in the first box he had opened. The correspondence and ledgers spoke of mundane business and family matters, but they had spoken directly to him as well. The writers had the daily problems of providing food, making a living, and dealing with their relations and dependents. They were concerned with larger issues of the economy and the government as well as small matters of gossip and the latest fashions.

Looking at the signatures, at the familiar family names, it had come home to him: these letter writers and ledger keepers were his ancestors. His very blood came from them. Without them, he wouldn't exist. He suddenly understood Edgar's desire to preserve the papers, the only remaining manifestations—indeed the embodiments—of the thoughts and lives of long-ago Jamisons. They would reveal his family to him in ways he might not yet comprehend, but he knew were important just the same. Oh, yes, he'd protect both the papers and his family.

Again, he experienced the enthusiasm, the rush of going into a good business deal. With the added plus of giving Lloyd a kick in the butt. But no need to tell the good professor any of it, especially not about Lloyd, so he went on with his explanation.

"I thought of what you said yesterday morning about being of mutual assistance to each other and concluded I agree with you. I propose the following: You spend the summer here with two tasks in mind. First, create a detailed inventory of the records. Organize them, when necessary, for easier comprehension or use. Second, at the end of the inventory, give me an evaluation of their contents and recommend the best repository for them. While you are doing this, you will be free to identify, copy, and begin your research on whatever records, journals, letters, you wish to use for your articles."

She'd never make a good negotiator, he decided as he watched her eyes widen and a smile start to form. She gave too much away.

"I find I share my grandfather's possessiveness about the records," he continued. "Like him, I don't want to let them out of my sight. Therefore, during the course of your inventory, you will stay here at the house, just as you planned to live at Windswept. There are several guest bedrooms upstairs."

He leaned forward to tick off the points on his fingers, consciously mimicking her previous actions. "Staying here offers you several benefits. By living with the records, you will have unlimited access whenever you want to work. You will also have minimal expenses, in addition to which I'll give you a grant of fifteen thousand dollars for your inventory and assessment."

She had frozen at the mention of the money, so he added, "If this were a matter of twenty boxes, or even the fifty you had originally seen, I wouldn't be making such a proposal. But getting through the mountain in the conference room is going to be real work, and I believe in paying for that.

"I'm traveling off and on these days and usually work out of my downtown office when I'm in town, so you would have few interruptions. Gonzales and his wife take care of the house, cooking and cleaning, and it would be no burden on them to do the same for you, no matter where I am. I'll be home in the evenings if you have any questions about your discoveries." And to keep an eye on you and what you find, he thought.

"That's my proposition. What do you say?" He sat back and waited for her answer.

Barrett was absolutely stunned. She could do nothing but sit and stare at him for a long minute.

"Dr. Browning? Barrett?"

His question broke the spell, but she couldn't sit still. She had to move or the excitement would burst her brain. She leaped off the sofa and paced in front of his desk. "Wait a minute. Let me get this straight."

She ran her fingers through her hair as she moved and felt the curls bounce. It was a wonder her hair wasn't sticking straight up from the shock of his proposal. Be professional, woman, she told herself, but, omigod, how his offer astounded her. She'd been hoping for partial access at best and would have been satisfied with only four hours a day. Well, not "satisfied," but accepting. She hadn't even considered where she might stay while compiling the inventory. To be actually *living* with the records, to be able to work on them whenever she wanted, for as long as she wanted, was her dream come true. She forced herself to collect her thoughts.

"You are offering me money to live here, in your house, catalog all the papers, use whatever records I want, my choice with no strings, for my research, and walk away from here with copies of any or all of it, and fifteen thousand dollars besides?" Hand to her chest, she stopped to take a deep breath. "I'm sorry, I seem to be babbling."

"Yes, you understand correctly." She heard a sly note in his softly drawled words. He had her and he knew it. "Is it acceptable?"

God, was it ever. Barrett stopped pacing as a thought struck her, and she voiced it before she analyzed it. "What's the downside?"

"I want *only you* to work on the records. I want one historian's view of the totality, not the piecemeal ideas of a clerk or grad student who's only been through a few of the boxes. If you think someone else can shed light on the meaning of a document or needs to appraise the worth of an item, fine, but only after you have studied it first. I particularly don't want a horde of people wandering around my house, even if they are historians."

"I have no quarrel with you about the idea," she said. "But what happens if I can't, simply physically can't, get through all those boxes by the time I have to report back to the university in the fall? I only have about two months free. As you pointed out, there's a whole mountain range of containers."

"Then you'll have to come back here on holidays and during the summers until you finish. If it takes another summer or longer, I'll renew the grant. I want a thorough appraisal, not a rush job."

She nodded. His request was reasonable and meant she wouldn't have to rush through the records. It would leave her time to write her articles also. The thought led to one of her most important concerns. "Just so there is no misunderstanding, our agreement includes my absolute independence about what I choose to write or publish—no censorship on your part. Whatever I write will be my version of history, not yours."

He considered her stipulation. "Agreed."

"You're sure? I've seen projects come apart because a family member or someone with a vested interest wanted their slant on interpretation, not the historian's. For my part, I'll bring as unbiased a view as I can."

"You don't have to worry about the family," he said with a small smile that for some reason gave her a small sense of foreboding until his next words clarified the situation. "Edgar left the papers solely and expressly to me to do with as I wish. I'm sure you'll do a fine job."

Barrett gave a sigh of relief. She felt like she could trust him. After all, he was well known in the business community for keeping his word. She had no basis for worry. Edgar had never hinted at any controversy among family members in regard to the papers. She banished residual anxiety from her mind.

But then he added, "I would prefer discretion about the records' extent or availability. I don't want to be bombarded by institutions pounding on my door in the hopes I'll give the papers to them. I don't want other scholars camped on the front lawn hoping for a look. I don't want feature articles about romantic plantation life in the *Houston Chronicle* or anywhere else. I'm not doing this for the publicity."

"Your grandfather did not put such a restriction on my access, and I should mention I've already told my department chair and several colleagues about the papers and about my plans to study them all summer. I didn't describe them in detail, but I know my enthusiasm came through and the fact of their existence did generate a little 'buzz' in the department. I don't know if word has circulated through the grapevine or made it off my campus yet, but it may have. I also don't know whom Mr. Jamison may have told. Once I submit an article to a journal or give a paper at a conference, news will definitely be out. Is any of this a deal breaker?"

He didn't say anything for a moment, simply stared and ran a finger over his mustache. Despite his stone-faced taciturnity she knew her news was not welcome, but she wasn't sure what difference it would make if others knew about the collection. He probably simply didn't want to be bothered. He was a busy man, after all.

"No," he finally said. "I don't know who Edgar told either, although the existence of our family papers is common knowledge back in St. Gregoryville. We'll have to live with it. If any 'grovelers,' as you called them, show up, I'll just have to run them off." He spoke in a bland tone, but smiled with a predator's teeth.

It was time to get down to details, Barrett decided,

and asked, "Would I work in the conference room? I'll need access to e-mail and the Internet at some point if I have to communicate with anyone."

"It doesn't matter to me if you work there or in the outer office. The computer on the desk has the latest version of word-processing and spreadsheet programs with a broadband line for Internet access. You'll have access also to the company network and can save your inventory there for safety's sake."

"That would work." She was almost talking to herself as she started pacing again. "Bring my laptop too. Shut down the townhouse for the summer, forward my mail, drive down right after I hand in final grades, and I could be here by . . . May twenty-first." She looked at Davis. "When would you want me to start?"

"Whenever you like. May twenty-first would be fine. Let Peggy Murphy know when you'll be here and she'll obtain anything else you need. I believe you met my executive assistant?"

"Yes, I did." Barrett sat down and studied the man across the table. She would be living in the same house with him all summer. Just the two of them, if you didn't count the Gonzaleses. A prickle of apprehension raced up and down her backbone and she frowned.

"Problem?" he asked mildly, but his gaze was intent.

"No," Barrett answered hesitantly, then, more

firmly, "not at all." His concentrated attention made
her once more abruptly aware of him as a man, a
downright attractive man, a man in whose house she
would be living. What would the History Department think of the arrangement? Who cared? What
about her overprotective brothers? She was a big girl;
they could just butt out. Barrett dismissed her linger-
ing apprehension. She had a job to do. Where she
stayed was nobody's business. She'd be professional if
it killed her.

Besides, she didn't have time for a man. The last
few years, she had concentrated on her career plan with
all her energy, and with tenure almost in her grasp,
nothing would sidetrack her from her goal, especially
a man.

Furthermore, who was she kidding? Herself? She
had no proof the man in front of her was interested
or even might be interested in her as anything except
a historian. She was simply a means to an end—a
cataloguing of his collection. He had looked at her
intently, with the exact same expression on his face,
since she walked into his office yesterday. It was probably his method of dealing with everyone.

Davis Jamison was offering her the keys to the
tenure kingdom. She didn't have time for nonsense.
And if he turned out to be other than the businessman

and gentleman of his reputation, well, her three very large brothers would take care of him—if there was even a greasy smudge left after she was finished.

She couldn't think of any other problems. She could live with the restrictions and understood his desire to maintain his privacy. "I'm just trying to take it all in," she told him. She took a deep breath. No guts, no glory. "You have a deal, Mr. Jamison." She rose and held out her hand.

Davis rose and shook it, pleased she had agreed so readily and completely to his plan. "*We* have a deal, Dr. Browning," he replied, giving in to the urge to hold on to her small hand a little longer than the polite norm. "I'll put the paperwork into motion immediately so everything will be spelled out in writing before you start. Will that be satisfactory?"

She nodded energetically, and the curls bounced again. Davis thought she looked like a kid who spotted the Christmas tree with the presents and they were all for her. Well, not quite. The more he saw of her, the more intrigued he became. Maybe she was *his* present. It remained to be seen what she would be like when he unwrapped her.

Chapter
FOUR

On the following Wednesday, Barrett stopped in the department offices to check her mail box after giving a final to her "Women in the Nineteenth Century" class. She plopped the stack of exam booklets on the table and took out a number of envelopes. One was a fat overnight delivery from Jamison Investments. She had verbal approval from Davis through Peggy Murphy for the department to announce the grant. This must be the written confirmation and some of the formal grant documents. She was considering opening it when she felt a presence behind her.

She turned to look up into the square, bespectacled face of Horace Glover. The man had obviously been reading over her shoulder.

"Hello, Horace. How are you?" she said as nonchalantly as she could while she put the envelope under her exams and gathered the bundle in her arms.

"Splendid!" Horace boomed. "Heard you received a grant to study those plantation papers you mentioned earlier. Congratulations!"

Barrett cringed inwardly. Horace's manner of perpetually projecting his deep voice as though he were in front of an auditorium almost hurt her ears in an enclosed space like the mail room. What a contrast with the soft-spoken Mr. Jamison. Davis made you think your hearing was going while listening to Horace made you wish it were.

"Thank you," she answered and maneuvered around his well-kept body to the door. He must have come from the gym and his well-known regular squash game; the scent of his after-shave was too strong to be hours old. Horace took care of himself; she'd agree there. For a man in his early fifties, he looked trim and fit. Too bad his mind wasn't as clean as the rest of him.

"So, tell me," he said with an earnest expression and a more modulated tone of voice, "is the collection as extensive as you thought it was? If I remember correctly, I wrote about a member of the Jamison family in one of my books on the war in Virginia. You know, at present I'm concentrating on the war along the Mississippi, and I'm very interested in any correspondence or accounts of life along the river—military correspondence, or better yet, a diary. I'm available this summer if you need any help deciding what might be valuable." He lowered his voice to a conspiratorial whisper and continued, "Or if you need help with anything else. I could still be a big help to your career, you know."

"I'll keep it in mind," Barrett said, keeping her tone as noncommittal as possible. "Excuse me, Horace, I have an appointment and can't stay to talk." She walked out of the mail room and down the hall as quickly as she could without appearing to run, but she could feel his pale blue eyes boring into her back. She'd better head home. It would be just like Horace to trap her in her office to discuss the scope of the Windswept collection or his ". . . help with anything else."

Damn! She thought she'd discouraged him on that particular idea. As for Windswept, how did he know about the grant already? She could only guess Horace had seen a copy of the draft memo she and the department chairman had sent to Houston. Like one of the generals he studied, Horace seemed to have spies everywhere. He'd probably charmed it out of one of the student helpers in the office.

But, what did he mean, ". . . as extensive as you thought it was?" She knew she'd never told anyone how truly rich the papers were. Horace must have simply been "reconnoitering," as he would call it in his military history jargon, scouting out the territory, testing her to see if there were any journals or letters worth "liberating" from Windswept.

Over her dead body. Conniving jerk.

She entered her office and closed the door. She didn't even turn on the light, just crammed the envelopes into her briefcase and shoved the exams into the shopping bag she'd brought to hold them. After ever so quietly opening the door and peeking carefully up and down the hall—good, nobody there—she locked her office and walked quickly to the back stairs.

As she made her way out of the building, she considered the situation with Horace. Why couldn't the man have made some other conflict besides the American Civil War his specialty? There were lots of good wars to study—world wars, Napoleonic conflicts, Viet Nam—to name a few. Why did he switch this year from studying the war in the East to concentrate on the Mississippi campaigns, a decision putting both of them literally on the same ground?

Wait just a minute. When had he made the switch? When she joined the department three years ago, Horace had been a strictly Robert E. Lee-Stonewall Jackson-Ulysses S. Grant-William T. Sherman military historian, concentrating on the war in Virginia, Tennessee, and Georgia.

Then, last summer, after their little *contretemps* over the "anything else," he'd announced he was going to do some research in New Orleans. A couple of her colleagues had muttered suggestively about Horace finding "hot sources in the French Quarter." She'd thought no more about him. But Edgar Jamison had called her in September to come to Windswept, and only after she had returned, all bubbly with anticipation, had Horace started talking about changing his theater of war.

What did Horace know about Windswept? He'd never mentioned it specifically by name, and Edgar had never mentioned him. Maybe he knew nothing except what he'd picked up on the department grapevine, and he'd decided to get back at her for her refusal to accept his "help."

Or maybe she was so hyper she was jumping to conclusions, acting like a conspiracy theorist who saw plots behind every bookshelf. She thought she'd outgrown that character flaw.

Maybe his change of focus was merely a coincidence. He was looking for a new topic to study and expanded on his existing knowledge base. He hadn't produced a book in several years, come to think of it, and she didn't remember announcements of any recent articles. Maybe he was looking for a topic to revitalize his juices—his historical juices, that was. Or did his other juices need a certain pill?

Or maybe she was letting her dislike of him color

her judgment.

And, most of all, why was she worrying about the man? She had enough to think about without wasting time looking for answers to unimportant questions.

She crossed the parking lot, dumped her briefcase and bag in the back of her car and drove home, running mentally through her to-do list and hoping she could make it through the exam papers by tomorrow. The sooner she finished her tasks, the sooner she could be in Houston and dive into the Windswept records.

———◆———

By the fifteenth of May, Davis was beginning to feel like he was back in control of his life. His grandfather's estate was proceeding toward probate, the investors for his latest project were enthusiastically coming on board, and his accountants and lawyers had established the grant for Barrett Browning.

She'd be here soon, and he wondered what his house would be like with her in it. He still felt uneasy about her being there. He hadn't lived with a woman for a long time. He'd made up his mind he never would again. But he wouldn't be "living with" Barrett, and she wasn't a guest; she had her own work to do. He doubted he'd see her much. The thought caused him a pang of disappointment, but he ignored it to think of the bright side of his situation.

Lloyd had not bothered him further.

Best of all, he could leave for Washington and New York in two days, secure in the knowledge his associates and Peggy Murphy could handle whatever came up at home.

He came back from lunch with plans for a productive afternoon ahead—until he walked into Peggy's office. His middle-aged assistant was smiling like a school girl at the man who sprawled in the chair across the desk from her. Then Davis recognized the guy—his brother Bill. His too-good-looking-for-his-own-good younger brother who could charm the socks, and other pieces of clothing, off any woman alive. His profligate, irresponsible, unemployed, living-off-his-trust-fund brother.

Davis ground his teeth and shook his head. He had to get Bill out of his office quickly or see all his efficient plans shot to hell. "What are you doing here?" he asked.

Bill turned and rose, an earnest expression on his face. "I really need to talk to you, Davis," he said.

Davis grunted. He thought he had a pretty good idea what was coming. Bill looked like an eager puppy dog—which never boded well. Better to get it over with. "Come on in."

He led the way into his office. "What got you off the golf course?" he asked when they were seated.

"I have an opportunity I think will interest you. I met a man named Bob Hochstapler at the Cooper's cookout." Bill proceeded to show him a brochure and lay out a proposal for a company in which he wanted to invest. "All I need from you is authorization to use some of my trust fund, maybe get an advance on my next quarterly payment. I never understood why Dad set up the fund this way, but since you're the administrator, I need your blessing. What do you say?"

"You know why Dad made me administrator, Bill. First, you weren't old enough at the time, and second, he didn't think you were developing the proper business abilities."

"I was only fourteen, for crying out loud. I'm twenty-eight now."

"And the principal's not yours until you're thirty and you still haven't exhibited the slightest bit of business acumen. My role as administrator is to save you from hare-brained schemes like this one. No, you can't have the money. Hochstapler is as shifty as they come, and this company is a crock, which you would have found out if you had done some homework on it instead of listening to a siren song from a con man." Davis was disgusted, but he wasn't sure if his feelings were directed at Bill for falling for the scam or at himself for not stopping the tale the minute he heard Hochstapler's name.

"But, Davis, I know this is a good deal. Look at the names of the people who are already investing." He pulled a piece of paper from the brochure and held it out.

Davis glanced briefly at the list and handed it back. "No, Bill, it's not a good deal. The word's all over town about what a shyster Hochstapler is. His list is as phony as he is. Did you try to call any of those people? Or do some research on Hochstapler himself? Don't you ever learn?" Davis felt himself growing angry and put a damper on his emotions. Yelling at Bill never went anywhere; the words just slid off his brother's expensively clothed back.

In the vague hope of reaching Bill's tenuous common sense, he said instead, "Do you remember what happened the last time? How much money you lost? Remember what I said then? The only way you're going to have any cash to invest in these idiotic deals is to stop living so high and save some. I can't control the money you receive once you have it, but I won't give you a penny out of the trust principal or an advance on the next quarter. Now, get out of here. I have work to do." Davis turned to the papers on his desk and pointedly ignored his younger brother.

Bill sputtered for a few minutes, but Davis, without raising his head, simply pointed his finger at the door. Bill left, and Davis looked after him for a few seconds. Bill had been the baby of the family, eight years younger than himself, four years younger than their sister. Their mother had spoiled him rotten.

Their father hadn't, of course. The old man had done nothing except work himself to death, and he paid hardly any attention to any of his children, except when they didn't meet his expectations to make something of themselves. And especially when they showed any signs of "weakness," manifested in lower grades or failure to excel in extracurricular activities. Davis had not been surprised when his father's will put him in charge of Bill's trust fund. Dad had always complained about Bill's lack of drive, ambition, and seriousness.

The result of their upbringing was clearly seen in the three of them. He and his sister were successful business people. They had majored in business subjects and both had MBAs. Dad had died when Bill was fourteen, and Mother had let her youngest do whatever he wanted, despite Davis's arguments to the contrary. All Bill had from college was a useless liberal arts degree. Their mother claimed he had simply "not found himself yet."

Well, Davis hoped Bill made the discovery before

he reached thirty in two years when the trust fund principal would be turned over to him. Davis would give his brother hell if he squandered the large sum the way he did his quarterly allowance. He'd protect Bill, all right, right into a decent job and a more sober outlook on life.

Davis shook his head at both of them, Bill for his naiveté and refusal to use common sense and himself for letting Bill sidetrack him from his work. He picked up the phone and got back to business.

Chapter
FIVE

The Journal of Mary Maude Davis Jamison
October 21, 1830
A blustery day with, thank goodness,
a hint of autumn in the air after the
oppressive heat of the summer.

I never realized how much work was required of a plantation mistress, especially for an establishment as large and thriving as Windswept. My summer revolved around the gardens, and I am pleased to write that our vegetable harvest has been outstanding. We are preparing the soil for the winter crop, and Edgar has supervised the building of three brick pits with sloping windowed roofs to act as hot houses for out-of-season vegetables. Mother has sent me seeds for some of my favorites from Mobile and I bought more on our last trip to New Orleans. I can't wait to plant them. Our herb garden was extremely prolific and the kitchen and laundry have drying bundles of plants hanging from almost every inch of their ceilings.

I do wish some of our servants were as easy to train as the bean plants and squash vines. Annie, thank goodness, is a wonderful cook, knows her business and does it. But Bertha must be watched or we would never have a clean set of bedclothes to our name. And little Evelyn, who so begged to be allowed to help in the house, is downright lazy. I must speak to Edgar about putting her to work elsewhere.

Edgar. Every day I love him more deeply. He has been so busy after firing the overseer. The man, a holdover from his uncle, was cheating us! Unfortunately, the scoundrel ran off (some said to Texas) before E could summon the law. Good riddance! And good news today when E told me he had found a new overseer, one with excellent references. Now I may see more of my loving husband.

I hope so, as we have been married for over seven months and our family is not growing. E, the naughty man, said he was looking forward to "long winter nights" to do something about that very matter. Even though the subject was risqué, I couldn't help laughing with him. In fact, we laugh together a great deal. Living with this man is downright pleasant.

E and his plans notwithstanding, however, I said a special prayer at services in our St. Gregory Episcopal

Church last Sunday. To have a child of our own—
heaven!

Present Day
Monday, May 21

Dressed in jeans and an SMU T-shirt and with a car
stuffed to the brim, Barrett was on the road by seven
and reached Houston's outer beltway around eleven-
thirty. She thought she had made good time—until
she became embroiled in a massive traffic jam on In-
terstate 45 just above the North Loop. Finally, at one
in the afternoon, a warm and frazzled Barrett drove
across the bridge to the Jamison house.

The home and surrounding greenery looked like a
cool oasis after the traffic, heat, and grime of the freeways. She parked her car where she had on her previous
visit, climbed out and stretched. She couldn't help but
grin as she walked up the three low, wide steps. She
was actually here, the Windswept papers were inside,
and her future was hers to control.

Gonzales met her at the entrance. "We are so
happy to see you, Dr. Browning. Mr. Jamison is out
of town, as you know, so I am welcoming you in his

name. Please leave your things in the car and I will take them to your room."

"Thank you very much, Mr. Gonzales. I'm happy to be here also. The box in the car marked 'Office Supplies' should go in the office."

"Very good." He indicated the woman standing at his side. "This is my wife, Eva. Eva, why don't you take Dr. Browning to her room so she can freshen up? If you'll give me your car keys, *maestra*, I'll put the car in the garage when I'm done."

Barrett smiled at the term *maestra*, Spanish for teacher and a title of respect. She gave Gonzales the keys and turned to his wife. "It's nice to meet you, Mrs. Gonzales."

"And you, *maestra*. Please call me Eva. If you'll follow me . . ." Eva, a short, roly-poly, cheerful-looking woman, led the way up the stairs at the back of the entry and along the balcony over the dining room.

They went past an open door through which Barrett saw a bedroom. She followed Eva into the next and last room on the end of the house. The beautifully appointed guestroom with its own attached bath contained an alcove seating area with a comfortable-looking chair and a television set.

"Lunch is ready, *maestra*," Eva said after showing Barrett where the towels were. "I thought you might like a light, cold meal after your long trip, so I prepared a shrimp salad with lime and avocado. Perhaps with some iced tea?"

"Sounds wonderful," Barrett replied. "I'll be down in a few minutes."

"Come down to the dining room whenever you're ready. Oh, and please let me know if there is any type of food you don't eat or if there is anything special you would like me to prepare."

"I'm not picky. Whatever you and Mr. Gonzales are eating will be fine."

"I was planning on a chicken dish tonight."

"Chicken will be fine," she reassured Eva.

"*Muy bien*," the housekeeper said. "Just come to the dining room when you're ready."

Barrett stopped to study her surroundings. She was relieved to see the room did not continue the relentless hard starkness of the contemporary living room. The conventionally styled furniture and the earth-tone colors in the walls, carpet, and bedspread were more soothing to her eyes than the vivid colors below, but the space was not without its drawbacks. She blinked when she realized the bland chamber could have been a room in a high-class hotel. So far the only warmth she'd seen in the house had been in Davis's office or around the pool.

The coldness didn't matter, she told herself as she walked into the bathroom. She didn't need coziness; she had Windswept.

She washed up quickly and hurried downstairs. She was ravenous.

The screen dividing the dining room from the foyer had been folded to provide entry. A long, black-glass table ran down the middle of the room under a chandelier Barrett could only describe as a chrome-bar-and-light-bulb contraption. Against the back wall, a stretch of black marble mirrored its opposite in the living room, but where that one had a fireplace and a painting, this one held what looked to be an iridescent crystal sculpture hanging from the ceiling to the floor. It wasn't a solid piece of glass, but looked almost as if it had been woven, with space between the threads. It seemed to ripple like a cloth tapestry also.

Eva came in through a door under the balcony with a plate and a large glass of iced tea. Barrett sat down at the lone place setting and Eva put the food in front of her.

"There's plenty more salad, *maestra*. Please, enjoy your lunch."

"Thank you. It looks delicious."

Barrett took a bite and couldn't help humming at the taste. The tender shrimp, piquant lime, and smooth avocado offset each other delightfully, and the flour tortillas added the necessary baseline. She'd have to ask Eva for the recipe.

She looked around as she ate. The room was large and the table quite long. The space felt as cold as the living room across the way, and it was not from the air conditioning. She wished she had brought a book to read, as she always did when eating alone. Even the presence of taciturn Davis would be an improvement. There was nothing she could do about it at the moment, however, so she applied herself to the meal.

Right when she decided she couldn't eat another bite, Gonzales came into the room. "I have unloaded your car and parked it in the garage. Here are the keys and additional keys to the kitchen and the front doors." He handed her the sets and continued, "Please allow me to instruct you how the alarm system works. Eva and I reside in the apartment over the garage, and we always set the system when we leave the house, usually between seven and eight, and you will need to disarm and reset it if you go out or return later than that."

"Certainly," Barrett said and followed him to the front door.

After she could turn the system on and off to her and Gonzales's satisfaction, Barrett unpacked her clothes and toiletries, then picked up her laptop case, boombox, CD collection, and briefcase and went down to her new office. She felt the tug of the boxes as she went past the conference room door, but resisted. "Be strong," she ordered out loud. "Be disciplined. Settle in first so you'll be organized."

A closet held supplies like paper and staples, a stack of new, still flattened, acid-free storage boxes and several cartons of acid-free folders, as she had requested. She'd transfer the records to them as she went along. The small round table and chairs by the windows offered a comfortable alternative to sitting at the desk. The L-shaped desk was clean and empty, and the chair was ergonomic, thank goodness.

She peeked into Davis's office. Peggy Murphy had told her he would be on a trip when she arrived. The news brought both a twinge of regret and one of relief. Regret . . . what? She wouldn't have an audience to astound with her expertise? He wouldn't be around to remove the awkwardness of being in a stranger's house without his presence? She wasn't sure where the feeling came from.

She knew, however, exactly where the relief originated. She could get to work without distraction. She'd have the papers all to herself. She wouldn't have to deal with his silences and intent, enigmatic looks.

Or with a possible attraction to the man. Her

inexplicable reaction in his downtown office had not repeated itself when she said good-bye at his house the following afternoon. Sure, his handshake had been warm, his smile transforming. His low voice had sounded more reassuring than hard. He'd actually spoken in full paragraphs, with declarative sentences, not interrogatory ones.

True, his statements had more of a "laying down the law" flavor, but it was to be expected. Edgar had done no less; in fact, the grandson had sounded remarkably like his grandfather when setting her parameters.

At least they hadn't parted with a meeting of the eyes that sizzled her blood. She wasn't sure how she would have handled herself if something similar had occurred. She'd been so high from making the deal her blood was already bubbling. It would have taken a powerful reaction to sidetrack her from her zeal for the papers. She probably wouldn't have noticed anything less overt than his grabbing and kissing her.

What? Kissing her? Where did she get such a notion?

Shaking her head at her screwy thought processes, Barrett turned back to her desk. Enough lollygagging.

It only took a few minutes to unpack her few supply items and boot the computer. An envelope from Peggy Murphy sat on the keyboard and held complete instructions for passwords, network access, and the like. Everything worked perfectly.

"Done. Showtime," she announced to the world and pushed back from the desk with a grin. "Now, finally, Windswept!"

She opened the door to the conference room and, for a moment, simply stood in the doorway gloating at her good fortune. She decided first to open a couple of the boxes to see what state the records were in. Then she could be more systematic.

The gloating turned to frustration, however, once she looked into several containers. As far as she could tell, the contents of each box were mostly coherent, with files in a rough chronological or alphabetical order—where there were folders at all. One held large envelopes with string ties, another held bundles of letters tied together with ribbons, some were filled with what looked like shoe boxes. To make the situation worse, the receptacles were stacked in totally random order and the labels were not helpful, or necessarily truthful. She couldn't even find the boxes she had worked on over the past holidays.

She stood back to consider her options. If she wanted to catalog the records in a coherent way and build her knowledge as she went along, instead of jumping from, say, 1880 to 1920 and back to 1845, she would need to do some sorting. "Looks like you're going to get some exercise, Barrett," she sighed.

In the supply cabinet she found some felt-tip markers, tape, and paper. She opened the first carton on the left, decided how to describe the contents, wrote notes and its dates on the paper and taped it to the outside. She hauled the carton into the hall as a starting point, and went back for the second one. She had been working for about an hour, grouping cartons by date in the hall, when Gonzales appeared in the door.

"Dr. Browning, what are you doing? You shouldn't be doing heavy lifting." He sounded horrified.

"It's all right, Mr. Gonzales." She blew a curl out of her eye as she placed an 1880 carton with its companions. "This is the only way I can organize these boxes. I'm quite strong, really. I would love some more iced tea, though, if there's any available."

"Right away, and I'll bring Ricardo to help you."

"It really won't be necessary. I prefer doing this by myself."

His expression was adamant. "Please, Dr. Browning. What would Mr. Jamison say if he saw you doing all this manual labor? He would blame me for not taking good care of you. His instructions were very strict. 'She should want for nothing,' he said."

Barrett gave in, not that it was much of a struggle.

She didn't want to get Mr. Gonzales in trouble, and knew her back and legs were going to start protesting the unfamiliar exercise pretty quickly.

Gonzales returned within minutes with a large pitcher of iced tea, glasses, and Ricardo, a burly young man with grass stains on his jeans. Barrett heard him give Ricardo instructions in Spanish not to let the *maestra* lift so much as one box.

When Gonzales introduced Ricardo, Barrett shook hands with the young man and spoke to him in fluent Spanish, explaining her organizational method. Gonzales and Ricardo both blinked, Ricardo smiled shyly, and Gonzales left the room with the admonition to dial "3" on the house phone line if she needed anything else.

By five o'clock, Barrett and Ricardo had made a sizeable dent in the cartons, Barrett looking and writing, Ricardo lifting and carrying. She called a halt to their exertions when Gonzales came in.

"Is everything all right?" he asked.

"Yes, we've accomplished quite a bit. Would it be possible for Ricardo to help tomorrow?"

"You have his help as long as you need it, *maestra*," Gonzales replied.

"I don't want to take him away from his regular duties," she explained.

"Please do not worry," Gonzales said. "Ricardo's duties are what I decide they are. We are both happy to be of whatever use we can. Dinner will be ready at seven."

The lonely dining room displayed another aspect of its character in the evening light, Barrett thought later as she finished Eva's delicious roast chicken with an apple-raisin-walnut stuffing, green beans with almonds, rice and freshly baked rolls. Over their tops, the chandelier's light bulbs had small chrome hoods which focused all the light downward to concentrate on the table. A dinner party with a colorful centerpiece and beautiful people would bring the room alive, she hoped, but until then, brrrrrr.

The glass sculpture climbing the back wall compounded the effect. It did more than glow or sparkle. Hidden spotlights in the ceiling far above shone directly on it. The glass "threads" had sharp angles and facets, and the light reflecting off the polished planes changed as one walked around the table. The result made the sculpture seem to move, to ripple down the wall like an icy waterfall.

It was an interesting effect, she decided, but it reinforced the feeling of coldness in the room, and she was glad she did not have to look at it while she ate. Thinking of eating . . . she and Eva had to come to a meeting of the minds about how much she could eat. She couldn't spend the next two months feasting without looking like the biggest Windswept box at the end.

Then she grinned to herself. On the other hand, being waited on was certainly a pleasure, a seductive one, almost. Certainly easy to get used to. She opened the book she had brought with her and read while she finished her meal—including a piece of lemon meringue pie.

She walked back to the office only to shut off the computer and the lights. Between the food and her very long day, she knew she would accomplish nothing for the rest of the evening. She didn't even watch any television, simply fell into bed and a satisfied sleep.

The next morning she rose early and went first to the dining room, then through the door below the balcony. She had assumed correctly; that way lay the kitchen.

She stepped into a sun-lit space and looked around at the glass-paneled oak cabinets, the stainless steel appliances, the butcher-block countertops, the windowsill with two big red ripening tomatoes and four small pots of green herbs. Yellow-and-blue Mexican canisters sat along the multi-colored tile backsplash. A cozy bay window boasted an oak table and padded chairs. Past the kitchen on the other side of the open counter, she could see a normal family room with comfortable chairs, a big sofa, a television, and a card table.

She blinked. The two rooms did not look like they belonged with the rest of the house. Real people lived here.

Gonzales and Eva were seated at the table, and both rose to their feet when she entered. "Good morning," Gonzales said. "What would you like for breakfast, Dr. Browning?" Eva inquired.

"Good morning." She fell into teacher mode. She'd decided last night she had to gain control of the situation or be doomed to the chilly dining room—alone. "First, I'd like to eat in this cheery kitchen instead of the lonely dining room, except when Mr. Jamison is home, of course. I assume I'll be eating with him for dinner. Otherwise, I'd be honored to share your meals.

"Second, I'd like to have a newspaper to read with breakfast. The *Houston Chronicle* you have here would be fine, if you're finished with it.

"Third, I'd like some grapefruit juice, Cheerios, if possible, with bananas or some fruit in milk, and a big mug of coffee to finish. And I'd like the two of you to relax and join me. Please call me Barrett. I'm not a pretentious person."

The Gonzaleses were staring at her with scandal-ized expressions, so she added, "Please go along with me on this. What I'm doing with the records can get lonely, and having human companionship around will be helpful. Okay?"

After they slowly nodded assent, she sat down at the table, picked up the comic section from the news-paper and started reading. Out of the corner of her eye, she saw Gonzales and Eva look at each other.

Eva nodded and told her husband to bring in the place setting from the dining room. While he went for the dishes, Eva poured a glass of juice and set it in front of Barrett. "Jesus tells me you speak Spanish," she said to Barrett in the referenced language.

"*Si, señora.*"

"*Muy bien.*"

After their exchange, all conversation was conducted in Spanish. By the end of the meal, Barrett and the Gonzales had reached a compromise on names. She was *maestra*, Gonzales was *don* Jesus, and his wife was *doña* Eva, but only when nobody else except Ricardo was around. In deference to Gonzales's sensibilities, formality was to reign otherwise.

Barrett and Ricardo finished the sorting late Wednesday and arranged the boxes in the conference room in the order in which she would catalog their contents. After the young man left, she walked around the room a couple of times admiring their handiwork and planning her next steps.

If she did nothing but inventory and organize box contents for the next two days, she could get a jump start on the process, establish her rhythm and make sure her methodology worked. The records began in the 1830s. If she could work her way well into the decade, she'd have some good leads for her own articles. Or, at least she hoped so. She'd follow those leads over the weekend and go back to the inventory on Monday.

She knew two items in particular she was looking for. Edgar Preston Jamison had shown her two journals as a starting point: one, the diary of Windswept's first Jamison master, Edgar John Jamison, and the other, a household account book kept by Mary Maude Jamison, Edgar's wife and mistress of the plantation. Barrett's cursory look into the boxes had not revealed either, but she knew they were there somewhere.

She looked at her watch and then at her hands. Almost five o'clock. And her hands and arms were filthy from handling all the old papers, her jeans were streaked with ancient dust, and her T-shirt smelled like old cardboard. She felt totally grimy. Walking

out into the hall, she gazed at the blue waters sparkling in the swimming pool. Just the ticket—a swim
to work off Eva's cooking, then dinner, then back to
work on the first box. She headed for her bedroom
and her swimsuit.

Chapter
SIX

A little before two on Thursday afternoon, Davis watched his house come into view through the limousine windshield. Damn, he was glad to be home from Washington. Meeting with all those Congresspeople and their staff members about the trade and foreign investment bills had been exhausting in the extreme. The talks had been partisan wrangling on one side and all the special interests jockeying for position on the other.

He wondered how his historian was doing and shook his head at the term "his historian." When had he started thinking of her that way? He'd not talked to her when he called the house on Tuesday, but Gonzales had apprised him of what was going on in the office wing. He had been puzzled about Barrett's attempt to move all those cartons by herself until he hypothesized she must not be used to calling on others for help. She just went ahead and got the job done. Totally unlike most of the women he socialized with. Those women usually wanted to be waited on hand and foot and didn't lift a finger if they didn't have to.

He still wasn't sure how he felt about someone living in the house with him, but there was nothing he could do about it now. Not without going back on their contract. He'd never reneged on a deal in his life, so the little professor was here for the duration of the project. He'd just have to put up with it.

Gonzales came out to take charge of the luggage while Davis paid the driver. In the foyer, the houseman said, "I put your messages and the mail on your desk as usual, sir. May I get you anything else?"

"Thank you. No, I'm fine. Where's Dr. Browning?" Davis asked, taking off his coat and tie and handing them to Gonzales.

"*La maestra* is in the office."

"How are y'all getting along?"

"*Muy bien.*"

Davis picked up his briefcase and strode toward the office. When he opened the door to the wing, he heard music. Sounds like Beethoven's Ninth, he thought. The normally open door to the secretarial office was closed also. When he opened it, he ran right into a wall of sound. The symphony had reached the section with the "Ode to Joy." "*Freude!*" the baritone sang.

Barefoot and wearing cut-off jeans and a University of Minnesota T-shirt, Barrett Browning was sitting on the floor surrounded by paper radiating out in all directions. One hand seemed to be conducting the symphony, which poured out of a large boombox. The other held a piece of light-blue paper covered with spidery handwriting. Barrett studied the item briefly, rose to her knees, stretched out over one string of papers, held herself up with her conducting hand, and laid the page between two others.

Davis felt lust give him a low blow. She stretched like a cat, every muscle taut, then recoiled and relaxed. He ran his eyes over her long wonderful legs and curvy little butt . . . and reined himself in with an effort. This wasn't the time or place. He took a step into the room.

Barrett must have seen the movement out of the corner of her eye because she jumped. She turned, snatched a remote control from the desk behind her and hit a button. The music stopped abruptly. "Oh! Mr. Jamison! I didn't hear you come in. It's good to see you. How are you? How was the trip?" She stood up, another cat-like move, and smiled in welcome.

"It's good to be home. The trip was boring. What is all this?" He waved at the papers strewn over the floor.

"Sometimes the floor method of organization is the only way to get the job done. This way I can see the contents of an entire box and easily put them in chronological or alphabetical order. This box appears to be all business correspondence. Let me clear a path so you can get to your office." She knelt and started picking up stacks.

"Don't bother. I can go this way." Davis moved around behind the desk. "Do you always play music so loudly?"

"Depends on the music and what I'm doing. This type of work is tedious and music helps get it done. Don't worry. I have headphones, so you'll not be bothered."

It wasn't the music bothering him. He shifted his briefcase and said, "No problem," as he walked into his office.

At three, Davis heard Barrett thank Gonzales. He stood up from the desk and came into the outer office just in time to see Gonzales deliver a glass of milk and a large brownie on a plate. The floor was clear and Barrett was at the computer with a stack of correspondence next to her. She carefully moved the papers away from the food.

"What's this?" he inquired.

"Mrs. Gonzales decided I needed fattening up, and when she discovered I liked chocolate, well, you see the results. Want a piece?" Barrett held up the plate for inspection.

"Sure. Eva's brownies are delicious."

"I'll be happy to bring you one of your own, sir," Gonzales interjected.

"No, I think I'll just have a bite of this one." Davis took the piece Barrett offered after she broke the brownie in two. "Thank you, Gonzales." The houseman left.

"How's the food been?" Davis asked as he watched Barrett take a bite of her piece. He did the same with his.

She chewed, swallowed, and took a sip of milk before answering. "Very good." She rolled her eyes. "Too good. I'm not used to eating so much. I've almost convinced Mrs. Gonzales to serve me what I consider to be a normal portion—about half the amount she was fixing. I've been using your pool to work it off. I hope it was all right."

He nodded while he finished the brownie. "Fine. Can I have some of your milk?"

She took two more sips and handed him the glass. "Take the rest."

He drank the remainder of the milk and gestured at the computer monitor. "Is this your cataloging table?"

"Yes, sir. Would you like to see it?" She swung around toward the screen.

He moved to look over her shoulder.

Barrett explained the table, displaying the various columns and pointing out the possibilities for sorting.

"I created this column to flag any document you or I might be specially interested in. If there's any particular item or subject you want me to watch for, just let me know. When I have the box inventoried, I run off a copy and place it in the notebook on the table, and I put another copy in the box itself."

"No, there's nothing I know to look for," Davis replied. He certainly didn't want to tell her about Lloyd's speculations of "something horrible" lurking in the records. He rested a hand on the desk and leaned over to read the screen more closely. "Looks like this one is mostly correspondence about cotton prices."

"Yes," she answered. "See here and here." She pointed out her designations for various business subjects.

His chest was almost touching her shoulder, and when he inhaled, her spicy feminine scent wound around inside his lungs and made him want to nibble on her neck to see if it was spicy also. Luckily, or maybe not, she moved her chair closer to the desk out from under his nose. He blinked to clear his head and straightened abruptly.

She must not have noticed his reaction because she scrolled the display down and indicated two more entries. He stepped back. The movement brought his eyes to her hair. All those dark brown curls beckoned to his fingers. He wondered if they were as silky as they looked, and he fought the impulse to run his hand through them.

This was ridiculous, he reprimanded himself. He hadn't had such an immediate reaction to a woman in . . . years . . . hell, never.

She turned and looked up at him. "Do you have any questions? Is there anything else I can show you in this?" She waved at the screen.

"Nothing I can think of at the moment." Not, that is, in the papers. As for the other things he would like to see . . . He cleared his throat. "Carry on. I have more phone calls to make."

He went back into his office, feeling like he was retreating. Damn, he had been right from the first: she was going to be a distraction. Then he licked his mustache to remove the last brownie crumbs and the action made him think of licking something else entirely. He shut his door firmly to block out temptation.

When his door closed, Barrett breathed a huge sigh of relief and slumped against the back of her chair. When Davis had leaned over her, his closeness had brought every single nerve in her body to attention. She'd almost gasped aloud, and a swift intake of breath only worsened her reaction because she could smell him, a blend of soap, woodsy aftershave, and himself.

She'd concentrated on keeping her voice and her

hands steady. She had looked only at the screen and tried to keep her body still. She thought she had done a pretty good job of hiding whatever it was rattling her to her core. Be professional, you idiot, she scolded silently.

She shook her head and pulled the stack of correspondence closer. She needed to get back to work. It was way too early to break for her swim.

⸻

That evening Barrett joined Davis for dinner in the dining room. Its coldness seemed to have retreated somewhat with both of them in the room. He was still in his shirtsleeves, and she had put on a pair of chinos and a cotton short-sleeved shirt after her swim. She hadn't been sure what to wear to dinner, but, since she was going to work tonight, she didn't want to put on anything the papers might soil. It looked like she'd made the right choice.

"Would you like some wine with the meal?" Davis offered as Eva served them stuffed pork chops with candied sweet potatoes.

"Better not. I'm going back to work after dinner. I'm trying to complete several more cartons before I allow myself to think of my own research. A promising box of family letters by Mary Maude, her mother and sisters did catch my eye for later, though."

"You're working nights too?"

"Yes, sir. And I plan on working this weekend, except for Saturday night. You were right. Staying here allows me all the time I want to get at the records. Not having to commute is great. Not to mention the fringe benefits of the Gonzaleses and Ricardo."

She decided to change the subject. She was tired of thinking about the records. Besides, she knew he could talk; he'd proven it when they were negotiating the deal. She wasn't going to sit there and let him ask questions while she rattled on. "How was your trip?"

"Tiring. Do you know why I was in D.C.?"

"No, sir."

He gave her a sidelong glance. "We need to get a couple of things straight. First, my name is Davis. If we are going to live under the same roof, call me Davis, Barrett. Second, why do you keep saying 'sir?' "

"I am a well brought-up person. I was taught to say sir and ma'am to my, uh—." She was about to say superiors, but the word didn't sound right.

"If you say 'elders,' I am going to be most upset." Davis chided.

"To everyone." She hoped she hadn't insulted him. He wasn't much older than she. Great, Barrett. Open mouth, insert foot.

"Good save. Now, please cease," he said with mock severity. "To answer your question, I was there to do some lobbying for the latest trade bill, especially with reference to foreign investments. I found the process more than a little frustrating. While some of our Senators and Representatives know their stuff, some of them can't find their asses with both hands and a mirror." He proceeded to tell her several anecdotes about his meetings.

"How much traveling do you do?" she asked, curious about when he would be at home, in the same house with her.

"It's very erratic and unpredictable and depends on the deal I'm doing. It looks like I'm home for a while. Why aren't you working Saturday night?"

"My three brothers live here. Since I moved to the DFW area, we don't get to see each other much, so we take every chance we can. We're having dinner at Greg's house. I grew up here in Houston, over in the Heights."

"What about your parents?"

"They're retired and in their RV in . . . Colorado right now, I think. They laugh about spending our inheritance seeing the country. They'll call at least one of us every Tuesday to check up." If he could ask about her family, she could reciprocate about his, she thought, so she asked, "What about you? Family, siblings? You mentioned a brother and a sister."

He nodded. "A brother and a sister, both younger. Mother passed away two years last February, but Dad died twelve years ago." His face took on a drawn look.

"Do you see your brother and sister much?"

"Not much. Martha's a successful realtor. And I don't see Bill unless he needs money." His lips flattened into a grim line for a moment before he concentrated on buttering a roll and said, "Tell me what you've found in the records so far."

Well, his warning was certainly clear enough. Stay away from family matters. His dad had been gone a long time; Davis must have been in his early twenties. Losing his father while he was a young man couldn't have been easy on him. She couldn't imagine how she would have handled a parent's death so young. She pushed the morbid thoughts out of her head and focused on answering his order. "So far, it's been mostly business correspondence, but there were some interesting letters and bills of lading and invoices for furniture. If the pieces are still at Windswept, the historical society will probably want copies for provenance and to show visitors."

"I should be seeing an inventory of the house's contents before too long," Davis said. "My Aunt Cecilia is the family representative working with the state people and the lawyers."

"Cecilia's your father's sister, if I have your family straight? Cecilia Walker?"

"Yes. How did you know?"

Barrett thought he looked almost as if he didn't want her to have the information, but she answered calmly, "One of the first things your grandfather and I did was put together a family tree. He had one, of course, on paper. I bought some genealogical software and we computerized the process. I can look up any family member I find in the correspondence whom I don't recognize. I can also add relevant information to each person's biography."

"Ah." Davis nodded. "I'm glad you put the chart into a computer. I remember the huge roll of paper Granddaddy had. Some of the ink was so faded, I never knew how he read it. How long is it taking you to finish a box?"

They spent the rest of the dinner discussing the records and then moved on to more general topics like city and state politics. He was clearly a Republican, she decided and hoped she could keep her Democratic temper under control. It wouldn't do to argue too much with the owner of the papers.

After dinner, she hit the records again. When she stopped at ten and went upstairs, Davis was still at work in his office. With the door again shut. She didn't interrupt him to say good night.

Friday morning, Davis came down for breakfast and found his usual place set in the dining room. It was a single setting. He walked into the kitchen to find out where his house guest was.

Barrett was sitting at the kitchen table, finishing a cup of coffee and arguing volubly in Spanish with Gonzales about the merits of one Astro over another for the upcoming baseball game with the Chicago Cubs. A wager was clearly going down. "How do I get a piece of this action?" Davis asked in the same language.

Gonzales leaped to his feet with a thoroughly embarrassed expression. "Pardon me, sir. I didn't know you were downstairs already. I'll be right in with your juice."

"Two will get you three if Alou goes hitless tonight," Barrett proclaimed.

"You're on," Davis took the bet and held out his hand.

"Sucker," Barrett muttered, put down her coffee cup and shook the offered hand.

Davis held onto her just a little longer than needful and grinned at her. "Corrupting my staff?" he asked.

"Hardly," Barrett said, retrieving her hand from Davis's grasp. "*Don* Jesus needs no help from me. I've already lost two dollars to this man. Besides, he knows the Astros too well. I'll be in the office if anybody needs me." She rose quickly and disappeared out the door.

Davis looked at Eva, who winked at him. "I'll have your breakfast right away, sir," the cook said.

When Davis came home Friday evening about five, he went straight to the office. No Barrett, although the computer was still on and several stacks of documents sat on the desk, waiting to be processed. "Where is she?" he mumbled as he passed her desk.

As he put his briefcase on his own desk, he caught a glimpse out of the corner of his eye of a movement by the swimming pool. He crossed the room to the window. Barrett was climbing out of the pool, breathing vigorously. She picked up a towel and began to dry her wet hair, which looked even curlier than usual.

The navy tank suit left little to the imagination, Davis observed, noting the water's effect on her nipples. He could feel his body responding, and he suffered a mild regret when she wrapped herself in the towel.

Just as Barrett put her sandals on, Ricardo came around the corner and shyly presented her with a yellow rose bud. Davis couldn't hear their words, but their body language was eloquent. Barrett thanked Ricardo with a warm smile, and Ricardo, in turn, practically keeled over in youthful ecstasy. The young man and the professor spoke briefly before she turned and went inside. Davis watched Ricardo watch Barrett and felt his mouth twist with mild irritation.

"What is this woman doing to my staff?" he groused out loud. First Gonzales made bets on the Astros, then Eva cooked brownies for her and winked at him, and now the gardener was bringing her roses—out of Davis's own garden, no less. She had them wrapped around her little finger and it hadn't even been a week. He walked back to his desk in a lightly annoyed state. The thought went through his mind again: she was going to be—hell, she had become—a distraction.

"How was your swim?" he asked at dinner.

"Wonderful," she replied. "Dealing with old papers makes me feel so dirty. And I needed the exercise badly after *doña* Eva's little snacks."

"You speak Spanish very well. Where did you learn it?"

"Partly school, partly the neighborhood. A couple of close friends are Hispanic and I spent a great deal of time with them growing up. One of my summer jobs in high school was clerking at a hardware store catering to Hispanic as well as Anglo customers. When I took Spanish in school, I had a lot of bad habits to overcome, thanks to my informal education. What about you?"

"Partly school, partly necessity when you're trying to make investments in Latin America or with Latinos in this country. It's good business to know the language and the culture."

"Do you like doing what you do?"

He was surprised at the question. Nobody had ever asked him it before. "Yes, I do. I enjoy the complexities of making a deal, helping a new company get its feet on the ground or an existing one to revitalize itself."

Warming to his subject, he told her most of his joys and some of his sorrows about his business activities. He talked about the psychology of deal making, the personalities involved on both sides, the satisfaction he felt when one came off perfectly, the frustration when a new company's management team could not get itself together. Each of her questions led him to another aspect of the business.

"What about the money?" she asked at one point. "How does it figure in with your satisfaction?"

"Money's just a way to keep score," Davis said.

"To some people, it's everything," she reminded him.

The saying brought to his mind a story of a man to whom money was everything. Before Davis knew it, Gonzales was taking away the dessert plates, dinner was over, and they were returning to their respective offices. As a test for himself—he *would* work without letting her distract him—he did not close the connecting door.

———◆◆◆———

"What in the hell is this?" he said about an hour later as he looked at the document attached to a piece of e-mail. "Barrett?"

At first he didn't think she heard him over her machine-gun typing, but she stopped and answered, "Yes?"

"You understand this damned word processing program, don't you? Would you come here a minute?"

She walked into his office and over to stand behind his chair as he scowled at the screen of his laptop.

"Murchison sent me this file for review. Look at this mess. How do I read this?" The document was full of lines of text in different colors, some with a line through them and some not. Some lines repeated those in black, some made no sense at all.

"This has been set up to track changes. It looks like several people passed the document back and forth between them and made revisions as they went. See, here's one and there's another. Somebody forgot to turn it off. It's not hard to fix." She leaned over his arm as she spoke, pointing out with her index finger the various authors by colors.

Her nearness had a distinct effect on his lower body. She smelled so good, like sunshine and flowers. If he raised his arm at all, he'd be touching her breast. It was almost a relief when she stood up straight. At least he could start breathing again. "Would you please fix this?" He started to push his chair back and rise so she could get to the keyboard. She put her hand on his shoulder to keep him in the chair, and he felt the jolt all the way to his toenails.

"Oh, no," she said. "I wouldn't be fulfilling my duty as a teacher if I did it for you. I'll show you what to do. You drive the mouse."

She must have noticed where her hand was because she removed it quickly when he sat down. "Yes, ma'am. What do I do?" He managed to keep his tone matter of fact despite the small zap jolting through his body when her hand had settled on him. He also noted her sudden nervousness.

Barrett stood above him, cleared her dry throat,

and tried to remain blasé as she showed him how to manipulate the screen display. She was careful not to lean over him again and to keep her hands on the chair's high back. As soon as he had a document without all the colors and strange symbols in front of him, she escaped to her own desk.

What happened when she got close enough to this man to touch or smell him? She didn't have such a reaction when she sat next to him at the dinner table. Of course, there was more distance there. But this morning at breakfast when they'd made that silly bet? Her hand had tingled from his touch all the way into the office. She'd immediately booted the computer, plugged herself into her boombox, and started typing so she could pretend she didn't seem him when he came through for his briefcase. But she was very aware of his presence then. And now.

Don't be an idiot, she said firmly to herself. Your reactions to him are way out of line. Be professional. She shook her head at her thoughts and turned back to the stack of papers. Although she managed to make a few more entries in the catalog table, it became quickly obvious her concentration was shot when she entered the same information twice.

Damn. She didn't have time for this sort of confusion. She leaned back in her chair and stared at the

computer screen. She needed to figure this out. Ana-
lyzing a problem had always worked to clear her mind
in the past. What could she conclude now from the
existing data?

One: She was attracted to him. He was a good-
looking, intelligent man and had turned out to be a
surprisingly interesting conversationalist—witty, observant, skilled. Her first impression of him has a
hard, cold negotiator was not wrong—she could still
see the underlying steel in him—but he was more. She
was looking forward to discovering more facets of his
personality. Furthermore, his deep drawl caused her
insides to shiver, and his touch make her hand tingle.
And he smelled good.

Two: Was he attracted to her? She had no evidence of reciprocation at all. He certainly wasn't
flirting. He was treating her with respect and seemed
interested in her work and her family history. But he
didn't seem interested in her in any male-female sort
of way. He definitely hadn't made any "moves" of any
kind. Lord knew, she could recognize those from a
mile away.

Three: Therefore, if there were anything going on
here, it was one-sided, all on her part, and she'd wear
herself out if she let herself wallow in unrequited attraction. Besides, she was too old for a crush. Why

set herself up to be hurt? Been there, done that. She felt her mouth twist as she remembered the T-shirt she'd left at home, the one her sisters-in-law had given her with the words, "A Man Is Temporary. History Is Forever."

Four: She was here to do a job, not have some sort of fling. She didn't have the time. She had to keep her mind on her work and her goals.

Five and Decision: She would continue to work on the papers, and she would be courteous and friendly with Davis, period. After all, she was a guest in his house. She had obligations to both him and the memory of his grandfather.

Finally: She couldn't help wishing again Edgar had not passed away. It would have been so much simpler studying the papers with him at the plantation.

She looked at her watch. It was late enough to quit for the day. Best to retreat to her room and read the mystery she had picked up last weekend. She closed down the computer and straightened the desk. Before leaving, she glanced into Davis's office. He was scowling at the screen and seemed to be totally absorbed in the document. As she left the room, she called a good night and he answered with an absentminded tone.

Davis leaned back to watch her leave the outer office. Something was definitely happening between

them, but he wasn't sure what. Up to now, she had
been treating him just as he imagined she would treat
anybody—pleasant, business-like, somewhat imper-
sonally. She certainly hadn't given him any of the
signals a woman usually gave a man she was interested
in—no flirtatious glances, no prolonged eye contact,
no small innocent touches, no standing just a little bit
too close.

But the sizzling eye contact when she was leaving after their first meeting and now every time they
touched, whether by handshake, as when they made
the bet, or by the contact with his shoulder, as when she
kept him in his chair . . . From the way she snatched
her hand from his shoulder, she had to have felt something too.

All right, he was attracted to her and she to him.
He'd very much like her in his bed. What was he
going to do to put her there?

It had been a while since he had had to work actively to pursue a woman, but he hadn't forgotten how.
This one might be trickier than most, however.

There were the ethics of the situation. She was a
guest in his house. She had not come here to share his
bed. Given her evident desire for access to the papers,
her manifest determination for achievement of her career goals, and her subsequent demeanor toward him,

he doubted she had any such notion in her head.

She also, in a way, worked for him. He definitely did not get involved with any woman whom he employed. On the other hand, this business relationship was more of an outside-contractor one, and it was a done deal. Her access to the papers did not depend on his access to her. They could work around any difficulty, he decided—assuming it even arose.

He had not invited her here with ulterior motives—well, not really. Attraction had been a very minor part of the package. Anything developing between them now would be between two consenting adults. If he kept control of the situation, kept it light with no strings attached for either of them, there would be nothing to worry about, he concluded. A summer affair would be a pleasant interlude for both of them.

Now, as to actual pursuit. He wouldn't, couldn't simply jump her bones. Not only was such a crude approach not his style or inclination, she would be at the least insulted, at the most pissed as hell. No, best to take it slow. He was a patient man and had all summer. He just needed to pursue her slowly, get her used to the idea of him as a man, as her lover. Build on their existing attraction, help her come to the conclusion she wanted to be, indeed belonged, in his bed. He wasn't sure how experienced she was with a lover, but her nervousness led him to believe, not very.

His campaign should be a slow, steady one, he decided. He had the distinct hunch, if he pushed too hard, too fast, she'd be gone, papers or no papers.

Another aspect added to his satisfaction with his plan, he thought as he ran it through his mind again. He enjoyed her company immensely. At dinner she expressed genuine interest in his business and the manner in which he carried it out. Her questions had been perceptive and penetrating. He was surprised to realize he had not talked so much about himself and the business to anyone, ever.

He had never had a woman as a friend before. He had certainly never thought of Sandra as a "friend." But it would be easy to become friends with Barrett Browning. They were already well on their way. He simply looked forward to making their friendship become more.

It was too bad Granddaddy had died. He would have enjoyed Barrett so much. But then, if Edgar had lived, the chances were good he, Davis, would either have never met her or certainly not met her in any circumstances where he could get to know her better. He remembered something else Edgar had said about the professor. "She's a good woman and a smart one. You treat her right, or I'll come back to haunt you."

"Rest in peace, Granddaddy," Davis whispered. "You were correct, she does know what to do about the papers. And I know what to do to take care of her."

Chapter
SEVEN

The Journal of Mary Maude Davis Jamison
April 24, 1831
A fine, fairly cool spring day.

The azaleas have almost lost all their blooms, but many of the roses show promise. I hope we can find the time soon to build our first greenhouse. Two of our Negroes, Heeba and her daughter Shallie, have been a godsend with the winter gardens and I believe they are looking forward to having more space to work with, just as I am. Heeba, a woman of perhaps 40 years, has been the midwife for our Negroes and it was she who concocted the medicines for them when James and Emily were alive. She claims her mother, who came from the West Indies, and her grandmother, who came from Africa, taught her the ways of herbs and medicinal plants. She has taught Shallie, and now she is teaching me.

I know, some people scoff that a servant could

teach them anything, but Heeba has proven to be quite knowledgeable. I have several books of home remedies by reputable physicians and herbalists and have checked all of Heeba's recipes. Every one for which there is an equivalent has agreed with the prescriptions in the books. Heeba has some tonics and balms not in the tomes, but our Negroes swear by them and will refuse more "modern" medicines. Under Heeba's guidance, we seem to be thriving, so I pay close attention and have begun a journal of cooking and medicinal recipes.

I must relate another, more difficult situation—this one with some of our neighbors. These women, who consider themselves to be the moral and virtuous leaders of our community, make me so angry. Last Sunday was a fine day and we went into town for church services. Two of the older women of the congregation, let me call them Mrs. K and Mrs. T, pulled me aside and filled my ears with gossip about Mr. and Mrs. P.

It appears Mrs. P took her husband to task in the middle of town for some of his "indiscretions." She went so far as to berate him in front of several bystanders outside his attorney's office before dissolving in tears. Our Episcopal pastor and his wife, who came upon the scene, were able to lead her away and take her home. According to Mrs. K, Mr. P is a known philanderer and has fathered several children by his Negro

servants. Rumors abound about his trips to New Orleans—for gambling and for visiting those places
virtuous women are supposed to know nothing about.
Mrs. T went on at some length about "poor Mrs. P."
Neither lady could understand why Mrs. P had reacted
as she did, thus bringing down scandal and ridicule on
the P family name.

I was absolutely appalled, first by the tale and second by the glee with which Mrs. K and Mrs. T related
it. I excused myself as quickly as I could and during
services offered up a prayer for Mrs. P.

Every married woman knows some men are unable to remain faithful to their wives. Indeed, my own
mother told me of these "facts of life" when she was
preparing me for my marriage.

I am very sorry for Mrs. P, but I can't help but
wonder where the P's marriage went so far wrong that
Mr. P turned to another woman. Thank God my marriage is such a wonderful one. Edgar and I profess our
love to each other daily and I cannot imagine my loving husband breaking our vows for the sake of what
must be a momentary pleasure or lapse in judgment.

Present Day
Saturday, May 26

Barrett rose at her usual weekday time, dressed, and went down to the kitchen. "Good morning," she said as she came through the door.

Eva was ladling coffee into the top of the maker. "Good morning. The coffee will be ready in a moment. I didn't expect you so early. Jesus just brought the paper in. It's on the table."

"Lots to do today," Barrett replied as she sat down and took the paper out of its plastic wrap. "What with shopping with my friend this afternoon and going over to my brother's this evening, I'm determined to spend the morning on research."

Eva handed her a glass of grapefruit juice, Gonzales came in with another "Good morning," and the three of them fell into what had become their breakfast routine.

Barrett hurried through her cereal and took the coffee mug with her into the office. Finally, she was going to do some of her own research. She picked up the notebook holding the printed box contents and her laptop and walked into the conference room. Half an hour later she was reading an 1830 letter from Mary Maude Jamison thanking her mother for sending the seeds and recipes she had requested. The letter also included a detailed description of Mary Maude's attendance at the St. Gregory Episcopal Church and of her fellow churchgoers.

She had been correct, Barrett congratulated herself. This collection was a treasure trove. Not only did it contain incoming mail, but many copies of outgoing correspondence. Mary Maude's parents had evidently kept all of her letters and returned them to her at some point. If even a small number of the letters were as rich as this one, Barrett would have no problem coming up with several solid articles—from plantation gardening to religion to community life—by the end of the summer. She added the topics and references to the list she was building.

She was reaching for the next letter in the file when Davis stuck his head in the door.

"At work already?" he asked with a smile.

"Lots to do. You, too, apparently." She pointed at the briefcase he was holding and told herself to ignore how charming he appeared when he dropped the stone-face routine.

"Still playing catchup at the office. You'll be out tonight?"

"Yes. Eva knows I won't be here for dinner."

"Did Gonzales give you a key?"

"Yes, and he showed me how to handle the alarm system also, but I don't expect to be too late."

"Good." He hesitated, looked like he was about to say more, but his expression blanked and he finally said, "I'll be here, so if you have any problem with the system, just let me know. Have a nice time."

"Thanks." She reached for the next letter again and heard him leave.

Barrett raised her eyes to the doorway and stared after him for a long moment. What had he been about to say? He'd had a funny look in his eyes—displeasure because she was taking the night off? She was surely entitled to some downtime. She was a guest, all right, but a working one.

Had it been loneliness because she wouldn't be here for dinner or because she wasn't taking him with her?

"Yeah, right," she muttered. Wouldn't it be a picture, Davis with her brothers? She was anticipating one of their usual go-rounds tonight. When were they going to let her grow up?

She shook her head to throw all thoughts of Davis, her brothers, and any other extraneous subjects out of her head and immersed herself again in 1830s Louisiana.

At Phil's house that evening, Barrett was having fun catching up on family gossip with her two sisters-in-law when all three brothers descended on them.

"Now the kids are down, we'd like to talk to you, Barrett, about this Davis Jamison," Phil said.

"Phillip," his wife Beth said with a warning note in her tone, "I thought we had agreed you all would leave Barrett alone."

"Yes," Greg's wife Chris agreed, nodding at her own husband.

Barrett looked at Phil, Greg, and finally unmarried Mark and sighed. She knew how determined her brothers could be where she was concerned. Sometimes she wondered how their wives and Mark's girlfriends put up with their overprotectiveness. "You don't have to worry," she told them. "I checked him out thoroughly. He's known for his honesty and integrity."

"Yeah, but . . ." Phil started to say.

She kept on talking over him. "I couldn't find anything to give me pause or stop me from staying in his house. I trusted his grandfather and know Edgar wouldn't have given Davis the plantation papers if I couldn't trust him also. Now, what's your problem? Did I miss a fact—like he's really an ax murderer?"

Phil put his hands on his hips and Barrett could almost see the wheels turning in his lawyer brain. "All right," he said. "I'll admit his business reputation is sterling. He's very successful and is known as a man of his word. I'm more worried about his reputation with women."

"His reputation with women? Does he have one?" Barrett asked as a tiny needle of despair pricked her heart before outrage buried it in angry heat. Here they went again. Although she wanted to yell, she kept her tone level. "Look, I'm not there to go to bed with him. I'm a working historian doing research. Furthermore, I'm an adult and what I do is my own business. What is it with you? I say hello to a man and you three start acting like you did when I was sixteen. Are you going to threaten him like you did the guys I dated in high school?" She assumed a mock-deep voice. "Touch our sister and you die, asshole!"

"Look," Greg put in. "We know you're an adult. But we worry about you. That guy, Wendell What-ever-his-name-is, we know he hurt you. We just don't want you to get mixed up with someone who will do the same again."

Barrett sighed once more. She wasn't about to re-hash Wendell Truman. She was long over him, and considering the speed with which Wendell's impor-tance faded from her life, she had never felt very deeply about him to begin with. Her brothers just exaggerat-ed all her relationships. Best to let them have their say and then they could all go back to enjoying themselves. "All right. Lay it on me."

"First," Phil said, assuming a stance like he was before a jury, "Jamison went through a very nasty divorce about five years back. I don't know who was cheating on who, but I heard lots of rumors at the court house. The settlement was all hushed up, but there were tales of a killer prenup—in his favor. Ex-wife took off for Dallas with a banker shortly after."

"Since then," Greg took up the tale, his cop face clearly on, "he's been playing the field, big time. Shows up at all the big social events with a different woman each time."

"So? The man is single and dates." Barrett put in. "Does he do drugs? Brawl at bars?"

"Not that I've heard of," Greg answered. "His police record is clean."

"Thank you, Sergeant Browning," Barrett sneered. "Did your HPD files come up with anything at all?"

When Greg shook his head, she turned to Mark. "What about you, little brother? Does Davis hang out with you football players around the Houston Texans? Get it on with the groupies?"

"Barrett, I'm on your side, like always," Mark said. "I told these bozos to leave you alone." He straightened to his full six-foot-five height and grinned at the shorter Greg and Phil. "Do you want me to make the point more forcefully?"

"No, it's not necessary," she said, waving her hand wearily. "He's divorced, and he dates women. Whoopee." She skewered the two older brothers in turn with one of her teacher looks, designed for students who had just come up with the most implausible excuses for not having their papers done. "Let me say this once and once only. I am staying at Davis Jamison's house to do a job, a job for which I am being handsomely paid. A job giving me the research I need to make my mark in my field. He has no interest in me other than my ability to catalog his family's collection. I have no interest in him other than as the owner of the papers. Now, unless the man is about to abscond to Brazil with his investors' money, would you three please *butt out*."

"But . . ." Phil said.

"But . . ." Greg said.

Mark just grinned at her.

"Enough," Beth said to the men in the voice she used when her two children were squabbling. "Change the subject. Now."

Phil glanced at his wife, then exchanged a look with Greg. Both men shrugged. "So, tell us about these plantation papers and how you're going to win a Pulitzer in history from this research," Phil said to Barrett.

Barrett hid a smile. It did her heart so much good to see her big macho brothers do what their wives told them. She described the treasures she had found and how she hoped to use them. Everyone was appropriately enthusiastic for her prospects, and she asked Mark about the Texans' chances for the next season to lighten the mood even more. Soon it was time to leave with hugs and kisses all around.

She thought again over her brothers' remarks on the drive to Davis's. They, as usual, were worried about nothing. At least they were supportive of her career goals; she wouldn't have expected any less of her family. They might all compete, but they stood by each other when needed.

Growing up, she had always thought success came more easily to her brothers than to her. They seemed to excel naturally in both schoolwork and sports. She had to study like a fiend, especially in math and science, to turn in comparable grades. In addition to wanting to keep up the family standard, she wasn't about to open herself up to brotherly taunts. "What's the matter, little girl. Can't you cut it?" still rang in her ears.

She'd almost despaired because she had never had the vision of her brothers about what she wanted to do with her life. Then she'd discovered history, real history, in college, and she'd known she'd found her calling.

Now to be as firm a success in her world as her brothers were in theirs.

Fortunately for them, the male members of the family had chosen careers where the rungs to be climbed on the career ladder were much clearer and judged more objectively than the slippery, foggy steps of academia. Every career had its politics, but deciding the worth of historical research could not be quantified like cases won, criminals caught, or yardage gained.

No matter, she thought as she made the last turn off Memorial Drive. She'd produce such articles and books that no one, not even Horace, could deny her right to tenure.

She grinned. Not a bad pep talk. She halted the car in the driveway and looked at Davis's house for a moment. Inside was all she could hope for—Windswept and the keys for happiness.

After putting her Honda in the four-car garage in between the Gonzales's Chevy and Davis's Lexus, she let herself into the house through the kitchen door and made her way to the stairs by way of the dining room. The house was quiet, and sconces on the stairs and down the hall toward the offices shed a dim illumination. She could see a light burning in Davis's office also.

At first she wondered if Davis was still working—

he was turning out to be a true workaholic, worse even than she was. She couldn't imagine him kicked back with a beer watching sports or an old movie on Saturday night. She took a step toward the office wing when a flash at the corner of her eye drew her gaze to the patio where only the pool and security lights were on. She moved closer to the glass and looked out.

Davis was churning up the water, swimming laps. She watched him make a smooth turn and with powerful strokes head back to the far end. The man has power to burn, she thought and felt her body tense at the sight of him, cutting through the water with a minimum of wasted motion as the pool lights gleaming off the water drops emphasized the muscularity of his arms.

Her brothers' warnings came back to her. Was the man a womanizer, a cavalier 'love 'em and leave 'em' sort? If so, she'd seen no evidence. Her research into gossip columns had mentioned his name in conjunction with several women, but never with a hint of notoriety—or of any long-term relationships. If her brothers couldn't find one iota of evidence against the man, and they'd surely tried, then she had nothing to worry about.

More evidence to the contrary was right in front of her: Here it was Saturday night and Davis didn't have a date. She sighed. Her brothers meant well. They didn't know Davis wasn't interested in her and the attraction was all on her part.

Willing her body to relax, she watched him for a few moments longer. She'd have to be careful about her reactions around him. She didn't have as much control over herself as she thought.

Should she report her return?

No . . . better not tempt fate, she decided. She'd managed to convince her brothers of her disinterest. Now if she could only convince herself.

Shaking her head, she turned and went up the stairs to her bedroom.

In the near end of the pool, Davis glided to a stop and rested against the side. A movement inside the house caught his attention. Barrett had returned. He watched her climb the stairs and disappear.

Damn! She was home earlier than he had expected. He had hoped to begin his campaign tonight, had planned to be reading in his office, to offer her a goodnight drink, have a friendly conversation. The empty evening had been long, and unable to concentrate on work, a magazine or a TV show, he had opted for a long swim to relax. Look where it had gotten him.

He threw himself back into the pool in frustration and floated for a while. Earlier he'd almost asked her how late she expected to be, but the question smacked too much of the notion he'd be sitting up waiting for her, like an over-anxious parent, or worse, a jealous man. He was certainly not the former and didn't have the right to be the latter.

He wondered about her three brothers. She must have been a handful for them. *A handful.* He'd like her to be a different kind of handful for him.

The thought stirred his blood, so he flipped over and swam another lap, then climbed out. He dried himself off and walked into his office through its sliding glass door. Before turning off his laptop, he checked his calendar. Tomorrow and Monday, the Memorial Day holiday, he had engagements for golf and dinners with some potential investors. Damn again!

Then the absurdity of his disgruntlement hit him, and he had to laugh. Patience, he told himself. *Remember, you have time.* What did he tell his staff when they wanted to rush into a deal? Take it easy. Reconnoiter the terrain before planning your moves. Find out what the other side wants. And, as was brought home tonight, don't assume the other party will act the way you want them to.

Now if he could only take his own advice. Shaking his head, he turned out the lights and climbed the stairs to his bedroom.

Chapter
EIGHT

$\mathcal{M}$onday afternoon Barrett hefted yet another box off the stack and carted it into the office. She was up to the 1840s, but it was slow going. The number of boxes was double that of the 1830s. As Edgar had proclaimed, the Jamison family were truly pack rats, saving every item from business letters to newspaper clippings, fabric samples to a packet of cotton seeds.

She stretched after putting the carton on the floor. It had been a productive Sunday and she had a good idea for her first article. With the Gonzaleses on their day off, she'd been able to eat—or not—when she felt like it. Thank goodness Davis was busy with clients and investors yesterday and today. She had accomplished so much more—two whole boxes—without his presence as a distraction.

She lifted the lid and sneezed. More dusty file folders and brown envelopes.

And, by the way, where *were* those journals Edgar had shown her? Particularly the first Edgar's book? She wished she'd paid more attention to their containers when he had pulled them out for her.

She was about to sit on the floor when the phone rang. She leaned over the desk to look at the set. Davis had multiple phone lines and an office-style system; the phone only rang in certain rooms, such as the kitchen and Davis's office. One of the Gonzaleses answered the phone when Davis wasn't home. Two buttons were blinking—one of them the intercom. She lifted the handset and pushed the button. "Yes?"

"There's a Horace Glover on line one for you, *mae-stra*," Gonzales said.

"Horace? Oh, ugh!"

"Would you like me to tell him you can't be disturbed?"

She sighed. "No, I'd better take the call. *Gracias, don Jesus.*"

"*De nada.*"

Barrett scowled at the phone, but she punched the button and managed to speak in a pleasant tone. "Hello, Horace, how are you?"

"Just thought I'd see how you were doing down there. I do take an interest in your work, you know. You're one of the up-and-comers in the department," he boomed in the cordial tone he adopted when he wanted something.

"Thank you," Barrett answered as she rolled her eyes. She decided to use a Davis tactic and keep her mouth shut. Volunteer nothing and maybe he'd come to the point.

After a few seconds of silence, Horace spoke again. He must not recognize the ploy, she thought.

"Let me get to the crux of the matter. Have you found any papers for a Edgar John Jamison, Jr., during the war? Correspondence, or the like?"

"Horace, I'm not at liberty to discuss the contents of the collection," she answered as she mentally thanked Davis for his conditions on her access.

"Why not?"

"Part of Mr. Jamison's parameters include my sole access until I have cataloged the entire collection." That wasn't absolutely true, she knew, because Davis had said she could bring in experts if needed, but she hadn't found anything to warrant the need yet. And the last person she'd bring in would be Horace.

"The old man didn't have any such limits when I talked to him."

"What old man?"

"I spoke with Edgar Jamison about the collection about a year before his death. Told him what I was looking for, and he said he'd get back to me, but he never did."

Dumbfounded, Barrett took a breath and closed her eyes for a moment. Edgar had never said one word about having talked to Horace. No, wait. Edgar had made one reference to "damn fool professors" who bothered him. Was one of them Horace?

"I'm sorry, but he never mentioned your request to me."

"How about if I come down and take a little look for myself? Just between us colleagues. Maybe get in a nice visit for the two of us?"

He sounded like a smarmy snake-oil salesman, and it gave her more pleasure than she wanted to admit to be able to answer, "I'm sorry, Horace, but I can't let you see them. It's against the agreement Davis Jamison and I made. You wouldn't want me to lose the grant, would you?" Hurrying on before he could answer the question, she tried to sound sympathetic to his request. "Please don't make a trip all this way for nothing. And you'll have to excuse me. I really have a lot of work to do."

"All right, but I'll give you a call later—just to see how you're doing, of course."

His voice insinuated his certainty she'd give in to his request later, but Barrett ignored the tone and said only, "Thank you for calling. Good-bye."

She hung up the phone and slumped down onto the floor beside the recently opened box. "Yuck! A nice visit. What a crock." She scrubbed her hands on the carpet. They felt dirty just from holding the phone during the conversation.

What was she to make of the news Horace had talked to Edgar? Horace evidently knew more about the papers than he let on. But what did it mean for her?

Whose correspondence had Horace been looking for? Edgar John Jamison, Jr., the first Edgar's son, born 1835. "Her" Edgar had talked about Junior being a hero in the battles along the Mississippi and Red Rivers after distinguishing himself in Virginia. Horace must be looking for some of his military records. Thank goodness Davis had placed those limits on her work. The last help she needed was from Horace.

She allowed herself a shiver of revulsion at the thought and turned her attention back to where it belonged, on the box in front of her.

———— ◆ ————

At dinner Tuesday evening, Davis worked hard at making Barrett more comfortable with him. In any negotiation, you had to understand the other party, their wants and needs, so he started there.

"Tell me, why did you go into history?" he asked after she told him her progress for the day.

"I had a couple of really great history profs as an undergraduate," she answered. "They made history come alive. It's not fiction. It's the story of real human beings. Doing my kind of history gets me right down to the personal level. Some of these people were absolutely extraordinary human beings without being 'great men' like Washington or Lincoln. They accomplished so much just by living, dealing with day-to-day life."

She laughed. "Of course, there are a goodly number of outright villains too. I love the research, finding out about all these people, trying to decipher them and their motives and actions. I like the teaching too. The writing is always a challenge, trying to explain how I arrived at my interpretations and convincing others to agree with them. What I am definitely not fond of, however, is the academic politics, but it goes with the territory."

"Is it difficult—the politics, I mean?" Davis was intrigued. "I know about regular politics and office politics, but very little about academia."

"It can get vicious, especially in the liberal arts where the pie of grants and budgets is so small, compared with the hard sciences and engineering. The tenure process can be rigorous." A bleak look crossed her gaze.

"You mentioned tenure when we first spoke.

Where do you stand?"

"I expect the History Department, the Dean, and the university will make a decision about me the year after this coming one. That's one of the reasons the Windswept papers are so important to me. There are at least a couple of articles in them and maybe a book. Getting them published would help my cause immeasurably."

"And you're determined to be tenured." He understood drive in a career. He had plenty of his own.

"Yes. It's next to impossible to get anywhere in the profession without it." Her determination was almost palpable.

"Here's to Windswept, then." Davis raised his glass and she joined him in the toast.

Later as he sat in his office, Davis listened to the rapid click-clack of the keyboard coming from the next room. The woman typed at warp speed. He smiled to himself before turning his attention to his e-mail.

A couple of minutes later, the phone rang. He picked it up. "Hel . . ." he started to say, but the caller interrupted.

"Davis, it's Lloyd," said his cousin.

Damn. "What do you want?" Davis asked.

"Is that professor going through the papers? Has she found anything yet?"

Davis almost sighed, but kept the disgust out of

his voice. "You're worrying for nothing. She's found lots of information, but nothing incriminating or even remotely scandalous."

"Well, she will. My mama is all upset about this. She's positive Grandmama told her some awful story was in those boxes. You *have* to let *me* look at the papers."

"No, I don't, Lloyd." He kept his voice calm and reasonable; he didn't want to give his cousin the slightest reason to pitch a fit and ruin his good mood. "You know the papers belong to me, not to the family as a whole. I'm following Granddaddy's wishes, according to his will and what he told me before he died. Dr. Browning is cataloging the collection and then she will write articles and books based on what she finds in them."

"What? Articles and books?" Lloyd yelped. "Hellfire, Davis! You never said she was going to write something about the family. I thought she was just doing an inventory."

"Yes, she's going to write academic articles, you know, real history, with footnotes."

"No, she can't! You don't know what kind of woman she is, what she'll write about us. I found out—."

"Calm down, Lloyd," Davis interrupted. "She'll write good, honest history." He kept his voice low but he was rapidly losing his willingness to continue the conversation. Lloyd was breathing so hard into his ear he couldn't hear Barrett's typing any more.

"But, but we'll be ruined!"

Davis shook his head. As usual, Lloyd was getting himself all wound up for no reason. At times like these, he really felt for Grace, Lloyd's wife. She was a nice woman and Davis wondered how his cousin had managed to attract and hold her. True love, he guessed, and marveled how Lloyd could be the beneficiary of such feelings. Davis himself had certainly never felt—or received—them.

Lloyd must be hell to live with, he surmised and not for the first time. He decided to do what he could for Grace to lessen her husband's anxiety, at least for the evening. He spoke with the tone of command and certainty he used with worried clients. "Listen to me, Lloyd. You know I have the family's best interests at heart. Do you really think I would allow publication of anything that might remotely hurt the family?"

"Well . . ." Lloyd's voice was ragged, but he seemed to be listening.

"Do you?" He kept his volume low and soothing.

"No, I guess not," Lloyd finally said.

"You tell Aunt Cecilia she can stop worrying."

"Okay, but . . ."

"I'll talk with you the next time I come over there.

Tell Grace hello for me."

"Okay," Lloyd said, but still sounded skeptical.

Davis hung up, leaned back in his chair and rubbed his right forefinger along his lip under his mustache. He might have a real problem with Lloyd. He hoped he had said enough to calm the man down, but he knew his cousin. Lloyd would go back to his mother and she'd get him all worked up again. Aunt Cecilia was certainly a piece of work. For the present, however, let calm prevail on Lloyd's home front. He turned back to his report on the upcoming merger.

In the outer office, silence reigned as Barrett sat stunned, fingers poised over the keyboard. What had she just heard? She hadn't meant to eavesdrop, but she had stopped typing to pull up the next stack of letters and Davis's conversation had come through loud and clear. He might speak softly, but his voice carried.

Lloyd must be the cousin she had met, Lloyd Walker, son of Cecilia. He had seemed a little hostile toward her at their first and only meeting, and when she had asked Edgar about him, the old man had told her not to worry about Lloyd. He'd said something about this particular grandson not "cottoning to outsiders."

But what had Davis told Lloyd? *You know I have the family's best interests at heart. Do you really think I would allow publication of anything that might remotely hurt the family?"*

What did his statement mean? Did what he told his cousin mean he would try to limit what she wrote?

No, she told herself. Davis would not do that. He was a man of his word, and he would honor their agreement—the same one she had had with his grandfather. She was to have full and complete control of the contents of her articles or books.

Lloyd must think some scandal lurked in the papers. She couldn't imagine what it might be. Evidence of collaboration with the Yankees? Confirmation of political shenanigans during Reconstruction or after? Proof of a secret murder, like how Scarlett had killed the Yankee marauder in *Gone With The Wind*? How ridiculous would that be?

The cousin must simply be one of those people who worried over nothing. She could ignore his anxiety. After all, he was in Louisiana, and she was here with the papers. She scoffed at herself for even thinking Davis would censor her conclusions or stop her publications.

Barrett turned back to the papers and worked through the stack on her desk. At nine o'clock, she decided she'd done enough for the day. She stuck her head in Davis's door, but he was on the phone again, so she just waved and went upstairs to bed.

In St. Gregoryville, after hanging up the phone, Lloyd leaned forward and put his head into his hands. Yesterday had been bad enough. There he'd been, enjoying himself at the family barbeque and crawfish boil on a fine Memorial Day, when his mother had interrupted his meal with more tales of possible malicious gossip and of even worse actual—but unspecified—deeds sure to ruin the family forever.

His wife, bless her heart, had coaxed his mother away so he could eat in peace, but he had lost his appetite. Grace had helped him restore his equilibrium—Thank God, some aspect of his life was working right—but this morning his mother had called, and it had taken him half an hour to calm her down.

Hellfire. The way she kept dropping little hints and innuendoes about doom with never any facts to back them up made him furious. He'd finally given her an ultimatum: give him some facts and he might be able to do something with Davis. Otherwise, drop the subject altogether.

Then this afternoon had brought a phone call from one of those professors who had been sniffing around Windswept before Granddaddy passed away.

Horace Glover. Lloyd had actually read one of his books about the military campaigns in Virginia because he'd mentioned Edgar Jr. Glover seemed like a nice enough fellow, and his book had the facts correct. However, the professor had related a tale Lloyd had not liked at all. According to the professor, he had approached Granddaddy about the papers with a request to look for correspondence and what-have-you from Edgar Jr. Granddaddy had snubbed him—oh, Glover hadn't said it in so many words, but Lloyd had been left with the distinct impression Granddaddy had been less than courteous in turning down the request.

That wasn't so bad, but then Glover had explained how he taught at the same university with the uppity Browning woman. What he told Lloyd about her, how inexperienced she was, how she was one of those "feminist" types, always looking to stick it to men, especially for the way they treated women in the past, how he was sure no good would come out of her digging around in the Jamison history—well, all the professor's statements on top of his mother's frenzy had caused him to finally call Davis.

And Davis had not even given him the time to make his case. His damn cousin had merely blown him off with platitudes. Davis was just like Granddaddy. Neither of them gave a shit about the family.

What was he going to do to halt this pending catastrophe, Lloyd pondered as he turned off the light in his study and headed toward the family room where Grace was watching television. He brightened when he looked at her. She'd help him take his mind off his troubles.

Chapter
NINE

*T*hursday afternoon Davis had just adjourned a meeting on the investment he was about to authorize and walked into Peggy Murphy's office when she answered the phone. She listened, then said, "Just a moment, please. I'll see if he's available." She pressed the hold button and looked up at Davis. "There's a Horace Glover asking to speak to you. He says he's a professor at the same university as Dr. Browning."

Davis frowned. "Glover? I don't know him." He thought a minute. "Granddaddy never mentioned him, and neither has Barrett."

"Shall I simply say you're not available?" Peggy asked.

"No, I'll take the call." He walked into his office, put his folders and legal pad on the desk, and sat down. This was exactly what he didn't want, to be bothered by historians or anybody else about those papers. He'd made it clear to Barrett, and she'd agreed, but she'd also warned him she'd spoken of the papers to members of her history department. This must be one of them. He made a bet with himself about what the fellow wanted and punched the button to activate the speaker phone.

"This is Davis Jamison," he said.

"Mr. Jamison, my name is Horace Glover. I'm a colleague of Barrett Browning."

The man's voice boomed out of the phone. Davis winced and hit the volume button a couple of times. "What can I do for you, Dr. Glover?"

"I understand Barrett is preparing a catalogue of the papers from your family plantation."

Davis said nothing.

Glover must have expected him not to respond because the professor rolled on. "I'm a military historian, Mr. Jamison. You may have read my latest book, *Manassas Marauders*, in which I related some of the heroic service of your great-great grandfather, Colonel Edgar John Jamison, Jr."

Glover paused, clearly expecting an answer, probably a complimentary one, but Davis decided to be truthful—and blunt. "No, I don't read much history."

"Ah." The flat statement stopped the professor's flow, but he rallied quickly. "Well, be that as it may, I'm turning my attention to the campaigns on the western side of the Confederacy, in which, as you undoubtedly know, Colonel Jamison played an important part. I talked with your grandfather about a year before his death concerning the collection, specifically regarding Colonel Jamison."

"Yes?" Davis said in a non-committal manner. He'd won his internal bet; Glover wanted access to the papers.

"I was doubly sorry to hear of your grandfather's passing. First, because he was such a fine man, and second, because I looked forward to working with him on the papers. Did he tell you he had promised I could search them for correspondence and other documents relating to Colonel Jamison's military career?"

Davis frowned at the ingratiating quality in Glover's voice and at his out-and-out lie. Promise? The only mention Edgar had made about anybody other than Barrett was to complain about "some damn fool professors" who were hounding him for access. He'd said the only promise he made was to himself to give them a kick in the ass off his property. Davis kept his voice placid as he answered, "No, sir, he said nothing to me about anyone except Dr. Browning."

Glover hesitated, then said, "That is unfortunate. Edgar and I spoke several times about the collection. Are you certain he left no notes or letters about our agreement?"

You know he didn't, Davis thought, but said only, "No notes, no conversations."

"Well then. Given my discussions with your grandfather, when may I peruse the collection for items about Colonel Jamison's career, specifically after he transferred from the eastern theater? He played a prominent role in the subject of my next book and I *certainly* want to do his memory justice." His tone implied Davis would *certainly* agree.

He had to give Glover points for sheer audacity. The man was assuming not only that Davis believed him about the "agreement" with Granddaddy but also that he was one of those Southerners who would do anything to see his ancestor's name in print. It gave him a certain satisfaction to be able to say, "Dr. Browning and I have an exclusive agreement regarding the papers. Until she completes the inventory and I know exactly what's in them, no one is allowed access."

"Let me ask another question, then." Glover's voice dropped in volume and took on a just-between-us quality. "Are you certain Dr. Browning is the right person to do the job? I don't mean to denigrate her abilities, but she has no experience in archiving old documents. Her main concentration in Women's Studies wouldn't prepare her for understanding the importance of the political, economic, or military aspects of the papers.

Her scholarship to date has been . . . 'acceptable,' but certainly not of the stellar quality you would want for a collection of the significance of the Windswept papers. Why, the woman doesn't even have tenure, and she isn't likely to get it, either."

Davis glared at the phone. The damned son of a bitch. There was obviously little collegiality among the members of the History Department, and this particular specimen was a real snake. It would be a cold day before this man laid one finger on the papers. He felt his temper flare, but held it firmly in check and asked with a purposefully frigid edge, "Are you implying my grandfather and I made the wrong decision concerning Dr. Browning?"

He must have gotten through to Glover, because the man backtracked rapidly. "No, no, not at all. I'm sure she'll do an adequate job. I'm simply offering my expertise if you need it."

"Thank you for your offer, Dr. Glover. I'll keep it in mind."

"Please do, and, uh, give my regards to Barrett."

"Good-bye." Davis pushed the button to disconnect. He swiveled his chair to the windows and leaned back, rubbing his finger under his mustache. Barrett had been correct: historians would be willing to grovel to get their hands into the papers. And lie. And cheat.

If he ever let this man in, he'd probably have to frisk him on the way out just to be certain this "good professor" hadn't finished the third part of that particular triumvirate of actions.

"Acceptable" scholarship? "Adequate" job? Glover had said the words the way a jealous competitor would praise a rival's work.

Sure, Barrett didn't have a lot of experience creating an archive, but she was smart and knew she'd have to bring in experts. She certainly had the motivation to do a good job. Granddaddy had investigated and chosen her. Everything Davis had seen so far indicated she knew what she was doing. Glover was full of shit.

Her "colleague" probably wanted to take over the inventory himself. Davis grimaced. The thought of Glover in her place left a sour taste in his mouth, and he'd only met the man over the phone. No way in hell would he invite such a person into his home.

But what did the son of a bitch mean, she wasn't likely to receive tenure? Sounded like sour grapes to him, Davis decided, but he had the sneaking suspicion he hadn't heard the last of Horace Glover. Maybe he should do a little research into Glover's abilities and reputation—to have the ammunition ready for the man's next foray. Good ol' Horace might be a military historian, but Davis knew a little about tactics himself.

He wouldn't mention Glover's call to Barrett, however. No need to distract her. He wanted her attention on two items only: the papers and him.

Friday afternoon a little after three-thirty, Barrett put the last of the files into the 1845-C box and carried it into the conference room. There were only two boxes left for 1845. Thank goodness. The C box had been all about cotton, cultivation techniques, prices, economic outlooks, reports from factors, and clippings from both Massachusetts and British newspapers about the cotton market. She knew someone over at Southwest Louisiana who would love to see this stuff, but as for her, she'd been bored stiff.

She walked into her office and looked out the glass walls at the pool's turquoise water glistening in the sunshine. It was time for a break. If she took her swim now, got her blood moving, blew the cobwebs out of her brain, she's be all set to work on her own research tonight. The set of 1832 correspondence between Mary Maude and her sister and two brothers had looked intriguing the first time through, and Barrett wanted to follow up on her idea for her first article.

She hurriedly turned off the computer and straightened the room. Within ten minutes, she was surfacing from a shallow dive. The cool water washed off the grime of the papers and cleared her mind at the same time. She swam six laps, then floated on her back and let her thoughts wander.

Talk about research heaven! She didn't know what she had done to deserve her situation, but she'd take it. A collection no historian had ever seen before, uninterrupted access, congenial company, family and friends nearby. All too often she had carried on research in places where she knew no one and filling the evening hours after the library or archives closed had been difficult.

And the food! Eva could cook in a five-star restaurant.

And the weight she must be gaining! Barrett turned over and swam another six laps.

When she was floating again, she couldn't stop her thoughts from returning to her host. She was enjoying their dinner conversations. They'd fallen into the pattern of telling each other how the day had gone—progress on their projects mostly. She was learning a great deal about the business world from him. In turn, Davis was showing real enthusiasm about history, and it seemed to surprise him. She had to chuckle; she'd seen the same reaction in several of her students after they were bitten by the "history bug."

As for the attraction she felt to him . . . She'd managed to temper her responses and had focused on placing him firmly in the category of a person, her host, possibly a friend, who happened to be a man. All she had to do was keep him there and the summer would be a piece of cake—dark, moist, chocolate cake with fresh strawberries on the side. She could do it, she decided, and congratulated herself on her resolve and intellectual approach to the problem.

Right now, she could float here in this marvelous pool, like a flower adrift on a tranquil sea and think up more awful clichés. Let's see, like a dandelion wafting on a summer breeze, like a hoop-skirted woman waltzing across a hardwood floor, like a fishing float bobbing on a peaceful pond, like a—

"Hello!"

Barrett sat up, or tried to, but her feet didn't descend fast enough and she went under. Sputtering, she straightened herself out, but she was in the deep end of the pool, so she had to tread water.

Davis, clad only in his swimsuit, put a towel on the patio chair and grinned at her. "Didn't mean to startle you," he said.

"No, not at all," Barrett coughed as she tried to

keep her eyes in her head. She usually didn't pay much attention to a man's physique, probably because her brothers were always wandering the house in one level of undress or another when they were growing up. She had developed a "seen one good looking male bod and you've seen them all" sort of attitude. She'd told herself she was more interested in what was in a man's mind than how his body looked.

But she couldn't ignore the man's body in front of her. All that sleek muscle, toned to perfection, a wide chest lightly sprinkled with dark hair, a flat stomach, slim hips and long powerful legs. Oh, God, he was gorgeous.

"Do you mind if I join you?" His white teeth flashed under the black mustache.

"Of course not," she managed to answer, hoping her fluster didn't show. She wasn't sure what to do, so she backed up to the pool edge and floated against the side to give him room.

He dove in cleanly and swam several laps before coming to her side. "You had the right idea," he said as he tread water.

"What idea?" She was confused and embarrassed by her confusion.

"To go for a swim. The summer heat is already building, and Lord knows, after the day I've had,

I needed to work off some steam." He moved so he could float beside her.

"Bad?"

"Just several unreasonable people. Nothing I want to talk about. Especially at the moment. It's too peaceful here to think about them."

Saying nothing, they floated amicably for a while, and Davis took her hand to keep them close together.

"Do you swim much during the school year?" he asked, righting himself to tread water close to her, then standing when he discovered he could touch bottom. The water was up to his shoulders.

Barrett used his hand to balance and told herself to ignore his closeness and the warmth of his hand. "No. My condo has an outdoor pool, and I don't use the university's indoor one. But your pool is so nice after a day in those dusty papers."

"I'm glad you're enjoying it." He pulled her a little closer to him.

"Oh!" she exclaimed when her arm brushed his. She tilted her body, trying to stand, but she was still out of her depth. He slid an arm under hers and held her up. Barrett told herself he was simply being cordial, friendly, helpful . . . yes, *helpful* to someone shorter than he was. Then she looked into his eyes— how could hazel glint with green and gold specks and be so warm at the same time?—and she felt her breath catch in her throat.

"Excuse me, sir," Gonzales said from the poolside.

Davis jumped almost as much as she did, Barrett noticed, but he didn't let her go.

"There's a call from Mrs. Murphy. She says it's important."

"Oh, hell. What happened now?" Davis asked. "Tell her I'm coming." He turned to Barrett. "Excuse me. This shouldn't take long." He made certain she could stand before he released her, then climbed out of the pool, grabbed his towel, and went inside.

Barrett didn't wait. The feel of him holding her up, their almost bare bodies touching along their lengths, his arm around her back, his hand splayed on her waist, had sent a bolt of electricity shooting through her. Going from placidly floating to instant awareness and accelerated heartbeat had unnerved her. "He's just a friend," and "Be professional," she told herself as she climbed out of the pool, picked up her towel, and went to her room to get ready for dinner.

On the phone in his office, Davis was not happy as he watched her leave the pool. He'd planned to return and take up where they left off. Even with Peggy blabbing in his ear, he couldn't help but smile as he thought of how she felt to him for the brief moment in his arms. And the way her nipples peaked under her suit when he put his arm around her. And how her blue eyes darkened when he looked into them. And how his own body responded.

Damn. He couldn't remember ever wanting a woman as much as he wanted Barrett.

The way her body had tensed when he held her up told him she was as aware of him as he was of her. But her eyes had a wary look in them, like she wasn't sure what he was up to. She was probably just cautious around men. With a mind and a body like hers, she must be hit on by numerous guys. No matter. He was certain he'd gain her trust. He'd just have to work especially hard at dinner to resume their usually relaxed companionship.

Chapter
TEN

Saturday right after lunch, Barrett sat on the floor of the office and jerked the top off box 1845-D. She hoped to God some decent records lurked in this one—anything to focus her mind, get it away from thoughts of Davis and yesterday. She didn't need this, this . . . distraction.

First, the episode in the pool had set her nerve endings tingling. Then he was just "good old Davis" at dinner, acting as though nothing at all had happened.

Obviously to him, nothing had.

But to her?

Second, she had trouble sleeping, and she *never* had trouble sleeping. Hadn't she slept like the proverbial baby the night before the oral exam for her Ph.D.? And before the defense of her dissertation?

Third? Ah, yes, third. Dreams. X-rated dreams, with a certain hazel-eyed, black eagle of a man.

Result? She hadn't been able to concentrate on her own research this morning, even with Davis out early to play golf. Rain was forecast for the afternoon, and he was trying to get in his game before the weather arrived. Barrett looked out at the gray overcast. The burgeoning clouds were churning across the sky and turning blue-black. She'd turned on the overhead lights and the one on the desk. There would be no swimming today.

She'd put on her most disreputable T-shirt—a University of Texas one looking, thanks to the holes in it, more burnt than orange—and a pair of cut-off jeans and kicked off her shoes to tackle the grungiest box in the collection. It was so heavy she had to ask Gonzales to help her move it into the office.

The two-by-three-by-two-foot receptacle was dented gray-green metal, not cardboard, with metal rings on each end and a makeshift wooden top tied on with old rope. She hadn't opened it in her initial sorting, but had assumed the "1845" label on the outside was correct. Gonzales had vacuumed the outside and cut the rope for her.

She laid the top aside and sniffed at the ribbon-tied brown envelopes filling the container. Good, no mildew smell and not as much dust as the exterior suggested. The envelopes ranged in size from eight-by-five to ten-by-twelve and were stacked flat, not on edge as in the other boxes. No notations indicated their contents or dates, either. With a sigh, she opened the first one and carefully pulled out the sheets it contained.

"Well, this is more like it," she murmured as she unfolded one after the other of the ten pieces. She arranged the pages chronologically on the floor under their original envelope. She quickly opened two more envelopes and spread out their contents in the same manner until she was surrounded on three sides by a semicircle of paper. Cross-legged, she leaned back against the desk and grinned. "Hot damn, you've found the bills of sale for the plantation's slaves," she said aloud as she raised her arms, waved her arms, and did a little seated victory dance.

A flash of lightning and a rumble of thunder drew her attention from the papers to the patio. It began to rain, and for a moment she watched the drops falling into the pool until its silvery surface danced from their impact. She hoped Davis had finished his game without getting wet. At least she and the papers were high and dry.

Another five envelopes later, documents covered the floor. She laid out the contents of the fifth envelope, stuck on a sticky note designating its year and tiptoed down the little path she'd left between lines of pages. She sat down in the middle and surveyed the scene. There was no order to the way the envelopes had been placed in the box; what she had spread out ranged from 1832 to 1854. The box was still half full and she had no more floor space, so it was time to record these before opening the remainder. She'd stack the envelopes in order when she returned them to the box. If there were bills of sale for even half of the four hundred slaves registered to the plantation in 1860, she had a long way to go. She reached for the first envelope's contents.

"Who are *you*?" a woman's startled and suspicious voice asked.

Barrett looked up to behold a vision. The woman in the doorway was beautiful, in fact, downright dazzling. She was tall, maybe five-nine or –ten, as nearly as Barrett could tell from her position on the floor. Slim and sleek, too. If she'd been out in the storm, she certainly didn't show it. She was impeccable from the top of her long, wavy blond hair highlighted with platinum streaks to the tips of her long red fingernails to the bottom of her creamy leather stiletto-heel sandals. The rest of her wore what Barrett surmised was at least a thousand dollars worth of designer pants suit. The suit's color was the light yellow Barrett couldn't wear unless she wanted to look like she had jaundice.

The vision's lipstick matched her fingernail color and emphasized the soft plumpness of her lips. The lips themselves went from the "U" shape in "you" to a straight line and her perfect brows drew together in a frown over light brown eyes as she glared down her small, straight nose at Barrett.

"Where's Davis?" she asked, but didn't give Barrett a chance to answer her questions. Instead, she turned her head slightly and spoke in the direction of the hall, "Gonzales? What's going on here?" She put one hand on her hip and waved the other at Barrett.

"Mrs. Reed," Gonzales said from behind her, "as I told you, Mr. Jamison is not here."

"And who is this sweet, young thing?" The woman pointed at the documents. "And what is all this mess?" She took two steps into the office and stopped with the toe of a sandal on top of one of the pages.

Barrett shut her open mouth and rose, thankful she was able to do so fairly gracefully. She knew her slovenly clothing had made the wrong impression, but her dress was no call for rudeness. And she certainly wasn't going to let this person, whoever she was, no matter how perfect, walk all over her documents.

"My name is Barrett Browning, and 'this mess' is part of the papers of the Windswept Plantation. Would you please step back? As you can see, some of the pages are in fragile condition." She pointed at the offending shoe and used her teacher tone of voice.

It seemed to work because the woman stepped back about six inches.

"*Maestra*, this is Mrs. Reed," Gonzales said, sounding embarrassed, "Mrs. Reed, this is Professor Browning. She is making an inventory of the papers from the plantation of Mr. Jamison's grandfather."

"Oh, yes, I read the old . . . 'gentleman' had died." She sniffed, took a tissue out of her purse, and dabbed her nose. "They certainly stink, don't they?"

If anything stunk, it wasn't the papers, Barrett thought as the woman's movement caused a swirl of air and carried the scent of her perfume over the box to Barrett's nose. The cloying smell reeked of sexuality. Mrs. Reed must fancy herself a femme fatale.

Barrett ignored the question and said instead, "It was nice to meet you. If you'll excuse me, I must get back to work." She accompanied the statement with a direct look to imply the sooner Mrs. Reed was gone, the better.

Mrs. Reed returned the tissue to her purse. With an expression of speculation, she stared at Barrett, then said, "Give Davis a message from me, Gonzales."

"Tell me yourself, Sandra." Davis's voice rang out from the hall, and he filled the doorway.

"Oh, Davis!" Sandra Reed exclaimed with a smile of seeming delight. As she turned toward him, she stepped back, her thin heel puncturing one of the papers under her feet.

"Don't move!" Barrett cried and carefully knelt so she could reach the document.

"What?" Sandra asked, and her other foot shifted, narrowly missing another bill of sale.

Davis grabbed her by the shoulders and held her in place. "Don't. Move," he ordered. "Barrett, can you take the document off her heel?"

"Just a minute," Barrett said, rapidly stacking the papers to the side. As soon as she had created a safe area around the skewered page, she put her fingers around the stiletto above the paper. "Okay, lift up your right foot and I'll slide the paper off." She glanced up at Sandra's smirking face and wished she could crack the heel right off.

Sandra did as requested, and Barrett maneuvered the paper down and away from the sandal. She rose and inspected the mutilation.

"Is it badly damaged?" Davis asked. He let go of Sandra and leaned to look over Barrett's shoulder at the document. "What is it?"

"It's a bill of sale for one of the slaves," Barrett replied as she smoothed the hole closed. "She didn't hit any vital information. We can still read the date, the slave's name and the price."

"Good." Davis gave her a grim smile, then turned to Sandra. "If you want to talk to me, let's go into the living room." He gestured at the door.

Sandra looked Barrett up and down once more, smiled brilliantly at Davis, and, head high, sailed from the room. His face set in uncompromising lines, Davis followed her out.

Barrett breathed a sigh of relief.

"I apologize, *maestra*," Gonzales said. "She walked in before I could stop her."

"Who is she, *don* Jesus?"

"Mr. Jamison's ex-wife." He said the words with a look of profound distaste on his face. Then he left.

"Oh," Barrett said to herself as she started to reorganize the papers. "The 'nasty' divorce Phil mentioned. Whoa. What a bitch." She took a minute to wonder how Davis could ever have married that woman and could only shake her head in puzzlement. Thank goodness she didn't have to put up with Mrs. Reed. "I'd show her what a 'sweet, young thing' I really am," she grumbled, "and probably get kicked out on my rear."

Davis ushered Sandra into the living room, but did not suggest she sit down. He wanted her out as soon as possible. He planted his feet and crossed his arms over his chest. "What's this all about?"

Sandra sauntered around the room, trailed a fingertip over the back of a Barcelona chair, and ran her hand over the smooth leather of the couch. Davis wondered if she was casing the joint.

She finally turned to him with one of her patented, down-her-nose expressions and a sly smile. "You know, this room looks as good as it ever did. I really did a marvelous job decorating the front of this house—and our bedroom, of course. I hope you haven't changed it either. But why didn't you ever let me do the same for the office wing? It still looks simply horrible, so plebeian."

He kept his face neutral, his eyes half-lidded. No way in hell was he going to make small talk or rehash old arguments. "Get to the point."

"I just wanted you to know I'm back in Houston—permanently."

"What happened to Joe Reed? Did he finally throw you out?"

"Oh, Davis, don't be crude. Let's just say we came to an amicable parting of the ways—much more harmoniously than you and I managed, I might add."

Davis grunted. It wouldn't take much for any divorce to be more civil than theirs was, but he wasn't about to give her an opening to discuss the acrimonious event again. Sandra looked like she was enjoying the conversation—a little too much for his comfort.

She wanted something. She *always* wanted something. Why else would she be paying him a call? She evidently hadn't learned that he'd give her nothing, ever again. But she was still playing those games of hers, and equally as always, she'd never come right out and tell him what she was after. He waited, keeping his negotiating face in place.

"And who is the little girl in your office? Such a cute thing, and so dedicated to those musty old documents. I thought she was going to break my heel when she removed that old piece of paper."

He debated not saying a word, but knew he'd get rid of her sooner if he answered a couple of her questions. "She's a professor of history. She's inventorying the Windswept papers for me."

"And she's staying here while she does?"

Sandra had certainly jumped to the conclusion quickly. "Yes. It's a big job."

She didn't look too pleased with the information, but she smiled with a patently false brightness and removed a card from her purse. "Here," she said, handing it to him. "My address and phone numbers. We must get together sometime, Davis . . . for old time's sake."

Davis took the card, glanced at it, stuck it in a

pocket. The address was a fancy high-rise condo not far from the Galleria. Her name was printed on the card as Sandra Hillsborough Jamison Reed. He wished once again he could have legally taken his name from her as part of the divorce settlement.

"Let me show you out." He turned, walked to the front door and opened it. A cold draft of damp air swirled into the entry hall.

Gonzales materialized from the back hall and handed him a wet yellow umbrella. "Mrs. Reed's."

"Thank you," Davis said and held it out, handle first, to Sandra. He stared at her until she shrugged and, with a smirk, sashayed up to him to take the umbrella.

She paused directly in front of him, flipped her hair back in that would-be seductive gesture she had, and ran a long red fingernail down his chest. "Let's see each other soon, Davis," she suggested in the low, breathy voice she used as a come-on.

Davis almost laughed in her face. Did she think, after what she had done to him, he was remotely interested in her? He remembered her seduction routine only too well. Her heavy perfume filled his nostrils. It had once ensnared him in a trap of gut-wrenching lust, but now it made him want to puke—probably not the reaction she was going for. He kept his expression blank, his gaze level, and his mouth shut.

When his nonresponsiveness registered, Sandra looked slightly shocked, certainly unhappy—like she almost couldn't believe she wasn't having her usual effect on a man. He opened the door a little wider and moved back. When she stepped outside, Davis shut the door and locked it. Through the peephole, he saw Sandra spin around and scowl at the door. Then she put her umbrella up and stalked off in the direction of her car.

Gonzales spoke from behind him. "I'm sorry, Mr. Jamison. She walked in right past me."

"It's all right. Both of us together probably couldn't have stopped her."

"Thank you, sir."

He grinned at Gonzales. "If she tries another stunt like this again when I'm not here, sic Eva on her. She'll get rid of Sandra without either of us having to lift a finger."

"Yes, sir," the houseman replied with a return grin.

Davis walked back to the office and halted in the doorway. Barrett was down on her hands and knees again, stacking the bills of sale into orderly piles. She stopped and looked up.

"I apologize for the . . . intrusion. I hope she didn't do any damage." Of any kind, he added mentally.

Barrett picked up a stack and rose. "There's no

need to apologize. As I said, her shoe didn't obliterate any important information." She walked around the desk, sat, fiddled with the papers and said, "Mrs. Reed is your ex-wife, *don* Jesus said." She flicked a glance up at him and back down to the papers.

Davis moved to the front of the desk, put his hands in his pockets and considered her reaction. Her voice was nonchalant, but her movements were jerky as she straightened the pages. She was curious, but too polite to ask the questions undoubtedly running through her mind. Although he hated to think about Sandra, much less talk about her, he owed Barrett some kind of explanation after the episode.

"Yeah, that was Sandra. We've been divorced over five years. She's been living in Dallas with her second husband, Joe Reed. They split and she's moved back here—why, I can't imagine because her family is in Dallas. But, Barrett . . ."

She looked up and he caught her gaze with his own. "You don't have to worry about her. She won't be back."

Barrett stared at him. His eyes had turned to hazel granite and his face to stone and she had no doubt at all he meant every word he said. Then he grinned at her, and what was becoming a familiar warmth returned to his eyes.

"Besides," he said, "if she comes back at all, I told Gonzales to aim Eva at her. They never liked each other, and Eva practically threw her clothes out the front door when she left."

Barrett had to laugh as the mental image of short, round Eva taking on tall, thin Sandra. "I had the notion Eva could be a whirlwind when she needed to."

Davis glanced at the bills of sale. "Now, what did you find?"

The subject of Sandra was obviously closed, Barrett thought as she handed him some of the documents. "We can compare these names to the census and other records for an accurate portrait of the slave population. These envelopes appear to be the slaves the plantation purchased. I haven't yet found any documents showing those Edgar Jamison sold."

Davis picked up the piece of paper Sandra had punctured and ran his finger over the hole. He read the spidery writing aloud. "*January 25, 1845. Received from Edgar Jamison, the sum of five hundred twenty-five dollars for Salome, a 20-year-old female in prime condition.*" A grim look on his face, Davis laid the page on the desk. "What a despicable business."

"Yes, it was," Barrett agreed.

A bright lightning flash illuminated the room and a huge crack of thunder caused the big glass windows to vibrate. Davis spun around in the direction of the patio and Barrett thought she must have jumped about a foot.

Davis turned back to her. "Looks like somebody agrees with us," he joked with a shrug of one shoulder. "I'm going to get cleaned up. What are your plans today?"

She waved at the papers. "More of the same."

"I have to catch up on my reading. I'll see you later." He gave her a small smile and walked out.

Barrett stared at the papers without seeing them as she reviewed the events of the past few minutes. The ex-wife. Another topic Davis didn't want to discuss. First his siblings, or at least, his brother, the one who wanted money. Now Sandra Reed. When he had come through the door behind Sandra, he had been the Davis she first met, the rock-hard, give-nothing-away, uncrackable monolith. The expression in his eyes and on his face currently proclaimed he was not carrying a torch for her—if anything, quite the contrary.

She sighed and slumped in her chair as a huge feeling of relief washed through her body.

Then she straightened. Why did she feel so relieved? It must be from knowing she wouldn't have to put up with another hostile person. Horace was difficult enough. The last disturbance she needed was for an unpleasant ex to wander in and out throwing caustic and catty statements at her or destroying documents.

Lightning flashed and more thunder rolled, this time farther away. She glanced out the windows again. A gloomy and melancholy day. Perfect for reading documents of the nature of the bills of sale, she thought as she turned to the computer. Sighing again, she pulled up the template for the inventory and started typing.

Chapter ELEVEN

The Journal of Mary Maude Davis Jamison
Windswept Plantation
December 4, 1832
A blustery winter day, not too cold.

My prayers have been answered. It is certain! I am with child! Edgar is beside himself with joy and cossets me dearly—when he is not railing about the political situation between President Andrew Jackson and South Carolina Senator John C. Calhoun.

But I care not for politics—not now. After almost three years of hoping and praying, we are going to have a baby. We are going to be a family. Edgar lost his parents when he was only 15, and I have sensed in him the longing for the love and stability only a family can provide. Rogue that he is, he has been teasing me about how much fun all the "practice" has been leading to this blessed event.

We are at this moment both sitting in his study,

I in a chair by the fire and he at his desk, diligently writing in our journals. He claims to be recording plantation business, but I think he is putting down his thoughts about the arguments over the right of states to nullify laws of the federal government.

I wasn't certain I would continue my journal when Edgar encouraged me to begin one, but now I cannot imagine being without the daily practice of ordering my thoughts and working out my plans and problems in writing. As no other white women live close by with whom I can easily share thoughts, my journal has become a friend and confidante.

Windswept Plantation
June 23, 1833
A beautiful summer day.

Elizabeth Caroline Jamison was born on June 20, 1833, a beautiful, 6-pound girl with blue eyes. I was surprised how easy the birth was. Oh, there was pain, of course, and I am tired, but the results are so wonderful. Edgar is a little worried because she has not a hair on her head, but Heeba assures him it will grow. Men seem to like women with long hair. Edgar certainly loves my long black hair and delights in running his fingers through it, draping it over his body and tickling me with it.

Heeba helped me with the birth. Edgar had wanted Dr. John Miller to attend me, but Elizabeth would not wait for him to arrive, and the absence of a physician did not bother me in the least. I know and trust Heeba, servant or not. As we have planted and tended the gardens, we have enjoyed many hours together. I was taught by my mother that one should always keep servants at a distance, but I simply can't do it with Heeba. From her I have learned so much about plants and herbal medicines, about teas and poultices, about beneficial and unwholesome combinations.

I honestly do not know if Edgar was disappointed his first-born child is not a boy. I do not think he was. When he came into the room to see us and his glance fell on his new daughter, a look of such wonder and awe came over him. But later, his roguish glint returned to his eye and he whispered, "Think how much fun we'll have making another!"

Present Day
Saturday, June 2

Rain fell steadily into the evening. At dinner, it seemed to Barrett they both tried to avoid any subject of consequence. Certainly Davis added no information about Sandra to the conversation. Barrett wouldn't ask, of course. After dinner, she returned to cataloguing her bills of sale and Davis tackled the mountain of business magazines and newspapers he had accumulated.

About nine o'clock, Barrett picked out the last of the envelopes from 1845-D. "Thank goodness," she muttered. She opened the envelope, spread out its contents and arranged the pages in chronological order. After stacking the contents and laying the stack on the desk with the others waiting to be typed into the inventory, she took time to stretch out the kinks. She reached high, tilted to one side, then the other, and finally bent over and touched her toes. The last maneuver brought her head down close to the box, and she glanced inside.

"Huh," she said, "I didn't notice that." The bottom of the box appeared to have a wrinkle in it. She knelt down and reached inside. The surface slid under her hands. It wasn't metal she was feeling, but an oilcloth of some sort, almost the same color as the box's interior. She worked her fingers around the edges. Whatever was in there was only slightly smaller than the box itself.

Now, if she could just squeeze her fingers under one edge on the long side, she might be able to get a purchase on it . . . There, one hand was ready, and then the other. She braced her knees against the base of the box and pulled. The object was heavy and tried to bend in the middle, but she kept steady pressure until it was vertical. The bottom side was laced together with stout twine through metal grommets.

She rose and tried to lift out the oilcloth-wrapped package, but it was heavy and she couldn't get a comfortable grip. She glanced at the inner office. No sense in breaking her back when help was right there. "Davis," she called, "could you come here a minute?"

"Sure," he answered and as he walked in, asked, "What do you have there?"

"I don't know, but it's too awkward for me to lift. It wants to bend in the middle."

"Here, I'll take this end and you take the other," he said. "Let's put it over there." He nodded at the table next to the windows and moved the chairs to give them room to maneuver.

Together they lifted the object out and placed it on the table, laced side up between them. He pulled one end of the twine and the simple slipknot opened. They each laid back their side of the covering.

Inside were two more similarly wrapped packages.

Barrett looked up and her gaze met Davis's. She could see the curiosity in his eyes and knew hers mirrored his.

"This is like a treasure hunt, isn't it?" He grinned and pointed to the package on his left, then his right. "You take that one and I'll take this."

They opened the packages simultaneously and spread wide the oilcloth to reveal two sixteen-by-twenty-inch, leather-bound ledgers in each bundle. The three-inch-thick books were tooled in gold filigree around the edges but displayed no titles or ownership.

"You open yours first," Barrett said as she scooted around to his left so she could see what he found.

With a flourish of his hands, as if he were a magician about to pull a rabbit out of a hat, Davis opened the cover to reveal words written in a flowing hand,

Windswept Plantation
The Journal of
Edgar John Jamison
1830–1838

"Hot damn," Barrett whispered. "I knew it was here somewhere. What's the one underneath?"

Davis was grinning as widely as she was while he slid the first ledger to the side and opened the second.

"It's for 1838 to 1847. What's in your stack?"

Barrett opened the top ledger. "More journal, this one for 1847 to . . . There's no end date. He died in 1854, so this must be the last one." She put the book on top of the other journals and opened the one below it.

"Oh, my God," she said, the words coming out in an excited whisper. "Look."

Around the edges of the first page hand-painted flowers and plants grew, some in orderly rows and some in abandon. In the center were the words:

The Herbarium
And
Pharmacopoeia
Of
Mary Maude Davis Jamison
Windswept Plantation

Barrett turned the page and read aloud what Mary Maude had written.

In this journal I will attempt to record all the plants cultivated at Windswept Plantation for both culinary and medicinal purposes. Rather than keep dried specimens of each plant here, I will draw and paint them to the best of my abilities. Dried speci-

mens will be kept in loose-leaf portfolios.

In addition to descriptions, I shall record here all the uses to which the various plants may be put, including recipes for medicinal and pharmacological concoctions. I will also note any special cultivation required.

Begun this day, February 24, 1832.

Barrett opened the journal to several places at random. A sketch, at times rough, at times filled out with still vibrant greens, yellows, and reds, portrayed an individual plant and a detailed description, often with a recipe for its combination with others or a comment on its contribution to health or a tasty dish.

A page titled "Marjoram" caught her eye. "Look at this drawing. Not only does she have the purplish-red flowers, but the detail even shows a hairy stem. And she writes, 'For disorders of the stomach and to relieve bloating.' I didn't know that. And she includes a recipe for a potion. Oh, Davis! These are wonderful." Without thinking, she wrapped her right arm around his back and gave him a side-to-side hug.

He reciprocated with his left arm around her shoulder and pulled her closer. "I had no idea looking through musty old papers could be so exciting," he said.

Barrett looked up and found herself caught in his gaze. In the bright light of the office, she could see the gold and green glints in his eyes. He was smiling, his lips quirking up under the black bar of his mustache.

For a few seconds, she stood transfixed in the warmth both from his eyes and from his body. Then he looked at her lips, and his head moved closer to hers, almost as if he were going to . . .

As she realized what she had done and how close they were, she hurriedly let him go and turned back to the journals. She had to take a breath before she could speak. "I knew Edgar's journals were here, your grandfather had showed them to me, but I never saw the Herbarium before." She sounded breathless to her own ears and hoped she wasn't making a fool of herself.

He squeezed her shoulder, and let her go, but she was still standing so close their arms brushed. She had to stifle the gasp that wanted to erupt as it seemed a spark flew between them. She busied herself with the oilcloth wrappings and used the excuse of folding the heavy cloth to move to the side.

Davis did the same with the wrappings from the journals he had opened and with the larger piece that had covered the four-book package. "Don't put these back in the box, okay? I'd like to take a look at Edgar's journal."

"I hadn't intended to stick them away. I want to look at them also, especially the Herbarium." She looked back at the metal container. "You know, finding these journals really makes me wonder what else is at the bottom of these boxes. When I was arranging them chronologically, I didn't take the time to delve into any of them. I didn't even look inside some. What else will we discover?"

She looked at her watch, then at the stack of slave bills of sale, and sighed. "But first things first. I'm going to finish these documents tonight, no matter what."

"And I'll start on Edgar. He has to be more interesting than what I've been reading." Davis gave her a wink, picked up the first journal and walked into his office.

Barrett let out a long breath as he exited. Stupid, stupid. Attracted to him or not, she had to be professional, and she'd practically thrown herself at the man. True, the Herbarium gave her reason to be exuberant, but she didn't have to hug him to show it. At least she hadn't used her other arm in a full hug. To have her body plastered to his would be too much for her equilibrium.

And he, poor man, to be subjected to her adolescent urges, had put up with her and had been kind enough to pat her shoulder in response. And then . . . ? Her imagination must really be working overtime if she thought he'd been about to kiss her.

Oh, God, she hoped he didn't think she was coming on to him like some love-starved historian who'd spent too much time in the library. She definitely did not want to engender any awkwardness between them. "Be professional," she muttered and forced her mind back on the tasks in front of her.

Barrett worked steadily for the next two hours and finished the bills of sale. She rubbed her weary fingers before filing the envelopes back in their box. There, done. She glanced over at the Herbarium as she stretched. Much as she would like to examine it tonight, she had to acknowledge it was too late, going on eleven o'clock, to start. Better in the morning when she was fresh.

As she was shutting down the computer, Davis turned off his office lights and walked in. He placed the journal on top of the others on the table. "Let me give you a hand with the box," he said.

They each took an end, carried the container into the conference room and maneuvered it into place. Davis clicked off the lights while Barrett went back to turn off the ones in the office. They halted in the hall by the stairs and looked out at the wet patio where the surface of the pool had returned to its usual placid state. It gleamed in the minimal illumination from the security lighting.

"It's stopped raining," Davis said.

"Yes," Barrett agreed and watched the droplets glisten on the tabletop for a moment. Then her eyes suddenly refocused and, instead of looking through the glass, she was staring at the reflection of the two of them. He was standing slightly behind her and the stairway sconces spilled enough light into the space to highlight the bones of his face, exaggerating its eagle-like resemblance.

She saw him raise a hand as though he might be about to touch her. No, she couldn't take another touch again. It would only aggravate her attraction for him. She pivoted and took a step toward the foot of the stairs. "What do you think of Edgar's journal?" she asked as a diversion—for her thoughts, if not his intentions.

She wasn't sure, but she thought he sighed before answering, "It's surprisingly interesting, especially the sections on enlarging the house. Edgar drew his own plans and the plantation produced the lumber. He mentioned his two master carpenter slaves, Horatio and Cletus. I can attest they knew how to build. Granddaddy said the house was always plumb, every right angle a true ninety degrees. Let me know if you find those drawings. I'd like to see them."

"I'll keep an eye out for them," she promised when they reached the top of the stairs, where she would go to the front of the house and he to the back to reach their respective bedrooms. "Good night. I'll see you in the morning."

"Barrett . . ." he began.

She raised her eyes to his when he didn't continue, but the shadows hid whatever he was thinking. He looked down at her for a long moment, lifted a hand and twirled one of her curls around a finger. When she felt the slight tug on her scalp, she couldn't have moved if the house shook, but he seemed to relax.

"You know the Gonzaleses will be off as usual tomorrow, and we're on our own for food."

She managed to nod. He released her curl and smiled with a look she couldn't interpret, but it drew a return smile from her.

"I have an idea I'll run by you in the morning. Good night." He turned toward his room.

"Good night," she replied and headed for hers, feeling absurdly as if an event had just happened she didn't quite understand. Damn, Davis Jamison was so hard to read.

Davis watched her turn the corner onto the balcony above the dining room before he walked into his bedroom and shut the door behind him. He shed his clothes, tossed them in the hamper, and brushed his teeth. He didn't allow himself to think about the evening until he was lying in bed.

Patience be damned. It had been all he could do not to return her little hug with a full-contact, body-to-body one of his own. The way she had dropped her arm and sounded so breathless had demonstrated clearly she felt the attraction between them.

He'd almost touched her while they were looking at the rain. He was actually raising his hand to put it on her shoulder and turn her around when she had walked straight out from under it. Something was causing her to . . . retreat? No, more like *deny* any inclination toward him.

He hadn't been able to stop himself from—finally—discovering if one of her curls was as soft as it looked. Well, he'd been proven wrong there. It was softer; the silky strand had simply flowed over and entwined itself around his finger. Touching it had brought him in scent range, and he marveled how stimulating was her mix of light spicy perfume, musty papers, and pure woman. Hell, he'd been instantly hard—and grateful for the low lighting.

What was he going to do? He liked the idea he'd had—to get her out of the house for a while. When she was here, she was so totally concentrated on those damned papers she could see nothing else. But he couldn't ask her out for a date. She'd never agree to it.

There was, however, one ploy she might go along with—if he negotiated carefully. He chuckled to himself and reached over to set the alarm so he would be up before she was. Now if the weather would only cooperate.

Chapter TWELVE

After a companionable breakfast with Barrett the next morning, Davis put down the financial section of the paper and looked out the window at a sunlit summer day. It was time to open his negotiation. "I have a suggestion I'd like you to consider," he said.

Eyebrows raised, puzzlement in her blue eyes, she looked up from the editorials.

He leaned back in his chair. "We both have been working pretty hard for several weeks—your finishing the school year, my traveling, and since you've come here and I've come home, we've been going at it nights, weekends, hell, in my case, even on the golf course."

She nodded, but didn't say anything.

"I, for one, need a break from business, and I'll bet you could use one too. It's a fine day. Let's play hooky from work and go to Galveston."

She frowned, and he could practically see her mind coming up with a list of objections.

"If not for yourself, do it for me," he said, playing

what he hoped was his high card. "I have a rough week coming and need to clear my head to come up with some innovative solutions to a couple of tricky situations. I need to 'not think' for a while. The papers aren't going anywhere. What do you say?" He gave her an encouraging smile.

She watched his smile—both beneath his mustache and in his eyes. The roguish Jamison glint flashed in the hazel depths. Was he serious? Did he have an ulterior motive? Of course not, she scoffed mentally. Her attraction to him was giving her unfounded ideas.

But what about her research schedule? "I should really take a good look at the Herbarium and Mary Maude's letters," she replied. "But . . ."

"But . . . ?" he asked with raised eyebrows.

She turned her head to gaze out the window at the flowers and bright sunny skies. The day appeared so inviting, especially after the gloom of yesterday. She sighed, and when she looked back at Davis, he was smiling wider, like he knew he'd won.

"All right," she acquiesced, and he grinned, the mischievous spark more evident. When she thought about the trip, she surrendered entirely. "It will do me some good too. I haven't been to the island in years. We can poke around the Strand, see some of the old houses, and—"

"And eat at Gaido's," he finished for her. "Let's change into shorts and look like real tourists."

———————◆◆◆———————

His idea had been right on the money, Davis thought as they waited that evening outside the famous seafood restaurant for their table. Barrett had proved to be a lively companion, interested in visiting a variety of attractions. She'd protested, saying she had no interest in war or its instruments, but she'd agreed to tour the World War II submarine in Seawolf Park.

Of course she'd bargained with him, trading the cramped quarters of the sub for the more gracious rooms of Ashton Villa, one of the few antebellum buildings still standing in the island city. Her knowledge of the way people lived in the nineteenth century and the questions she asked the docents enlivened the tour for all the participants.

"Would you have liked to live back then?" he'd asked her as they left the building.

"No, I much prefer modern conveniences," she'd answered with a grin, "but some of the architecture in Victorian houses is wonderful. The homes can be so warm and welcoming. Have you ever thought about living in a renovated one today?"

"Too much bric-a-brac and gingerbread," he'd answered. "Too hard to keep up."

She'd said nothing, only looked back at the villa and sighed.

On the Strand, the restored historic mercantile center, they had wandered in and out of the art galleries. One shop displayed several Texas beach scenes, and Barrett had spent a number of minutes staring at a picture of dunes, wispy grasses, and the sea beyond.

"Like it?" he'd asked.

"Yes, it calls to me somehow."

He had looked at it more closely. "Yes, I see what you mean. It's quite good."

"You like it?" she'd asked. "I thought you were more of an abstract-art person—from what's in your house, I mean."

He'd shrugged. "I guess I am, but I have no problem with representational art."

Remembering the conversation, he frowned. Did he have any representational artwork, where objects, or people, or places could be recognized for what they were? He'd grown up with family portraits and landscapes that had seemed dull and stodgy to him even as a boy. When he'd found his present house, he'd appreciated its clean lines and ease of upkeep. Then there was Sandra's influence. He shook his head. He certainly didn't want to think of her at the moment.

But he had liked the coastal painting Barrett had been studying—enough to make a mental note of the gallery and the artist.

"Jamison, party of two!" came over the loudspeakers. He put the thoughts out of his mind as he took Barrett's hand to help her up and they went to their table.

They didn't do much talking on the way back to Houston after dinner. Full with good food and the memories of a wonderful excursion, Barrett relaxed and her mind drifted, replaying the day.

Davis had been the perfect gentleman—always opening doors for her, asking what she wanted to see, willing to go different places—after some negotiation, of course. And, she had to admit, the submarine had been interesting. She couldn't imagine being one of its crew cramped together in the depths of the ocean; she was strictly an on-top-of-the-water person.

He had definitely shown his lighter side today. They had conversed about so many subjects, from war to the shrimp industry, Victorian living to sculpture, seashells to T-shirts. Not only had he talked, he'd *listened*. So many men, certainly most of her male colleagues, did not listen to what a woman had to say. They lectured, they interrupted, they pontificated.

They told you what to do or how to solve your problems as though you didn't have a brain in your head.

Davis, on the other hand, had let her finish her sentences, made comments contributing to the subject matter, and asked questions showing his attention to her statements. They had, in a word, conversed.

He hadn't touched her except once or twice, like when he helped her over the granite groins stretching out into the Gulf to retain the beach sand. And he'd held her hand while they walked on the seawall. And he'd been behind her with his hands braced on the railing on the ferry over to Bolivar Peninsula and back. And he'd put his hands on her shoulders when they stood, surrounded by other tourists, in Ashton Villa. And he'd put his arm around her shoulders as they walked back to the car from the restaurant.

My goodness, more times than she'd thought. A small tingle ran down her back as she remembered how good, how right her hand in his had felt. How safe and protected she'd been on the ferry. Had she leaned against him without realizing it? She had an impression of a hard, warm body against her back.

But she had to be serious. He didn't mean anything by the hand-holding or any of the other touches, she assured herself. He just had good manners.

He simply needed to get away from work, and she

was a handy companion. Anything else was all in her imagination.

It wasn't like they were on a *date*.

She glanced at him sideways. He drove with easy confidence, his long-fingered hands resting lightly on the wheel. The dashboard lights emphasized the harsh planes of his face, the dark slashes of his eyebrows and mustache, the slightly hooked nose. He could easily be a pirate at the helm of his frigate sailing through tropical waters or a starship captain guiding his craft through space, intent on his course.

She was close enough to smell him too. Despite the cool air circulating through the car, or perhaps because of it, the scents of sun and beach and man swirled through her nostrils every time she inhaled.

She knew her imagination was getting the better of her, but her thoughts resulted in a sudden intense awareness of his presence, his very male presence in the car. For a large Lexus, the car seemed to have shrunk and his body was very close to hers.

"Wouldn't you like to run your fingers through his hair and down those broad shoulders?" asked a little voice deep inside her. "Don't you wonder if his mustache tickles?" She told the voice to shut up, but her hands twitched anyway. She clasped them together in her lap before she did something stupid. She tried to concentrate on the soft jazz playing on the radio.

Davis saw the glance, the twitch, and the fidget. His tactics were working. She was becoming more aware of and curious about him, not as the owner of the papers or as her host, but as himself. It had been all he could do to keep his touch somewhat impersonal during the day. She hadn't shied away, had even leaned back against him on the ferry. He wanted her accustomed to his touch—and much more. He felt his body respond to the thought and wondered how much longer he would have to—or could—wait.

"You know I'm throwing a party at the house on Saturday in two weeks, sort of a thank-you to clients and an introduction to prospects?" he asked.

"The G's mentioned it," she acknowledged.

"I hope you are planning to come."

"Thank you. I'd like to. What's the dress? You know, what will the women be wearing?"

He shrugged. "I don't have the slightest idea."

"I'll call Peggy. She'll know."

"I'm sure she will."

"She was a big help arranging my stay here. We hit it off right away. She's an interesting woman. Did you know she studied to become a concert pianist?" When he shook his head, she continued, "Yep. She had plans when she was in college, but she met Jim

Murphy and fell in love. She gave up on her dream and switched careers to put him through school in engineering. I don't think she regrets it. I can hear the love in her voice when she talks about him."

How does she do it, he wondered. How in the space of a couple of phone calls did she and his assistant become so attached, sharing such personal details? Peggy had worked for him for seven years and he had no knowledge of her former ambitions. The comment made him wonder about something else. Barrett was certainly ambitious; she'd made it clear, but . . . "What would you do, if you had to face her kind of choice?" he asked.

"Career or the man?" She was silent for a few seconds. "Peggy was a young woman in the middle of college and didn't have an established career. She told me she didn't know if she had really the drive or the talent to follow the music route. 'Probably not' is my guess. My friends truly talented in the arts are driven by their talent. It won't let them settle for anything else."

"I know what you mean," he said.

"My situation is very different from Peggy's," she continued. "I have a fairly well established career, and my livelihood is tied to academia. I can't see myself giving up my career under any circumstances. I don't need to. I can teach and research history anywhere—

and publications, tenure and an associate professor title will make me more marketable if I decide to leave my present university."

Along with the determined tone that usually crept into her voice when she mentioned tenure, there was a note he couldn't identify, and he shot a glance at her, but she was looking out the passenger window.

Before he could pursue the idea, she turned back and asked in a bright voice, "What are your travel plans these days? Going anyplace exotic soon?"

Although he wasn't certain why, Davis would have liked to press her a little more on the first subject, but he went along with her question. "No, I'm sticking close to home for a while. Will it bother you if I work out of the house on occasion?"

"No, of course not."

"Good." A picture formed in his head of her working in the office, headphones on her head, typing like a fiend, oblivious to all going on around her. "You know, you concentrate more fiercely than anyone I've ever seen. Sometimes I think a bomb could go off and you'd never hear it. How do you do it?"

"Comes from growing up in a noisy house with three brothers. It was either block out everything or never get any studying done."

There was a light in the Gonzales's apartment

when they drove into the garage, and Davis remarked on it.

"Yes, they're probably deep into *Masterpiece Theatre* or *Mystery*," Barrett said. "You'd never know it to look at Eva, but she loves all those British shows. She has all the tapes for *Upstairs, Downstairs*."

"You're kidding!" Once again, she knew his staff better than he did.

"Nope." Barrett shook her head as she looked at the incredulity on his face. Didn't the man ever talk to the people who worked for him?

She took a deep breath as she opened the door and climbed out. The warm and humid night air felt almost good after the air conditioning in the car—or was her reaction simply relief at being out of its close quarters? She should be nonchalant, not give away her attraction to him. She had to play it cool, so she grinned at him. "Don't forget my seashell T-shirt."

"I haven't," he replied as he opened the trunk and removed the bag. "Now I know how you accumulated such a collection. I think we went into every T-shirt tourist trap on the island."

"No, we missed at least two," she teased.

She went to take the bag out of his hand, but he just said, "I've got it," and led the way into the house.

He was behind her in the hall, however, and up

the stairs. At the landing where he should have gone in the other direction, to her surprise he gestured toward her room and followed her down the balcony. After she opened her door, hit the switch for her bedside lamp, and turned back to him, he relinquished the bag and took her free hand.

"Thank you for going with me today, Barrett," he murmured, raising her hand to his lips. He kissed her knuckles lightly.

His mustache *did* tickle, and goose bumps skittered up her arm. The touch of his lips on her skin caused her to gasp as her body came to attention. Trying to ignore her reaction, Barrett stared up into his eyes, which were almost black in the soft light. She couldn't seem to move, could only wait to see what he was going to do, but she managed to say softly, "You're welcome, Davis. I enjoyed it too."

Davis bent and lightly brushed her lips with his— once, then returned to linger for a few seconds longer. The mustache tickled again, but his lips were soft, and the kiss was over before she knew it. He smiled down at her. "Good night, Barrett," he said, turned, and left.

Transfixed, hardly breathing, Barrett stood in her doorway until she saw the stair lights go out. She inhaled a huge breath as she went inside, closed her door and leaned back against it.

Holy . . .! What had just happened?

Davis Jamison, that hard, enigmatic, gorgeous man, the man she was having so much trouble reading, had just kissed her. The man to whom she was thoroughly attracted, but who, she had decided, did *not* reciprocate her feelings, had just *kissed* her. Twice.

Brief as they were, those were no thank-you kisses. She'd been kissed before. She knew what one of those felt like, and it wasn't like *this*. A thank-you kiss didn't take your breath and leave your body tingling. A polite, courtesy peck on the lips did not shut down your mind and make you want him to do it again.

Trying to force her thoughts into order, she pushed off the door and dumped the T-shirt she had bought out of the bag. She tossed the bag in the trash can, folded the shirt and put it in a drawer. Her mind still swirled in confusion.

"All right," she said aloud as she sat on the bed and took off her sandals, "what's going on here and what can we conclude from the facts?" She almost laughed because the question reminded her of one of those "trace the development of" questions she asked on history tests.

First. Davis was attracted to her. Those touches and those kisses were absolute proof. He clearly wasn't a touchy-feely sort of man who treated all women the

same, who bestowed kisses here and there and who
didn't mean anything by it. Oh, he probably wasn't
attracted as much as she was to him, but there was
something going on in the head behind his mustache.

Second. He wasn't rushing her, pushing her,
coming on to her—not blatantly. He had to be too
sophisticated to simply jump her bones. She couldn't
imagine him being heavy-handed in any endeavor.
No, Davis was the type you wouldn't see coming—as
he had just proved.

Third. What did he want? That kiss said more
than friendship. A simple summer affair? With a con-
veniently located woman? It was too soon to tell. She
had to be careful not to jump to any conclusions like
she knew she was inclined to do.

Fourth. What did *she* want? What if she fell for
him? Given her present attraction, wouldn't she fall
far, fast, and hard? Ah, now those were good questions. She wanted . . . not to be hurt. Not to have to
put herself back together. Not to be the object of pity
or scorn. Not . . .

She flopped back on the bed and drew her knees to
her chest. She was thinking in the negative. What did
she want in the positive? She couldn't simply answer
"Davis" to her question. She didn't know yet how far
she wanted to go with him. She did want his friend-

ship, she enjoyed his company, but after that?

Priorities, she had to set priorities. Above all else, she had to catalog the collection and gather her own research. Accomplishing those goals was still first and foremost and was going to take all her time and energy. She didn't have time for an affair, no matter how convenient.

Professional. She had to be professional. What if—oh, God, she hated this idea—they had an affair and it went sour? Where would it leave her, not with Davis, not even with her own feelings or self esteem, but with the ability and access to inventory the papers? What would it do to her professional reputation if he kicked her out of the collection, especially if it got around she'd been sleeping with the owner? Besides "bye-bye, tenure," she'd have a horrible time finding a job in the future.

Conclusion. She had to call a halt to . . . what? Something that hadn't really started? She'd have to talk to him, discourage any . . . advances. Explain her situation. She couldn't get involved. He was a reasonable man and they had a contract. He had to understand.

The question was, when would she do it? It was not a conversation she particularly wanted to initiate. She'd just have to pick her time carefully.

She sat up, feeling somewhat more in control. Her

course was clear—or clear enough.

But when she was lying in bed relaxing into sleep, she couldn't help replaying those two small kisses and the look in his eyes. And the tickle of his mustache on her upper lip.

Davis flicked off the stairway lights and closed his door behind him. He chuckled to himself as he remembered the stunned look in Barrett's eyes after he kissed her. She had not seen it coming. For a very intelligent woman, she had missed his cues.

Her friendly but impersonal demeanor was probably the way she handled men in general. She didn't let them get too close. She ignored subtle overtures. As for more obvious ones? He chuckled to himself. He could see her turning her "teacher" look on and hear the "teacher" edge to her voice. No man would stand a chance against her weapons.

Except for him.

He'd made progress today, he was certain. By the time they entered the restaurant, she'd become accustomed to his casual touches and seemed to be taking them for granted, even welcoming his hand in hers.

He hadn't been sure if he'd kiss her tonight, but her blue eyes had darkened when he kissed her hand, and she looked so appealing . . . and her lips had parted with her gasp, and he had to have a taste, even if it was just a tiny one.

He had her attention now, and although he still planned to take it slow, build their relationship with care, he was looking forward to the days to come.

Just as he fell asleep, he wondered what she thought of his mustache.

Chapter
THIRTEEN

About four-thirty Monday afternoon, Davis completed a phone call and looked at the work still to be done. He'd take it home. If he left now, he might be able to join Barrett in the pool. She'd tried to be "business as usual" at breakfast that morning. She had not brought up their excursion or displayed any of the usual indications of "interest" he was used to seeing from women. Instead, she'd snuck surreptitious glances at him from behind the newspaper. Wary and, at the same time, determined glances.

He had no doubt he'd win through her wariness. But what was she determined about? He grinned to himself. Finding out could be fun.

He reached for his briefcase just when Peggy appeared at the open door.

"Excuse me," she said with an unhappy note in her voice. "Lloyd Walker is here again."

"Let him in," Davis said. He stood and walked around to the front of his desk. He wasn't going to let his cousin get comfortable this time.

"Davis." Lloyd tried his threatening glare again as he came in. He stopped when he was about five feet from Davis and crossed his arms.

Davis leaned back against his desk and crossed his arms as well. "What is it now, Lloyd?"

"You *have* to let me go through the plantation papers," Lloyd stated, pale blue eyes glittering as he drew himself up and thrust out his chin.

Davis recognized Lloyd's mood. Whenever he was ready to fight, Lloyd always got a look of pompous righteousness on his face and a fanatical gleam in his eyes. Davis decided to be deliberately impassive; he knew it infuriated Lloyd and besides, old habits formed in childhood died hard. "I've given you my answer on the matter."

Lloyd put one hand on his hip and used the other to point at Davis. "Listen here. My mother is driving me crazy. She's absolutely certain Grandmama and Grandmama's mother both warned her there was bad news, disastrous information in them. Now my mother has talked to Aunt Phyllis." He said the last sentence as if he were announcing the end of the world.

Davis stifled a groan. Just what he needed—more family pressure. Cousin Taylor's mother was a notorious gossip who prided herself on her ability to root out secrets.

A note of triumph entered Lloyd's voice when he continued. "Aunt Phyllis corroborates Mother. She says *her* mother warned her about bad blood in the Jamison family when she married Uncle William, but she married him anyway."

"Wait just a minute," Davis interrupted. "Aunt Phyllis's family has no grounds for slinging mud, not with their rum-running exploits during prohibition."

"I know," Lloyd spat, "but the evidence is mounting."

"No, it's not. Has any one of these sources offered any details? *Who* exactly did *what*? When? Where? How in hell do you expect to find whatever it is when you don't know where to look? Do you have any idea how many boxes are sitting in my house? Do you have any inkling how long it takes to go through even one box? Dr. Browning has been working hard and she's only up to the eighteen-forties."

Lloyd looked disgruntled for a moment, but he rallied. "I have some questionable reports about her too. I still think she's unqualified."

"Questionable reports? From whom?"

"I have my sources," Lloyd said as if he were a member of the CIA. "The word around her department is she won't get tenure. How will it look if we rely on her judgment and she's a second-rate historian?

How can we trust it?"

Lloyd must have been talking to that asshole Glover, Davis surmised, but he said only, "And you can do better? You with no training in history?"

"I've had training. I was pre-law in college. We had to take a lot of history. I'll get to the bottom of these tales and Mother's fears. Whatever it was had to happen before the year Granddaddy was born. That narrows it down."

"Yeah, to only about ninety years." Davis shook his head. "It doesn't matter. I am not letting you have access to the papers." He watched Lloyd turn redder in the face at his declaration.

"You don't give a shit about the family, do you? Well, let me tell you something." Lloyd whipped out his pointing finger again and shook it at Davis. "You'll pay for this. Something in those papers will ruin us all."

Davis straightened off his desk and looked down at his angry cousin. "Don't be so melodramatic. If the family withstood the Yankees, the boll weevil, and the Great Depression, it can stand up to anything in some musty old records—assuming, of course, all this bother is not just some ghost story or misunderstood tale from Grandmama's youth. You're working your-self up over nothing, and I don't have the time to waste on it. Now, get out of my office and let me get back to my business. That's where you should be too, tending to your own affairs."

He took a step toward Lloyd, who backed up and opened the door. He didn't leave, however, without a parting shot.

"Mark my words, Davis. I *will* investigate those papers, and I *will* find out what Mother and Grandmama are so afraid of. When it all comes to light, you are going to be lucky if anyone in the family ever speaks to you again." He walked out, slamming the door behind him.

"Good riddance," Davis said aloud as he rounded his desk and sat down. Lloyd was really getting wound up over nothing.

Or was he? Could there be any bit of news, any evidence of wrongdoing, an act so awful to justify Lloyd's or his mother's premonitions of doom? Nah, he scoffed, and began to gather his files. The past was the past, and Davis had no patience for those who lived in it. He had enough to pay attention to in the present.

By the time he reached the elevator, Lloyd wished he had done something to wipe the superior look off

Davis's face, even if it meant his larger cousin would have knocked him on his ass. At the same time, he had to admit he'd blown his own game plan.

He'd worked it out so carefully after Dr. Glover's call yesterday with the news Granddaddy had promised the professor access to the papers and his cousin had refused his request. He meant to be calm and collected, the way Davis always was, to lay out his arguments like a legal brief, to make it clear it was going against Granddaddy's wishes for Glover to see the records. After all, the man wanted to add to the glory of Edgar Jr.'s name. What was wrong with that?

Then he'd use the historian as his entrée to the papers. Even if Davis refused to let his own cousin study the things, said cousin would have a spy in the enemy camp, *his* captive researcher willing to do his bidding.

But instead of rehearsing his arguments, he'd thought about the mess he was in all during the long drive from St. Gregoryville. His car's air conditioning wasn't working properly, and the miserable Houston traffic didn't help his disposition either. By the time he'd handled the snooty bitch who guarded Davis's office and then faced the sneering bastard himself, he'd been too angry to maintain control.

Now he had to head home. Home. Where one of his apartment properties needed renovation so badly

the city inspectors might condemn it—and he didn't
have the cash or credit to fix it. And where he had to
prepare for an upcoming idiotic lawsuit which he had
been unable to talk his fool client out of and for which
he wouldn't see a penny for months.

Home, where his accountant had died, dropped
dead of a heart attack at the age of fifty-one, only six
weeks ago. Two weeks ago the man's son and inheri-
tor of the business had informed Lloyd of his father's
dereliction of duty with regard to keeping up with
business. The late accountant had been sicker than
anybody realized and had left all his clients' books in
total confusion. God only knew what Joe Blinford
had been doing, but he hadn't balanced the accounts
in six months.

Blinford Jr. had been extremely apologetic and said
he'd straighten everything out at no charge to Lloyd.
When the books had been balanced, however, Lloyd
found himself in worse shape financially. Nobody
seemed able to account for some receivables. Junior
thought his father had simply deposited them in the
wrong accounts and they'd turn up when he finished
with all the clients. Well, crap, what was Lloyd to do
in the meantime? How would he pay his bills?

On top of it all was this damnable mess of the
Windswept papers. His mama called him daily, pre-

dicting ruin, but not coming up with any real facts despite his pleadings. He felt like screaming at her to get off his back. Blowing up wouldn't work, of course. She'd just lay a guilt trip on him even Grace wouldn't be able to talk him out of.

What was so sacred about those records? They should belong to the entire family. If he could only get his hands on them, he knew he'd be able to find what Mother was talking about, no matter how many boxes he had to go through. But his cousin, smug in his possession of the family heritage, refused to give him access.

Damn Davis! Damn him to hell!

Lloyd stomped through the parking garage, but stopped when he spotted a black Lexus. Wasn't it Davis's car? He walked over to it and looked in the driver-side window. A folder with the Jamison Investments logo sat on the passenger seat. It was his cousin's. His look-down-his-nose, so-superior, younger cousin's.

Damn Davis! He gave the door a kick and dented the side.

The release of frustration felt so good, he kicked the car several more times. Davis thought he was so smart, huh? Wham, another dent!

He heard someone coming and rapidly walked to his own car, parked fortuitously only six cars down, but he still shook with rage. A few kicks were not enough to punish his cousin for his highhandedness. He'd show Davis he didn't rule the world.

He saw the man he'd heard get into a car and drive off. He stood for a moment, but nobody else was in sight or hearing. He opened his trunk and took out his daddy's hunting knife he always carried in his toolbox. He walked back to Davis's car and checked again. Nothing moved and the only sounds were those from the street below.

With the razor-sharp knife, he quickly slashed all four of Davis's tires and gave the other side a couple of kicks for good measure.

There. Let Davis have something to worry about for a change. Lloyd restored the knife to its place, climbed in his Cadillac and backed out of the slot.

Several ideas occurred to him as he paid the parking fee. He'd talk to his mother again. He wouldn't tell her about his financial difficulties—hellfire, he hadn't brought himself to tell *Grace* the true extent of those. But if Mother wanted him to get the papers, then she would have to help him pay for the effort. And he'd tell the fool client—the *rich* but stingy fool client— he wouldn't take his case without a stiff retainer. He wasn't doing anything on contingency.

And he had something else to do—one more ploy

to try—before he went home. He turned the car toward the cheap motel he remembered up close to the North Loop.

Chapter
FOURTEEN

The Journal of Mary Maude Davis Jamison
Windswept Plantation
October 17, 1835
Still warm, but we're all hoping for
cooler weather soon.

We have a wonderful son, born October 13, and Edgar is beside himself with joy. Edgar John Jamison, Jr., is a strapping boy and came forth exercising his lungs. Edgar said he could hear his boy announcing his presence all the way down in the library.

I do not know what I would have done without Heeba as this birth was a little difficult. Edgar Jr. did not want to be born for quite a while. I am still tired, but I can feel my strength returning daily.

Thinking of Heeba, I have learned so much in the past 3 years from her about plants: plants for food, plants for medicines, mixtures for healing, and herbs for cooking. I have taught Annie, our cook, how to prepare some dishes as the chefs do in New Orleans, and she has proved an apt pupil. Edgar delights in inviting fellow planters and their wives to dinner and has often told me how proud he is of our accomplishments—well, he really said 'my' accomplishments, but I can't take credit for it without acknowledging Annie and Heeba and the other servants' work.

Windswept Plantation
September 15, 1840

Another very hot day, after three weeks of unrelenting heat and dryness. Ominous clouds are massing in the south, and several of the older servants think a big storm is brewing. If it would only bring relief!

The weather, however, cannot dampen my spirits. We have another son! Davis Wade Jamison was born September 2. I thought Edgar was happy when Rebecca was born in 1838, but his joy at another son seems immeasurable. The man takes such delight in his children. He is already training Edgar Jr. in his own footsteps, taking him on his rounds of the plantation. Edgar Jr. sits on his own pony, a precious copy of his father. I even caught him trying to paint a mustache on his lip with Elizabeth's water colors so he'd look just like him. I am so proud of my men.

Each birth has been harder than the last, and after
Rebecca two years ago, Heeba was apprehensive about
my having another child. But God blessed us with
Davis, and I am ecstatic, although I agree with her that
my labor was very difficult. I am certainly not recuper-
ating as speedily as in the past. Heeba warned me more
severely this time, however, and will teach me how to
mix certain plants and herbs to prevent a reoccurrence.
I am of mixed feelings about this, as I would like as
many children as God will give me, and I know Edgar
would be totally against my taking such measures.

And I probably shouldn't write this, but we take
such pleasure in the marriage bed. Edgar is mine and
I am his, for all time. I am so blessed with my husband, whose faithfulness is legend.

At the Galliard plantation three months ago, my
heart went out to Marie, whose husband has a dread-
ful reputation among the ladies for his dalliances in
the quarters. There, before the eyes of their assem-
bled guests, stood the youngest house servant, a lad of
seven, the spitting image of her husband Samuel and
almost a twin of her oldest son Martin. I don't know
how she can bear to see those children (yes, there are at
least two more), but in all honesty, I don't know what
she can do about it. The Bible and the Church teach us
to submit to our husbands. There are at least two other

ladies in the parish with the same situation.

I said a prayer for all of them. I don't know what I would do in their shoes. Thank God, I will never be.

To thank me for his new son, my dearly beloved husband has given me a new botanical book with beautiful illustrations, a wonderful addition to our library. Heeba scoffs at my reading as a way to learn about plants and their healing properties, but I gain much knowledge and insight from them. She won't admit it, but I have even taught her a thing or two!

Present Day
Monday, June 4

Hoping he would be in time to join Barrett in the pool, Davis left the office a few minutes before five. He knew he'd shocked Peggy by leaving early, and he grinned as he approached his car.

All it took was one glance to replace his high spirits with cold, hard anger. Who in the hell had vandalized his Lexus? Dents on both sides and four flat tires. Somebody really let him have it. Somebody had been really pissed . . .

Lloyd.

The vandal had to have been his cousin. Of all the low, miserable . . . Davis hoped to high heaven Lloyd had gone home, because he'd like nothing better at the moment than to beat the shit out of the man. A dozen curse words and phrases ran through his head, but he didn't voice them. He refused to give Lloyd the satisfaction, even in absentia, of causing him to lose his temper. He simply turned around and went back to his office.

"What's the matter?" Peggy exclaimed after one look at his face.

He told her what had happened. "You call the parking garage management and my insurance company, and I'll call the police and the Lexus dealership," he said. He'd better call home also to alert Gonzales he might be later than usual.

The police officer who responded asked if he had any idea who would vandalize his car, but Davis did not mention his cousin. He could not prove Lloyd was the culprit, and none of the garage staff had seen or heard anything. The dealership hauled his vehicle away and left him a rental in its place.

He made it home just in time for dinner—and a couple of words with Gonzales before Barrett came down. He told his houseman to be extra vigilant and make sure the security system was turned on, just in case Lloyd had any more destructive ideas. They also decided not to tell Barrett and Eva about the incident. If asked about the change in his car, they'd say matter-of-factly he had car trouble and leave it at that. No need to worry the women.

At dinner Barrett didn't seem to notice anything out of the ordinary. In fact, she was bubbling over with excitement about a phone call from a high school friend. As he listened, he realized her happiness acted as a balm to his spirits and helped erase his crazy cousin from his mind. He took a bite of his pasta and let her words roll over him.

"Angela found out from one of my sisters-in-law that I was in town," she said. "She really let me have it for not letting her know. Well, she's getting married this Saturday. Big, big wedding. I never received her invitation, it's probably in my mail being forwarded, so it's a good thing she called. It'll be great to see her whole family again, especially her mother. The woman was like a second mother to me when we lived next door to each other."

"So you're going?" he asked.

"Wouldn't miss it for the world."

"The bride's last name is Tejeda? Her father runs the restaurant chain?"

Barrett nodded. "Yes. The groom is Diego Morales.

His family own the furniture and import-export stores. Why?"

"I've met Diego. His father and I have collaborated on several investments and he's bringing his son into the business. I have an invitation to the wedding also." Looking at his weekend schedule just this morning, he'd known his attendance at the wedding was mandatory for building more connections in the Hispanic community with an eye toward investments here at home and in Latin America. Since then, he'd been trying to figure out how to talk Barrett into going with him. For once today, it appeared the gods were smiling on him. "Would you like to go together?" he asked.

"Could we? I hate going to weddings by myself."

She looked so thoroughly pleased with the idea Davis felt like kissing her right there at the dinner table. Then he thought of his cousin and knew he'd do whatever it took to keep Lloyd, his crazy ideas, and his erratic anger away from her.

———◆◆◆———

Tuesday morning, while Brahms' First Symphony played in the background, Barrett was on the carpet, deep into organizing a box of business papers, invoices, factor reports, and other accounting records. When she noticed a movement out of the corner of her eye, she looked up to see Eva in the doorway—an Eva who seemed distressed. Muting the boom box, she turned to the housekeeper.

"Is anything wrong, *doña* Eva?" she asked as she rose.

"Please come quick, *maestra*," Eva exclaimed, wringing her hands. "Mr. Davis's cousin, Lloyd Walker, is demanding to see you. Jesus told me to come get you so he could watch Mr. Walker."

Eva's statement didn't make much sense to Barrett, but she stepped over the circle of files and papers and hurried out to the entrance hall with Eva on her heels. She remembered meeting Lloyd in Louisiana when he came by to see his grandfather. She also remembered the conversation she had overheard between Davis and his cousin. She had a pretty good idea what Lloyd might want and braced herself to do battle.

When she rounded the corner into the front hall and came up to the two men standing like pit bulls eyeing each other warily, tension and dislike seemed to be ricocheting off the walls. "Hello, Mr. Walker. Is there a problem, Mr. Gonzales?" she asked as she looked at Lloyd.

Gonzales started to speak, but Lloyd cut him off. "Yes, *Dr. Browning*, there is a problem." He emphasized her name nastily, as though he wanted to spit it out of his mouth. "I demand to see the Windswept papers, all of them and right now!"

"I'm sorry, I don't have the authority to show them to anyone," Barrett countered. From the tone of his voice alone, she decided he'd see them over her dead body.

Lloyd looked her up and down, an insulting, sneering scrutiny of her cut-off jeans, Northwestern University T-shirt, and bare feet. "I'm Edgar Jamison's grandson just as much as Davis is. I have as much right to those papers as Davis does, and I want to see them now!" He took a step in her direction, but Gonzales moved in front of her, slightly to one side. His posture stated clearly Lloyd would have to go through him before he'd get to Barrett.

"I'm sorry, Mr. Walker," Barrett repeated, feeling just the opposite. She assumed her professional and slightly stand-offish professor attitude, as if Lloyd were a student asking for special treatment. "I cannot allow anyone access to the Windswept papers without Davis's express permission. In addition, the documents are not in any state for casual perusal. Are you looking for something in particular?" She thought he blanched at her question, but she ignored the reaction and continued. "I could tell you if I found it already or I can keep a lookout for it and Davis could let you know when we find it."

"No! I have to be the one to look. I'm the only one who can find it." His answer came quickly and too loudly for the circumstances, she thought.

Sweat popped out on his forehead, and he took a handkerchief out of his pocket and wiped his brow. A crafty gleam flashed through his eyes, his voice dropped, and his drawl deepened. "Look here, honey," he said through a clearly fake smile, "why don't you and I just sit down here in the living room and talk about this. I'm sure you'll see my point of view. What harm can I do to these dusty old papers? After all, I'm part of the family."

He turned to Gonzales and looked down his nose at the shorter man. "You're dismissed. The professor and I can talk on our own."

Gonzales didn't move, except to roll his shoulders like he was anticipating throwing Lloyd out bodily.

"We really don't have anything to talk about, Mr. Walker," Barrett said. "I can't give you access, and if Davis were here, I'd recommend against letting anyone go through the papers before they're inventoried." She played what she hoped might be her ace in the hole. "Shall we call him to see what he says?"

"That won't be necessary," Lloyd growled. He turned to the door, but swung around when he reached

it, pointing a finger at the two of them. "You tell Davis
for me I'm going to see those papers, one way or the
other, and I don't care what I have to do or who I have
to climb over to get them!" He threw the door open
and stomped out to his car. The tires squealed as he
tore out of the driveway.

"Well!" Barrett exclaimed. "What was that all
about, *don* Jesus?"

Gonzales relaxed as his eyes followed Lloyd's
progress onto the road. "Mr. Walker and Mr. Davis
do not get along." He shut the door.

"No fooling!" She grinned at Gonzales, and he
shrugged with a smile. "I'd better get back to work."
She walked off toward the office, but turned to the
older man after a few steps. "I'm glad you were here,
don Jesus. I wouldn't have liked to try to get rid of him
by myself."

"It was my pleasure, *maestra*." Gonzales bowed.

———————◆◆◆———————

Hoping to talk with Barrett before dinner, Davis came
home early. When Gonzales had called him to report
Lloyd's visit, hot anger at the son of a bitch had flashed
through him. When his houseman had told him what
Barrett had done, pride in his historian cooled him

down. She had handled his cousin beautifully, but Davis wanted to make certain Lloyd had not upset her. She, however, had already taken her swim and was changing in her room when he arrived.

He asked Gonzales to bring him a bourbon, and he strolled out to the pool. A light breeze ruffled the water, bringing the scent of the roses to him. The temperature was mild, but it wouldn't be long before the patio was too hot a place to sit until the sun went down.

He took off his jacket and tie and stretched, feeling his muscles finally begin to relax for the first time since the phone call. When the houseman brought him the drink, he sat at the table. He concentrated on his surroundings, particularly a chattering mockingbird, to avoid any thoughts of his unwelcome visitor.

The door behind him opened and Barrett walked onto the patio. "Davis? You're home early." She looked from the glass in his hand to his eyes. "That kind of a day, huh?"

"I hear you had a similar one. Can I get you a drink?" It made him feel better just to look at her, all chocolate-brown curls and long legs. He wondered how much longer he could be patient.

"No, I'm fine. I have some good news too. I'm almost through the eighteen-forties." She sat down next to him at the table.

"I'm glad you're making progress." He took a sip of his drink. "Gonzales called me after Lloyd left. I'm sorry you had to put up with him and his crazy demands."

"Davis, there's no need to apologize. It certainly wasn't your fault. I hope I did the right thing, not letting him have access to the papers."

Yes, it was his fault, but he wouldn't belabor the point. "You made the absolutely correct decision. Lloyd and I have had it out several times now about the papers. Edgar left them to me alone, with complete control over their disposition."

"Lloyd became very agitated when I asked if he wanted to look for something specifically. He must have an idea, but he refused to tell me what it was."

"He has an unfounded claim from his scatter-brained mother there's something scandalous in the papers. She maintains this mysterious information will ruin the family name."

"What, after all this time? Something not already part of local lore? I haven't come across anything remotely of an infamous nature. And your grandfather never intimated any awful revelation lurked somewhere. What could it be?"

"God only knows. He claims his mother heard the tale from our grandmother, but nobody's said anything concrete. Granddaddy always said Lloyd's mother, her mother, and her mother before her all shared the same trait: They were all inordinately proud of and worried about the family name and convinced the slightest blemish would ruin them in society, among the 'people who matter.' "

"And I'll bet your father, his father, and his father before him didn't give a damn," she teased.

Davis shot her a glance as he took a swallow of his bourbon. She certainly had them all pegged. "Correct. And I don't either, not in the context Lloyd does, at least. I care about my family's honor and honesty, and I'll do what I can to help and protect them from real threats or hardship, but I'm not going to help them maintain their place in the social register."

A frown crossed her face and she clasped her hands in front of her on the table. "So our rules about access stay the same."

"Yes. No one gets access until the inventory is completed, and then only on my say-so. You can still call in experts as needed, but that's all. If, and this is a very large if, we let Lloyd close to the things, I want to be there, doling out the pages one at a time. I wouldn't put it past him to try to steal some."

"He won't lay a finger on even a scrap, then," she said with an emphatic nod. He thought she looked relieved.

"Agreed." He put his drink down and covered her hands with his. When he began to rub his thumbs over her knuckles, she tensed and raised her eyes to his. It would be so easy to drown in the deep blue of hers, he thought, but he remained serious and concentrated on the situation at hand.

"I don't want to frighten you," he said, "but I do want you to be careful where Lloyd is concerned. He had a peculiar look about him when he came to my office, and from what Gonzales said, he was almost out of control here. From now on, if I'm not here, neither Gonzales nor Eva will let him into the house. If he comes back again, one of you is to call me immediately." He gave her fingers a little squeeze for emphasis.

"I was very glad Gonzales was here today," she said, and her gaze turned apprehensive. "Do you really think Lloyd would try to force his way in? He did make a threat when he left, but I assumed it was bravado and bullying on his part."

"I don't want to take any chances," Davis said. "We used to fight all the time as kids, and he always pitched a fit when he didn't get his way. He's seemed more unstable lately, like he's on a hair trigger. I called his house before I came home, and his wife Grace said she expected him back home this evening. He had gone to New Orleans about a law case, according to her. I didn't tell her he was actually here.

"If he calls you or tries to contact you in any way, let me know immediately. I don't trust him at all, and I don't want you in the middle of the argument between him and me. Agreed?"

"Agreed." She nodded.

He gave her hands a squeeze and smiled when she returned it. He couldn't help raising one and kissing the back of her fingers. "Agreed."

She started, but didn't pull out of his grasp. Her blue eyes darkened, and she wet her lips. He watched her pink tongue retreat into her mouth and thought about how it would feel to follow it with his. He saw the questions in her eyes, and he smiled. "I'll take care of you, Barrett," he murmured and leaned nearer to her.

"Dinner is ready, Mr. Jamison," Gonzales announced from the doorway.

Davis sighed inwardly and sat back. He and Gonzales were going to have to talk about interruptions. He rose and held the hand he had kissed to help Barrett rise. "Thank you," he said and led Barrett into the dining room.

Two hours later Barrett sat staring at her computer

screen. She'd managed to put Lloyd's visit and the questions it had generated out of her mind—until Davis came home. And took her hands in his. And kissed her fingers. And promised in those deep velvet tones, "I'll take care of you."

A shiver ran up and down her backbone and she wriggled, rubbing against the back of the chair until the tremor subsided. Then her hand tingled where he had kissed it, so she rubbed it too.

Now she had more questions, but not about Lloyd. Davis was going to stand up to his side of their agreement, she had no doubt about it. She hadn't raised the matter of publication of her findings again, but she didn't distrust him on the point either.

No, her questions revolved around their, their . . . what? Relationship? Friendship? Arrangement? What did one kiss on the hand, one kiss on the lips—no, two on the lips—and another on the hand, accompanied by mustache tickles add up to? What did eyes that went from hard, cold granite to warm, persuasive, charming, gold-and-green-flecked hazel pools signify?

He was after more than just an inventory.

The attraction between them was not a figment of her imagination. Neither was it one sided.

The man was subtle, she had to admit. At dinner, he hadn't mentioned Lloyd or any other member of his family. He's steered the conversation from city politics to sports to her reminiscences of her friend who was getting married. He hadn't touched her again.

He didn't need to.

A tension hung in the air—slight, wispy, invisible, but not undetectable. Enjoyable, not offensive. Exciting—oh, yes, exciting. Titillating.

What was she going to do about it? About him?

What had happened to the priorities she had set just the other day? She'd never discussed the situation with him, brought it out in the open, as she had decided she had to. Somehow the opportunity hadn't arisen.

Or, she'd been chicken. *Bwuck, bwuck, bwuck.* She formed the words with her lips, but didn't say them aloud.

It was so easy to go along, doing her work, enjoying his company, letting the days slide by, especially when he'd made no overt move forcing a discussion. What he'd done up to now could be explained as his normal attentiveness to a woman, any woman. Except she couldn't see Davis *normally* kissing "just any woman" on the lips or the fingertips, or telling "just any woman" he'd take care of her while looking at her with a gaze hot enough to incinerate every last scrap of the Windswept papers.

They needed to talk.

She had to think about the situation and come to her own conclusion, in her own best self-interests.

But not now. Not right this minute. The combination of Lloyd's visit, the accompanying adrenaline rush, and the conversation at the pool and *its* adrenaline rush had scrambled her brain. Better to finish this small stack of papers and get a good night's rest.

She turned to the pile and resolutely began entering the first letter's information into the table.

Bwuck, bwuck, bwuck sounded in her head, and she shook it vigorously. She wasn't a barnyard fowl. She merely had to pick the opportune time.

———◆◆◆———

The next afternoon, Davis tracked down his cousin on the phone at his office in St. Gregoryville.

"Lloyd, stay away from my home, Barrett Browning, and the Windswept papers," Davis said with no preliminaries. "You have no 'right' to the documents, and your empty threats waste all of our time."

"Now, see here," Lloyd sputtered. "I won't let you ruin the family."

"I'm not going to."

"Yes, you are, if you let that little nobody mess around in our history."

"All you're doing is making vague accusations and wild statements with no facts to back them up. Why should I believe you? Your mother and Aunt Phyllis haven't given you any details about this reputed 'awful thing,' have they? Lloyd, you're a lawyer, for God's sake. Think, man, you have no evidence of any wrong-doing by anybody."

"My mother's word is good enough for me."

The discussion degenerated from there, despite Davis's attempts to maintain some kind of control. Lloyd simply refused to listen to reason. He finally threatened legal action, and Davis told him to go ahead and waste his money.

The word, "money," seemed to penetrate Lloyd's temper, and he suddenly shut his mouth. Davis let the silence hang in the air for a few seconds. Then he said, "Lloyd, you know I always protect the family."

"Not this time, you won't. That woman and what she writes will be the ruin of us. I'm the only one who is willing to save the family name, and I am going to get my hands on those papers, no matter what," Lloyd shouted into the receiver.

"No, you aren't," Davis said as evenly and calmly as he could.

"Go to hell, Davis!" Lloyd hung up.

Davis threw the receiver back on the hook and sat

down at his desk. Damn! Lloyd was an idiot. He was beginning to worry about his cousin's stability also. He sounded more out of control than he had ever before in one of their arguments.

Davis rubbed his face with both hands. One of these days, he supposed he'd have to go over there and get the whole family together to thrash this out. But he'd wait until Barrett worked her way through more of the papers and he could prove there was nothing there. For now, at least his cousin was back home and unable to bother them, and Davis could tell Barrett to relax. But he'd tell Gonzales to keep the security alarms on.

Chapter
FIFTEEN

Saturday afternoon, as Barrett dressed for the wedding, she reflected on the last three days. Davis hadn't mentioned Lloyd again, and she certainly hadn't brought up the subject. Her host had been the perfect gentleman, the comfortable friend, the interested on-looker in her historical quest. They'd discussed subjects from politics to baseball at dinner. He hadn't repeated his kisses, either on her lips or her hands. He hadn't touched her at all.

She—*bwuck, bwuck, bwuck*—hadn't forced the issue, hadn't brought up the subject of a "relationship" either.

But still . . . that tension, awareness, whatever it was, continued to surround them both and heightened each encounter, even the trivial ones.

On Friday at the bottom of yet another oversized trunk filled with 1840s correspondence, she'd found the rolled-up architectural drawings for the plantation house expansions from the first Edgar's bedroom wing all the way to the addition of the kitchen and installation of modern bathrooms. If she didn't know better, she'd have thought his grandfather hid them. Had "Grand-daddy" been playing games? If so, to what purpose?

She and Davis had spread the plans out on the long table in the conference room after dinner and studied them, standing side by side.

"Look here," Davis had said, pointing to the kitchen diagram. "I never realized the present kitchen wasn't added on until the nineteen-twenties. They must have been still cooking in the original unattached kitchen up to then."

"And probably still using the fireplace as the stove," Barrett had added and she'd rummaged through the plan scrolls. "Wait a minute, I think . . . Yes, here it is." She'd pulled out a five-foot-by-four-foot paper and anchored the corners with the scissors, a utility knife, a yardstick, and a roll of tape. "This is the master plan. See, it shows the other buildings."

Braced on one arm, she'd leaned over the table to study the structures at the top of the sheet and pointed to the various buildings with her free hand. "Here's the milk house, the laundry, and the old kitchen. The laundry shows the water pipes, the sinks, and I think this round object may be a washing machine or a per-manently placed tub." She had rested her finger on the drawing.

"Right." Davis had leaned over also. "There's the fireplace in the kitchen and the baking oven in the wall next to it. This area in front is designated 'hearth.'" He tapped his finger on the objects. "I don't see any indication of even a wood-burning stove or an additional chimney for it, do you?"

"No," she had said after studying the drawing, "I don't." She had raised her head and found herself looking straight into his eyes, their heads no more than a foot apart, their shoulders almost touching. In the cool air-conditioned room, the warmth of his body had been palpable and oh, so alluring. Her gaze had fallen to his lips, and when she had raised it to his eyes again, the heat in the hazel depths had been scorching. She had felt the strongest need to move into his arms and claim his incandescence for her own.

Only by the absolute application of her will had she managed to pull back and straighten. She'd made some comment—probably an exposition on open-hearth cooking, but she couldn't remember any more—and busied herself with another drawing while she'd tried to calm her suddenly galloping heartbeat. When she'd finally summoned the courage to glance back at his face, he was studying another plan, but a satisfied smile had lurked under his black mustache.

The man was a devil, no doubt about it.

His pursuit of her wasn't her imagination. They had to talk soon. But first, the wedding.

She pulled the gauzy, light blue dress over her head and zipped up the back. Then she twirled before the mirror. The full short skirt flared; it was a wonderful dress to dance in. The V-neck, deeper in back than in front, set off the slight tan she was acquiring from her swims. Thank goodness the dark blue jacket made it proper to wear in church.

She put on her silver earrings with the sapphire drops and the matching pendant necklace, a gift from her parents when she received her B.A., slipped on her shoes and the jacket, and gave herself a once-over, front and back. She'd tamed her curls as best she could, and they'd just have to do.

Picking up her purse and the present she'd run out to buy yesterday, she took a deep breath and opened her door. Time to go to the wedding.

Davis was talking with Gonzales in the foyer as she came down the stairs. He was wearing one of his power suits again, this one navy, with a crisp white shirt and a small-patterned, red-and-blue tie. He must have heard her step because he glanced up and seemed to freeze for a moment as he ran his gaze from her curls to her shoes and back up. She could almost feel the heat from his eyes and she stopped, transfixed. He looked both formidable and fascinating.

Then he broke the spell by grinning. "What? No T-shirt?"

"I didn't have one with frills and lace," she retorted with an answering grin.

He took the present from her and gestured at the door. "Come on, then, Cinderella. Your carriage awaits."

———◆———

She did feel like a fairy-tale princess, she thought later, as she whirled around the dance floor in Davis's arms. In a ballroom full of handsome men, she was certain she was dancing with the prince—and to a waltz, no less.

She detected the fine hand of the bride's mother in the selection of dance tunes, which were ranging from old-fashioned waltzes and fox-trots to the latest cha-chas, rumbas, and sambas. The swing, jitterbug, and plain old rock and roll were yet to come. Elena Tejeda had always loved to dance, whatever the music. She'd taught all the neighborhood children too.

Mama Elena also liked handsome men, and when Barrett had introduced her to Davis in the receiving line, she'd sized him up immediately and given Barrett a wink. Of course, when Davis had bowed over Mama Elena's hand and murmured, "It's always a pleasure to meet a beautiful woman," he had won her over completely. She had whispered in Barrett's ear, "This is definitely the right man for you."

Since Barrett knew the bride's family and Davis was acquainted with the groom's, they had no problems fitting in with the crowd, a number of whom had gone to high school with Barrett and Angela. Davis didn't seem to mind listening to their reminiscences. In fact, from some of his conversations with her friends and their families, it looked like he had attracted possible new investors.

She wasn't surprised at this turn of events. A gathering such as this would be an excellent opportunity to further his business interests. She had noticed the cordiality with which the groom's father greeted Davis. Evidently their investments had gone well.

The waltz ended and he ushered her back to their table with his hand on the small of her back. They were back to touching again, she realized. Nothing overt, just holding hands every once in a while, or his arm was around the back of her chair at the table, or he was standing just slightly behind her so their arms touched.

He was pleasant to her male friends, but she caught the exchanged "looks" from time to time. It reminded her of her brothers' attitudes when they were dating the women who became their wives—definite "stay-away-she's-mine" orders. She soon had confirmation. When she was dancing with a classmate, he asked her if she and Davis had something going. She replied in the negative; she was simply studying some old papers Davis owned. With a very dubious note in his voice, her friend said, "I don't know . . . The look he gave me said I'd better return you to him safe and sound." She scoffed at the remark, but she also noted he didn't delay escorting her to Davis after the dance.

Guys' games, she thought and stifled a snort. But did Davis think he had a right to do it? They'd have to talk soon.

Davis stood when she returned to their table. He took her hand and said, "Let's circulate. My mother taught me to always dance with the hostess."

While Davis danced with Mama Elena, Barrett was Papa Jose's partner. Jose proceeded to question her closely about Davis and didn't seem to like her bland off-putting answers. When the music ended, he told her, "I have discussed Davis Jamison with Juan Morales and a few others. This is a good, honorable man, Barrett. I worry about you. It's about time for you to marry and settle down."

"Please, Papa Jose," she begged, feeling heat rise to her face, "I'm fine. You don't need to worry on my account."

"Now, Barrett," he said. "Angela finally found her Diego. You will find your man too. Besides, your parents couldn't make it to the wedding and asked me to look out for you. What kind of neighbor would I be if I didn't follow their wishes?"

"Thank you," she said and asked a question to change the subject. She didn't need a matchmaker.

Davis was dancing with Mrs. Morales when Barrett returned to the group around the Tejedas' table. His absence seemed to have its own effect, as one man after another asked her to dance. The result was she remained on the floor through several sets, moving from one partner to the next. She had to smile. She'd always been popular, but never like this. None of the men held her close or even flirted much, but several asked questions, mostly business related, about Davis.

After yet another dance with yet another old friend, Barrett decided she needed something cool to drink and headed for the bar. As she sipped some cold water, she looked around for Davis and saw him in deep conversation with Jose Tejeda, Juan Morales, and several other men important in the Hispanic community. He was obviously too busy to dance with her and she felt vaguely disappointed. She put the thought aside to talk with two of the Tejeda sisters.

Several minutes later, the band started a tango

and Davis appeared in front of her. With the grin of a rogue reminding her again of his grandfather, he asked, "Do you know how to tango?"

"Yes," she replied. "It's Mama Elena's favorite, and she made sure all of us know how." She nodded at the couples, the Tejedas among them, already beginning the dance.

He held out his hand and she went with him.

Once on the dance floor, he took her in his arms and swung her into the long gliding steps and dips of the tango.

Barrett gave herself up to the music pulsating with the beat, the feel of their bodies brushing, touching, moving in close unison, and the man gazing at her with dark eyes. He led with mastery, with subtle but clear indications, with understanding of the stylized sensuality of the dance.

But the way he held her, looked at her, pulled her to him had nothing to do with the conventional elegance of the tango and everything to do with its heat, its glamour, its passion. She was entranced when the final chords sounded and he laid her back in a low dip.

As the band segued into a slow, sultry song, Davis raised her without a word. He kept her close, drew their clasped hands to his chest, and moved into a languid step that became little more than a sway as others packed the floor.

When he laid the edge of his jaw against her temple, Barrett shut her eyes and floated. She could feel the heat of his hand on her back, his thumb rubbing her bare skin just above the back of her dress. She could smell his woodsy after-shave and the pure male beneath the suit. She was beguiled, she was enticed, she was . . . seduced. She'd analyze all this later, she decided. Right now she'd just enjoy. She sighed and ran her left hand up over his shoulder.

As he felt her palm slide across to the collar of his coat, Davis smiled. She smelled so good, a subtle blend of warm woman, heated from the dance, and light, floral accents. She had looked so pretty when she appeared on the stairs ready to leave. The blue jacket complimented her eyes, and the swirling skirt showed off her legs. But when she'd taken the jacket off at the reception to reveal the deep V of the dress and the smooth sweep of her back, he'd almost growled. He'd made certain to warn off any men with possible designs on her. Now he had her in his arms, so he tested a theory and rubbed his thumb up over her backbone. Yep, warm silk.

He smiled to himself when she shivered slightly and moved even closer. With her high-heeled shoes, they fit together perfectly, danced smoothly, as if they'd

been partners for years. He'd have to take her dancing again soon. On the other hand, if they danced
much closer, she would hardly miss the effect she was
having on him—and neither would anybody else.
Control yourself, Jamison, he ordered. Wait until you
get home.

The song ended and he held her a few seconds
past the last note. He pulled his head back and gazed
into her heavy lidded eyes. Her mouth, with her lips
slightly parted, was so tempting. He was lowering his
head to brush a kiss across those lips when the ballroom lights came up and Juan Morales called all the
guests to bid the bride and groom farewell. Barrett
blinked, visibly shook off the spell they had both been
in, smiled rather tentatively, and turned toward the
raised platform where the wedding party stood.

Davis could only take a deep breath and shake his
head. What was it with these interruptions every time
he got close to her? He hoped to high heaven this was
the last one.

On the way home, Davis glanced over at Barrett
as she babbled about the wedding and the friends she'd
seen. She was definitely nervous, probably about him.
She'd never run at the mouth before. In fact, her ability
to speak succinctly was one of the attributes he liked most
about her. And she could be companionably quiet.

She seemed to realize what she was doing, because after a couple of minutes, she stopped in the middle of a sentence and sighed. "Sorry," she said, "I guess I'm still jazzed from seeing everybody again."

He stopped the car at a red light, reached over, and brought her nearest hand to his lips. "No problem," he murmured. "Meeting your friends was interesting." He brushed her knuckles with his mustache as he kissed the back of her hand. He heard her breath catch and turned his head to smile at her. She didn't say a word, just looked back with those big beautiful blue eyes, as if she were waiting to see what he did next.

The light turned green and the driver behind them honked. Davis had to grin. His luck with interruptions was holding—it was all bad. He kissed her hand again quickly, returned it to her lap and gave it a squeeze before letting go. The car behind honked again as he stepped on the gas pedal.

After a few minutes, Barrett cleared her throat and said, "I think you may have some potential investors calling you next week. Several of my friends mentioned they were looking for opportunities."

"Yes, I agree. I gave out a number of cards. Juan Morales, Jose Tejeda, and a couple of their friends are coming by on Tuesday with a start-up proposal. All in all, the event was enjoyable on several levels." He shot a glance at her, but she was looking straight ahead. She didn't say anything else.

Barrett stared unseeing out the windshield as she castigated herself for acting like a discombobulated nincompoop, blathering on nonsensically. Yes, she was nervous. The last dance and now the kiss on the hand yelled loud and clear that Davis, the black eagle, was hunting tonight. She had to keep her wits about her. The man had a powerful effect on her; it would be so easy, too easy to end up in his bed. And lead to possible disaster. On several levels.

On the other hand, she had to admit she was curious about what kissing him would be like. Really kissing him, not the little bitty sample of last weekend. She knew what his hands felt like—those long fingers had already caused tingles up and down her backbone when they were dancing. It took scant creativity to imagine them elsewhere on her body and she had to suppress the shiver the thought generated.

She mulled over scenarios for saying good-night—kiss or not, go farther or not, or—*bwuck, bwuck*—simply run upstairs and lock herself in before he could do anything. Wouldn't the last idea go over well? Talk about making a fool of herself.

Then her eyes focused and she realized they had arrived. He parked in the garage and took her hand as they walked to the house. She almost giggled. Could he read her mind? Did he think she was going to run away?

"Would you like a nightcap?" he asked as he reset the security device when they were in the kitchen.

"No, it's late. I think I'll just turn in," she replied and moved toward the door into the dining room.

He simply nodded and followed.

Only the light over the sink was on, and Davis flicked its switch as they went through the door. The wall sconces along the hall and stairway cast their usual low illumination to highlight the path through the darkness.

Barrett glanced up at Davis as they climbed the stairs side by side, his hand on the small of her back. He must have seen the movement of her head because he gazed back as they came abreast of one of the fixtures. The light reflected off the hard planes of his face but left his eyes in shadow. Barrett was struck once more with the avian-like resemblance, but then he smiled, and pure warmth and charm surrounded her.

"I had a good time tonight," he said in his deep velvet voice. "Did you?"

"Yes, I did too," she replied, but couldn't think of anything else to say as they continued up the stairs.

And then they were at her open door. Her bedside lamp cast a muted light onto the balcony.

She swung around to face him. "Davis . . ." was the only word she could get past her throat when she looked up into his darkened eyes.

He put his right hand on her waist under her jacket and wrapped one of her curls around a finger on the left. He glanced at the curl she could feel him playing with, then lowered his gaze to her eyes. "Barrett . . ." he whispered.

And then he was kissing her.

Softly, tenderly, with great care. And skill. And persuasion. And . . .

And she was enthralled.

His mustache tickled, and his mouth heated hers. When he caressed her lips with his tongue, she parted them for his entry. He swept in, claiming, tasting, daring her tongue to play with his. When she responded with forays of her own, he tangled his hand in her curls and, widening his stance, used the other to draw her into him.

She was abruptly swimming in his embrace, and she had to hold on to him as the only means to stay afloat. He tasted dark, mysterious, incendiary. She slid her right hand around his waist under his coat and splayed it across his back. His muscles were hard and smooth and she could feel them shifting as he pulled her closer until they were pressed together from thigh to chest. She raised her other hand to his shoulder and then to the back of his neck. Her movements served to bring them even more intimately together—enough to feel the strong evidence of his desire.

When her hips met his, he made a satisfied sound deep in his throat that she could feel resonate within her. When he brought his hand up her back from her waist, above the V, to glide over her bare skin, a wave of heat accompanied the stroke and warmed her to the core. When he deepened the kiss and slid his hand down, down to press her more tightly against him, she heard herself repeat the sound he had made. She was melting, flowing around him, into him, and she had to hold him even more tightly to remain upright.

Davis thought he had his wits about him until he heard her small sound of surrender and felt her body become pliant in his hands. Triumph coursed through him: she would be his.

But then she returned his kiss, kneaded his back muscles, and fisted her hand in his hair. Her tongue danced with his as he deepened the kiss even more. Her taste—heady, sweet, provocative—swirled through him.

And his blood heated and the world contracted to only the two of them in each other's arms.

And he kissed her the way he'd been wanting to— slowly, thoroughly, taking the time to savor, to enjoy, to possess.

And she kissed him back, with softness and fierceness and passion. The passion he'd wondered about when they met. The passion he'd definitely uncovered. The passion as he'd never felt it from another woman—honest, forthright, real.

He ended the kiss and held her to him, taking the time to delight in the feel of her breasts against his chest, her softness against his erection, his fingers playing with her curls. She didn't say a word, probably couldn't if she was in the same shape he was. He doubted he could have stood alone.

He felt her take a deep breath, and he relaxed his arms but didn't let go. She loosened her grip and brought both hands to his chest, resting one on each side of his tie.

She raised her head to meet his eyes with a solemn gaze. "Davis . . ." She licked her lips.

"Barrett . . ." he said and smiled into her eyes.

She cleared her throat and frowned at him—she looked perplexed, as if she were searching for words, but it was a frown nevertheless. Not the reaction he was hoping for. He braced himself.

"Davis, this is not a good idea."

He would not pretend to misunderstand her. "Why not? Our attraction for each other has been obvious. The kiss we just shared is proof of it."

She shook her head. "That's immaterial. Acting on our attraction is not a good idea." She tried to take a step back.

He let her take half a step. "I don't agree." At least she wasn't denying the magnetism between them. He leaned back against the door jamb and put both hands on her waist to keep her positioned between his legs. She left her hands on his chest, but otherwise they weren't touching. "We're both adults, single, and unattached. Where's the harm?"

Barrett stared into his eyes and marshaled her thoughts—not an easy task with him so close, but she wasn't going to act like an affronted virgin and try to wrench herself out of his arms. She spoke as evenly as she could. "Davis, this is not professional behavior."

He raised his eyebrows at the term.

"I'm here to do a job, create an inventory for the Windswept papers, not to . . ." She floundered, not sure what to call whatever it was between them. After their kiss, "attraction" and "temptation" weren't strong enough terms.

He evidently had no confusion. "Enjoy the summer? Have sex with the owner? Make love with me?"

"Exactly!" she said before she really thought about his words, especially the last ones. She had to explain,

to make him understand her situation. "I can't afford a
. . . relationship right at the moment." She hurried the
last three words when he opened his mouth to supply
some. She couldn't let him define the terms in this negotiation. "I'm under a deadline. I have to concentrate
on my career if I have any hope of receiving tenure,
and while I'm grateful, very grateful to you for the opportunity you've given me to use the papers, . . ." Oh,
Lord, what was she going to say next?

Again he furnished the words, this time with a
frown of his own. "You're not *that* grateful? Barrett, I
don't want *gratitude* from you, and our having—or not
having—sex is in no way tied to the papers or your access to them, so get the idea out of your head. Let me
state it categorically. Whatever happens between us,
you will always have access to the papers as we agreed.
If you become uncomfortable living here, I'll pay your
expenses for wherever you want to live while you're
working on them. Satisfactory?" He gave her waist a
little squeeze with his question.

"But my professional reputation will be worth
nothing if it appears I'm sleeping with you for access,"
she countered, at the same time absurdly relieved by
his statement. "I'm certain speculation is already floating around the department simply because I'm staying
at your house."

"The inventory and the articles you write will bolster your professional reputation and get you tenure," he said in an assured tone. "Any speculation will die under the weight and quality of your work. As for what goes on in this house between the two of us, nobody will know, with the possible exception of Gonzales and Eva, and I know they won't say anything."

"But what about your cousin?"

"Lloyd? What does he have to do with us?" He looked genuinely puzzled by her question.

"He struck me as the type to spread rumors, any rumors if he thought they'd get him access or stop me from completing the inventory."

"You don't have to worry about Lloyd. He's at home and won't bother us. If anything, he's my problem, not yours."

She thought furiously and came up with another idea. It was somewhat puny, but she couldn't resist. "What about because I work for you? How would it look for you to be sleeping with an employee?"

He chuckled. "But you're an independent contractor. And our sleeping together is not a condition of your access or a requirement for the grant. You're not going to cry sexual harassment, are you?"

"No, of course not." So much for that idea. She snuck a glance at his face. The scoundrel looked like he was enjoying the situation. Well, why shouldn't he? Davis Jamison lived for negotiating, didn't he? And after their kiss he had a pretty good idea how tempted she was. What was she going to do now? She crossed her arms and glared at his tie.

He took the initiative with a finger under her chin to raise her face and her gaze to his. He used his other hand to pull her a little closer. "Barrett, I'm not going to rush you, and I certainly don't want you in my bed because of a misguided sense of gratitude." He said the last word as if it tasted bitter. "Think about it, about us. We enjoy each other's company. We're sexually attracted to each other. I'd like to take our enjoyment to the next level. For both of us."

"But . . ."

"And I'm not going to drop the subject, or let you ignore me. I don't think I'm capable of it. I want you too badly and I'm going to do my damnedest to persuade you."

"Wait a minute," she objected, trying at the same time to ignore the thrill his statement had given her. She couldn't let him take control. She had to think about it, come to her own conclusion, get used to the idea he was as attracted as she was. They were negotiating. She had to state some conditions of her own. "We have to treat each other professionally, as equals, as adults. I am not here for . . ." She shied away from finishing the sentence. Whatever she said might be too revealing. She regrouped and hurried on. "I am here to work, not fend off lecherous advances. No ambushes. No chases around the desk. No gratuitous gropes."

He laughed. "All right. I'll act . . . we'll both act . . . professionally." He gave the word an ironic twist.

She nodded, thinking she could handle that—until he added, "During working hours," and covered her mouth with his again.

He kept this kiss light, she realized, but it weakened her knees just the same. She had to fight not to clutch his lapels. When he ended the kiss, he held her to him for a long moment. Then he nudged her back a step, straightened, and whispered, "Good night." He turned and walked to the stairs.

"Good night," she answered softly and watched him turn the corner.

She closed the door and walked to the closet on shaky legs. Her whole body tingled, her breasts felt heavy, and there was an ache between her legs. She had never imagined being so attracted to a man. And his mustache brought a whole new dimension to kissing.

While she washed her face, she repeated all the reasons she couldn't get involved with him—career goals, reputation problems, and the worst possibility—

the relationship would flounder, go wrong, end horribly in anger, and with it would go all her professional dreams.

But what about her personal ones? Did she even have any?

She did expect to get married and have children— some day. But first came the career. She was no Peggy Murphy who would subordinate her dreams to a man. Peggy might be happy, but she, Barrett, never would be. She was too ambitious, too goal oriented. Her brothers had succeeded in their chosen fields; she would too.

No, she wouldn't think about a personal life. This was her career-building summer and she had to concentrate on her goals.

But here was Davis Jamison, bigger than life, as handsome as sin, and more tempting than a hot fudge sundae. Wanting her, enticing her, offering her . . . what? Oh, she knew she'd find pleasure in his lovemaking. It was obvious, from the way she felt in his arms and from his kisses.

On the other hand, did she have to say no? If she was careful, really careful, what did she have to lose by, what was his term, *enjoying the summer*?

She mulled it all over while she put on her huge Houston Texans T-shirt she'd "borrowed" from her younger brother and got into bed. She usually slept nude, had gotten into the habit in her first apartment with the lousy air-conditioning, but it didn't feel right to go without clothes here. She switched off the light, settled into the pillow, and pondered the question.

They had a deal for the papers. From all their dinner conversations about his business and from her own research, she knew he was a man of his word. He wouldn't renege on an agreement, no matter what happened between them, and he'd confirmed it again just a few minutes ago. If worse came to worse personally and they couldn't tolerate being around each other, she could always come to the house only when he was at work, or he could put the papers at a neutral site.

What if their affair lasted only for the summer? He certainly wasn't thinking long term, and she shouldn't be either. A long-distance situation wouldn't work anyway, with her up there and him down here. They'd be lucky to see each other once a month. She just had to be sure they parted amicably in August. She wouldn't count on resuming anything but the inventory when she returned to finish it.

But what if . . . Oh, Lord, she was so attracted to the man. What if she fell in love with him? What if he didn't reciprocate her feelings?

Disaster. Unmitigated disaster.

How could she bear to be around him then? Longing for him, unable to touch, acting like a total fool. How could he stand to have her in his life, this idiotic woman, mooning over him all the time—or worse, acting shrewish like his ex? Either way, she'd remind him of his mistake in having anything to do with her in the first place.

She would simply—simply, hah!—have to make certain she did *not* fall in love with him. Keep her wits about her. She had no trouble doing it with every other man she'd ever dated. She'd treat their attraction as nothing more than a pleasant interlude.

Just as he was doing.

No thinking long term—except about completing the inventory, of course.

As he was doing. He probably wanted nothing to do with a long-term relationship. That bitch of an ex-wife was enough to make anybody think twice about a serious involvement. And her brothers had said he currently played the field.

Fine. They could both live with an enjoyable summer then.

She wasn't going to simply fall into his arms, however. She didn't surrender to any man, from her brothers on down. She'd concentrate on the inventory and her own research and see what happened. She'd

never been seduced before. She couldn't help giggling
at the idea. It might be fun.

Chapter SIXTEEN

After a long, difficult labor a month too early, our fifth child was stillborn on November 3. Edgar buried our third son, John Calhoun Jamison, in the church graveyard while I watched from a pallet in the back of a wagon. I refused to stay in my sickbed and let Edgar bear the burden all alone. The dull, gray, autumn day chilled our souls and reduced us all to tears. Even the heavens wept as the tiny coffin was lowered into the ground.

My convalescence has been slow, and Heeba is plying me with all sorts of potions and teas to restore my health. She has not said 'I told you so,' and I thank her for her silence. Edgar has brought in a doctor from New Orleans and encouraged me to concentrate on becoming well. I don't think much of the doctor's nostrums, however, and Heeba absolutely scorns them, so we are pouring them out when Edgar isn't looking.

Edgar is saying things like, "Don't worry, Mary Maude, you can still have another child." I know he is trying to cheer me up, but I don't know if I can bear another one, either physically, or, God forbid, mentally if I were to lose another baby. But I won't speak of my reluctance to Edgar. He needs all my support and love right now.

And we must prepare for Christmas, a usually joyous time in our household. The children are sad, of course, but their normal high spirits are returning. I must be happy with them and for them. I must!

Windswept Plantation
February 27, 1845
A frigid day, spent huddled around the fire,
trying to read the Bible for solace.

I suffered a miscarriage (the excess bleeding could have been nothing less) on February 15. Having been too busy to even think about my regularity—or lack thereof—I didn't even know I was carrying a baby. At first Edgar was angry, claiming I had been working too hard in the greenhouse, preparing for planting, and should have taken greater care, but he finally understood I hadn't known my condition. He has been remorseful and solicitous ever since, spoiling me at every turn.

As for me, I am tired, but not totally exhausted. Sad because of what might have been, but (dare I admit) somewhat relieved not to have to face child-birth. I honestly do not want to go through it again. I am thirty-four years old and have four healthy chil-dren. That is enough for me. Pray God it is enough for my husband.

The doctor Edgar brought from New Orleans when dear John was stillborn will be my ally, I think. He was most insistent then that my bearing another would be dangerous. I will ask Edgar to bring the doctor back and enlist his aid in speaking with my husband.

Heeba told me she had suspected, but wanted to wait a little longer before confirming her diagnosis. As I write this, she is preparing some of her fortifying tonics and her concoctions to prevent conception.

I think the child was conceived during the New Year celebration (especially Edgar's and my private welcoming of the new year) when I was not as careful as I might have been. I know there must be ways to enjoy each other without running such a risk. I must speak with Edgar about this. I will certainly be care-ful from now on!

Present Day
Sunday, June 10

Davis woke up Sunday morning at his usual early time and lay there grinning. He was looking forward immensely to the next step in his campaign. Those kisses last night had left him aching, but extremely optimistic.

She hadn't said no, she hadn't left his house. What were her terms again? No lecherous advances? The words sounded like a "historical" phrase—or out of a bad novel. No ambushes. No chases around the desk. No gratuitous gropes. He chuckled at her "deal breakers."

Then he sobered. What had she put up with from men before? He'd show her how real men operated. What real men? How *he* went about courting. Courting? Another "historical" word, one implying more than just a roll in the hay.

No matter. The end result would be the same: Barrett in his bed.

When he walked into the kitchen, Barrett was reading the papers and drinking coffee at the table. She had on her usual uniform of jeans and a T-shirt, this one from Notre Dame, and looked so cute he wanted to scoop her up and carry her off. But he couldn't—it was too much like an "ambush"—so he strolled up to her, leaned down, and gave her a quick kiss. Then he took a gulp of her coffee while she frowned at him. He returned a grin.

"I was just about to fix myself some breakfast," she said with a tinge of exasperation in her voice. "Do you want some?"

"No, I have an early golf game. I'll grab something at the club house with the guys. I'll be home about one, probably. What are your plans?"

"I'm going to read Edgar's journal and compare it to what Mary Maude was writing to her parents and sisters. I have a couple of ideas for articles, and I want to see if I have enough data to put one together."

"Sounds good." He rummaged through the sections of the paper to find the front page and read the headlines.

"Davis, I'd like to get something straight about 'working hours,'" she said in a firm tone.

He put the paper down and looked at her. Unlike someone else he could name, Barrett certainly faced everything head on, brought it right out in the open, and he admired her for it. He was coming to love negotiating with the woman. What had she thought up now? "Okay, what?"

"Since I'm inventorying the papers both day and night, I consider 'working hours' to be highly flexible and define them as any time I am engaged in the inventory or research, be it research for the papers or for my own publication. Also included in this characterization is when I am actively writing my articles. Is this definition acceptable to you?"

She tried to keep her expression neutral, but he could see her satisfaction. She thought she was putting boundaries around him and his persuasive abilities. He kept his face straight, but it wasn't easy. "Let's see. That would mean from eight in the morning . . ."

"I usually start my day before seven-thirty."

"From roughly seven-thirty to five in the afternoon? Time out for a swim and dinner, back to work between seven and eight to . . .?" He raised his eyebrows at her.

"The last is flexible, depending on what I'm working on," she answered. "Usually between ten and eleven, but it could easily be later if I'm writing and it's going well."

"What about lunch?"

"I eat it at the desk, since I've talked Eva into making me simple sandwiches or salads."

"And on the weekends?"

"Oh, the weekends . . ." She looked a little disconcerted for a second, like she'd forgotten those two important days, but she rallied quickly. "I consider Saturday and Sunday like any other day."

"If I have my calculations correct, leaving dinner out of it, you will have time for me between five and six in the afternoon, and from ten or so at night to six or seven in the morning." He rubbed a finger along his mustache, trying to make the impression he was pondering the situation. It was really to hide his smile. "All right," he said after a long pause during which she did not move a muscle, "it works for me." He held out his hand to shake on the deal.

She regarded his hand with suspicion, then slowly accepted his grasp. They shook. He didn't let go, but turned her hand over and kissed the back of it, taking care to give her knuckles a little brush with his mustache. He felt the tremble ripple up her arm. He kept his face perfectly straight as he gazed into her blue eyes and said, "What I want most are your nights."

She gasped and jerked her hand out of his grip.

Before she could do anything else, he leaned over, gave her open lips a quick kiss, straightened, and headed for the door. "I'll see you later," he said as he went through and closed it behind him. He heard a muffled "Mmmmmmmgh!" and a bang like she'd hit the table with her fist. He grinned all the way to the garage.

Davis returned home around one, not particularly happy about being waylaid at the club. Now he had to ask Barrett to do him a favor and he hoped she wasn't angry after their "working hours" deal. No, she wouldn't be angry, but she would be plotting how to get even. His sister always had when he played a trick on her.

He found her in her office, sitting at the round table with one of Edgar's big journals open, taking notes on a pad. "Hi, how's it going?" he asked as he took a seat across from her.

"Well enough, I think. I'm at the end of the eighteen-forties. I'm finding plenty for several articles, but unfortunately, they would be all about Edgar and his life and not about Mary Maude and hers. He doesn't write much about her, except about her gardening abilities and the renown her home-grown exotic fruits and vegetables bring to their entertaining. And of course his pride when she gave birth to another child."

"I only read the first volume. What do you think of Edgar so far?" Davis was beginning to see how she had gotten so caught up in history itself, the studying and interpretation of individual lives. He had learned much about the art and craft of writing history listening to her reports and observations at dinner. Her talking about his own family added a personal touch, and the stories made him more and more curious about her findings. He had not expected to be so fascinated. He'd always been bored by history in the obligatory school and college courses. Maybe it was the teacher.

"He's put a lot of himself into this journal," she answered. "It's more than just a report of weather, crops, and expenses. Edgar Jamison was a proud man, proud of his accomplishments with the plantation, proud of his family, his four children. His pride comes through more in the second volume as the kids get older."

She stopped to stretch and he enjoyed the play of her breasts under the T-shirt.

She gave him a strange little smile when she noticed where his gaze had gone. One of those "Gotcha" smiles just like his sister's when he fell into one of her traps. Was Barrett teasing him?

She resumed a bland expression and continued, "Some of the entries lead me to think he probably had a touch more arrogance than the average man, and his correspondence will tell me more. He seems to have run his plantation with a strong hand. Politically, he stood with John C. Calhoun and the more radical Southerners. From his portrait back at the plantation I'd say he was a handsome man, but I don't know if he used his looks in a lady-killing way."

"Why do you say arrogant?"

"In his journal he positively crows about besting some of the other planters with his horses and his success at building Windswept. It's in the words he uses when reporting a satisfying success in anything. And when he rails at someone's stupidity. You can say Southern planters were arrogant by definition, but I think Edgar saw himself as above average in everything." A twinkle appeared in her eyes. "Speaking as a direct descendent, do you think you inherited any of his arrogance?"

"Definitely," he responded laughing. "I'm also autocratic, egotistical, and vain." He paused. Now was the time to be humble. "Listen, I have a large favor to ask."

"What can I do for you?"

"I have to take a couple of prospective investors and their wives to dinner on Wednesday. I ran into one of them, Al Pendleton, at the club, and he said the other one, a long-time friend, is coming here from his home in Atlanta on Tuesday. I've been trying to get together with both of them for God knows how long. To make a long story short, they're both history buffs, big on the Civil War and their ancestors who fought in 'the recent unpleasantness.' I mentioned Windswept, the papers and you. Al said he'd like to meet my 'tame' historian . . ."

Barrett's eyebrows almost touched her hairline.

"Uh, 'captive' historian?"

Her eyebrows drew together in a frown.

"*Consulting* historian." Her brows resumed their normal position over deep blue eyes that were definitely laughing at him. "Anyway," he continued, "would you come with us? I hate to ask this, but . . ."

"It would be my pleasure," she said. "Can you find out who the ancestors were? I can do a quick research job on them. Some Southerners are notoriously protective of their forebears' place in history and I'd like to go prepared. But you'd better warn them: I don't *do* battles, you know, fight them using the silverware for cavalry and infantry. I'm not a military historian."

"I'll owe you for this. We'll be dining, and then the wives want to go dancing, so be prepared."

———◆◆◆———

Barrett watched Davis warily the remainder of the day, but he didn't make a move on her, just worked in his office. She stopped feeling stupid for leaving herself so open to his shenanigans in the morning. *All he wants is the nights!* He didn't fool her. He'd take it any time he could get it. Or her.

Having skimmed much of the last volume, she

gave up on Edgar's journal around four. She wasn't going to find what she needed with this particular Jamison. He, a self-centered male, barely mentioned Mary Maude's contributions to Windswept's success. He was proud of his children, especially the boys, but spent most of his time either overseeing plantation activities or taking part in politics in Baton Rouge when the legislature was in session. As many wealthy planter families at the time, the Jamisons had made several trips to New York and Europe over the years, but except for noting the purchases they made, Edgar said little about what they had seen or whom they had met—outside of prominent politicians.

If only Mary Maude had kept a journal. But if she had, nobody, including Davis's grandfather, had said anything about it, and Barrett hadn't found even mention of one. She'd just have to make do with the correspondence.

She sighed and glanced out at the pool. The aquamarine water, rippling from a little breeze, beckoned. Could she chance it? What would Davis do? What else but join her? And . . .?

No, she decided. No sense in putting such temptation in front of him—or her. She didn't know if she could resist all the alluring, unclothed masculinity of Davis in a bathing suit.

Feeling slightly letdown, she went back to looking over her notes for possible article ideas. If she wrote something on Mary Maude's Herbarium, she could use the plantation mistress's own illustrations. She liked the idea the more she thought about it. She'd need some reference books on herbs and plant medicines, so she fired up the computer to search.

She had just placed her order for a book shipment when Davis walked in. "How about dinner?" he asked. "Eva left us a casserole, or we could order in pizza."

"Pizza," she answered as her taste buds started tingling for cheese, tomato sauce, and pepperoni. "With everything."

After pizza, salad, and a couple of glasses of Chianti, Davis joined Barrett in her office and sat at the table. He opened the second volume of Edgar's journal and started to read. She continued her Internet search for information on early nineteenth century folk medicines, downloading some articles and making notes of references to check.

About ten, she shut off the computer and Davis closed the journal. He turned to her. "I see what you mean about Edgar's arrogance. The man was very sure of himself, at least in his writings." He waved a hand at the book.

"Do you remember any family stories about how

Edgar died?" Barrett asked.

Davis thought for a moment. "No, I don't. Why?"

"I'm just curious. He died in eighteen fifty-four, only fifty-two years old. He records his illnesses in his journal entries, but seems pretty healthy until the final two years. Then he was ill off and on. He was clearly frustrated because no doctor could diagnose him and he didn't seem to be able to get well. A couple of times, just when he thought he was over whatever it was, he'd have a relapse, despite careful nursing by Mary Maude. If the Herbarium is any indication, she was quite knowledgeable about medicines, both folk and those endorsed by the medical establishment. She frequently added descriptions to her notes which could only have come from medical books of the time. But he died, despite her best efforts."

"Of course, back then people died of all sorts of commonplace ailments we think nothing of today. No antibiotics or such." He shrugged and stood up.

"Yes, and they often blamed illness on a 'miasma' or unhealthy night air." She came around the desk and preceded him into the hall. He switched off the overhead lights and followed.

She could feel him behind her as they walked through the dim hall illumination to the stairs. All they had done was turn the corner, and they were suddenly in their own world, full of soft shadows and quiet possibilities. It had been like this the night before, but something was different this time. She couldn't bring herself to continue their conversation—not about death when she felt so full of life.

Anticipation of a good-night kiss gripped her and silenced her—and him too, she surmised. They both knew what was coming this time, knew what a kiss stirred between them, knew what fires a touch could ignite. She had to admit she was looking forward to it and curious about the outcome. But she wasn't ready to succumb to him just yet.

He didn't wait to reach her room, however. Instead, at the top of the stairs where the decision had to be made of going to her room or his, he drew her into his arms. "Barrett . . ." he murmured and kissed her.

This kiss was different also. The previous night's had been soft; this one was hungry. Last night's had explored; this one plundered. That one had savored; this one ravished.

At first Barrett's whole being concentrated on what he was doing to her mouth. Nothing else mattered, and she wound her arms around his neck to keep him right where he was as she responded with demands of her own.

Then . . . she felt him move. He loosened the

steel bands of his arms and brought his hands to her shoulders, then down her back to squeeze her butt and pull her hips against his erection, and finally around to her ribcage to rest just under her breasts.

He raised his head just the slightest bit, his lips two inches above hers. When he wouldn't let her pull him down, she opened her eyes enough to meet his heavy-lidded gaze. She was about to ask him what was wrong when he traced the lower curves of her breasts with his thumbs and slowly, ever so slowly, rubbed them back and forth across her nipples. Her suddenly engorged, highly sensitive nipples.

She moaned, a soft, aching sound she didn't recognize, didn't know she could make.

"Davis . . ." His name forced itself out of her. She fisted her hands in his hair, pulled herself up, and took his mouth, demanding, yearning, wanting . . . oh, yes, *wanting*.

Oh, yes, *craving* just what he was doing as he covered her suddenly heavy breasts with his hands, massaged them slowly. Oh, yes, *needing*, desperately needing as he took her nipples between his thumbs and fingers and squeezed. Every muscle in her body clenched in response.

She had no idea how long the kiss or the sweet torture went on, but when he wrapped his arms around her and lifted his head again, she could only cling, surrounded by his heat, until their heartbeats and breathing had slowed. Her sluggish mind took forever to come back to itself. Her body simply luxuriated in his strength and warmth. When he separated them, she almost protested.

His hands on her waist, he nudged her back a step, and she looked up. He was not smiling. On the contrary, his face was stark and tight, his eyes black in the low light.

"Good night, Davis," she whispered.

"Good night, Barrett." He gave her a soft, quick kiss and let her go.

Somehow she managed to turn and walk to the balcony and her room without her insubstantial legs failing, but she had to hold onto the balcony edge before she made it to her door. It was obviously going to be harder than she thought, not to simply fall into his arms.

Davis watched her turn the corner onto the balcony and let out a long breath. All of his body ached with the strain of letting her go, of not taking the kiss to its logical conclusion. He had never had such a strong response to a woman before. Not one that locked his muscles, constricted his breathing, left him hard as granite.

He had to stand for a couple of minutes, willing

his body to calm down, before he could walk into his room.

At least Barrett seemed to be as affected as he was. Did she have any idea what she was doing to him? She certainly wasn't trying to use her "feminine wiles" on him. He was an expert on women's enticements, both real and fake, and Barrett was simply being herself.

In fact, during the afternoon and through the evening, she had reverted to the easy friendship and conversation they enjoyed before the kiss yesterday. She'd made no reference to it or their subsequent discussion.

She didn't seem apprehensive any more about the possibility of his refusing her access to the papers, so she must trust him to be true to his word. That was good. He wanted her to trust him. He couldn't see her getting into bed with him unless she did, on several levels.

And once in bed . . . Lord have mercy, he hoped he could maintain his control. If she could make him hot as a habenero pepper with denim and cotton between them, what would happen skin to skin? He felt his body start to react to the mental movie in his head and he dragged his mind to his appointments on Monday. It was either that or a cold shower.

Chapter
SEVENTEEN

$\mathcal{B}$arrett was happy to see Monday morning arrive. For one thing, Davis was out from under foot, and she could get some work done. She'd finally arrived at the records for the 1850s, and there were boxes and boxes of them.

She was working her way through a big folder of Edgar's political correspondence when the phone rang on the house line. Gonzales informed her Horace Glover was asking to speak to her.

"I'll take the call," she told him, but made a face at the phone before she punched the button. "Hello, Horace."

"Hello, Barrett," he boomed. "Just thought I'd check on how you were doing. Finding any juicy subject matter? Anything on Colonel Jamison?"

What did he mean by "juicy subject matter," she wondered. Had Horace been talking to Lloyd? It didn't matter, but she'd rather not have the two collaborating. "I can only repeat what I told you the last time you called. I can't discuss the papers with you. All I can tell you is that the work is progressing."

"Has Davis Jamison decided what to do with the records when you're finished, you know, perhaps open them to scholars?"

"No, he hasn't made a decision yet."

"Look, I'm going to be down there at the end of the week. Why don't you and I go out for a nice lunch, or better still, dinner? Get caught up with what we're doing, plans for next year, that sort of thing. I have a couple of ideas for your research I'd like to run by you. You need to be thinking about publishing. Your tenure vote is just around the corner, and I'd like to do what I can to help." His voice had started out with a cordial tone, but lowered in volume and pitch to a slightly husky, almost intimate, certainly insinuating murmur by the time he uttered his last sentences.

Yeah, right. Like she believed him. Barrett rolled her eyes, happy she didn't have to guard her expression. He was, however, a full professor, so she'd respect the position—but she'd ignore his comments and unsubtle hints. "Thanks, Horace, I appreciate it, but I'm very busy and lunch is just out of the question. I also have commitments for all my evenings."

"Well . . ." he started.

She wasn't about to let him ask her what she was

doing with her busy-ness or commitments, so she interrupted. "Thanks for asking. I hope your research is going well. I need to get back to work. Nice talking to you. Good-bye."

She hung up before he could reply. "Mmmmmmmgh!" She allowed herself a small angry squeal and shook her fists at the phone. A visit from Horace was the last thing she needed. Especially over dinner, invitations to which she had always managed to evade. She wondered idly where he would have taken her. The word around the history department was, if Horace wanted to come on to a woman, he took her to a really nice restaurant, a dark and "romantic" one. If he wanted what was in the woman's mind, not her body, they went to a cheap joint—once, according to rumor, even to a Denny's—and it was Dutch treat.

Chuckling, she returned to her stack of correspondence, but not without a small prayer Horace would stay away.

———◆◆◆———

Monday and Tuesday seemed to set the pattern. She worked, she swam, Davis came home, they ate, they worked in their respective offices. They said good night with searing kisses that left her with melted bones.

He didn't move a hand toward her breasts again, but seemed to content himself with playing with her curls and holding her as tightly as he could against him. She knew he was affected. If the hard evidence against her abdomen wasn't enough, he was breathing as roughly as she was, and she could feel his heart beating as strongly and rapidly as hers. Where her body wanted to melt into a puddle of desire, his felt like a pillar of granite, scorching hot granite.

It was almost enough to make her scream. Her attraction to him grew with each encounter. She wanted him to go farther, take the next step, increase the intimacy. She ached in several places, and she knew only his touch would alleviate her "condition."

As seductions went, this one was certainly taking a long time, she complained to herself as she dressed for the dinner with his investors. But maybe . . . he was proceeding exactly according to plan.

Anticipation was a marvelous mechanism for ratcheting up the tension between them. Did he think he only had to arouse her and she'd fall into his arms, begging him to take her or she'd explode? No, damn it.

If he wanted a game, she'd give him one. Anticipation worked two ways. So did seduction.

Dinner with the investors went well. Barrett had done some homework and, when it was clear she wouldn't rehash battles, both wives instantly perked up and began asking questions about women's lives in the war and telling tales from family history. By the time they finished eating, even the battle enthusiast had been won over, especially when Barrett mentioned some of his family and their travails by name. Davis sat back, feeling extremely smug about having included Barrett in the first place. Once more she had effortlessly wrapped people around her little finger. He had no doubt these investors were hooked.

Dancing later, he smiled down at her. "I should hire you, you know, to handle my investor relations. And my Hispanic relations. And me."

She seemed to consider the offer seriously for a moment. "Thank you, but no, Davis. I'm too happy doing what I do to follow the siren call of business." Then she grinned. "And I doubt anyone could *handle* you."

He couldn't resist that one. "Lady, you can handle me all you want." He pulled her closer and twirled her around as she gave him one of her teacher looks. She couldn't quell his enthusiasm, however. "Nothing to say?" he whispered in her ear.

She didn't say anything. Instead she raised up on

tiptoe and flicked his earlobe with her tongue. It was the last thing Davis had expected her to do, and he jerked, his body tightening as desire roared through him. When he heard her chuckle and whisper back, "I'll take it under advisement," he could only wince. He'd asked for it. Then he chuckled. He needed to step up his campaign of persuasion. He did not doubt victory now; the lady was obviously willing.

As they were walking to his car after saying good night to the investors, Davis's cell phone rang. He frowned at the caller ID displaying his home number and punched the button to answer. "What is it, Gonzales?" he asked.

"There's been a break-in here, sir."

Davis relayed the information to Barrett and said into the phone, "Are you and Eva all right?"

"Oh, yes, sir. When you gave us the night off, we went to visit my sister. When we came home, we found the police here and the alarms going off."

"We'll be there in twenty minutes." He hung up.

When they drove up to the house, the driveway was full of police cars. Davis identified himself, and an officer escorted him and Barrett into the house. They found Gonzales and two other officers, one in plain clothes, in the living room.

"What's happened?" Davis asked of all three.

The tired-looking man in the rumpled beige suit spoke. "I'm Lieutenant Leonard Gilroy of the Hunter's Creek Police, Mr. Jamison. Your alarms went off at 10:08. Officers responded and reached the house at 10:22. We found the kitchen door broken open, but no sign of the intruders. Mr. Gonzales arrived just as the officers were exiting the house. From the tracks on the walkways, it appears the burglars backed up a good-sized truck to the rear door. This implies they were planning to steal something more than jewelry or a television set."

"I've checked the house, sir," Gonzales interjected. "They did take the TV set from the family room, but nothing upstairs is disturbed."

"What about the office?" Davis asked. He glanced at Barrett; she looked pale, but composed. He could feel anger rising in himself and clamped down on it.

"Some boxes are rearranged in the conference room and stacked in the hall, but I don't know if any are missing," Gonzales answered.

"Oh, no," Barrett said and headed for the office wing. Davis followed.

Several boxes were in the hallway, a couple even on a dolly. One lay sideways on the floor, as if it had been dropped in haste. A police officer was dusting them for fingerprints.

"Did they get any of them?" Davis asked as Barrett started counting out loud, pointing to the boxes as she went.

"Eighteen-thirty A, B, eighteen-thirty-one A, B, C . . . and all the other years and letters are in sequence. I don't think so." She turned and walked into the office. "Edgar's journal is still on the desk, and the computer is still here."

Davis came up behind her and put his hands on her shoulders. She slumped back against him. He could feel her trembling.

"What's all this?" Gilroy asked from the hall as he surveyed the boxes there and in the conference room.

Davis gave Barrett a squeeze and they returned to the hall. "The records from my family's plantation in Louisiana. My grandfather died recently and left them to me. Dr. Browning has been inventorying them for me," Davis replied. He introduced Barrett.

"Well, it certainly looks like the perpetrators were going to load these up. Why would anyone want old records? Are they worth anything?" Gilroy opened a box, looked in, and closed the lid again. His watery blue eyes had a puzzled look.

"Not in monetary terms." Davis debated with himself, then decided to tell the whole story. If Lloyd would go to such lengths as burglary, Davis wasn't going to protect him, family member or not. "The only person interested in them is my cousin, Lloyd Walker. He's been badgering me to let him have access to them. Lloyd lives in Louisiana."

"Would he go to such trouble to get them?" The detective was plainly skeptical.

"I don't know, lieutenant. He's been threatening a lawsuit, even though as a lawyer, he ought to recognize an ironclad bequest when he sees one. But I can't see him driving a truck and loading the boxes himself."

"This was no one-man job, Mr. Jamison. Not only would you need muscle to move all these boxes, but one of the responding officers said he thought they saw a truck's taillights down the road just before they turned into your driveway. The burglars probably had a lookout. It would be too easy to get trapped back in these dead-end roads by the bayou." Gilroy looked around and waved his hand at the situation.

"Also, they hit while no one was at home. This implies someone has been watching the place. Is the house frequently vacant?"

"No, and especially not during the week," Davis answered.

The officer who had been looking for fingerprints spoke up. "There's a few partial prints, but mostly smudges, Lieutenant. Not much usable."

"Okay, Collier. You can take off."

"What else can I tell you, Lieutenant?" Davis asked.

"Your cousin's address and phone number. At the moment, he's the likeliest suspect, but if he's in Louisiana, I doubt we'll be able to prove anything against him unless we catch one of the crew who broke in."

Davis supplied the information, and the police left. He and Gonzales shored up the kitchen door as best they could. The task completed, he looked around the kitchen and said, "I don't think we can do any more with this tonight. Let's get some sleep and tackle the mess in the morning."

"I'll take care of the cars, sir," Gonzales said. "And I'll arrange for the door repair tomorrow."

"Good. Thank you. We have to put in an insurance claim too. Peggy has all the information at the office and she'll call you. No need for a new television for the family room. I never watched it anyway." Gonzales left and Davis put his arm around Barrett's shoulders and turned her into the hall. "Come on, Barrett. It's late."

When they arrived at her bedroom door, Davis took her in his arms and gave her a hug. "Are you all right?"

"I'm fine, especially since they didn't take any of the papers," she said, leaning back into his embrace.

"Do you really think Lloyd instigated this?"

"I honestly don't know. Can you think of anybody else? A crazed historian, for example?"

She shook her head. "No, not even . . . well, nobody. A historian would have to cite his sources. What's he going to put in the footnotes, 'Letter from Edgar Jamison to John C. Calhoun, stolen from the Windswept Collection?' "

"You have a point." He sighed, more in disgust than anger. "If it was Lloyd, something else besides fear of a scandal must be driving him to go to such an extreme as house break-ins. I'll have to call a cousin or two back in Louisiana and see if they know what's going on."

He pulled her a little closer. "This wasn't the ending I had planned for this evening, Barrett."

She put her hands on his shirtfront and glanced up at him from under her lashes. "I haven't said yes yet, Davis."

"You will." He kissed her long and deep and when he had her—and his—heart racing and breath coming fast, he drew back and put a bit of devilment into his smile. "You will, Barrett." He kissed her again quickly before sauntering nonchalantly off to his room with a cheery, "Sleep tight." And thinking he needed another cold shower—badly. The damn things were becoming a habit.

The next day everybody was moving sluggishly. When he came home, Davis reported that Lieutenant Gilroy had found Lloyd in Mississippi when he called, so there was no proof of any wrongdoing on his part. The kitchen door had been fixed, the insurance people had been called, and all the other tasks connected with the break-in underway or completed.

After dinner, Barrett and Davis went back to the office. Barrett yawned mightily as she sat at her desk and looked blearily at the screen. "I finished another box," she told him, yawning again.

"Why don't you call it a day, and go to bed," Davis suggested.

"Good idea," she answered, turning off the computer.

"Want some company?" he asked hopefully.

"No." It was a flat statement, and he was clearly disappointed. Then she walked around the desk, plastered herself to him, and pulled him into a scorching, demanding, tantalizing kiss he felt in every molecule of his body. His arms went around her automatically, and, although he tried, she didn't let him take control. Instead she drew back, stepped out of his arms, turned him around, and gave him a push toward his office. "Good night, Davis." And she sauntered out the door.

Taut and aching in every fiber, he watched her go, those hips swinging a little more than usual, and a great grin spread over his face. Turn-about was unfair play, he guessed. For the second time in two days she had surprised him. What could he do in return?

Chapter EIGHTEEN

The Journal of Mary Maude Davis Jamison
Windswept Plantation
June 22, 1846
A warm summer day

Something is wrong, but I don't know what. The children and Edgar are all healthy and seem happy. The tutor we employ to teach the children is doing a wonderful job, even convincing the boys to stay with their studies when they would rather be outdoors. The crops are growing well, and there are rumors of good prices for cotton this year. My garden is bountiful, and the roses we imported from England are splendid, a riot of color. I have fully recovered my health, although last year at this time, I wasn't sure I ever would. My husband loves me and we enjoy each other's company as much as we ever did—although Edgar chafes at times over the precautions we take to avoid another child.

So, what is nagging at me, teasing me, making me

restless?

Edgar has been going to a number of meetings lately, as he takes more interest in the political situation, what with Texas having been admitted to the Union as a state and the Mexican government complaining. If he's home and not in Baton Rouge, he's been staying up late, long after I have gone to bed, corresponding with our Congressmen and state legislators.

Maybe that's it: I wish he were home more often. But no, loneliness is not the right feeling. It's something else, but just beyond my reach.

Oh, well, time to go to bed myself. Whatever is bothering me will come to me or come to nothing, I'm sure.

October 29, 1848

Finally, a break from the heat as clouds black as pitch and rain as heavy as Noah's deluge roared over us, leaving brilliant blue skies and a brisk cool air in their wake.

I have been in the doldrums all summer. And I have no reason for it. The children are healthy and growing. It is hard to realize my oldest is fifteen and my youngest is eight. Where have the years gone?

Edgar is his usual loving self. When I see him.

He is so busy with politics and the plantation and other business interests, always working late or traveling to Baton Rouge or Washington. Sometimes it seems we only see each other at dinner, if then.

At the rate we are going, I do not have to fear the possibility of bearing another child. Why does the thought make me sad? And which part of it—another birth might do me irreparable damage, or my husband and I seldom share our conjugal bed for anything but sleep?

———————◆◆◆———————

Present Day
Saturday, June 16

Saturday evening Barrett stood before the full-length mirror in the bathroom and turned back and forth to check out her new dress. Her shopping trip on Friday with her sister-in-law had truly paid off. Beth had taken her to a boutique on Westheimer Road where she had found the perfect dark blue-green cocktail dress for the party. The sleeveless dress had a scooped neckline and a short slim skirt—deceptively simple, it showed off her "assets," as her mother used to say, in an elegant manner.

The stylish red-haired store owner had suggested

just the right accessories too—a silver necklace with shimmering blue and green stones and matching drop earrings. She had even offered some make-up tips to emphasize Barrett's eyes so they took on overtones from the dress. Pleased, Barrett blinked at the mirror; her eyes had never looked so blue. A pair of strappy, high-heeled, dark blue sandals completed the ensemble.

She held up a hand mirror to view her backside and nodded in satisfaction. All the swimming she was doing was having a good effect on her body. It even—a miracle—seemed to be slimming her hips. She'd have to remember to kick more during her laps.

After making certain she had left nothing personal in plain sight, she walked out onto the balcony and closed the door firmly behind her. Davis had said guests sometimes used the bathroom in the other bedroom next to the stairs, but they wouldn't come any farther, certainly not through a closed door. She had decided to be cautious anyway. As for the office wing, Davis had locked the conference room, so she wasn't worried about any curious guests being able to disturb the papers.

She glanced over the railing. A bar had been set up directly below her. The caterers, under Eva's eagle eye, were laying all sorts of delicious-looking hors d'oeuvres around a multi-hued floral centerpiece on the long dining table. Silver and glass gleamed and the crystal waterfall shimmered with the reflections of the colorful array of food and flowers. For once, the dining room seemed, if not totally welcoming, at least warmer.

Davis was talking to Gonzales in the foyer. Last night Davis had said good night with another of those kisses that left her legs wobbly, but as before, he hadn't intensified his caresses. She, however, couldn't help running her hands over his back and shoulders and pressing her hips against his blatant arousal. He'd held her for a long moment and smiled under his mustache, then stepped back, turned her around and given her a nudge toward her room—exactly as she had given him the night before.

Okay, tit for tat—so to speak. What would to-night bring?

She hurried to the stairs and descended. Both men turned in her direction.

Gonzales smiled and, hand on his heart, bowed as if he were a *caballero*. She wished she had a *señorita's* fan to flirt with, but settled for smiling at him before he departed.

She turned to Davis. He was not smiling. He looked wonderful in his navy suit, snowy white-on-white shirt, and red power tie, all tall and dark and handsome, but his intent expression clearly said the black eagle was hunting again. She suppressed a shiver, then had to fight a stronger one when he lifted and kissed her hand and his mustache worked its magic.

"Good evening, Barrett. You look . . . spectacular."

The velvet rumble of his voice tickled her nerve endings and it was all she could do not to fling herself into his arms. She satisfied herself by stepping up to him, careful to *not quite* touch along the lengths of their bodies. She inhaled carefully; he smelled as good as he looked—fine clothing, faint spicy aftershave and his own particular self. "Thank you," she breathed, doing her best imitation of a sultry femme fatale. "So do you. Is there anything I can do to . . . help . . . you in any way?"

He grinned, pulled her close, said in a husky voice, "Not right this minute, but I will definitely need some . . . help . . . later." He stepped back as a couple of the catering staff passed them and continued in a normal tone, "I think the Gonzaleses have everything in hand as usual. I'm making one final round. Come with me and see if I missed anything." Holding her hand, he walked her into the living room.

A tiny spotlight shining on the long painting against the far wall drew the eye to the bright colors, and the soaring glass walls reflecting the interior made the room seem even larger. Flower arrangements on the coffee tables of the two seating groups offered some softening effects, but Barrett thought the room still had its aloof, unwelcoming edge. She hoped having it filled with people would make it more comfortable, but she said only, "Everything looks fine."

She glanced out at the patio where candles and torches flickered, and the exterior garden lights shone on tables on the lawn and the path down to the bayou. "How many are you expecting?"

"Anywhere from forty to sixty, what with my staff, investor clients, heads of the companies we invest in, and all their spouses." He waved at the interior and included the exterior in the gesture. "We usually fill up the space inside and outside. Thank the weather gods for no rain and some breeze to keep the mosquitoes away."

The doorbell rang. "Time to go to work." He gave her hand a squeeze before releasing it and heading for the door.

The first to arrive were members of his staff, including Peggy Murphy and her husband Jim, an average-sized man with brown hair and friendly eyes. Barrett wasn't able to exchange more than a few words with Peggy before guests started coming and Davis asked her to help welcome them. She watched him metamorphose into the perfect host, greeting all by name and asking the kind of questions which demonstrated he knew them as friends as well as business associates. He introduced her as "the historian who's helping me with my family's plantation records," and before long, she found herself separated from him and in conversations about his guests' family histories. Everybody had a story to tell.

From time to time, Davis sought her out to introduce someone. As he did so, he touched her arm or back, and more than once she felt his eyes on her across the room while she talked with his guests. A couple of times, when she was talking with a man by herself, especially a single man from his office, Davis appeared at her side and placed a proprietary arm on her shoulder or took her hand in his. Men and their games, she thought, raising her eyebrows at him after one such encounter. He grinned merrily, a flash of white under the black weapon on his upper lip. She knew his office would be buzzing with speculation about her on Monday.

About an hour into the party, Barrett had just finished munching on some of the cold shrimp, lobster puffs, and Eva's spicy tamales when an absolutely gorgeous couple approached her. The man was movie-star handsome and the woman, in addition to being drop-dead beautiful, was wearing a little designer creation Barrett knew cost more than she herself would spend on five complete outfits. At the same time, they looked disconcertingly familiar.

When they introduced themselves as Martha and Bill Jamison, Davis's sister and brother, she understood. No wonder they looked familiar—same coloring but different eye shades, similar facial structures. Neither had their grandfather's nose nor any of the predator look so obvious in Davis. Bill had Davis's height and Martha topped Barrett by at least three inches. She wondered briefly why Davis had not mentioned they were coming to the party. All she could remember him saying about them was Martha was a realtor and Bill always wanted money.

"We heard you were here," Bill said. "We knew he was arranging for the Windswept papers to be organized, but we practically had to drag the information out of him. I must say you're nothing like what we expected in a history professor shuffling a lot of boring old records." He looked her up and down appreciatively. His grin was distinctly Davis-like, only more flirtatious.

"Bill, don't be a jerk. I'm sure she hears those old non-jokes all the time." Martha whapped him on the arm before turning to Barrett. "Please excuse him, Dr. Browning. He's the family idiot. Always speaks before he thinks."

Barrett chuckled. "It's a pleasure to meet you

both. The name is Barrett, and I have three brothers of my own." She was getting tired of the stale compliment, though, having heard it at least half a dozen times already.

"Then you know how difficult being a sister is." Martha rolled her eyes, then asked, "How is the work going?"

Feeling like she'd found a friend, Barrett answered, "Well, but slowly. Cataloging is always tedious."

"Found any family skeletons yet?" Bill asked with a mischievous smile.

"Not yet. Do you know of any?" She was serious, but knew he wasn't.

Davis appeared at her elbow before Bill could answer. "I see you've met the rest of the family."

"Davis, why didn't you tell us Barrett is so charming? I'll be happy to take a few days and help her, you know." Bill's look was guileless.

"I'm sure you're quite busy, Bill. Barrett doesn't need your help."

Barrett thought his hands-off order was clear to all of them, but Bill merely grinned at his older brother. She and Martha exchanged a glance, shook their heads.

"Brothers' games," Martha muttered.

Davis paid no attention. "Now, I need to introduce her to someone, if you'll excuse us." He grasped Barrett's elbow and steered her toward a couple standing nearby.

She smiled at the two Jamisons as she allowed herself to be taken away. "It was nice to meet you," she managed to say.

Before she could question Davis about his rudeness, she was in a conversation with the couple, both of whom were avid genealogists. Pleading he had to greet other guests, Davis excused himself after five minutes. It took Barrett another twenty minutes of comparing websites of census data, ship manifests, and immigration records before she could make her escape. She couldn't blame Davis for abandoning her, however. He had been surprised to discover the couple's avocation; they had only discussed business matters in the past.

She was beginning to feel like she was working at this party, acting as a source of information much the way a physician would be in similar circumstances. At least nobody wanted to tell her about his gall bladder.

Barrett was crossing the foyer down by the stairs when a hush fell over the guests closest to the front door. A man and a woman entered. He was tall but a trifle portly, possibly mid-to-late sixties, with thinning, iron gray hair and a conservative suit and tie. She was . . . Sandra, the ex from hell. And in a tight, short, cut-down-to-there, show-off-the-tan, shimmering white dress, with diamonds sparkling at her neck, ears, and wrists. She looked as beautiful, and as hard, as the crystal waterfall in the dining room.

Davis, who had been standing just down the steps in the living room, turned to the newcomers, and Barrett watched his expression change from friendly host to poker-faced negotiator. He approached the pair, shook the man's hand and smiled—but only at the man. He barely glanced at Sandra. Barrett could see the grimness behind his greeting and the rigidity in his stance. Davis and the man spoke, but too quietly to be heard.

When no fireworks erupted from the trio, the other guests resumed their conversations—at a slightly louder volume than before the interruption.

Barrett considered blending into the crowd to avoid Sandra all together, but when she saw the blonde, smiling like a shark spying a fat swimmer, reach out a hand and stroke Davis's right arm from shoulder to elbow, she felt anger bubble up inside. Davis didn't move until Sandra's fingers continued down his sleeve and curled into his hand. Or attempted to. He smoothly moved his hand out of reach around his back as he listened to Sandra's male companion.

An irritated look flashed across Sandra's face, but she recovered quickly and assumed a look of amused haughtiness. She glanced around, and her eyes met

Barrett's. Her disdain became contempt as she flipped her long blond hair off her shoulders and turned her attention back to the men. She smiled brilliantly and laughed at something her companion had said.

The bitch! Barrett felt icy rage streak down her backbone. *No way* would she let Davis face that harpy alone. It was time the hellcat got a little of her own back.

Feeling as though a green-eyed devil were sitting on her shoulder, Barrett sauntered up to the trio, insinuated herself on Davis's right side between him and the woman, and took his right hand with her left. Davis gave her hand a squeeze, but whether in warning or thanks, she didn't know. With a surprised look, the other man had stopped talking at her approach. She held out her right hand to him. "Hello," she said with a cheery smile. "I don't believe we've met. I'm Barrett Browning."

"Milt Callahan," he responded as he shook her hand. "This is . . ." He nodded toward Sandra.

"Oh, Sandra and I have already met," Barrett said, turning her gaze to the blonde. "*How are you*, Sandra. That's such a *pretty* dress. We're *both* so happy you're here." She put so much saccharine into her delivery her teeth felt gritty, but she smiled with fake delight at the woman who was now scowling—a most unbecoming look for one so beautiful.

"Milt's a retired banker," Davis told her before Sandra could speak. "He and his late wife were with me at the beginning of Jamison Investments. Without his help, I wouldn't have gotten off the ground." He looked back at the older man. "Barrett's a history professor and is cataloging my family's papers for me, Milt. I'm glad you could come tonight. It's been too long since we saw each other. You're looking good. How are you doing?"

As he talked, Davis slid their clasped hands behind her back and pulled her closer. Barrett relaxed a bit when she felt some of his tension drain away. She concentrated on Milt and pretended Sandra didn't exist.

"Oh, not too bad," Milt said vaguely as his gaze moved back and forth between Barrett and Sandra and noted the half embrace between Davis and Barrett. Barrett could see the moment he realized the awkward situation he'd created. "Uh, Davis, I hope I didn't overstep any bounds bringing Sandra to the party . . ."

"No, of course not, Milt," Davis said. "I know some of your old friends here will be as happy to see you as I am. The Kramers are over by the fireplace, and the Turnbulls are outside on the patio. Help yourself to a drink and go talk to them. I'll catch up with you later."

"Right. Good idea," Milt agreed and turned to Barrett. "It was nice to meet you, ma'am." Then with a

"Come on, Sandra," he practically dragged the woman to the bar.

Her reception evidently not what she had expected, Sandra went without a word. She only flashed a viperous glance at Barrett, who turned her back, the better to ignore the malicious bitch.

"I wouldn't have thrown her out," Davis said in a low voice. "I wouldn't embarrass Milt—and she knows it, which is probably why she inveigled him into bringing her. I do appreciate your defusing the situation, but I really didn't need help in handling her."

"I know," she replied, "and I may not be a military historian, but I also know it always helps to have reinforcements after a surprise attack." She glanced beyond Davis to the living room. "Speaking of reinforcements . . ." She gestured at Martha and Bill who were standing at the bottom of the steps looking like the cavalry about to charge.

Martha and Bill nodded at Davis and walked away in the direction of the patio.

"Looks like all of us have your back," Barrett told him.

"That's nice to know," Davis murmured.

He gazed down at Barrett, feeling a bit stunned. What a woman she was, coming to his "rescue" like she did. He'd never had such support before, someone stepping forward to take part of a burden, social or otherwise, even from his family. When Sandra had pawed him, he'd felt his skin crawl. He'd had no idea how to get rid of her without hurting Milt. Then Barrett took over, declared without being obvious he was *hers*, not Sandra's. Milt, no slouch, had picked up the hint and the awkwardness of Sandra's presence immediately.

Sandra, for once, had the sense to keep her mouth shut. After all, what could she say? Barrett was being perfectly hospitable. Sandra must have realized throwing a fit here would put her on several society blacklists, not because it would embarrass him, but because everybody loved Milt. She also must have realized Barrett was no pushover.

His "tame" historian was turning out to be not a harmless scholar at all, but more like a hit woman. She was certainly dressed to kill. When she had come down the stairs, all deep blue eyes, curvy body, long legs and curls, his breath had caught in his throat and his mind had gone blank as the blood in his body rushed south. It had taken him several long seconds to regain control—all the while wanting to sling her over his shoulder and climb the stairs to find the privacy of his bedroom.

Take it easy, he'd told himself. She's not going home with anybody but you. He raised their still clasped hands, kissed her knuckles and winked. "I'll have to thank you properly later."

Before she could reply, Gonzales opened the door to admit more guests, and Davis released her hand as they turned to greet the new arrivals, the couples from the Wednesday dinner party. "We have a surprise for you two," the man from Georgia announced. "Look who showed up on our doorstep this morning."

The couples parted to reveal a fifth member of their group, and Davis heard Barrett gasp. He shot a glance at her. She seemed frozen in place for a moment.

"Horace," she said, almost under her breath. Then she plastered on a smile so false it looked like it might crack her face.

"Davis," the client continued, "let me introduce Dr. Horace Glover. We met several years ago when he was kind enough to include two of my ancestors in his military histories. He heard we were in town and gave me a call. He's a colleague of Barrett's and I didn't think you'd mind us bringing him along."

"The professor and I have spoken on the phone," Davis said, shaking Glover's hand. "And no, I don't mind you bringing him. There's always room for one more. Welcome to my home, Dr. Glover." He felt his teeth grind together as he said the words. So this was the snake—a reptile with a square jaw, trendy eyeglass frames, and a toothy smile.

"Thank you," Horace boomed. "That's true Southern hospitality. And Barrett, how are you, my dear?" He held out his hand and when Barrett took it, he pulled her to him and would have kissed her on the mouth if she hadn't moved her head so quickly.

Davis felt rage ripple through him, but he put on his negotiating face as Barrett said something inconsequential and hurriedly stepped back. He put his hand on her waist, drew her into the curve of his arm, and gave her a surreptitious squeeze. Some of the stiffness went out of her spine, but she still didn't say anything.

He saw other guests entering behind Glover. "Please make yourselves at home," he told the clients, with a wave at the bar and the food. "The other investors for the project we discussed on Wednesday are here, and I'll introduce them as soon as I welcome the people behind you."

The five went to the bar as Davis shook the hands of the latest arrivals and introduced them to Barrett. She seemed to be back on track as she smiled and bantered with a guest who made a fatuous comment about not having any teachers like her in school. He signaled to one of his associates who took the newcomers off his hands.

"Are you all right?" he asked Barrett when she

closed her eyes and took a deep breath.

"Yes," she replied and opened her eyes again. "Seeing Horace here was just a surprise. He's called me
twice, asking to get a look at the papers. I told him no,
of course, but I didn't think he'd have the gall to show
up without permission. He's very sneaky. Nobody
knows how he gathers his information, like knowing
those people are your clients and are in Houston, but
some department members claim he has a network of
spies—former students—all over the country. Whatever the truth, I'm certain he didn't 'just happen' to
drop in on your client by pure chance." She ran her
hand over her forehead as if to soothe a pain. "You've
spoken to him before?"

"Yeah, he called me at the office the other day
with an absurd claim that Granddaddy had 'promised'
him a look at the papers. And no," he continued when
she jerked her alarmed gaze back to his, "Granddaddy
never promised and I refused him access."

He glanced over her head and saw Bill and Martha heading their way. "I'll handle Horace. You talk
to the other Jamisons. Bill's always good for a laugh.
And don't worry. I know exactly the people to sic on
Glover to keep him occupied."

"You mean the couple who've traced their ancestors back to the Stone Age?" Her eyes began to take

on a mischievous twinkle. "The ones who claim kin-
ship with the Lees of Virginia *and* English nobility
and want to tell you all about every single member of
the family?"

"Precisely. Now, go." He gave her a nudge toward the living room and went to join the clients with
Glover. The man was pontificating about something
and Davis could clearly hear him over the voices of his
other guests. It didn't take him long, however, to lure
the professor into the genealogists' web and see him
safely ensnared.

Davis looked around for Barrett. She was engrossed with one of his favorite clients. Then he
noticed Bill and Martha talking intently with Peggy
Murphy and her husband. The foursome grinned at
one another and split up, each heading to other groups.
What was that all about? Davis shook his head. He
didn't have the time to find out. He first had to make
sure his clients were talking with the entrepreneurs
he'd invited them there to meet.

Chapter NINETEEN

*A*bout an hour later, Davis stopped by the foot of the stairs to check with Gonzales about food and beverage supplies. After being assured no one would go hungry or thirsty, he stood for a moment surveying the crowd around the pool. He needed to circulate with those folks, now that it looked like there'd be no more arrivals. He stepped aside to let a woman pass and watched her walk toward the powder room between the office wing and the family room behind the kitchen.

As he turned back around, he frowned. What had he just seen? Something had been out of place or not quite correct. He faced the office wing again. Its door was slightly ajar. He knew he had closed but not locked the door. Too often at this party, someone asked for specific information or a private word, and he took them to the office, so he had not locked the wing. He had locked . . . only the conference room. Where the Windswept papers were.

He stalked down the hall, opened the door, and

flicked the light switch. The sudden illumination revealed Professor Horace Glover standing in the opened conference room door with his hand on the knob—a knob from which a wire protruded.

"Can I help you, professor?" Davis asked in a calm, soft and—he hoped—deadly voice.

Glover whirled around, his eyes bugging out, his mouth open.

Davis shut the office wing door behind him and waited for Glover to speak. He watched several emotions—fear, anger, contempt—play across Horace's face as the man decided what to say, how to explain himself.

"Well," Glover finally said with a hint of phony embarrassment in his tone, "I guess you've caught me." He held out his hands as if in supplication. "I plead temporary insanity. I couldn't stand being in the same place with the fabled Windswept records and not sneak a peek at them. I throw myself on the mercy of the court and ask you to put me out of my misery and let me see them."

Davis let ten seconds go by and watched the professor fidget before he asked, "Why should I break the conditions of the agreement I have with Dr. Browning?"

Glover drew himself up and said with what sounded like the utmost sincerity, "Because I can do a much better job of the inventory than she can." He assumed a just-between-us-men manner and continued, "I have to tell you, Jamison, she's out of her depth here. Way out of her area of expertise."

"And I need experience like yours . . . or what will happen?"

"I've seen thousands, tens of thousands, of pages of primary source materials like your papers. I understand what I'm looking at. I doubt Barrett can say the same for her 'women's studies.' " He put a sneer into the last words. "Furthermore, I am a recognized authority. My name on the inventory will enhance the reputation of the papers, make them more valuable for you, gain you more and better publicity when you decide to donate or sell them. Scholars will know they can trust the inventory to be correct and complete."

Putting answers in lists must be an occupational hazard, Davis observed, but he kept his tone reasonable and resolute when he said, "Dr. Glover, the answer is still no."

"Mark my words," Horace said, his face flushing as he pointed his finger at Davis, "you're making a mistake. Letting a little no-talent, no-tenure nobody with a feminist ax to grind, with no conception of what makes good history, loose on your family records is to head straight for disaster. Especially if you let her use them to write articles or books. There's no telling how she will twist the Jamison story to make your ancestors into something other than the heroes and fine people they were."

Davis watched, fascinated at how Glover was working himself up. What a pompous ass! He thought about refuting the man's words, but knew it would do no good. Arguing with Glover would be like arguing with Lloyd; neither man would listen to contrary opinions.

Glover kept talking, his voice falling into a conspiratorial tone as though he were imparting confidential information. "If she's done to you what she's done to me, led you on, dropped salacious hints, offered you false promises or 'her charms' for helping her gain a place in the field, beware. She'll never deliver. I can promise you she'll never be offered tenure, not at our university or any other, not with my influence against her. You should have heard what the professors said at the university where she received her doctorate. I think there's something fishy about her work there also."

Davis felt his anger boil up past indignation, past fury and reach the level of wrath, but he leaned back against the door and spoke softly and carefully. "What exactly are you claiming, Glover? Barrett is dishonest? Incompetent? Untrustworthy? A poor historian? A slut and a whore?" He shook his head in fake wonder.

"What do you take me for? Do you think I would

let just anybody into my home or my family's history? I had her thoroughly investigated. Everyone speaks extremely highly of Dr. Browning. Except for you. Isn't it strange that you are the only person with such accusations, in fact, with any derogatory statements at all?

Letting some of his contempt show, he looked the professor up and down. "And isn't it interesting that you, with all your supposed sterling reputation, should have broken into a locked room in my house, having wormed your way in by trading on an acquaintance with good and honorable clients of mine?"

Glover's face darkened from pink to red. "Now, listen here . . ." he boomed, but stopped, obviously searching for his next words.

Davis didn't give him the chance for rebuttal. He stood straight again, his hand on the doorknob. "Let me suggest a scenario, Glover. Let's say a certain professor tries to block the tenure appointment of another historian and uses false claims and spurious evidence to do so. Let's say someone holds security recordings of this certain professor breaking into a room, a locked room holding records to which everyone knows he has already denied the professor access. Let's say someone makes those tapes, which also record sound, by the way, available to the relevant authorities of the university."

He paused. Glover appeared too stunned to speak.

"Tell me," Davis continued, "Do you think the professor's accusations would hold any water in those circumstances? What chance would a professor have to retain his position in the light of such unethical, illegal conduct? Even tenured professors can be removed for cause. What would happen to his reputation under any circumstances? I wouldn't be surprised if Dr. Browning didn't have grounds to sue him for slander as well."

"Tapes?" Glover squeaked, his usual boom completely busted, his face suddenly pale.

"Surely you don't think I'm the type not to have excellent security," Davis chided with a wave at the air duct at the end of the hall.

Glover glanced at the grillwork and lost even more color. "But . . . but that's blackmail."

"I prefer to call it 'job security,'" Davis answered. "Did you drive yourself or come with your friends tonight?"

Glover looked befuddled by the change in topic, but replied, "I followed them."

"Good. I suggest you tell them you don't feel well and are going back to your hotel. Then you get the hell out of my house!"

With his last words, Davis yanked open the office

wing door and, with a sharp gesture, pointed in the direction of the front. And heard Barrett say, "Davis?" When he turned his head, she was standing right on the other side of the threshold, her hand out as if she were about to grasp the knob.

She took a step in before she saw Glover and the open conference room door. "Davis?" she repeated. "I saw a light back here and . . ." Her voice petered out as she looked from one man to the other.

"The professor was just leaving," Davis said. He turned to Glover and pointed the way out again. "Your friends are in the living room."

Glover drew himself up with, to Davis, a pitifully inadequate attempt at bravado. Scowling, he stalked past the two of them. Barrett stepped back as if to avoid the man's possible touch.

Gonzales appeared at the foot of the stairs and looked a question at Davis. He beckoned his major-domo and said, "If Glover isn't out of this house in three minutes, let me know." Gonzales nodded and followed the professor.

Davis drew Barrett into the office wing hall and shut the door. She glanced at the open conference room and asked, "What's going on? What was Horace doing in here?"

Davis went to the door and took the wire out of

the keyhole. It was a common paper clip. "The professor decided to 'sneak a peek' at the Windswept papers. He picked the lock and was about to walk in when I caught him. I just threw him out." He studied her while he talked. Her expression went from incredulity to anger. He wondered how much she had heard before he opened the door.

"Why, the underhanded son of a bitch! I never thought he'd stoop so low as to break in. What on earth did he expect to find in a few minutes? To read carefully through the master list could take at least an hour."

"I don't know," he said. "Whatever it was, he didn't have the chance to open so much as a single box. And don't worry. He won't be back, I promise." He made sure the conference door lock was activated and shut it firmly. "He did show me I need to have better locks than these flimsy ones if I want to keep the papers here."

"Oh, Davis," Barrett sighed and came over to put her hand on his arm, "I'm sorry this happened."

"It wasn't your fault," he said, relieved she had probably heard none of the previous conversation. She surely would have said something if she'd heard those ugly threats of Glover's. He didn't want to discuss Horace now, so he put briskness and good humor into his next words. "We have a party going on out there,

and we need to get back to it." He gave her a quick kiss
and with his arm around her shoulders, led her back to
his guests.

———————◆◆◆———————

Eventually the party wound down, and the only people
left were Davis, Barrett, Bill, Martha, and Peggy and
Jim Murphy at the far end of the living room. His back
to the fireplace and his tie loosened, Davis stood next to
Barrett's chair. In the background, the caterers swiftly
dismantled the bars and took care of the leftovers.

"How do you think the party went?" Davis asked
the whole group after he and Peggy discussed the people with whom he or one of the staff needed to follow
up on Monday.

"Better than last year," Martha said, "until Sandra
showed up, that is."

"Yeah, but we took care of her," Bill said, rubbing
his hands together like a man who'd just made a mil-
lion-dollar deal.

Davis shot a glance at Barrett, who returned his implied question with an "I don't have the slightest idea"
shrug. "Okay," he said to Bill, "what did you do?"

"I started it, I'll tell it," Martha interrupted. "I
was in the dining room and overheard the Hendersons

talking about Sandra and a derogatory statement the bitch made about Barrett. So I asked them about it. It seems Sandra, when she wasn't with Milt, was telling everybody Barrett was a gold digger, a little nobody who'd latched onto you, Davis, for a meal ticket. The Hendersons said Dr. Glover had been in the group with them and *he* said Barrett wasn't even a real professor, just out for what she could get, too green to be inventorying an important source like the family records. Oh, and *then*, Sandra informed them how much she *pitied* you and wondered how you could have lost your edge. After all, if you couldn't see straight through Barrett, what did it say about your business abilities?"

Davis, instantly furious, clamped a wall around his temper. Before he could open his mouth, however, Bill held up his hand. "There's more. Just wait for it, Davis."

"So," Martha continued, "I grabbed Bill and Peggy and Jim and we hatched a plan."

"Yeah," Bill said. "It was great. One of us was always with Sandra or Glover, refuting what they said. The others circulated, talking up Barrett and how good and smart she was *and* how well Jamison Investments are doing. And by the way, wasn't it awful how Sandra had played on Milt's good nature to persuade him to bring her tonight? Everybody knew your split was not the most amicable, so what could be her motive for coming here except to make spiteful trouble? We also asked—all very innocently, of course—what she was doing back here and what had happened to the guy she left you for."

"A couple of people with Dallas connections had heard he kicked her out. The prevailing consensus is for cheating on him," Martha interjected.

"By the time we finished," Bill continued with a frown at his sister for interrupting, "Sandra was stymied. If she brought up Barrett's name, either the people had already talked to Barrett and thought she was great. Or, if they hadn't, they were primed not to believe anything Sandra said. It worked like a charm." He leaned back on the couch and grinned at Davis.

"Is that why you made me recite all my academic credentials for you?" Barrett asked.

"Yep," Bill answered, "we needed the facts to back us up."

"Milt, bless his heart, caught the tail end of one of Sandra's catty little remarks and hustled her out before she could do any more damage," Peggy put in, "but by then, she didn't have a friend in the place. You were out on the patio at the time, so Milt said to tell you he would call you to apologize. He was very embarrassed."

"I kept after Glover," Jim put in. "He has a grand

scheme to bring in a herd of graduate students to do the inventory when you turn the papers over to him. I lost track of him for a while, but when he left early, I figured we had taken care of him too."

"So, what do you think, big brother?" Martha asked with a grin on her face. "Did we do good?"

Davis honestly didn't know what to say to this turn of events. He simply sat down on the raised hearth and looked at each of the four plotters in turn. They all smiled back, obviously proud of coming to the rescue.

Another rescue.

Without his help or orders.

To protect him and, more important, Barrett from Sandra's and Glover's viciousness.

His anger faded away, replaced by feelings of humility and gratitude that, for a moment, he wasn't sure how to handle. He was used to being on the giving, protecting side. He found it harder to be on the receiving end than he thought it would be.

"Thank you," he said finally. "Thank you on my part and for what you did for Barrett."

"Glad to be of help," Martha said.

"It was fun," Bill added.

"It certainly added some excitement to the evening," Jim said.

"Just doing my job," Peggy said. "We can't have

people losing confidence in us." She rose and pulled her husband up. "Now it's time for this woman to get some sleep. We'll see you Monday, boss."

Chapter TWENTY

As Davis closed and locked the front door after the group left, Gonzales appeared and turned out the living room lights. Eva came in from the kitchen and announced, "The caterers have left, and everything is secure. We'll give the rooms a good cleaning on Monday as usual. Will there be anything else tonight?"

"No, thank you both. Everybody loved the food, and the party ran like clockwork. You did a spectacular job. Rest up tomorrow. You deserve it. I don't even want to see your faces in this house. By the way, did you save any tamales for me?"

"Yes, sir. There's at least two dozen in the refrigerator."

"Good. I'm looking forward to them."

"Thank you, Mr. Jamison. Good night," Gonzales said.

"Good night," Barrett and Davis said together.

Davis watched Gonzales turn out the dining room lights and the two disappear into the kitchen. The hall sconces offered their usual shadowed illumination when he drew Barrett into his arms.

She came eagerly, and he contented himself for a while with simply holding her. She seemed to find the embrace as comforting as he did because she wound her arms around his waist under his jacket and held on tight.

After enjoying the feel of her against him for a few moments, he drew back and gazed down into her eyes. She smiled up at him.

"What did you think of my party?" he asked.

"It was fun, but I didn't expect a conniving woman or a thieving scholar among the guests. Are your gatherings always this exciting?" she asked with a mischievous gleam in her eyes.

"God, I hope not."

She turned sober. "Davis, what happened between you and Horace back in the office? If I hadn't seen it with my own eyes, I wouldn't have believed he could stoop so low as to break into the conference room."

He turned her and, with an arm around her shoulders, started her walking toward the stairs. "The 'good' professor, and I use the term advisedly, is evidently jealous of you and wants to get his hands on the papers in the worst way. When I wouldn't agree to let him in, he made a number of false, malicious, and disparaging accusations about your work and you personally. What Martha and the others heard was just part of it. He even threatened to work against your appointment to tenure."

She gasped, stopped in her tracks, took two steps away from him, then swung back. "Conniving bastard! What a two-faced, pusillanimous, sorry excuse of a human being!" She raised and brandished her fists as if she wanted to hit something but didn't have a target. "Mmmmmgh!"

"Barrett." He clasped her fists in his hands and shook them gently to get her attention. "You don't have anything to worry about. I took care of him."

"How? How can you stop his innuendoes and downright lies?"

"Blackmail."

"What?" Her voice went up a couple of octaves with the question.

"I threatened to reveal all to the university—backed up, by the way, with audio and video recordings of him breaking into the conference room and bad-mouthing you afterward." He couldn't help letting a little smugness seep into his tone.

"What recordings?"

"There aren't any, of course, but I led Glover to believe I have state-of-the-art security all over the house." He shrugged. "And he's afraid that not only will I shred his vaunted reputation, but you will sue him for slander."

She stared at him for a moment, then her eyes started to twinkle and a smirk played on her lips. She shook her head slowly. "Oh, Davis. Oh, no."

"Oh, Barrett, oh, yes," he mimicked, but nodded just as slowly. "You should have seen the look on his face. I only wish I really had a camera."

"Oh, me too."

"He looked like this . . . and then . . . and then . . ." Davis made Glover-like faces of shock, innocence, and anger. She started laughing, he joined in, and by the time he portrayed anger, they were howling, holding on to each other to stay upright.

"My hero," she gasped when they came up for air and climbed the stairs. "You saved me and the papers from the evil Dr. Glover."

"Ah, but you're my heroine. How you handled Sandra was absolutely beautiful. I've never seen her speechless before."

"And I *did* see the look on *her* face." She skewed her face into a more-than-passable imitation of Sandra at her most snooty.

Her mimicry set them off again, but with an arm around each other, they managed to stagger up the re-maining steps to the point where the hall led in two directions—to his bedroom or hers.

As they turned to face each other, their laughter subsided. She raised her head, and he felt her breath catch as their eyes met and their gazes locked. In a heartbeat, he felt them come to the crucial question. Tonight?

He placed his hands on her shoulders and took a deep breath as her scent—subtle perfume and something uniquely Barrett—worked its way into his every cell. Even in the shadowed light, he could see her pupils expand until only a small rim of blue showed. She smiled, a slow, very feminine smile. He felt his cock grow hard, then harder still.

God, how he craved this woman.

When she stepped closer and he felt her soft breasts against his chest and her belly against his erection, desire dealt him such a fierce blow, it almost took him to his knees. A violent need to take her right here, against the wall, on the floor, rampaged through him and tightened his muscles to the point of pain. Clamping down on the primitive urge, he assuaged it some by wrapping his arms around her and pulling her tighter to him.

She offered her mouth and he took it. When her tongue greeted his, when she made a small purr of agreement, when her body went pliant, the hunger he'd been suffering burst its bonds and erupted into ravenous starvation. He greedily thrust his tongue hard into her mouth, to claim, to devour, to possess.

And found himself possessed in return. She returned his kiss with a wild passion, an aggression, an avarice to match his own.

He slid one hand around her neck and behind her head, threading his fingers through her curls to hold her still. The other, he ran up her back, then down to press her hips even tighter against his rock-hard arousal. And he took the kiss deeper still, down to the hot darkness where only need and want and desire existed.

How long they stood, wrapped in each other's arms, he didn't know.

It wasn't long enough. He could stand here, kissing her, forever.

No, it was too long. The compulsion to see her, touch her, smell her, taste her without the barriers of clothing grew strong, stronger, then overwhelmed him.

He raised his head enough to free his lips. "Barrett," he whispered.

"Davis," she breathed the word more than said it.

"Come to bed with me."

"Yes-s-s-s." She tried to pull his head down into another kiss.

He resisted. He wanted much more. "Come," he said.

He stepped back, took her hand and led her to his bedroom above the office wing. He opened the door and drew her inside, down the long room to his big bed against the far wall. The bedside lamp he'd fortunately left on cast a warm glow and gave him what he wanted—the ability to see her, all of her. When they reached the bed, he brought her back into his arms and looked down into her heavy lidded eyes. The passion, the desire in them staggered him. She wanted him as much as he wanted her. She was his woman, he knew it in his heart and his soul.

Barrett gazed back at the black eagle before her. He was so fierce, so intent, so concentrated on her. In return, she could look nowhere except at him. Her mind had no room for thoughts of her surroundings or anything else except her need for him. His kiss mesmerized her. His touch ignited her blood. She wanted him with every ounce of her being. She'd never felt like this before, so focused on, so needful of anyone. She had to have more.

Running her hands up his shirt front and around his neck, she pulled him down into another kiss. Davis could kiss like no man she'd ever known. She was becoming addicted to his warm, pliant mouth on hers, their tongues dancing, his mustache tickling and enhancing each caress. She indulged herself and kissed him back with all the fervor she was feeling inside.

But kissing quickly became no longer totally satisfying. She wanted, needed, yearned to touch his bare
skin, stroke the hard muscles moving under his shirt,
be warmed by the heat of his body, and realize the
wonder of coming together without any barriers.

Without breaking their kiss, she pushed at his
shoulders and then at his jacket until he loosened the
steel bands of his arms and shrugged off the coat.
The motion moved them apart, but only long enough
for him to whip off his loosened tie. Between small,
tantalizing kisses, she went to work with trembling
fingers on his shirt buttons. He took care of his cuff
links, pulled the opened shirt out of his pants and off.
Breathing heavily, he stood still and she could at last
touch his bare skin.

"Mmmmm," she hummed. Better. She splayed
her hands across his broad, hard chest, through the dark
curly hair. She leaned in, inhaled—oh, he smelled so
good—and kissed his skin just above his solar plexus.

He shivered, cupped her head in his large hands,
tilted her head back, and kissed her until she thought
she'd explode. Then he released her lips and murmured, "My turn."

She was the one to shiver as he reached behind her
and unzipped her dress. He took a step back, grasped

the shoulder straps, and drew the dress down to her waist, then over her hips. When he let it go, it pooled around her shoes. He looked her up and down, his glance almost a physical caress as it traveled over her lacy strapless bra, panties, and thigh-high hose.

He slid his hands from her waist, behind her again, and released the back catch of her bra. As it fell away, he straightened and his gaze dropped to her bare breasts. His eyes gleaming, he looked for a long moment before reaching out to cup them gently. With his touch, she felt them grow heavy and tight, their peaks pebble and swell. Then he weighed them, flicked their nipples with his thumbs, and the intense tingling sensation spreading through her from those two points stole her breath. She closed her eyes and heard herself whimper.

When he bent and kissed first one tip, then the other, she had to grip his shoulders to remain upright. When he took one nipple in his mouth and suckled, she rose on tiptoe to offer him more. When he transferred his attentions to the other, she moaned, arched against him, held up only by her clinging hands.

By the time he pulled back, kissed his way up her neck to her mouth, she could only hang on. And want more.

He bent, picked her up, and placed her on the big, high bed. Leaning over her on braced arms, he kissed her, another hungry but too short kiss. Then he straightened and ran his hands down her rib cage to her waist and lower to her thighs. After he removed the hosiery and the thong—so slowly she thought she'd burst from anticipation and the slide of his warm hands on her legs—he stood again, and his gaze roamed her body as if committing it to memory.

She made no attempt to cover herself; she felt no need for modesty with him. She did have a need to see all of him, however, and she did her own share of looking as he removed the rest of his clothes. Within seconds, he stood before her, wonderfully nude, his sex jutting proudly toward her.

He was beside her before she had seen her fill, but it was all right. In fact, it was more like heaven when, lying on his side, he took her into his arms. He thrust his top leg between hers and hugged her tight. For a long moment, they simply held each other, cheek to cheek, hardly moving at all. She felt giddy from inhaling his scent—woodsy aftershave and musky man.

Oh, how glorious to touch along the entire length of their naked bodies, to entwine around each other, to feel his searing heat warm her down to the marrow of her bones. How marvelous to run her hands over his hard back, his firm buttocks, to sense the strength in his muscles, in the man himself. How exquisite to feel his hand kneading, first her breast, then her bottom, then sliding down and up the entire length of her leg.

He lifted his head, and she felt fever rise within her when she met his darkened eyes. Their lips came together and their kiss turned from merely hungry to voracious in a flash. Wildfire burst forth in her blood. She was liquefying, flowing into a molten lake of desire.

When he left her lips, made his hot, openmouthed way down her neck to her breast, and laved, then dropped kisses all around the areola, she groaned. When he rubbed his mustache across the aching tip and then suckled hard, she arched against him with a wordless cry.

It was too much. No, it was not enough. More.

He turned his attentions to her other breast and she writhed, pushing her hips against his when she felt his slick, damp penis slide against her wet core. He shifted, moving over her, turning her onto her back while he knelt between her legs. Braced on stiff arms above her, he kissed his way up from her breasts and found her mouth again.

His move gave her access to his chest, and she rubbed and kneaded, traced his hard muscles, tested the resiliency of his skin, brought his flat nipples to tight pinpoints. He seemed almost to purr at her ministrations. She reached lower.

When her fingers closed around him, he lifted his
mouth, went still, watched what she was doing. She
caressed him, measured his thickness, his length with
her fingertips, then took him between her palms. She
could feel his blood pulsating; hers beat in unison. She
squeezed gently and he grew longer, harder. She felt
her own sex swell, ache, long for him. She raised her
hips, searching for him.

"Wait," he grated as he sat back, captured her hands
and brought them to either side of her head. He let
her go, leaned over to the night stand, opened the top
drawer, pulled out protection, and swiftly applied it.

He shifted again, back to his original position, but
braced on one hand.

With his free hand, he fondled her breast, then
moved lower, over her nest of curls to her swollen folds.
He raised his eyes to hers as his finger found the engorged knot of nerve endings under its hood. When
he rubbed it, she gasped as all her muscles tensed.
When he pressed it, her hips bucked of their own ac-
cord. When he stroked lower, she wrapped her legs
around his hips and rose to meet him.

Their gazes locked, he withdrew his fingers, positioned himself and pressed in. And in, and in. She felt
herself stretching as the broad head of his erection slid
into her. Stretching more as he filled her slowly.

And finally he was in, to the hilt. She was panting, as was he. Poised above her, he looked triumphant. She felt the same.

"Hold on to me," he said, his voice low and rough. She raised her hands to his shoulders, grasped tightly. Then he began to move, again slowly, almost out, all the way in, almost out, all the way in.

She could feel her internal tension increase and her muscles clasp him tighter with each stroke as he increased his rhythm, but only in small increments. She could see in the rigidity of his face and feel in the tightness of his body the price his control was costing.

But she didn't want control. She wanted heat, passion, the Davis she knew lurked beneath his granite surface. She wanted all that and more. She wanted him. Now.

She reached her hands around his head and pulled him down and herself up and into a ferocious kiss. He seemed as solid as stone for a second, but when he groaned and his tongue thrust possessively into her mouth, she knew she had succeeded in breaking the bonds of his restraint. Beyond hunger, they both feasted, he as ravenous as she. His taking only increased her need to give. His giving only led her to take more.

They broke the kiss. They had to, to breathe.

Instead, they stared into each other's eyes, and the thought flashed through her mind: his concentrated attention was the most erotic thing she'd ever seen.

She tightened herself around him—once, twice. Her movement triggered something in him, and he began to drive into her, faster, harder, deeper. As determined to take him as he was to have her, she rose to meet him. Their bodies pounded together, and the powerful force of his thrusts almost lifted her off the mattress. Her legs wrapped around him, she rode him as much as he did her.

Yes, this was what she wanted. Power, fire, ferocity. She let herself go, surrendered to the increasing tempo, to the building tension, to the man above her. Her body clasped his tight, then tighter, and she cried out as she shattered beneath him and tumbled into ecstasy.

Through a haze, she felt him thrust even harder, faster, more urgently, then lock himself to her as he climaxed. Then he gave a low groan, his arms buckled, and he relaxed on top of her.

As his breathing slowed and his heartbeat returned to normal, Davis came back to himself. His head was on the pillow next to Barrett's, his nose in her hair and his lips barely an inch from her earlobe. Her hands caressed his back, and her legs were wrapped around his hips. He was still buried deep inside her.

God Almighty, what a ride. He had never lost control like that in his life, taken a woman like a berserker. He'd never had such a lover before either—one who gave of herself so completely, who urged him on so demandingly, who wrung him out so thoroughly. He inhaled and smelled a light floral perfume, warm woman, and hot sex. He could stay here forever.

He nuzzled her neck, kissed her earlobe. She squirmed slightly, and he tugged on her dangling earring to provoke another twitch. He'd taken everything off except her jewelry, and the thought of her wearing only precious metals and gems appealed to him—probably to his baser, more primitive instincts.

When she wriggled and trailed her fingernails down his back, he realized he must be heavy. But he couldn't resist just a couple of seconds more of bliss. He knew his time was up when she gave him a hug with arms, legs, and the muscles sheathing his cock.

He raised up on his elbows and looked down into her face. She wore a sober expression, but her eyes were big and blue and soft, and when he kissed her lips, he felt her smile against him. He smiled back when he lifted his head.

"Stay the night with me," he murmured. "I want to wake up with you in the morning." He gave her what he hoped was a persuasive kiss.

She smiled again, ran her hands up and down his ribcage, seemed to be considering his request. He could almost see the wheels turning in her head and he watched her practicality resume control of her mind. For a moment he was afraid she'd refuse, but she finally said, "I'd like it too. I need to wash my face though, and take off my jewelry."

"Fine." He kissed her again, had to stop himself from eating her up as desire unexpectedly woke again. He wasn't surprised at its return, rather at its speed. He shrugged mentally; just more proof of how much he wanted her. He rose on hands and knees and withdrew from her body. They both made little sounds; was she as sorry as he was to be disconnected?

After he got off the bed, she sat up and looked around. Her eyes grew bigger as she took in his bedroom furnishings, but she didn't say anything, only climbed down.

"I'll take care of this—" he said, waving at his lower body, "—and meet you back here. Okay?"

"Okay." She nodded.

When he came out of his bathroom, she hadn't returned, but her clothes were missing from the floor. He picked up his own, hung up the suit and tie and put the rest in the hamper. He was turning back the bedspread when she came in.

He couldn't help but smile. She was wearing a huge, ugly, faded, multicolored robe. It missed dragging on the floor by only an inch, and although she had rolled up the sleeves, her hands barely peaked out past the cuffs. It was the least seductive garment he'd ever seen. Then his body let him know she could be wearing a barrel and it wouldn't matter.

He met her at the foot of the bed, kissed her, and reached for the robe's sash. Once it was undone, he opened the garment and slid his hands inside around her waist. Her naked waist.

"Good," he muttered against her lips.

"Good, what?" she asked when they finally parted.

"You didn't put on a nightgown. I prefer you just as you are."

She just grinned up at him and, waving at the bed, asked, "Which side?"

He pointed to the left side and they climbed into bed. He switched off the lamp and a soft glow from the security lights around the pool permeated the room through the sheer curtains—just enough to see her shape, her hair dark against the white pillowcase, and to find her lips with his. Leaning on one elbow over her, he kissed her and cupped her breast in his free hand.

When she returned his kiss, he grew hard again.

When she moaned and turned to swing her leg over his, he pushed his erection against her.

"Oh," she said.

"Oh," he replied before he started kissing, licking, nibbling, and brushing his way down her body. This time he'd take it slowly, take time to savor, take her until she cried out his name.

And he did.

And she did.

And she fell asleep in his arms.

Chapter TWENTY-ONE

The next morning Barrett woke up but didn't open her eyes for a while. She was so comfortable lying next to Davis she didn't want to move. She was on her back and he was on his side toward her with his bottom hand tucked under his pillow and the top splayed over her abdomen. She smiled; he evidently wanted to know exactly where she was. Or to keep her there.

She smiled more broadly as she replayed scenes from the night on the back of her forehead. As she suspected from his kisses, Davis had proven to be a consummate, passionate lover. He'd drawn reactions and feelings from her she hadn't known she possessed. Neither of the other two men with whom she'd had sex came close to making her feel so, so . . . satisfied, or cherished, or aroused, or complete.

Now, in the hazy light of day, did she have any second thoughts about what she had done?

No, she didn't, she decided. They would find mutual pleasure together during the summer. When she left, she'd have the research for several articles and a friend to see when she returned. She could and would keep her head on straight where Davis was concerned. And guard her heart.

Yes, especially the last.

She nodded to herself in confirmation of her decision and opened her eyes.

Yep, she was still in the big four poster. His furniture hadn't been an hallucination. She cradled Davis's hand in both of hers—he grunted and laced his fingers with hers—and sat up. She'd paid no attention at all to the room last night. Davis had more than filled her vision. Now she studied it in the dim morning light.

It was a large room, probably the length of the two offices below combined. On the windowless back wall opposite the glassed wall stood a large marble-topped dresser and a tall armoire that barely fit under what must be a ten-foot-high ceiling. The dark mahogany and ornate carvings in the furniture contrasted sharply, but in a complimentary manner somehow, with the abstract paintings and the glass wall overlooking the pool. The paintings picked up the colors in the oriental carpet; only at the edges could the light oak hardwood floor be seen.

The wall behind the bed held long slits of glass on either side to allow a view of the bayou behind the house. The living room wing to the east and the sheer white draperies kept the room shaded from the morning sun. Against the glass, two modern armchairs flanked an oval marble-topped table with a lamp on it.

All in all, there wasn't much furniture for such a big room.

As she examined one of the paintings, she felt Davis shift. She looked down at him, and he put his free hand on her back and rubbed it gently.

"Good morning," she said with a smile. With his dark beard stubble and disheveled hair, he resembled a pirate more than an eagle at the moment. A complacent, satisfied buccaneer.

"Good morning," he replied in a low, velvet drawl. He searched her eyes for a moment, but seemed satisfied with what he saw as he tugged her down into his arms.

She relaxed against him, but kept hold of his hand. She had a question and didn't want to be distracted before she had an answer. She gazed up at the top of the bed posts and wondered how to formulate her query.

She didn't have to because he said, "You're probably wondering about the furniture in this room, aren't you?"

"Well, yes," she admitted. "It's quite a contrast to the rest of the house."

He took a deep breath and let it out slowly, al-

most as if he were putting off an answer, but he said,
"I bought the house before I married Sandra. She decorated the living and dining rooms—and this room.
The furnishings here were in keeping with those
downstairs. I never let her touch the offices, and she
never got around to the kitchen or family room."

He paused, took another deep breath, let it out.
"When I caught her in this room in our bed with another man, I threw her out and all the furniture with
her. I slept in the room you're in for a while. Then
Granddaddy came for a visit, took a look around, and
said I needed to sleep in my own bedroom. A couple of
days after he want home, all you see here, except for the
two chairs by the windows, arrived from Windswept.
The bed, chest, armoire and nightstands are a bedroom
set Mary Maude had made in New York in the eigh-
teen-fifties. She took it when she moved to the dower
house after the war and Edgar Jr. married. The original
set she and Edgar used stayed in the big house. Mary
Maude must have liked a large bed. I had to have the
mattress, springs, and linens made to fit."

His expression solemn, he raised up on an elbow
and leaned over her. "This bed has a lot of history,
Barrett, but where Sandra is concerned, it has none."

She felt absurdly relieved to hear those words, but
the last thing she wanted to talk about at the moment was

his ex, so she asked with as straight a face as she could muster, "Can I at least hope for a ghost in the wardrobe? An interview with a Jamison from the past would really help my research. Talk about a primary source!"

He started laughing, gave her a smacking kiss and rolled over, taking her with him until she was sprawled across him. "I'm afraid the only Jamisons around are living ones. And I'm the one you have to put up with."

"I guess I'll just have to manage, then." She made herself comfortable on his hard body, not a difficult thing to do, she discovered, and kissed him. When they surfaced, she had captured his fully aroused erection between her legs.

"In the drawer," he rasped between gulps of air.

She had to move off him to reach the drawer and its contents. Kneeling by his side, she tore open the foil-wrapped package and looked from the condom to Davis and back again. She'd never performed this particular task before, but how difficult could it be? She knew the basics and applied them.

Davis watched her as her earnest expression, slightly open mouth, and fumbles almost sent him into orbit. By the time she had him fully prepared, he was in throbbing pain. When she mounted, he grabbed her hips, positioned her, and pulled her down until he was completely sheathed inside her.

They both sighed at the contact.

She was so beautiful poised there above him, her brown curls going every which way and her pink nipples like raspberries, almost calling for him to taste them. She braced herself on her arms and bent down to kiss him. He reached up to fondle her breasts as she began a slow rise and descent along his stiff cock. Up and down, up and down.

It was heaven. It was hell.

This woman drove him crazy. Finally he couldn't take anymore. He reached again to her hips and held them steady while he moved against her. She flung her head back and arched as the heat built between them. He felt himself get closer and closer to the peak and knew he wouldn't be able to wait for her when she suddenly stiffened and climaxed around him. He fused her to him as he followed into sweet oblivion.

Sitting cross-legged on the office floor that afternoon, Barrett stared blindly at the letter in her hand. She was having a horrible time trying to concentrate, and she knew the reason. He was sitting two feet away from her.

They'd finally gotten up, but before she could put

on her robe, he'd pulled her into the shower in his
bathroom and made sure they were both thoroughly
clean. They'd dressed and fixed themselves a breakfast
of eggs and tamales. Davis said it had become a tradi-
tion of his to have Eva's tamales after the party. He
threw some nopalitos into the mix, which delighted
her as she'd forgotten how good the slightly sour pick-
led cactus was with eggs.

While reading the Sunday papers, Barrett had
decided to carry on with her planned activities as if
"nothing" had happened. Her old self-instruction,
"Be professional," seemed to hold new import as she
tried to stay on an emotional even keel. Keeping
her hands off Davis when they were itching to touch
wasn't easy either.

As for him . . . although he had a possessive gleam
in his eyes, he hadn't touched her since the shower.

Well, what had she expected? He'd chase her
around the kitchen table? Grab a grope while she was
filling the coffee pot? Strip off their clothes and make
love in the middle of the floor?

She certainly wasn't going to do any of those things
to him. But . . . wouldn't it be fun . . . no, better not
to think about it.

So, she'd tried during the morning to pull together the first article she had outlined, and, although

she'd made fair progress, she'd given up after lunch when she'd found herself staring into space, thinking about Davis's hands instead of life in nineteenth century Louisiana.

Inventorying a box required less concentration and focused her attention more concretely. When she'd pulled one into the office, Davis had looked up from his desk and offered to help. She'd accepted. For one thing, his aid would make the work go faster. For another, they'd be in the same room, where she could sneak little peeks at him. She only hoped the contents weren't too boring for him.

Fortunately, this one contained a bushel of political correspondence to and from prominent men in state and national government. The letters were gossipy, at times caustic, once or twice probably libelous. Davis had taken to reading the juicy parts aloud.

"Who's this fellow?" he asked, holding out a letter and pointing to the signer.

She looked at the date and the signature and shook her head. "I don't know, but the name's familiar somehow. The deeper we get into this box, the more I think we have a potentially important cache here. But I don't know for certain. I'd like to call in an expert on Southern and Louisiana antebellum political history to look these over. It would be faster than my researching the authors."

"If you stop to find out who every correspondent is, you'll never get through the inventory. Call whomever you like—except for Glover."

"Don't worry. Besides, it's not his area of expertise." She paused to reflect for a moment. "I know a couple of people, one at LSU and the other at Southwestern Louisiana, who might be able to help. I'll give them a call Monday or Tuesday."

Davis filed the letter in its proper sequence and leaned back on his braced arms. "I've been meaning to ask you, why does Glover have it in for you?"

She thought a minute and sighed. "I think it must be a combination of events and circumstances. Horace Glover has quite a reputation around the department as a ladies' man. He's been married and divorced three times, each time to and from a younger and younger woman. Until I arrived, or so I've been told, he never had anything to do with a History Department woman, even a secretary."

Davis frowned and stated in a low, dry tone, "He made a pass at you."

"Oh, he was very subtle about it in the beginning— happening to run into me in places, suggesting a cup of coffee between classes, asking my opinion about a question, offering to help me get settled in department matters. In a way, it was flattering to be the object of attention from a well-known historian. Fortunately, the chairman of the department and I hit it off from the beginning, and he dropped a few hints to warn me about Horace. Since I wasn't attracted to the man and was terribly busy creating lectures and grading, I didn't have any problem turning him down."

"A little rejection couldn't be enough to bring out all his venom," Davis put in.

"I wouldn't think so either." She shrugged. "He left me alone until the school year ended. Then he talked about how much 'help' he could be with tenure. I also overheard a couple of the secretaries say Horace was having trouble finding dates and how they hoped most of the campus women had his number by this time."

She leaned forward, resting her elbows on her knees. "It was also last school year he suddenly announced he was changing the focus of his research from the eastern to the western theater of war. He said he'd studied all he needed to in Virginia and Georgia and wanted to look closely at the Mississippi River campaigns. A couple of our colleagues mentioned, rather unkindly, it didn't matter what he researched, because he hadn't published a well-received or ground-breaking book in several years and had lost his edge. One even called him "Has-Been Horace.""

"Glover told me he'd spoken to Granddaddy," Davis said. "He could have called during the spring or summer of last year. The papers' existence is well known in the parish, and LSU has hinted how much the university would like them. Granddaddy never did explain why he kept the papers, but Glover could have found out from a number of sources."

"Then I started corresponding and visiting with Edgar, and he probably picked up the news from the department grapevine."

"Yeah, and he started hitting on you as a conduit to Granddaddy," Davis said with a disgusted expression.

"And when he couldn't 'charm' either you or me, he turned on me." She grinned at him. "And, thanks to you, and Bill, Martha, Peggy, and Jim, he failed."

"Damn right," Davis said with an answering grin that included more than a little menace. "It was a pleasure to throw him off the property."

She stacked the pages they had put in order and rose to start entering them into the inventory. The claims and invective they'd been reading reminded her of something. "Davis," she asked as she turned on the computer, "do you think there could be any validity to Lloyd's or his mother's claims?"

"No, of course not," he scoffed. "What made you think there could be?"

"Just looking at these letters, I guess. Passions could run high, as you can see. Men still fought duels over statements like we've seen here."

"As far as I know, no Jamison ever fought a duel, or killed anybody, unless it was in a war. Now, I'm not going to say, 'Don't bother your pretty little head about it' . . ."

"Thank you."

". . . but I really don't think you have anything to worry about." He looked outside, then back at her. "I have an idea. Let's get through this box and then take a swim. The Gonzaleses have gone to her sister's, and nobody's here but us, so we can go skinny dipping. What do you say?" His waggling eyebrows and the grin under his mustache encouraged her to agree.

She stared at him for a moment and wondered where her work ethic had gone. But it was a hot summer day, and the pool beckoned, and here was Davis . . . "Okay," she said, with a smirk of her own.

They finished the carton in record time.

Chapter TWENTY-TWO

The Journal of Mary Maude Davis Jamison
Windswept Plantation
August 4, 1850
A blistering hot day, a horrible day,
devastating, painful, and revelatory

I don't know if I can write this down, but I must. Perhaps seeing the black ink on the white page will help me come to grips with the situation.

Cleopatra gave birth to a baby girl this morning. Although I usually do not go out to the quarters unless there is a dire emergency, Heeba was at a neighbor's helping with a difficult birth, so I brought the mother and new babe some fortifying nostrums. The baby is a healthy, very light-skinned girl. At first this surprised me, and I wondered who the father could be as all of our male Negroes are medium to very dark and Cleopatra is a medium brown herself. Then I looked at Cleopatra's 2-year-old son, whom I had never seen.

He is the exact likeness of Edgar Jr. at that age.

I was struck dumb. I had absolutely no doubt in my mind that Edgar is not only this boy's father, but also the father of the little girl. I don't know if any of the servants noticed my reaction, but Cleopatra had a look on her face combining fear and arrogance. I returned to the house as soon as possible. By the time I arrived, I was in a state I can only describe as distraught. I hurried here to my room, hoping to calm myself by writing my fears away.

It isn't working.

Thank God, Edgar is off at one of his political meetings. I must get hold of myself, as I rage between devastation and anger. How could he do such a thing? How could he come to my bed and then go to hers? How could he profess to love me while he ruts with her?

Is this what has been bothering me for so long? Some premonition we were not right between us? How can I share the same bed with him now? What am I going to do?

Windswept Plantation
August 7, 1850
Another terrible day,
after an even more terrible night.

It is all true and worse than I thought. Yesterday, after much pleading on my part, Heeba confirmed my fears and made them worse. Edgar has lain with not only Cleopatra, but Salome as well. Salome also has a child by my loving husband.

I feel like such an idiot, such a fool. All these years, I have listened to ladies gossiping about the husbands of the neighboring plantations, how Mr. X had fathered numerous children, and Mr. Y had three mistresses in the quarters. I thought, I believed, I swore my husband remained true to me. I was above all the gossip.

I must confess, I was proud to assume I alone among all these married women had held my husband's interest. I was more perfect, more virtuous than those whose husbands wandered. The women themselves were, must be, at fault for their husbands' adultery.

I was blind to what was right before my eyes.

Yesterday I would not countenance even the suggestion of my husband's infidelity. I simply refused to consider reality. Despite Heeba's testimony, I had almost convinced myself I was wrong, and Cleopatra's son does not look like Edgar Jr. But the idea ate at me, fear gnawed at my stomach like a wild animal trying to escape a trap. By last night, I could stand the uncertainty no longer.

I confronted Edgar, and our marriage came crashing

down. Not only did he admit his philandering, but blamed me. He claims my fear of childbirth has dampened my ardor and his, made our lovemaking a 'chore' for him. He had to turn to others to 'assuage his animal passions.' After all, he is a lusty man and needs an outlet. It's not as if the women meant anything to him. Oh, no. He was trying 'to save me.'"

I could hardly believe the words coming out of his mouth. God gave us free will and the ability to reason, and Jesus taught us about resisting temptation. Has Edgar no sense of my honor or feelings? How dare he besmirch our name, our marriage, our home?

I have borne his children, made him a home, and gone willingly, eagerly to his bed. I have loved him with all my heart and my body. And yet . . . and yet . . . he has trampled on all that and me for momentary pleasure.

At times, his revelations caused me to almost double over with pain, but I resisted such weakness. I am a strong, capable woman. I will not accept this catastrophe as a defeat. I did not accept what he was telling me.

We talked long into the night. At first, he did not understand my upset until I brought up the concept of honor and our marriage vows to forsake all others. How would he feel if I had a lover? The question incensed him at first and he made comments like: "You could not do that," and "I'd kill the bastard," and "You belong to me." As I was no less angry than he, I refused to back down from my position or accept his "arguments" as "the way of the world." After many words, he finally seemed to realize the humiliation his actions had caused me and he became very contrite, begging my forgiveness for his misdeeds.

He swore never to turn to another woman again as long as he lives, and he trod as on eggshells all day, solicitous to the extreme. I have sworn to forgive him. As a Christian, I must, but it will not be easy.

He offered to sell the two Negroes and the children, but I told him not to, as the children are innocent victims, and his blood, after all is said and done. But they must be kept out of my sight.

What will I tell our children if they notice the resemblance? Edgar Jr. is already fifteen. Does he have any inkling of his father's actions?

I am determined to do nothing in haste. Marriage is forever. We can work this out over time.

But how can I share the bed with him now?

Present Day
Monday, June 18

Davis went to his office Monday morning in high spirits. Making love with Barrett was all he had anticipated and more. He could hardly wait to get home that evening. He was standing in front of Peggy's desk going over everyone's assignments when his brother walked in. Bill never showed up this early. Davis felt his good mood start to evaporate.

"What do you want?" Davis asked as Bill followed him back to his office.

"Just thought I'd stop by and see if anything else happened with Sandra or the professor."

Standing while he unpacked his briefcase, Davis looked at his brother suspiciously. He was up to something. Had to be. "No, nothing."

"I was at a barbeque yesterday and somebody brought up Sandra's name. The real story's coming out of Dallas. Reed caught her in bed with another man, but he didn't have the sense to have her sign a prenuptial agreement, and he got burned in the divorce. She's on the prowl again, for sure."

"What does that have to do with me?"

"You, nothing. But I got to thinking about Milt. You know how lonely he's been since his wife passed away, and he did bring Sandra to your party. Milt seemed to be disgusted with her mischief, but you know how persistent, not to mention devious and convincing, she can be."

Davis thought about possibilities for a minute. He didn't like any of his conclusions. "You have a point. I'll give him a call this afternoon."

Bill hovered.

"Anything else?" Davis asked, putting an edge on the words.

"Well . . ." Bill assumed the falsely serious expression he always used when about to make a pitch for money.

"I've said all I'm going to say about your financial situation," Davis interrupted and sat down at his desk. "I refuse to listen to another fool scheme you've heard about at a party."

Bill swallowed whatever he had been about to say, but recovered from his disappointment enough to ask, "How's Barrett?"

"She's fine. Now, get out of here and let me get to work."

Instead of arguing, Bill suddenly brightened like he'd thought of a good idea, said good-bye, and left.

"Good riddance," Davis muttered and studied his follow-up list from the party. Who should he call first?

He had made only three calls when Peggy announced Mr. Walker on line one. He picked up the receiver and said, "What now, Lloyd?"

"This is your last chance, Davis." Lloyd sounded like he was in control of himself, but his tone was venomous. "Give me access to those papers, or you and Barrett Browning will be sorry. She'll drag our good name through the mud. If she publishes any false stories, I'll have the law on you, and that poor excuse for a historian will never get another job as long as she lives."

"If I were you, I'd be careful what lies I spread about her. Barrett Browning could give you lessons in honesty and certainly in integrity," Davis growled through gritted teeth. "You may find yourself on the receiving end of one of those lawsuits."

"You're mighty protective of her, Davis," Lloyd came back in a snide snarl. "Hellfire and damnation. You've got her in bed, haven't you? That's why you're letting the little slut ruin our family's heritage and good name."

"Lloyd, I won't dignify your statement with an answer. If you want legal action, contact my attorneys. But stay away from Houston, me, Barrett, and my house." Davis slammed down the phone.

"Peggy!" he called through the open door. When she appeared, he said, "I am not in to my cousin. Refuse all his calls. You have my whole-hearted permission to hang up on him. If you see him in the building, call Security and have him thrown out."

"Yes, sir! It will be a pleasure," Peggy answered with a grin as she closed his office door.

A little later she buzzed him again. "Taylor Jamison is on line two. Do you want to talk to him?"

"Yeah, I'll take it," Davis grumbled. Taylor was another cousin, the grandson of Edgar's youngest brother. He had always liked and respected this cousin, and they shared the same low opinion of Lloyd. "Hello, Taylor," he said into the phone.

"How're you, Davis?"

"I'm fine. How are Corinne and the kids?"

"The family's fine, at least most of my branch of it. I called about another member of our more extended relations." Taylor's raspy drawl sounded disgusted.

"Lloyd, right? What's he done now?"

"He called me yesterday, complaining about your having those plantation records. He wanted my help to get them away from you. He went on and on about some sort of dire happenings if they were left to your loving care. What the hell's going on with him, Davis?"

Davis leaned back and threw his pen on the desk. Here we go again, he thought and said, "You know about as much as I do. So far neither Aunt Cecilia nor

Lloyd has offered me any detailed information. Did he say anything specific to you? Did he tell you your mother agreed with them?"

"No and yes. I talked to my mother, and all she really remembers is a vague rumor and admits it could have been started by another suitor of hers. Lloyd's just blowing smoke, as usual hearing what he wants to. I tried to tell him if anybody had committed a crime, it certainly couldn't have been kept a secret this long. Not from all those gossips in St. Gregoryville, where they're still talking about Emma Louise Miller running off with the Yankee carpetbagger in 1869. I never understood why anyone was surprised since her family had been Yankee collaborators for years." Taylor sighed. "Anyway, to come back to the point, Lloyd sounded really mad, and he made some threats against you and the female professor you've got going through the papers."

"What sort of threats?" Davis began to get angry all over again.

"Vague sort of things, like law suits at first. Then he talked about teaching you and her a lesson, but he didn't get explicit about it. I always thought Lloyd had a few holes in the top of his screen door, if you take my meaning, but something about the way he was talking made me think he might try violence. You know how he gets red in the face? Well, he sounded just about purple. When we were kids, he'd always swing at someone after that." Taylor's worry came through the phone lines in his tone of voice. "I'd hate to see anybody get hurt."

"I appreciate your concern and this call, Taylor," David said. He decided not to alarm his cousin further with tales of the car vandalism or the break-in. "But I think we have things covered here."

"Well, if you're certain . . . Look, you let me know if I can do something. My branch of the family, including my mother, thinks you're doing right by Edgar and the papers. I went over to visit him last year and he was raving about how great this Dr. Browning was. I hadn't seen the old man so interested in living in years. I told Lloyd about my visit and also told him not to bother any of us with his ideas; we're all on your side. I'll keep an eye on him though, just to be on the safe side."

"Thanks. I'll let you know if I need anything. Say hello to Corinne and Aunt Phyllis for me."

"Will do. Take care." Taylor hung up on his end.

Davis slowly returned the phone to its cradle. Damn, Lloyd was getting more unstable. If he would just stay in Louisiana . . .

And if Bill would find himself a job . . .

Damn. Family. And Granddaddy had charged him with protecting them all. "I can manage with outside threats, but I can't save them from themselves," he muttered as he swiveled back to his computer screen.

But no emergency existed at the moment, thank God, and he could return to his more pressing business tasks.

———◆◆◆———

Barrett was pleased with herself by dinnertime. She'd woken up energized—thanks partly to Davis, she was sure. The knowledge of their mutual desire, the experience of lovemaking with him, and probably also the comeuppance of Horace had combined to clear her mind for work. She'd accomplished so much today, and she couldn't wait to tell him.

All it took, however, was the sight of him to tone down her exuberance. He radiated weariness when he joined her in the dining room and gave her a light kiss and a distracted smile.

After Eva had served them and left the room, she asked, "Are you okay? You look a little grim."

"It's been a day of interruptions. Then, on the way home, I was thinking about my family—all the parts of it. Lloyd called this morning." He grimaced and shook his head.

"What did he want?" Barrett felt a little shiver of premonition run down her back like an unwelcome icy drop of rain.

"Just more ranting about the papers. I also heard from another cousin who said Lloyd's been trying to bring the rest of the family to his side, but nobody's buying. Lloyd still has no facts and he's in Louisiana, so he can't bother us." He paused, took a sip of water. "I'm more worried about Bill."

Barrett raised her eyebrows in question. Inwardly part of her was elated. Davis was finally talking to her, sharing his life, not cutting her out. Another part was not happy. He must be really worried if he was telling her. "What happened?"

"Bill came to see me this morning. His excuse was to tell me some gossip he'd heard at a party on Sunday. His real reason was to ask for an advance on his quarterly allowance. I stopped him before he could get that far, but I expect a return visit." He explained about the trust fund from his father. "Bill has never settled down in a job, but every grifter and con artist in the state knows his name. Martha and I saved him a couple of times, but now neither of us will give him a cent and I won't let him use the principal in his fund for these fly-by-night schemes."

"Has he ever worked? What did he study in college?"

"Outside of summer temporary ones, mostly for the fun of it, he's never held a job. And all he has is a useless degree in English."

"Hey, there's nothing wrong with the liberal arts," she said in mock outrage, hoping to lighten the situation.

"Point taken. But you did something with it. Bill's never seemed motivated to do anything but live high. How long his principal will last when he gets his hands on it in two years is anybody's guess. I know he resents me for telling him 'no' all the time, but I promised our father I'd take care of him. I just wish he'd do something with his life. He's very smart, everything has always come easy with him, and he can charm the pants off anyone. But the man's twenty-eight, and he won't grow up."

"I'm sorry for him then. If I think of anything to help . . ."

"Thanks, but he's not your problem." He must have heard the curtness in his statement because he added, "I'd appreciate any ideas, but I don't know if Bill will listen to anybody."

"I'm willing to give it a try if you want me to. My brothers claim I have a second Ph.D. in laying down the law to men."

He shot her a glance and chuckled as she hoped he

would. "I'll bet. Speaking of which, laying down the law, I mean, I talked with Milt Callahan. He sends you his apologies for bringing Sandra to the party."

"He has nothing to apologize for."

"That's what I told him. Sandra conned him with some cock-and-bull story about wanting to get back together with me. After he saw the real situation and hustled her out of here, he told her in no uncertain terms not to call him again. I think we've seen the last of Sandra."

"Good," Barrett said. "I'm not sure I could control my reactions if she damaged any more of the papers." Or made a move on Davis, but she didn't say the words out loud.

"Nor could I." He waved his hand as if brushing the subject aside. "But enough of this. Tell me about your progress today."

She began talking about the letters she had found and her calls to the political experts, one of whom would come in a couple of weeks to assess the correspondence. He listened and asked questions as he always did, but she knew the problem of Bill would continue to perplex him. She only wished she had an answer.

Davis still looked a little bleak when Barrett came into his bedroom that night. She had gotten ready for bed in the guest bedroom where her clothes and personal items still resided. Looking at him standing by the window gazing into the darkness with his hands in his pockets, she felt a little apprehensive. She did not think she knew his moods well enough yet to predict his responses. She walked over to stand by his side.

"Davis?" She put a hand on his arm.

He simply put his arms around her and held her close. "Hmmm?"

"If you want to sleep alone tonight, it's okay."

An incredulous expression on his face, he leaned back to frown at her. "Didn't I tell you yesterday I want you in my bed every night? Where did you get such a preposterous idea?"

"You look like you have some thinking to do, and I don't want to be a hindrance or anything. Sometimes people like to be alone . . ." He stopped her with a kiss, a long, thorough, arousing kiss.

"Does that convince you I want you in my bed?" he asked huskily when he finally raised his head. "Now take off the horrible robe you're wearing. On second thought, let me help you." He untied the sash and reached inside.

At the touch of his hands, Barrett decided she could help him get over his problems in another manner.

His lovemaking was so tender and fierce at the same time, Barrett almost wept, she was so happy.

Chapter TWENTY-THREE

*A*bout eleven Tuesday morning, Barrett was sitting on the office floor surrounded as usual by papers when Martha Jamison breezed into the room—followed by a perturbed-looking Gonzales.

"It's okay, Gonzales," Martha said airily. "You don't have to announce me. How are you, Barrett?"

"Thank you, *don* Jesus," Barrett told the houseman and looked up at the other woman. "I'm fine, Martha, how are you?" She just knew Davis's sister had come to check her out. Good. She wanted to know Martha better herself.

"I was in the neighborhood and don't have an appointment until three. I hoped we could have lunch. Do you have the time?" Her smile was hopeful, optimistic, and innocent. Barrett bet Martha could sell anything to anyone with her smile.

"Sure, but I'm not exactly dressed to go out." She indicated her jeans and U.C. Berkeley T-shirt.

"We can run over to Goode Company on the Katy

Freeway."

Barrett licked her lips at the thought of excellent, tart, spicy barbecue. "You've twisted my arm. Let me put on my shoes and tell the Gonzaleses I'm going."

Over chopped beef sandwiches, coleslaw, and iced tea, Martha and Barrett discussed the realty business and the writing of history. They were finishing their iced tea before Martha finally got down to business.

"Of course, the real reason I asked you here was to discuss Davis," she said in a confidential manner.

Barrett raised her eyebrows. She didn't mind talking about herself, but she wasn't sure she wanted to talk about him with his sister. Well, too late, she was in it now. "Oh?" she asked in what she hoped was a noncommittal way.

Martha ignored her reserved tone and stated, "I saw the way he looked at you at the party. He's never looked that way at another woman in his life. Even Sandra. Especially Sandra. God, what a bitch. She really dug her claws into him. They met when he was twenty-eight. His business was beginning to take off, I was on my feet, and Bill was in college. Mother was doing well also."

She sighed. "I think he finally felt free from all the responsibility that fell on him when Daddy died. Davis assumed the protector role then and took care of all of us. He's still doing it where Bill is concerned. Granddaddy helped, but he was in Louisiana and we were here. Davis did a fine job. I imagine, now Grand-daddy's gone, Davis will step into his shoes, looking out for all the Jamisons, here and in Louisiana. As you can probably tell, family is pretty big with us."

"Us too," Barrett interjected.

"Right. Then you know what I'm saying. Now, where was I? Oh, yes, Sandra. Davis looked around and there she was, a golden, gorgeous goddess. He de-cided she was it, the woman he'd marry. Why, I never figured out."

Martha shrugged, rattled the ice in her glass. "Maybe he thought he was in love, maybe he thought she was the perfect woman to fill the role of his wife, maybe he was simply in lust, I don't know. I always thought she was a cold-hearted bitch, but what could I say? He did listen to my advice about a pre-nup, thank goodness. And the rest is history, as they say. I've been worried about him in the past couple of years. Oh, he's dated, but I know he's been lonely." She leaned back, studied Barrett.

"Then Granddaddy died, left him the papers, and here you were. Quite frankly, I think you could be the best thing for him." She shot Barrett a sharp glance. "And don't say you don't know what I'm talking about.

It sticks out all over you."

Barrett laughed and felt a blush creeping up her neck. She sighed. She was thinking only in the short term; Martha was way out in the future—where she had resolutely refused to go. "Look, you're jumping to a conclusion too fast. In my trade, we call it theorizing ahead of your data. I do like Davis. A lot. But we're really only friends. I'm doing a job for him. That's all it is. At the end of the summer, I'll go back to my life, and he'll go back to his." A small arrow of sadness shot through her at the statement, but she was careful not to let it show.

"I know what I see," Martha said firmly. "Davis needs somebody like you, someone who's fun and smart, who can take him away from business, from himself, who has other interests than clothes and so-cializing. And anyone who can squelch Sandra like you did has my vote. He's been carrying a load all by himself for a long time. I think I've been successful enough so he doesn't worry about me any more, but Bill is another matter."

"Yes, he told me about your brother last night."

"Bill drives both of us crazy." She began to gather her things. "Well, I've said my piece. I hope you're around for a long time, Barrett. I like you and I think you could do a lot for Davis. Tell me about your family while we go back to the house. I especially want to compare notes on brothers."

"Thank you," Barrett said, grateful Martha wasn't going to belabor the subject of her relationship with Davis. She wouldn't know what to say; she hadn't truly decided anything about it—like what would happen in August when she went back to school. Enjoy the moment, she thought. The future would have to take care of itself.

Davis felt more like his old self at dinner Tuesday evening. Somehow sharing his thoughts about Bill with Barrett had helped restore his good spirits. Certainly sharing his bed had contributed also. Their affair was going exactly as he had planned.

He was feeling smug and complacent until Barrett said Martha had dropped by. What was his sister doing, meddling in his . . . situation, he decided was the best word. He wouldn't come right out and ask the question, however. "Oh?" he said.

"Yes. We went out to lunch."

"That's nice."

"Yes, it was. We had a good time. She wanted to know about the papers, and we discussed the real estate business here and in the DFW area. She's very knowledgeable and must be good at her job."

Barrett's tone sounded intentionally blithe, but Davis knew Martha wouldn't have come over without an agenda. "Did she have anything else to say?"

She smiled, innocence personified. "Oh, we did discuss the attitudes and shortcomings to be found in older brothers. Younger ones too."

Davis groaned. "I suppose she told you a lot of scurrilous tales about me."

"A few. Did you really terrorize Eric, her first boyfriend in high school? Threaten him with a big Bowie knife?" She was grinning, an evil sister grin. God, he felt for her brothers.

"Not exactly. He was a senior and she was a freshman. He was too old for her and had a questionable reputation. I happened to have with me the hunting knife Granddaddy gave me when I discussed Martha with the horny son of a bitch. I simply told him he'd be singing soprano if he touched her. End of problem."

He tried to give her a haughty, I'm-a-big-brother-don't-mess-with-me look, but she started laughing, and her delight was so contagious, he ended up joining her. He'd laughed, chuckled, and downright howled more since Barrett came than he had in the previous year, he realized. There was just something about this woman that made him happy.

But then she said, "You know, Martha and I should get together more often. We both need support dealing with our brothers."

"Heaven help us." It was a heartfelt prayer.

They adjourned to their respective offices after dinner. About eight-thirty, the internal line rang in his office. Gonzales announced, "There are three gentlemen with the last name of Browning here asking if they can see you, sir. They ask you not tell *la maestra* of their presence."

This could only be Barrett's brothers. There must be something in the air this week. If it wasn't one brother, it was three. "Thank you. I'll be right out," Davis replied. Barrett had her head down, reading, when he passed her desk. As usual, she was concentrating so hard, he did not think she noticed him. Good.

The brothers were large men, one Davis's height and the two others taller. He could see the family resemblance in their facial structures, eyes, and hair color. None had her curls, though.

"I'm Davis Jamison." He shook their hands as they introduced themselves. Phil, the oldest, was the shortest. Greg was in the middle in age and height. Mark, the youngest, was the largest, and Davis remembered he was the pro football player. "If you

don't want Barrett to see you, we can talk in here."
He led the brothers into the dining room and turned
up the lights.

"What can I do for you?" he asked once they were
seated.

Phil was the spokesman. "Barrett has talked so
much about you and her job here that we thought it
best to get to know you ourselves. We like to look out
for our sister, if you take my meaning."

Davis smiled. In fact, he was so amused he almost grinned. He could not remember being checked
out by a girlfriend's family since high school. The
conversation from dinner also went through his mind.
He hoped none of them had a hunting knife. "What
would you like to know?" he asked, leaning back in
his chair.

"Mainly we wanted to make sure she was safe in
every definition of the word. Barrett can be too trusting, and we don't want to see her hurt," Phillip stated.

"I have no intention of hurting Barrett. In fact, I
expect to take very good care of her. Gentlemen, she is
safe here." If they wanted to know what his intentions
were, they were going to have to state it explicitly. He
hoped they wouldn't; he himself wasn't sure what they
were. He heard someone coming down the hall. Uh
oh. It didn't sound like Gonzales.

It wasn't. Barrett came around the corner of the stairs and halted, a look of surprise on her face. Her expression quickly turned to one of anger and exasperation as she stomped into the foyer and stood for a moment on the top step scowling down at them. Davis watched her carefully and felt a flash of apprehension on behalf of the other men. He was thankful he was totally innocent in the situation.

Her sudden appearance did not disconcert her two elder brothers. Mark, however, appeared chagrined. She stalked to the end of the table and glared at each brother in turn. "I have to go to my room for something and what do I find? My busybody brothers have come to call," she said, her voice low, calm, and acid-tinged. "My apologies for my brothers, Davis. They look like normal people, but they don't have a brain among them. I am very tired of their playing the big brother game."

"Now, Barrett." Phil tried to get a word in, but she was having none of it.

"Do not tell me I'm jumping to a conclusion here. I do not intend to repeat our usual conversation about your oversight of my activities," she continued. "It obviously does no good. In the future, I will maintain contact with my sisters-in-law and *their* children, but, Phil and Greg, it will be a very long time before we are on speaking terms. I refuse to put up with this embarrassing charade ever again." She made a slashing gesture with her hand.

"But you, little brother," she pointed a finger at Mark. "Your ass is mine." She grabbed hold of his shirt collar and dragged her brother up into the foyer. He was bent almost double but made no attempt to use his obvious advantages to break loose.

They heard the front door slam.

Davis traded glances with the two and managed, only with difficulty, to keep a straight face. "Gentlemen, I think you have a problem."

"Yeah, I think she means it this time." Greg shook his head. "Let me come to the point, Jamison. There are two of them. First, Barrett got involved with an asshole named Truman three years ago. She got hurt, and we don't want to see it happen again. Second, and most important, I'm with the Houston PD and Phil's an Assistant District Attorney with Harris County. We heard there was a break-in here and a possible nut case out to get you, connected to these papers she's studying. We will not have Barrett caught in any crossfire."

Davis sobered up immediately. "Let me assure you I am taking every precaution possible with regard to my cousin, even though I do not expect violence from him. We have security alarms on the house, and my staff is fully alerted. I've been downplaying the situation with Barrett, so as not to worry her, and I would appreciate it if you did not belabor the subject. There's no sense in causing her undue alarm." He was not going to address the subject of this Truman fellow, and he certainly wasn't going to discuss with her brothers what he and Barrett had between them. "Having her hurt is the last thing on my mind."

"I think we can agree there," Greg said. "If I thought the situation was really bad, I'd try to take her out of here, but with the plantation records here, I probably wouldn't have a snowball's chance of her agreement. That leaves us depending on you. You know you can count on us if there's any problem?"

The front door opened and closed again. All three men turned to watch Barrett stamp past them toward the office without acknowledging their presence in any manner.

"Yes, I do, and I appreciate the help." Davis said after she had passed. "I'm keeping a close eye on my cousin. Any problems are really between him and me. Barrett has nothing to do with our argument." Lloyd would be insane to try anything against Barrett personally. Surely he knew Davis would kill him if he did. "But what are you going to do about her? She's thoroughly pissed with you."

"She'll come around," Greg said. "She always does. Come on, Phil, let's go see if she left any hide on Mark. He didn't like the idea of coming here in the first place. I hope she didn't worm out of him our knowledge of the break-in. She'll go ballistic if she knows we've been keeping an eye on her. Thanks for your time, Jamison." He rose and held out his hand.

"Don't worry about Barrett," Phil said. "She'll be all right when she cools down. After all, *you're* not the object of her anger."

Davis saw the brothers out and went back to the office. Barrett was standing, looking out at the pool, her clenched fists on her hips, her posture stiff with anger. He walked up behind her and started massaging her tight shoulders. She shrugged, as if to throw off his hands, but he kept rubbing. After a minute, she relaxed. In the glass reflection, he saw her close her eyes.

"Better?" he whispered in her ear as he put his arms around her and drew her back against him.

She took a deep, deep breath and let it out. "Davis, I really want to apologize for my brothers. I hope they didn't embarrass you too much."

He chuckled and kissed her ear, then nuzzled her neck just above the T-shirt until she wiggled. "It was an enlightening experience. I haven't been checked out by a woman's male relatives since I was a teenager. Facing your formidable brothers reminded me how good old Eric must have felt when I warned him off Martha."

He turned her in his arms so he could see her face. "And, speaking for brothers, they do have your best interests at heart."

She punched him lightly on the chest and gave him a disgusted look. "Oh, please. Do you have any idea how sick I am of them acting like Neanderthals in the name of 'what's good for Barrett?' I'm not twelve years old. I'm a grown woman."

"You certainly are." He pulled her closer, rubbed against her.

She frowned, thumped him again. "Don't change the subject. Why did my brothers come here tonight? I know it was for another reason than to torment me—or you."

He gazed down at her while he tried to formulate his answer without bringing up the burglars or Lloyd. He wasn't fast enough.

"Oh, wait," she said, comprehension causing another scowl. "I know. Phil and Greg have been keeping tabs on me, haven't they? Greg knows a couple of officers at Hunters Creek, and they told him about the break-in, didn't they? Or Phil has someone watching for our names in the police database. Right?"

"I can honestly say, I don't know the answers to those questions," he said with a straight face.

"What about this one? Did they know about the break-in?"

Davis stared down into those blue eyes and reminded himself how intelligent he had thought the brain behind them was. He was proven right again. "Yes, they knew about it. They just wanted to be sure you were safe." He gave her a little kiss.

"And?"

Damn, she was hard to distract. He kept his tone bland. "And I told them you were and I would keep you that way." He tried another kiss. A longer one.

"And?"

"And they said nothing else." Another kiss, this time using his tongue.

She pulled back and her gaze concentrated on his mouth. Good, it was working.

She licked her lips and said, "Nothing about us, you and me . . ."

"No." This time he took her mouth and plundered. And started an inferno that carried them up the stairs and into his bedroom.

Where there was a minimum of talking and a maximum of Barrett.

Later, Davis lay awake while she slept in his arms.

He'd meant what he said to her brothers. He'd keep her safe, from Lloyd, from Glover, from Sandra, from anyone who tried to hurt her.

What had happened with the guy the brothers mentioned—Freeman? Thurman? No, Truman. Three years ago? He'd seen no indication she was pining for anyone. He doubted he had any serious competition from the pathetic son of a bitch. What a jackass the jerk must have been, to let Barrett get away.

He certainly wasn't going to let that happen. He'd keep her right here, in his house, in his bed.

In his life.

Wait a minute. What had he just decided?

To keep Barrett in his life. To have her with him permanently. The idea felt right, like a good business deal and investment. He smiled and felt his mustache and another part of his anatomy twitch in agreement.

Chapter
TWENTY-
FOUR

Late in the afternoon Thursday, Barrett looked up from her place on the floor to watch dark gray-blue clouds roil across the sky above the patio. They looked ready to unleash another deluge on top of what had already fallen during the day. Before she opened the new box, she shivered and slipped into her sneakers. She didn't like to wear shoes while organizing the papers on the floor, but her feet were cold.

She was deep into the files when Gonzales announced Bill Jamison wanted to see her. Disgruntled at the interruption—she really wanted to complete this carton today—she agreed. After all Davis had told her about his brother, she wondered what he could want, but she wasn't about to deny him entry either. When he came in, she remained sitting on the floor, surrounded by correspondence, and gestured him into one of the chairs against the windows.

"Hi, Bill," she said but tried not to sound too cordial. "Be careful where you step, please. As you can see, I'm kind of in the middle of things right now. What can I do for you?" She looked him up and down. Polo shirt and tailored khakis, high-end loafers, and an expensive watch. What Martha and Davis had said about their little brother came to mind. The man was really too handsome and charming for his own good, but compared to Davis, he looked . . . soft.

"I was in the neighborhood and thought I'd drop by for a minute. I wanted to tell you how great you looked at the party." He appeared calm, but an odd nervousness seemed to lurk under the surface, like he was trying not to fidget.

"Thanks, but you didn't need to do that. And thanks for your help with Sandra and Horace. I really appreciated it."

"You're welcome." He leaned forward to study the correspondence. "These are the infamous Windswept papers? Found anything juicy?"

"No. Do you know of any scandals in them?"

"Nope. The only stories Granddaddy ever told me were all about military ancestors and the Yankees. Historic heroics, Jamisons through the ages." He picked up a letter and read it.

"Bill, I'm really busy. Could you please come to the point?" Barrett put down the sheets in her hand. "Why are you here?"

Bill grimaced and dropped the paper back on the floor. "I have a favor to ask. I know I don't have the right, but I'm hoping you'll give me some help." Definitely nervous now, he didn't look her in the eyes.

Barrett said nothing, simply waited.

"It's about this project." Bill launched into a description of what he called "an investment opportunity" and painted it in glowing colors. He was only about thirty seconds into the description before Barrett knew the whole thing would be risky at best and a disaster at worse. "Well, what do you think?" he asked.

She wasn't going to make it easy for him. "What exactly is the favor you want from me?"

He took a deep breath. "Well, I was hoping, seeing how close you are and all, you would help me approach Davis about a loan from my trust fund." He ended with what he clearly hoped was an ingratiating smile.

Although she'd suspected what was coming, his cavalier attempt to use her against Davis infuriated her instantly. She sprang to her feet. "Why on earth should I do that? I have no influence over Davis on anything other than the Windswept papers."

"Oh, yes, you do. I've seen the way he looks at you. The man's a goner. I don't need much, just ten thousand . . ." Bill pleaded, looking like a puppy eager for praise. He'd probably want a tummy rub next.

Barrett stepped carefully over the papers to Bill's chair and leaned toward him, hands on her hips. "In the first place, I would never ask Davis to do such a thing. Your family finances are none of my business. In the second place, the scheme sounds absolutely awful." She reeled off five reasons why. "This snake-oil salesman clearly has you bamboozled."

She straightened and looked him up and down. "What *is* the matter with you? I know you were well and expensively educated, but to ask me intercede with your brother? Do you have the sense, common or otherwise, God gave a pineapple? In the third place, how old are you, twenty-seven, twenty-eight?"

"Twenty-eight," he mumbled.

"What a waste of human potential and money. Well, it's about time you did something to prove it. From what I've observed, your brother and sister don't think much of you as a man. They show little respect for their own brother. Doesn't it bother you? Do you think respect grows on trees? Davis and Martha both work very hard for their money and their success. Are you thinking those things grow on trees too?"

She paused, then thought of something else. "You haven't signed anything, papers for this con man, have you?"

"No, but . . ."

"Good. Then walk away from him, tell him not to call you. Get yourself a real job, make your own money, and you won't have to ask Davis for it, if you really want to invest in these idiotic messes."

"But I can't do anything anybody would hire me for." He looked downright woebegone.

"My God, you are so pathetic. I can't take more whining and self-pity, I won't ask your brother for money for you, and I don't have time for this. Will you please go?" She pointed at the door.

"But, Barrett, I need your help." He slumped in his chair.

"You only need my help to get out of here." She grabbed him by the shirt collar, pulled him out of the chair, and hauled him down the hall to the front door. They passed Davis, who had come in through the kitchen.

"Barrett! Bill! What in the hell?"

"Stay out of this, Davis." She reached the front door, flung it open, and pulled Bill to his car.

When they got there, the wind whooshed through the trees, and a pelting rain followed, drenching both of them instantly. Between the volume of water and the sound of its passage, Barrett felt like she'd stepped under a waterfall, but she ignored the elements be- cause she'd had a brainstorm as she towed Bill down the foyer.

"Listen up, Bill." She pulled his face down to her level and shouted to be heard over the rain. "I'm not going to tell Davis a thing about what you asked me to do. But I will if you *don't* do something about yourself *or* if you ask him for money for this hair-brained scheme. Damn it! Get yourself a life that means something." She jerked on his collar for emphasis.

"Here's an idea. You have the looks, charm, and contacts of a born fund-raiser. Hook up with a good charity, like a homeless shelter, literacy, bone-marrow transplants, food banks, something specific. Not a big umbrella organization, but one where you as an individual can make a difference. Volunteer to raise money, but not through those damned highfaluting parties. Go one on one with donors after you've done some time in the trenches with the real volunteers."

She gave him a little shake. Even with the water dripping in her eyes, she could tell she had his attention. "You don't need a salary, you've got your damn trust fund to live on. There are numerous people out there who would love to give you money for a good cause. Little old ladies would fall all over themselves. Fund raising is respectable, and you'd be doing some good in the world.

"And you'll make so many more contacts, people

will be begging to hire you once they see you're serious about something and they recognize your abilities. Then sit down with Davis and talk about how to recognize these scam artists so they can't bamboozle you again. I know he'll help you if you ask for advice instead of money. So will Martha."

She gave him a shove toward his car. "Go home and dry off." She spun on her heel and headed back to the house. She thought he had listened to her. What he did with the suggestion was up to him.

Davis had watched Barrett give his brother a piece of her mind, but the rain was coming down so hard he couldn't hear what she said. "Barrett?" he said as she squished into the hall.

"Not now, Davis, I'm too angry to be coherent." She took off her sneakers and ran up the stairs with one in each hand. She turned right at the top of the stairs and headed to her bedroom.

Davis looked at Gonzales, and the houseman returned his raised eyebrows with a shrug of confusion. He heard Barrett stomping on the balcony above him. The woman was a tornado. First she grabs her brother and hauls him out, now his brother gets the same treatment. Where had he gotten the idea she was a "tame" anything? He shook his head and asked, "When will dinner be ready?"

"In an hour, sir."

"Good." Davis took the stairs two at a time. As he walked into her bedroom, he heard two *bonks*. Probably her shoes hitting the bathtub. He stopped in the bathroom door to watch the spectacle before him.

Standing with her back to him, Barrett was muttering to herself as she removed the wet clothing.

"Brothers!" *Schloop* went the Harvard T-shirt when it hit the tub.

"Strangle them all at birth!" *Schlurp* went her jeans.

"A case of arrested development!" Her socks made little wet *thuds*.

"My God, I'm wet clear through." She struggled a moment with her bra clasp before it yielded and the bra silently joined the socks.

"And I'm freezing." Her panties came off with no problem and made a tiny *plop*.

She grabbed one of the big fluffy towels and, bending over, buried her face and head in it to dry her dripping hair.

The sight of her bare bottom was too much for Davis. With the swiftness of a lightning bolt from the storm outside, raw possessiveness surged through him. He moved up behind her and pulled her back against his rapidly growing erection.

Barrett froze. She'd had no idea he was behind her

until she felt his warm hands and then his body against her cool skin. "Davis?" she asked through the towel.

"It better be."

She dragged the towel off, straightened, and stared into his eyes in the mirror above the sink. The heat in his reflected gaze warmed her to her core. Their bodies were a study in contrast: hers completely naked and his completely suited, hers pale pink, his dark blue. She watched his hands travel up her ribcage and around to cup her breasts. The eroticism in the picture almost made her moan.

He bent his head, kissed her neck, then nibbled his way down her shoulder, his mustache clearing the way. Between kisses, he said, "I've just been watching one of the most provocative strips I've ever seen."

He turned his attention to her other shoulder, then took the towel from her limp hands and threw it into the bathtub. When he cradled her breasts again, he smiled at her in the mirror. "You smell like rain," he murmured.

Barrett sank into him and put her hands on top of his. She gasped when he skimmed her nipples with his thumbs and she felt an electric tingle all the way to her toes. Laying her head back against his shoulder, she watched his gaze travel down her body. The intensity in his eyes, in his touch, was almost too much to bear.

Closing her eyes, she rubbed her bottom against his hard arousal.

"I'm in need of an appetizer before dinner," he whispered in her ear. "How about you?"

She arched against his hands as he massaged her breasts. Her breathing and heartbeat increased as arousal prowled through her. She wasn't cold any longer. "Yeesss," she said on a long exhalation.

He skimmed a hand from her breast to her dark nest of curls and probed gently, provocatively. At the jolt of sensation his fingers caused, she gasped again and pushed into his hand. His hands moved to her hips and she was expecting him to turn her around. When he pulled her back a step and used his body to bend her at the hips, she opened her eyes and looked back at him in the mirror.

"Brace yourself on the counter," he said.

Surprised, she did as he asked, her hands on the edge, arms slightly bent. She'd never made love this way, and she found the idea both interesting and exciting. She watched him in the mirror take a condom out of his pocket, unbuckle his belt, and drop his pants and boxers. He swiftly applied protection, nudged her legs farther apart, and then was sliding between her legs.

She arched her back at the intimate contact, and he entered her in one long, deep thrust. Locking eyes with her in the reflection, he held her hips and began stroking. He moved slowly at first, taking his time, prolonging the experience. Although his face was set in sharp, hard lines, he seemed to enjoy the moment. She certainly did. Her body began to tense, and her interior muscles tightened, clasped him as he moved in and out.

Then he reached around her hip, touched a finger-tip to the sensitive nub hidden in her curls, and thrust harder and faster.

"Davis!" she whispered and closed her eyes. An earthquake of a climax rippled through her, stealing what breath she had left, leaving her shaking from its power, her wobbly legs barely able to keep her upright.

Davis held her to him with one hand and watched her throw back her head in ecstasy. She was tight and hot, and it felt so damn good to be in her. He would have laughed with joy if he'd been able. She milked him so intensely he could only thrust once more before his own release hit him like a hurricane-force wind. He didn't know how he kept them from falling, but he managed to brace himself with one hand on the counter and the other around her as she sagged, almost limp. He withdrew slowly, straightened, and brought her up also to rest against him as he hugged her.

She put her hands on his arms and slowly opened

her eyes. Their gazes met in the mirror again. She smiled, a slow, sultry parting of the lips accompanied by a gleam in her eyes that Eve must have used on Adam to indicate her satisfaction with his love making.

And he knew in that moment his decision of the previous night had been the right one: he would never, could never let her go. She was his.

She turned in his arms, rose on tiptoe, and molded her body to his, her arms around his neck. "Some appetizer," she mumbled against his lips, punctuating her comment with kisses.

He let his hands rove over her body, settle on her buttocks, and knead lightly. He grinned with his own pure satisfaction. God, he couldn't get enough of this woman. "We'll take on the main course tonight."

Somehow they managed to make it to dinner on time.

Halfway through the meal, Davis could stand it no longer. "Are you going to tell me what was going on with Bill?"

"No." She took another bite of the spicy chicken.

One thing about this woman, she wasn't wishy-washy. "Why not?"

"Because it was between Bill and me and I told him I'd keep his confidence. If the time comes I can tell you, I will. What we said to each other has nothing to do with you and me or anything else we're involved with. I have nothing more to say on the subject." She looked absolutely determined.

He understood keeping one's word. "I can live with that," he said. But as he thought back over what he had seen, he wondered if she'd just performed another rescue.

Chapter TWENTY-FIVE

Friday was another gloomy day with intermittent showers, and Barrett started the morning standing in the conference room surveying her progress on both the inventory and her own research.

She had originally planned today to outline an article on plantation life as seen through the correspondence between Mary Maude, her mother and her sister who had also married planters. The women had established a system whereby the writer sent duplicate letters to the two others. Barrett had worked her way up to 1855, so she had more than twenty years of family guidance, instruction, and suggestion—and triumph and defeat when actions taken succeeded or not. The article could be an interesting glimpse, both of women's lives and of family dynamics as the sisters matured.

Barrett looked first at the stacks of photocopies she had made of the correspondence, then let her eyes roam over the boxes, and finally she shot a glance at the door beyond which were the hall, her office, and . . .

Davis's office. In which he sat, having decided to work from home rather than deal with Houston's wet, clogged freeways.

Her hands in the back pockets of her jean shorts, she paced the room, up and down the narrow corridor between the stacks of boxes and the long table. If he weren't present, she'd be able to work at her usual pace, concentrate on the minutia of the documents, have the article blocked out by noon.

As it was, all she seemed able to do was think about him and yesterday in the bathroom and then at night in bed. She hadn't expected him to follow her, had been thinking only about getting out of her wet clothes. Then, there he stood, a pirate of the corporate variety. And she didn't have a stitch on. And before she knew it, he was in her and she'd had the strongest orgasm in her life. And he'd never even undressed.

But when he'd hugged her to him afterward, and she'd felt how he was shaking, she'd never felt so wanted. He'd been in a playful mood that evening too. Main course, indeed.

Now she was hungry for him all the time. She couldn't get enough of him. What she really wanted to do was walk into the back office, haul him out of his big executive chair, strip his clothes off, push him down on the desk, and . . .

"Stop it!" she muttered. "Be professional."

But, oh, how nice it would be to have all that wonderful male flesh under her hands. And other places. She felt herself grow hot simply thinking about him.

She wouldn't even have to worry about protection. When she'd asked him last night how he "just happened" to have a condom in his pocket when they were in the bathroom, he'd replied, "I started carrying them around on Sunday. One never knows when one is going to get lucky, does one?"

And he'd grinned under his mustache like a Johnny Reb who'd spotted a Yankee supply train full of gold.

And she'd grinned right back.

Barrett stopped pacing and leaned on the back of a chair. Her head was spinning—or was it her heart? She had been stupid to imagine, even for a second, she could maintain internal equilibrium where Davis was concerned. He was inside her in every sense of the word. Especially inside her heart.

She might as well admit it. She was in love with him.

And she was right back in the position she'd been in before he'd declared his interest in her—attracted to him, wanting him. Only now it was worse. Now, despite her career ambitions, despite knowing she had no time in her life for anything except achieving tenure, she craved him. Not only for the summer either, but long term.

What did he want? He'd given her no indication he was thinking beyond the end of the summer.

What if he was? History was what she was meant to do. Her career, her advancement, fulfillment of her dreams lay in North Texas. She wasn't about to give that up; she'd worked too long and hard. How would her failure look to her family? How disappointed in her would they be? How would she be able to live with herself if she didn't pursue her profession with everything in her?

Could she have both Davis and tenure? A long distance romance, much less a greater tie, would not be easy, probably damn near impossible. She ran through several scenarios for maintaining, no, intensifying, a relationship—oh, how she despised that word of many meanings. She dismissed most as untenable or unworkable and tried to analyze two or three remaining. She finally slumped against the chair. No matter what arrangements they made, they would always be working or traveling and have little time—or energy—left for each other.

Assuming he wanted more than the summer.

What did they have between them? More than just a physical attraction, and she was certain he would agree. They enjoyed each other's company too much to have only a sexual bond. He wouldn't have opened up to her about his family and Sandra if all he wanted from her was sex. No, they shared a friendship, a work ethic, possibly a sense of humor, and a growing—on his part—fascination with history, at least as far as his family was concerned. Were those elements enough to sustain them?

She leaned back and stretched, trying to loosen tightened muscles.

What a dilemma. How was she going to resolve it?

Or should she look at the situation another way? Did she have to decide immediately? She had at least another six weeks before decisions had to be addressed, much less made. Their relationship was new. Who knew what would happen by August? For now, she would just enjoy the ride. So to speak.

A faint *bwuck, bwuck* sounded in her head.

She turned back to the boxes in disgust. Who was she kidding? With all these thoughts going through her head, she wasn't going to get any meaningful work done this morning. Better to continue the inventory. She could concentrate on each paper in turn without having to think in a straight line or follow a thought to its conclusion.

The next installment was not in a box, but

contained in a very heavy, black-metal trunk, a little bigger than the one holding the Herbarium and Edgar's journals. A worn label on the outside said "1855" and she had given it the designation "F." This was the container she hadn't opened at all, indeed, had been unable to open. Its lock looked rusted shut. It was also heavy as sin, having required both Gonzales and Ricardo to move it into place. What was in it?

Maybe that's what she needed, a new mystery, to get her mind off Davis and their situation.

She hoped it wasn't more funerary pieces. She'd been through one box filled with letters and condolences, newspaper clippings and obituaries. At the bottom had lain two embroidered "mourning" pictures pertaining to Edgar's death in 1854. The depressing subject matter and the flowery language quickly became tedious in the extreme.

The only bright spot, if it could be called that, had been a copy of Edgar's will and the probate documents. They clearly illustrated the difficult position of women, even a widow with minor children, in the hierarchy of the day. Eighteen-year-old Edgar Jr. had inherited the bulk of the estate. Mary Maude, who had contributed as much to Windswept's success as her husband, had been provided for, as had the younger children, but the technical power was all in her son's hands.

In fact, Mary Maude was lucky Edgar Jr. was deemed able to take over the plantation since the legal system did not permit women to handle business affairs. From what Davis's grandfather had said, she had continued to run the plantation until Edgar Jr. had enough experience to take over, as she had during Edgar Sr.'s long illness. If Edgar Jr. had not been old enough, Mary Maude would probably have had to put up with a court-appointed trustee. Barrett had read enough of the plantation mistress's opinions to know Mary Maude would have hated such a situation, no matter how qualified the man or how close their blood relation.

Barrett was tired of the mournful correspondence, however. She'd welcome even cotton price information on this dreary day. Anything to brighten her mood.

She called Gonzales, and he and Ricardo moved the trunk into her office. Ricardo brought some tools and played with the lock for a few moments. To everyone's surprise, it opened with a soft, well-oiled click. Just as the two left, Davis came in from his office.

"What's going on?" he asked.

"Another mysterious trunk," she replied as she tugged open the lid. The first thing she saw was a tray full of black-bordered correspondence. "Oh, no . . ."

"What is it?" He picked up one of the envelopes and pulled out the letter.

"Please tell me it's something besides another condolence over Edgar's death," she pleaded, plopping down on the floor.

"'Dear Mrs. Jamison,'" he read aloud, "'Let me express my profound sympathies over the death of your beloved husband . . .' Sorry." He put the page back in its envelope and handed it to her.

She looked out to the patio. It began to rain. "Perfect."

He chuckled, leaned down to kiss the top of her head, said, "Hang in there," and walked out toward the front of the house.

Barrett stared at the trunk for a moment. Maybe, if she was very, very lucky, and the history gods were shining on her, even if the sun was not, maybe other types of correspondence, shipping orders, something interesting, *anything* different lurked in the bottom of the trunk. With a little prayer, she lifted off the tray and set it to the side.

And looked at gray-green oilcloth tied together with twine through metal grommets.

With slightly shaking fingers, she pulled the twine end and the slipknot unraveled. She spread back the oilcloth. Two sixteen-by-twenty-inch, green-leather-bound ledgers sat side by side.

She rose on her knees and lifted out the book on

the left. Like Edgar's journal, it was tooled in worn gold filigree. The leather felt smooth and supple to her fingers, as if it had been much handled.

She took a deep breath, opened the cover, and read the title page.

Windswept Plantation
The Journal of
Mary Maude Davis Jamison
1830–1835

"Oh, my God," she whispered as she traced the writing with her fingertips. "Oh, my God, oh, my God." She hugged the book to her chest and started laughing. She was soon laughing so hard, she literally fell over, still clutching the book.

The next thing she knew, Davis was on his knees beside her holding on to her shoulders to stop her rolling from side to side. "Barrett! What's the matter? Are you all right?"

She opened her eyes, but he was all blurry through her tears. She was too breathless to speak, so she reversed the book so he could read the first page and pushed it under his nose. He let go of her to take the journal and when he read the title, he gave her a big smile. "This is what you've been hoping for, isn't it?"

Barrett levered herself up into a sitting position and nodded. After wiping her eyes with the tail of her shirt, she said, "Yes! And look at all of them. The trunk's full. If she's half, even a quarter, as chatty in her journal as she is in her letters, this is a gold mine. No, this is a *tenure* mine." She felt slightly drunk as she grinned at him.

He handed the journal to her and grinned back.

"And I have you to thank." She rose to her knees and gave him a big, smacking kiss.

Davis kissed her back and got to his feet. "No, it was all Granddaddy's doing. You indulge yourself. I'm going back to work."

Barrett barely nodded to him. She immediately sat back down, turned the page and began to read.

My name is Mary Maude Davis Jamison and this is my journal, a present from my beloved husband, Edgar.

Chapter TWENTY-SIX

The Journal of Mary Maude Davis Jamison
Windswept Plantation
January 23, 1852
Bitterly cold. In more ways than simply
the temperature.

Edgar has broken his promises and been to the quarters again. I was up during the night with Davis, who has a cold, and from my son's window I saw my husband returning to the house. When I retired, he said he would be working late in his study. He came to bed still smelling of his consort, whether Cleopatra or Salome, I know not and care not. It was all I could do to pretend to sleep, as far away on the bed as I could be.

This is the second time I have caught him during the past year. The first time he claimed drunkenness as a defense. I asked for no explanation last night or this morning. What good would it do? He is a liar and a cheat and I cannot trust him.

I no longer enjoy our (thank God) infrequent conjugal relations. Yet I cannot refuse him altogether as
it would only give him an excuse for more frequent
liaisons with those women. I am trapped.

In public or with the children, the strain between
us is barely perceptible, I believe. We have both carried
on as though all was tranquil. But I seek out ways to
exhaust myself during the day so as to fall asleep immediately. I cannot allow myself to dwell on what Edgar
does or my anger seeps through my blood like poison.

Windswept Plantation
April 8, 1852
A pleasant spring day. Warmer than usual.

I am so angry I am cold with it.

At the Winslow's spring party, I overheard two
of the most notorious gossips in the county discussing Edgar's bastards. Oh, how mealy-mouthed they
were, pitying me and the children. They pretend their
own husbands' "natural children" dropped down from
heaven with no connection to them at all. I took some
meager satisfaction in the fact no one asked them to
dance, while my dance card was full.

But it is clear: Edgar's transgressions are common
knowledge.

Then while working in my garden, I had a glimpse of Salome and another servant who asked when her baby was due. I believe the exact words were "When you gonna give the master his next child?" and the answer was "In time for the harvest."

Our marriage vows mean nothing to Edgar. My honor and the honor of the children mean nothing to him. His own children mean nothing to him. I mean nothing to him. But what can I do about this?

Windswept Plantation
July 19, 1852
Hot, hot, hot. Man, beast, and
plant all wilt together.

I would leave this place in a moment, if only I could take the children with me. But no court in the land would allow it.

To begin with, I am sick unto death of the cloying solicitous attention I receive from the "good women" of our church and neighboring plantations. Yesterday the hypocrites were out in force. They all know I have joined their secret sorority of wronged wives, but we maintain the polite fiction: none of us recognizes the status. Our play-acting, however, is by no means the worst part. What our husbands are putting us through is.

At least Edgar and I do not pretend with each other any longer. We are civil and polite, but nothing more. Claiming a problem with my back that requires a very hard bed, I have moved out of our bedroom to one upstairs overlooking the back of the house. My relocation, however, has given Edgar license to come and go as he pleases—and allow others to do so as well. The heat woke me this morning an hour before dawn. It was too hot even to light a candle. As I was attempting to cool down with tepid water from the basin, I heard whispers below my window. I carefully peeked out and witnessed Edgar in his robe giving Cleopatra a pat on her backside as he sent her back to her quarters.

I will never sleep in our marriage bed again.

Windswept Plantation
September 25, 1852
Some rain at last. We all rejoice.

I have a new book of herbal medicines and have spent many happy hours discussing its contents with Heeba. She distrusts some of the recipes and claims they are the reverse of what they claim to be, in other words, noxious instead of efficacious. She was particularly suspicious of one, a mixture normally effective for stomach disorders, but combined in the book with the parts of two plants known to cause death if in high enough amounts. The recipe is very dangerous because the original mixture will totally mask the taste of the poison. I have written to the author and publisher of this tome and asked if they have made a mistake.

Windswept Plantation
October 5, 1852
Still warm.

I am at my wit's end.

Edgar brought one of his doxies into the house again and this time Rebecca, who is only fourteen years old, found them together.

When I confronted him, he was so falsely contrite that I could have vomited.

His total disregard for the children is the last straw. I must do something.

Present Day
Sunday, June 24

At ten o'clock Sunday night, Davis looked over at Barrett, who was wrapped up in the afghan on the couch in his office, engrossed in Mary Maude's journal. She had done nothing except read the books since she had discovered them on Friday.

He couldn't blame her. He understood completely what the journal meant to her. It was more than a ticket to tenure; it was the opportunity of being the first historian to find and investigate a new, extremely rich source. He would have the same reaction if he found a start-up company with a brand new process or product.

She'd read bits and pieces to him from time to time. His great-great-great grandmother was evidently quite a woman—bright, literate, observant, straightforward. In fact, she reminded him of Barrett herself.

Davis rose from his desk, stretched, and yawned. "Come on, honey, let's go to bed," he suggested as he walked around the desk.

"Hmm?" She surfaced enough to focus on him. "Oh, I'll be up in a minute. I just want to finish this section. You go ahead," she answered vaguely and returned to the journal.

Davis looked down at her and couldn't help smiling. When she was concentrating, he was lucky if she even heard him. "Don't read too long." He kissed the top of her head before he left the room.

Upstairs, he prepared for bed, propped up the pillows, and began a book Granddaddy had once given him about the Civil War. "It's a good one, even if written by a Yankee," the old man had said. Edgar had been correct; Davis was soon immersed.

Some time later, he woke up, at first disoriented. He looked at the clock: two in the morning. The light on the nightstand was still illuminated, his book had fallen to his side, and Barrett was not in bed with him.

Muttering to himself about absent-minded professors who forgot to sleep, Davis put on his robe and went after her. She was still cocooned on the couch, but a giant box of tissues was on the table, and she was crying.

"Barrett! What is it? What's wrong?" He sat down and pulled her, cocoon and all, into his arms.

"Oh, Davis," she whispered. "Mary Maude killed him. She murdered Edgar!"

"What? Murder?" The word hit him like a sledgehammer blow, and he leaned back so he could see her face.

She reached for a tissue and blew her nose before answering. "She discovered Edgar had been visiting the slave quarters and had children by two of the women, Cleopatra and Salome."

She sniffled again, and Davis handed her another tissue. "That must have been devastating," he murmured while his thoughts came back to and swirled around the word *murder*. Mary Maude a killer? Barrett had to be mistaken.

Barrett nodded. "Mary Maude confronted Edgar, who first denied his infidelity, then claimed he had gone to the other women to spare her, his wife, from his 'animal tendencies' and to protect her health. He swore he'd never do it again. Then she overheard people at church talking about his infidelities and pitying her. Her situation worsened when it became clear that Edgar was not keeping his promises."

"Go on," Davis said while he tried to assimilate what she was telling him. He had never heard one intimation, not a rumor, not a whisper of Edgar's death from anything except natural causes. Although the family knew the first Edgar had been no saint, they had always revered him as the honored patriarch of the family. And Mary Maude as his loving, devoted wife.

"Your great-great-great grandmother was a proud woman, Davis," Barrett said after blowing her nose again. "She hated being an object of public ridicule, and she hated Edgar for betraying her, but she was faced with a fearful dilemma. She couldn't leave him, she had no money of her own, even if divorce had been an option. She wouldn't burden her parents or her sister by going to live with them. And she had the children to think about. At the time, children in a

marriage were the *property* of the father, and she knew
Edgar wouldn't give up his children, not under any circumstances. All the laws and social customs of the
time were against her.

"So, Mary Maude decided to teach him a lesson as a
way of preserving her honor and her children. She made
the decision when, after she moved into another bedroom, one of their daughters caught her father with one
of the women, in the house, in the master bedroom."

"She wrote all this in her journal?" Davis asked.
"Why put such incriminating statements into writing?"

"Her journal was her outlet. You can see over the
years how the journal goes from a record of plantation
happenings to her diary of innermost thoughts. There
were no other white women on the plantation, with the
exception of the overseer's wife, and they didn't seem
to be friendly—different classes and all. To whom
would she confide such a plan? Certainly not a friend
or her sister. She had to let her feelings out somehow,
so she used the diary.

"You can tell how affected she was by his infidelities. Her handwriting even looks angry—her normal
copperplate calligraphy spikes and jerks like it's all she
can do to keep the pen on the page to record the words.
Also, nobody would dare to read them. Edgar seems to
have discounted her 'scribblings' and ignored them. I

doubt anyone else knew what the journal had become."

"How did she kill him?" Part of him was denying his own ancestor could have done such a deed, but the other part was fascinated by Barrett's story. Who would have thought it possible?

"Poison. She was a botanical expert by then, with all she'd learned from Heeba, her gardens, her library, and her correspondence over twenty-some years. Mary Maude poisoned Edgar slowly. She didn't start out to kill or torture him, though. She records several confrontations about his continued trips to the quarters, and he promised each time to quit. But when he didn't, she resumed the poisoning.

"She says she was trying to convince him his illness came from his unfaithfulness and drew his attention to the idea several times. Her plan didn't work, however, as he refused to change his ways. When the second woman, Salome, became pregnant again during one of his 'healthy' periods, she came to the conclusion he would never change and she had to protect her children, so she gave him a fatal dose. I think she thoroughly loathed him by then. She wrote several times, 'He is not the man I married.' "

"Didn't anyone suspect anything?"

She shook her head. "Not that I can tell, not even Edgar. You've read his journal. He doesn't even speculate in it about his illness. How could anyone else? The doctors prescribed 'cures' of questionable efficacy, and many people, both white and black, wholeheartedly endorsed Mary Maude's potions. He had been 'sick' for so long—this illness-recuperation-illness went on for two years. Besides, people died back then from relatively simple causes, and frankly, nobody would suspect Mary Maude. She had a reputation as a healer, had been her husband's faithful nurse, and seemed to be doing everything she could to help him."

"Are you absolutely certain she *murdered* him? Could she have made a mistake with her potion recipe? Could you be misinterpreting something she wrote?" He felt like he was grasping at straws, but he couldn't simply accept what she had told him.

"She closed this volume with these entries," Barrett said as she flipped back a page and started to read.

October 19, 1854

Edgar is dead by my hand. He died this morning peacefully in his sleep after I gave him the fatal dose last night. I cannot mourn, I cannot grieve, I do not feel satisfaction, I do not feel freedom. I refuse to feel guilt. I move through the house with as much emotion as a machine. Indeed, a cotton gin has more sensibility than I do.

October 21, 1854

I buried my husband today in the family plot of the St. Gregoryville Episcopal Church. On the gate to the plot, the willow tree wrought in iron wept more than I did at the ceremony. Several friends remarked how "brave" I was, how "well" I was holding up, how "awful" it must have been to nurse Edgar through his illness. Even how "relieved" I should be since Edgar is beyond pain now. And how "thankful" I should be that Edgar Jr. is of an age to take over the running of the plantation.

As for Salome, Cleopatra, and their children, I do not want them here, reminding me every day of Edgar's faithlessness, but selling them will only cause the gossip's tongues to wag anew. I don't care what the laws against manumission may be, I will have them all taken north and set free there with enough money to sustain themselves until they can find work—or more likely, other men to care for them.

None of this, after all, was the fault of these women or their children. How can I condemn them when it was all his doing? This horrible system we live under has punished both the Negro women and me for his lack of integrity. The innocent children are, after all, Edgar's, and as such, linked by blood to my own dear ones. We are all slaves to this iniquitous system.

Edgar Jr. agrees with my plans and, mercifully, has not asked any questions. He has not spoken of his father's indiscretions, and his silence leads me to think he knew of them, but when or what he learned, I do not know. It doesn't matter.

No one has any inkling of my crime—except myself, and perhaps Heeba. She will, I know, be silent.

As for me . . . As I watched Edgar's coffin lowered into the ground, I looked at the spot next to his and realized my penance for killing him will be to lie next to my "beloved" husband for eternity.

It is a fitting atonement.

Barrett closed the book and put it on the coffee table, but said nothing.

Davis wrapped his arms around her and held her close. She wasn't wrong. He had to accept the truth: Mary Maude had committed murder.

He felt suddenly weary. Barrett's discovery had to be the horrible scandal Lloyd was harping about, and they had to discuss the revelations and what they meant for the present-day Jamisons.

But not now.

He nudged her back so he could see her face. She looked exhausted. "It's after two in the morning," he said. "Let's go to bed."

She didn't argue, only nodded, unwound her co-coon, and rose when he did. Hand in hand they shut off the lights and climbed the stairs.

He didn't let her go to her own room to get ready for bed as she had done on past nights before joining him. He didn't want her out of his sight, even to brush her teeth. It was more than not wanting her to wake up enough to start talking about Edgar and Mary Maude. He didn't stop to analyze his reasons, but led her to his room, helped her take off her clothes, and tucked her into his bed. He joined her and on an elbow, leaned over her, gave her a soft kiss.

"We'll discuss all the ramifications tomorrow. Okay?"

"Okay," she answered. She looked for a moment as if she wanted to say something else, but she only gave him a kiss back and snuggled closer.

He turned out the light and settled her in his arms. She fell asleep immediately, but he lay awake for long minutes thinking about those "ramifications."

She'd want to publish her findings, of course. The story of Mary Maude the murderer would make all the best-seller lists, he was positive, even if written in dry-as-dust historical language. Somehow he knew, by the time Barrett finished such a book, it wouldn't be bor-ing history, but a vital, engrossing tale. Hell, it would probably win a Pulitzer, to boot.

He could almost hear the radical feminists crowing over one of the slave-owning plantation masters receiving his comeuppance at the hands of his own wife. He could almost see the talk-show hosts and pop psychologists having a field day with his ancestors' failings. The news would definitely make the papers and magazines, and God only knew what the tabloids would do with it. Probably something like: "You Men Who Play Around—What Are Your Wives Feeding You Tonight?"

Then there was his family.

He could definitely hear the screams of outrage from the Jamisons in Louisiana, particularly Lloyd and Aunt Cecilia.

What was he going to do?

Granddaddy had made him the protector of the family—bequeathed him the post, in fact. The old man had meant for him to protect its members as much from themselves as from outside forces—probably more.

But he had a deal with Barrett to let her use the information in the papers as she chose. To go back on a deal, on his word, would diminish him in his own eyes. God knew what reneging would do to him in Barrett's.

What about Barrett? Such a book could make her

career and get her tenure with no trouble. That's what she wanted, wasn't it? What she'd been driving for, day and night, working on the papers? He rarely saw such determination in anyone these days. Why was she so driven? It didn't seem to be sheer ambition, the thirst for position he'd seen in so many men. Was it the security of a tenured post? Would her determination get in the way of their being together?

What about Mary Maude's story? What if he asked Barrett to withhold the information about the murder? No, it wouldn't work. She'd talked too much about the duty of historians to tell the truth about events, not shy away from uncomfortable realities. And there was no way he could see to downplay a murder. Unfortunately, also, no doubt existed that Mary Maude had poisoned Edgar. Her confession was right in her journal in her own handwriting.

No matter what he decided, could he trust Barrett to be sensitive to his family? Could he trust her with their history? Could he trust her, period?

Or would she be like Sandra, care about nothing, not his feelings, not their relationship, be ready to pack up and leave after using him and his family for her own purposes?

And to think just the other day he'd been contemplating something permanent with Barrett. Could he be with her at his family's expense?

What was he going to do about her?

But what would he do without her? Without her infectious laughter, her genuine interest in him and his work, her generous help with his family, her sexy presence in his bed? The possibility of losing her opened a chasm in his chest into which his heart plummeted like a cannonball down a deep well.

The object of his thoughts turned over on her side with her back against his ribcage and her butt against his hips. Davis resolutely threw the questions out of his head and pulled her a little tighter against him. He wouldn't try to make a decision now. Tomorrow would be soon enough for answers.

Chapter TWENTY-SEVEN

Davis was gone when Barrett woke. She looked at the clock and groaned. Ten in the morning. She groggily struggled out of bed, slipped into Davis's robe, grabbed her clothes and staggered around to her own room. In the bathroom, she stared at herself in the mirror.

Damn. Swollen eyelids, bloodshot eyes, splotched skin, Medusa-like hair. She only hoped Davis had not taken too close a look at her before he left.

In the shower, she vaguely remembered him giving her a good-bye kiss and telling her he'd be home early. They certainly had important issues to discuss. The news about Mary Maude would hit his family like a bombshell. How could it not?

Lloyd Walker, for one, wouldn't be happy, but he was Davis's concern, not hers. Davis would explain how the secret was out now and covering up the past never worked. Besides, they had an agreement: no censorship of her work. A brief flurry of excitement on the part of the family shouldn't make any difference to her project.

And what a project! Few historians ever had such an opportunity before them. The journals were so rich, so detailed, so complete. Added to all the other papers? She knew how treasure hunters felt when finding a gold-laden Spanish galleon. She'd do a complete biography of Mary Maude, detailing her change from a demure bride to strong matriarch of the family, despite everything from a cheating husband to war and reconstruction. Set her in her times, bring in everything from medical to legal practices, tie in the politics to day-to-day life.

She scrutinized her image in the mirror while drying off. She was looking more human, and she grinned in exultation at the future before her.

What a story, what *history* she'd write.

What a glorious beginning for her career.

She finished dressing and hurried downstairs, eager to read more of Mary Maude's journal.

She was sitting on the couch in Davis's office with one of the journals on her lap when Davis walked in about two o'clock. She watched him as he put his briefcase on the desk, took off his coat and dropped into one of the chairs across the coffee table from her.

His face was drawn, his eyes hooded, and he looked more like the Davis she'd first met than the lover with whom she shared a bed. He definitely had not liked her news about Mary Maude. Or maybe he was just tired from lack of sleep.

"Hi." She gave him a welcoming smile. Better to assume the best than a looming disaster.

He gazed at her for a long moment and, despite her optimism, a shiver of unease crawled its way up her backbone to lodge as a cold spot between her shoulder blades. He returned a smile more resigned than pleased, but the change to his face from implacable negotiator to more of an interested neutral eased the chill.

He leaned back, tented his fingers under his chin with his elbows on the chair arms. "Tell me the story again," he said in a low, dead calm voice.

She repeated what she had told him in the early morning and closed with, "I've skimmed the next two volumes today, going through the war. No one questioned Edgar's death. Ever." She made a negating gesture with her hand to emphasize her point.

"Not while Edgar Jr. was off at college, not after he returned and took over his father's place in running the plantation. Then the war came and I doubt anybody, except for family, even thought of Edgar. Mary Maude never mentions her husband again."

She tried to keep her voice matter-of-fact, tried not to let her enthusiasm show, but she was fairly bursting to tell him how Mary Maude and Windswept had survived through the war. Those years alone would fill a book. They, however, were not the point of the discussion. She folded her hands together on top of the journal and waited for his response.

"This story has to be what Lloyd and his mother have been talking about," he finally said, looking straight into her eyes. "How Grandmama and Aunt Cecilia came up with their idea of a long-ago scandal lurking in the papers, I haven't been able to find out. Maybe it was Granddaddy's mother who got it from her mother, or somebody in the past read the journals and passed it on. Something said at the funeral may have set off a recollection for Aunt Cecilia, but if she had real knowledge, Lloyd would have gotten more out of her than he did. I'm sure no other member of my generation or the previous one ever heard a whisper otherwise."

He frowned, looking more puzzled than angry. "What I don't understand is . . . Granddaddy read every piece of paper in the collection. He must have read these journals, must have known about Mary Maude and Edgar. If he was protecting the family from the truth, it might explain why he didn't open the papers to scholars. Yet he never said a word, never hinted at Mary Maude's deeds to me or to you. He kept the family secret truly secret."

"Yes," she agreed, "he did. And then he let me in."

"What do you intend to do?"

She couldn't contain her excitement when she answered, "Write a full-fledged biography of Mary Maude, incorporate all the documents, letters, the Herbarium, the journals. As I go, I'll produce my already planned articles: the correspondence with her mother and sister, the working life of the planter's wife, the dynamic development and interaction of the plantation community over time. Everything added together will be a complete study of her, her life, and her times."

He rubbed his finger along his mustache for a few seconds. "What do you think will be the response to the story of the murder?"

She studied him carefully. He was back in negotiator mode—showing no emotion, offering no observation of his thoughts. She had an answer to his question, but he had probably come to the same conclusions. All she could do now was bring the problems out into the open. "I imagine it will cause quite a bit of excitement in several circles. First, your family. Second, the media, both mass and scholarly. Third, feminist and anti-feminist organizations and advocates. Fourth, historians of nineteenth-century America with any number of specializations, from legal to social history. I'm sure there will be more."

"That's pretty much what I thought. A circus." He said the last word with utter conviction—and disgust.

"But I believe it can be a manageable and short-lived one," she countered. "The tale is a very old story. The participants are long dead. After the initial announcement, interest should die down quickly. The only people then studying Windswept should be the academics."

And if not? Davis's expression implied even the slightest bit of "excitement," scholarly or not, was unacceptable. What did his disapproval mean for her purposes? Her unease turned to dread, and the chill in the middle of her back dropped ten degrees.

"Lloyd, his mother, and a couple of other aunts and uncles are going to hit the ceiling," he said in a voice she thought suspiciously bland. "They're going to claim you're bringing shame and ridicule down on the family by publishing such a tale."

"It's not my intention to hurt the Jamison family, but I can't do anything about their feelings, or about what others may say or write." She put the volume on the coffee table and leaned forward. What she said next was the crux of the matter, and he needed to understand it—and her. She put every ounce of conviction she had into her next words. "All I can do, *all I will do* is tell the truth. All I can do, *all I will do* is write good solid history, put Mary Maude in the context of her culture and environment, and let her speak for herself. I don't want to have my narrative or interpretation become a diatribe for or against any cause. I'm not going to write lurid, melodramatic books or articles. Hers is an important story even without the murder. But I can't gloss over her actions. I can't pretend they didn't happen."

"What if I asked you to?" Again that low tone with no inflection.

"What?" She sat up straight as an icicle of shock stabbed her in the back. "What do you mean?"

"What if I asked you to leave out the murder?" His expressionless face and voice gave her no clue where he was going or what answer he wanted.

She almost couldn't believe he had asked the question, and she heard her outrage tinge her reply despite her attempt to keep her voice level. "I'd refuse. I won't whitewash the story. I was explicit on the point when we first met. You agreed I would decide what goes into my writings with no censorship from you. To leave out the murder would be a great disservice to Mary Maude. Not to tell her complete history is to disparage the woman, make her less than she was. Davis, these events happened over one hundred and fifty years ago. What could possibly impact the Jamison family now? Or is it . . ."

He didn't ask what, merely waited.

"Does your request have anything to do with the Jamison branch of the family you didn't know you had?"

"Edgar Sr.'s progeny who were moved north? No," he said, "we've all come to terms with the reality of bi-racial relations. No family with a history of owning slaves could do otherwise. The white side of the family has always known about Edgar Sr.'s proclivities. They extended to more than the two women Mary Maude knew about. A number of African-American Jamison descendants still live in the area."

"Why didn't you tell me about them?" She felt more puzzled than angry at the omission.

"I didn't think about it before," he said with a shrug. "Their existence has never been a secret. But it's not my 'distant cousins' who are the problem here."

"Then what is? Are you asking me to leave out the murder? Are you going back on our verbal deal? Even if it's not part of the formal grant agreement?"

His eyes turned to hazel granite and his face to stone at her question. All her research on the man, all her observations of him had convinced her he was a man of integrity who stood by his word. Even to suggest he would renege on a deal would insult him. She, however, needed to make sure the rules between them were as clear as the evidence in the journal.

"I'm asking you to give me some time to think about it and tell the family first," he said.

She pondered the request for a moment. The situation wasn't as simple as his appeal made it out to be, and she had to be sure he understood and acknowledged her point of view, her purpose, so she said, "Consider this too, then. I am here to write *history*, not sensational articles for the tabloids. I would agree to keep the murder a secret until publication, but I have no control over what a publisher might want to do.

"You mentioned your grandfather's knowledge of the collection, of the 'family secret.' I think you're correct—he must have known the whole story. But *he* made no limitations on my research in the deal I had with him, and I do *not* believe he would have hidden the journals from me. If he were alive, I'd be publishing Mary Maude's entire story."

When Davis didn't say a word, didn't move a

muscle, didn't even blink, Barrett knew further discussion would be fruitless. They could go round and round on the topic and never come to a conclusion satisfactory to them both. She needed to know he would not stand in the way of her writing the complete story. He needed to know not only how the other Jamisons thought, but also, and more importantly, to determine if he wanted the truth to come out at all. She'd stated her position. Good negotiating tactics said it was time to let him think.

What had Martha called him? *The protector of the family?* He was certainly playing the part.

She rose and picked up the journal volume. "Let me know what you decide. I have an inventory to work on." She walked out of his office and closed the door softly behind her.

She crossed the room slowly and laid the book on the table where Mary Maude's journals were stacked. Looking out the glass at the shimmering pool, she hugged herself and tried to force her mind to think around the ice that had permeated her brain at his request.

He hadn't given her an absolute answer when she'd asked him point blank if he was going back on the deal; he'd only asked for time to think about it. In her experience, when a person made such a wishy-washy statement, he was looking for a way out.

He was going to protect his family. He was going to ask her to at best ignore, at worst actively hide, Mary Maude's crime.

And she'd refuse and he'd kick her out, not only of the papers, but of his house and his life.

Where did it leave her? If, to stop her publication, he shut her off entirely from the collection, she would see her career ambitions come crashing down. Oh, she could write about the murder, but without the actual documents to back her up, the original documents any scholar could look at, how could she prove it?

And the possibility of tenure would go too. She couldn't even imagine the difficulty of making tenure with superficial articles or a biography with a gaping hole at its core—whether or not anyone knew of the falsehood.

She wouldn't falsify the record. She flat refused to lie about Mary Maude in print or any other mode of communication. To do so went against every fiber of her being, both her personal code of honor and her re-sponsibility as a historian. She had to tell the truth.

It all came down to Davis. What would he de-cide? Why was he hesitating?

What was "the problem," the *real* problem, if not African-Americans with Jamison blood or a murderess in the family? He had not explained his statement.

Why would he refuse to let her tell the truth?

Didn't he understand publishing a lie would be the equivalent of his putting out false financial information to an investor?

Was he trying to protect his family? From what? Some negative publicity only lasting until the next scandal came along? She knew from her research and her friends who grew up in them that small towns could be hotbeds of gossipy backbiting, but this was the twenty-first century. Did anyone really care about what their ancestors may or may not have done? She knew a couple of people who took positive delight in their rapscallion forebears.

Or was it because he didn't trust her? Did he think, despite her promises, she would publicize, sensationalize Mary Maude's transgressions? Would write hurtful, spiteful words about Edgar Sr.? Would run his family name through the mud, just to sell a few books and make a big name for herself?

The man didn't know her at all. What was the matter with him? Had he been deaf and blind to her all this time to come up with such a crazy notion? Or, was she just one of his staff like Peggy or the Gonzaleses whom he didn't really know? Or, worse, did he think she'd betray him somehow?

He'd trusted her enough to take her to bed. Or

was that just about sex? Was she simply a convenient bed partner? She began to feel warmer as the heat of anger replaced the cold of rejection.

And to think she was in love with the man.

She'd admitted it to herself and then, to make it worse, had daydreamed about having both him and tenure, about how they would work out the long-distance relationship. She'd assumed he wanted her the way she wanted him.

In the heat—oh, definitely the scorching blaze—of the moment, she had done what she never did when researching: she'd theorized ahead her data, assumed facts not in evidence, jumped headlong to a conclusion, just the way her brothers accused her of doing when she was younger. She thought she'd learned not to leap when studying history. Evidently not, because she was living with the consequences now. All it had taken was one, no, two questions from him to show her beyond doubt, she was living in a fairy tale.

Oh, God, she was. Icy waves of despondency washed over her again and she bent over, clamping her hand over her mouth to stop a building need to whimper.

"No. Stop it," she said out loud. "Don't start bawling like an idiot." It was better to discover his lack of trust now. Before she would be even more badly hurt. It was not the time to give in to despair. She straightened and glanced around the office.

She had to get on with her life, work toward her professional goals. They had a contract, verbal and otherwise. She'd live up to her side of it, no matter what he decided. She'd negotiate from now to next Christmas to maintain her access and their publishing agreement.

And right at the moment? She had a job to complete.

She stood tall, threw back her shoulders, and marched into the conference room. The trunk where the journals had lain hidden was in a corner and could stay there. With a grunt, she picked up box 1855-G, hauled it into her office, and got to work.

Chapter TWENTY-EIGHT

Davis watched the door close behind Barrett and leaned forward to scrub his face What a mess. He rose, walked to the glass wall, and stood gazing out at the tranquil pool, putting his thoughts in order.

Or, God knew, trying to.

Off and on all morning he'd thought about the repercussions the story would have among the various Jamisons. Ordinarily, he wouldn't care what the family thought, but his grandfather's death had changed things. The words of that particular Edgar came back to him again: *"You're the protector of the family now."*

Some protector he was, about to tear down the family name by revealing its founding mother as a murderess, a cold-blooded killer, no matter how she portrayed herself as acting to preserve the family honor.

To hint, even slightly, that one of the primary Jamisons had murdered the other would bring the wrath of his relatives down on his head. The culprit's written confession would mean nothing to them, would be explained away as the writings of a widow distraught in her grief, feeling guilty for not being able to nurse her husband back to health. But if he allowed Barrett Browning, an outsider, to publish the truth, even in a scholarly manner? He'd be thrown out of the family.

And Barrett? What would he do about Barrett?

He hadn't answered her question, *"What's the problem?"*

Pick one.

The problem was the family in an uproar, beating—figuratively, even literally—on him for shaming them by publicizing their secrets. The problem was his being unable to protect them from ridicule and notoriety unless, another problem, he went back on his agreement with Barrett—his written agreement and his *word*.

The problem was he could lose Barrett over this debacle. It was clear she was mad as hell at him for even suggesting she ignore the facts. He knew from their talks she was a woman of integrity, a historian who wouldn't hide the truth, no matter how unpleasant.

What had he expected? She'd agree to pretend Mary Maude's journal confession didn't exist and they'd all live happily ever after? Why had he even asked such a damn stupid question? Where were his wits? He'd known she would never consent to such a proposal.

Hell, he could remember every word she said when they were negotiating the contract.

"Just so there is no misunderstanding, our agreement includes my absolute independence about what I choose to write or publish—no censorship on your part. Whatever I write will be my version of history, not yours."

Being in a state of ignorance, he agreed, and then he'd told her he was the sole owner; he could do what he wanted to with the papers. Now here was his opportunity.

"Shit!" he said aloud and sat down at his desk, picked up a pen and rolled it between his hands.

Granddaddy had known the true facts about Edgar's death, he was certain. Why hadn't the old man brought them out in the open earlier? Protecting the family again? Or too old and tired to get into the fight sure to ensue? Or, more likely, he'd simply run out of time and life before he could accomplish what he meant to do. After all, he had invited Barrett specifically to Windswept to inventory and research the papers.

Another problem: what had Granddaddy meant to do in the end; let her publish?

It sure as hell looked like it. Barrett had spoken the truth when she said Granddaddy wouldn't have hidden the journals from her. The old man had trusted her. *"She knows what to do,"* he'd told Davis.

But did *he*, the present owner of the papers? This confusion, this indecision was totally unlike him, Davis thought. He was a decisive, take-charge individual. His course of action always came to him as a crystal-clear path. But this one meandered, forked, came back on itself, and finally slid off into a swamp full of alligators.

What the hell was wrong with him?

He gave a short bark of laughter as the answer came: in a word, *Barrett*.

He had gone from wanting her physically as a summer dalliance, to wanting her physically for far longer than two or three months, to wanting her mind totally concentrated on him, wanting her company, her teasing, her laughter, her joy. Her body and her soul. Forever.

A wave of longing and possessiveness swept over him so swiftly he almost gasped as his body tensed, ready for a fight—or sex.

He could come to no other conclusion: He was right where he'd never thought to be again—in love with a woman. No, that wasn't right. He was never in love with Sandra. Lust, maybe, self-delusion, certainly. Not love. Not like the way he felt about Barrett.

How he felt brought up yet another problem, probably the deal killer. Did he trust her enough to let her write Mary Maude's story? He'd sworn after Sandra never to trust another woman. Could he trust Barrett? If he didn't, would she leave?

Only one answer to the last question: yes, in a heartbeat.

"God damn it, what a mess!" He threw the pen down and pushed himself back in his chair.

Okay, okay, get a grip. Look at this like a business deal. He wouldn't make a decision without more information. He'd asked for more time and she'd more or less granted it.

First, he had to tell the family. He'd put off any other determinations until later. To deal with the coming uproar would take all his energy.

What were his "talking points?" How would Barrett list them? He ticked them off on his fingers. The truth had seen the light of day. He wouldn't hide it from them or anybody. The Jamison family was a strong one. They deserved to know the facts and would weather the storm of publicity sure to follow.

As for his cousin? Lloyd and his mother were unduly upset. Hell, once the titillation over a murderess in the family wore off, nobody would say a word against them. Not with all the dirt going back four generations ready to be slung against gossip. No one in St. Gregoryville was without sin.

He was informing the family of her—no, their—findings. He wasn't going to let them blame her for their own family misdeeds. Even if he let Barrett start writing today, the book wouldn't be published for months. They'd have the time to come to grips with the situation, have ready answers when anybody mentioned Mary Maude and Edgar.

He'd emphasize that the decision to publish was his alone to make and he hadn't made it yet. No, leave out the last part if possible. If they thought they could still influence him, he'd never hear the end of it.

Okay, those points made sense to him. Before he made the calls, however, he needed some factual backup. He rose and walked into the other office.

Barrett was on the floor, organizing the contents of another box. She wore her headphones and was humming with the music from her boom box.

He said her name, but she didn't respond, so he squatted down beside her and put his hand on her shoulder.

"Oh," she said as she jumped. She snatched off the headphones and turned to him, but said nothing. Her big blue eyes held no anger, no plea, no regret—nothing by which he could gauge her feelings.

Her expressionless face angered him slightly. Damn it, he was doing the best he could to handle a difficult situation. He didn't let his frustration show, however. Instead he rubbed her shoulder lightly, ignored—by sheer strength of will—how good it felt to touch her, and said, "Before we do anything else, I have to let the family know what we've found. Would you do me a favor?"

"Of course." She could have been talking to a complete stranger who'd asked if the bus stopped here.

He extended the rub across her shoulders and down her back. She shivered slightly. Good. She wasn't immune to him. "Would you photocopy the relevant passages from Mary Maude's journal so I can refute their disbelief with her own words?"

"When are you going to make the calls?"

"I'll begin as soon as you give me the copies. Do you want some help?"

"No, I know exactly where the entries are." She put down the papers she'd been holding and, easing out from under his hand, rose to her feet. "I'll have them for you in a few minutes."

"Thank you." He stood up and watched her step over the papers to the table and pick up a volume. Her shoulders were slumped and her face looked momentarily forlorn. He wanted to take her in his arms, but knew they'd end up in bed if he had his way. He had the most absurd feeling they needed to restore and reassure at least the physical bond between them. This was not the time, however; he had to concentrate on his first task.

"Barrett?" he said, pausing in the doorway.

She turned to him.

"We'll get through this."

She stared at him a few seconds, frowned, nodded, and walked across the room to the copier.

He went into his office mulling over the best approach. First Taylor in Baton Rouge, then Lloyd. No. Martha first. She might have some good ideas for handling the others. Bill could wait. As he was jotting down the sequence of events as Barrett had related them, she brought in the journal copies.

"I highlighted the relevant passages," she said.

"Good, thank you. Is this in the correct order?" He finished the last point and handed her his notes.

She read them, gave the page back, and said, "Yes, that's correct. I'm going to take a swim."

"Chicken?" he joked, hoping to tease some reaction from her.

"Excuse me?" She looked taken aback for a second.

"I don't blame you. I don't want to be around either when Lloyd starts yelling."

She gave him a puzzled look and departed.

———◆◆◆———

"Wooooeeee!" Martha's voice squealed in his ear after he related the tale. "She certainly taught old Edgar the First a lesson, didn't she? Way to go, Mary Maude! But, uh oh, this won't go over well in Louisiana."

"Look, I need some help here," Davis said. "Any ideas on breaking the news to the bunch over there?"

She was silent for a few seconds, then said, "Let Taylor tell Aunt Phyllis and his side of the family. No sense you calling them all individually. I could call . . ." She named another two aunts and a couple of cousins.

"Agreed. I'll take . . ." He read from his list and ended with, "I thought I'd let Lloyd tell his mother."

"Chicken." It wasn't a joke, but a flat statement.

"Correct. I know the second I hang up, he's going to beat me to Aunt Cecilia on the phone, or he'll go looking for her if she's not home. He's going to garble the story, but I can't help it. The only alternative I could think of was to drive over there, call a family meeting, and tell them all at once. I don't like the scenario because I'd want to bring Barrett as my expert and I won't put her through the arguments sure to follow."

"So, you *are* going to let her publish the truth."

"I haven't decided yet, but don't tell anyone. Here

are the relevant facts." He read off his list of the events.

When he was done, Martha asked in a phony blasé voice, "How is she, by the way?"

"Fine." He looked out at the pool where Barrett was swimming. How he wished he were with her.

"One piece of advice, brother dear. Don't blow it with her." She said the last sentence slowly and distinctly, the way she used to talk to him when she thought he was being a teenaged idiot.

"She's none of your concern." He practically growled the words, heard himself and purposefully changed his next to a calmer tone. "I have to call Taylor and Lloyd. I'll let you know how it goes. Will you tell Bill?"

Martha said she would and Davis hung up the phone.

On to Taylor. This cousin wasn't happy, but he took the news well, listened to the details, and agreed to tell his mother and his siblings. "Any chance of Dr. Browning, uh, 'suppressing' the facts?" he asked.

"No, not voluntarily. She wants to write a biography of Mary Maude."

"This story is bound to be big news, at least around here." Davis heard his cousin sigh and then ask, "How much control do you think we'll have?"

"Over what gets said in the media? None. Over

what people think of the family? Over what all those good neighbors in St. Gregoryville will say? Again, probably none. But if we present a united front, it should be easier—I hope. You know what my Grand-daddy always told us: 'People will think anything they want to. All any of us can do is tell the truth.' "

"Yeah, and mine said, 'Never explain. Your friends don't need it, and your enemies won't believe you.' I don't envy you being in this position, but I'll stand by your decision. I'll do what I can with the family too. I was going over to St. Gregoryville this coming weekend anyway. I'll make the rounds, try to keep things cool."

"Thanks, Taylor. Tell everyone they can call me if they have any questions. And I'll send you a copy of Mary Maude's journal entries so you can see what she wrote for yourself."

"Good luck with Lloyd."

"Thanks." Davis hung up the phone and stared at it for a minute. Then he looked out again at Barrett. She was floating, serene. Then she flipped over, swam to the ladder, and climbed out. He let his eyes roam over her body, enjoying her curves. He was already looking forward to the night, when he would make certain they were still together. He watched her dry off and go inside. Damn. There went his plans to join her in the water.

But now . . . It was almost five. Lloyd should still be at his office. Davis lifted the receiver and punched the buttons.

"Hello, Lloyd," he said after the receptionist put him though. "Sit down and listen. I have some news to tell you."

After he finished explaining what Barrett had discovered, Davis waited for his cousin to speak. When the silence lasted too long, even for him, he said, "Lloyd? Lloyd. Are you there?"

"Hellfire and damnation," Lloyd croaked in an old man's voice. "Mary Maude *murdered* Edgar Sr.? *Poisoned* him?"

"That's what she wrote in her journal. Do you want me to read the passage again?"

"No. I heard it the first time." Davis could hear him take a deep breath before he burst out with, "We have to *burn* those journals and fix it so Barrett Browning *never* mentions a word of this to anyone."

"No, we don't and we won't," Davis responded. "Barrett's planning to write a biography of Mary Maude. A *scholarly* biography. No sensationalism, no tabloid literature. But she's not going to lie or sweep the facts under the rug." He knew he was implying publication, but he kept his mouth shut about his own indecision.

Whatever he concluded, he did not want his cousin thinking for a moment he had a say in the matter.

"You listen to me," Lloyd snarled. Davis could practically hear his teeth grinding. "This news will destroy the family, our good name and standing. We'll be laughing stocks, or worse, be called killers. People will say,"—he assumed a snide falsetto—"'There goes one of those Jamisons. If they all take after Mary Maude and her bad blood, you can't trust even one.'" His voice fell back into its usual register. "Nobody with any sense will have anything to do with us. You won't feel anything over there in high-and-mighty Houston, but here in the parish, we'll get the brunt of it. You don't know what it's like over here. I'll be ruined!" He was wailing by his last words.

Davis tried to stay calm and rational, but it wasn't easy. His cousin was as volatile and unreasonable as ever, and Davis wanted to reach through the phone and give him a good shaking. "Lloyd, take it easy. Nothing's going to come of this except a little publicity. And it will be at least a year before any of it appears in print."

"Why are you doing this, Davis? Why are you being so mean and ruthless? The family never meant anything to you, did it? Granddaddy was crazy to leave you all the papers. He didn't care about the Jamison name either. He must have known all this scandal would come out. It was always you who was his favorite. He never liked me, but I didn't think he'd try to get me from the grave!"

"Hey!" Davis yelled back. "This is not about you or me. It's history, our family history. It happened over a hundred and fifty years ago. Nothing coming out of this can hurt us."

"I'll sue! I'll take you and the bimbo to court!"

All Davis's weariness came back and hit him between the eyes. "All right, Lloyd," he said and heard his voice come out in a flat, disgusted tone. "You do that. I told you about Mary Maude out of courtesy so you could get used to the idea before the book and articles come out. I'll be over there in a couple of weeks to talk with the family. But this plan is going forward, and you can't stop it." He hung up on Lloyd's sputters.

He didn't have a chance to think about what he had just told Lloyd because the house line rang immediately. "It's your Aunt Phyllis Jamison on line two," Gonzales announced.

"Thank you," Davis replied. "I'll take it." With an inward groan, he punched the button. "Hello, Aunt Phyllis. I guess you've heard the news from Taylor."

Chapter
TWENTY-NINE

At dinner, Barrett picked at her food while Davis related the account of his phone calls. Jamison family reactions ranged from a vehement "Destroy those journals!" to a wailing "How could Mary Maude shame the family so?" to a know-it-all "I always thought there was something wrong with the way Edgar died," to a celebrity-hungry "Do you think the story will make *People Magazine*? Will we be on television?"

She didn't really care what his relatives thought. The most important Jamison, the one with the power, was sitting beside her. Davis, however, gave no hint of his probable decision. She was determined not to ask. If this was a true negotiation, she could not put herself in the vulnerable position of beggar.

Bwuck, bwuck, bwuck. She couldn't even delude herself. The truth was, she didn't want to hear or have to deal with a negative answer. He'd been right when he'd asked her if she was chicken.

"Could you do that?" Davis asked.

Barrett dragged her mind back to the table. "What? Oh, make copies of her journal entries to send to everyone? Certainly. I'll do it tonight."

"Thanks. Even though they'll try, Lloyd and Aunt Cecilia can't refute her own words."

He had the grim hawkish look about him again, she thought as she watched him cut his meat. Whatever he was about to say next, if it was about the murder, she didn't want to hear it, so she started talking about Windswept's trials and tribulations during the war. Davis seemed relieved to change the subject and contributed some family tales about Yankee visits to the plantation.

After dinner, while she copied Mary Maude's journal, she could hear him in his office on the speaker phone cajoling, soothing, joking, explaining, arguing, repeating, repeating, repeating—whatever was required according to the demeanor of the person on the other end of the line.

While he reiterated over and over the decision to publish was his alone, he still didn't state what his decision would be. Instead, he talked about the need for a united front and the strength of the family. Most of his relatives seemed to go along with what he was saying, but a few lambasted him for even considering the idea of letting the truth out. The latter worried Barrett the most, she realized, especially the thoughtful ones who never raised their voices. She had no idea how much influence they carried with him. She snuck a glance in while he was talking to one of them, and the bleak look on his face didn't encourage her about the outcome of the situation.

As she collated the copies, she took a deep breath and slowly let it out. She felt like she'd been trampled over by a whole troop of Yankee cavalry. It was time to go to bed.

Bed.

But whose?

After all the events today, with all the inconclusiveness of the situation, with all her fears of mistrust on his part, how could she share his bed? She wasn't angry any more, so she wouldn't pretend it was spite keeping her away. Was she trying to teach him a lesson? Or, worse, blackmail him? No journal, no sex? No booky, no nooky? She shook her head. Damn, now her mind was going.

No, she just needed some distance, some separation to keep her own mind clear if he denied her. Above all, to keep her poor, downtrodden heart guarded.

Bwuck, bwuck, bwuck said the idiot piece of poultry in her head. "Oh, shut up," she told it and carried the copies into his office. As she laid them on the coffee table, he hung up the phone.

He leaned back and stretched, and she had to force her eyes off his long body as her own reacted to the sight and to the memories of being in his arms. She cleared her suddenly scratchy throat and said, "Here are the copies."

"Good, we'll mail them in the morning. Barrett . . ." The phone rang again, he picked it up, listened, and asked the caller to hang on. He covered the mouthpiece and turned to her.

Before he could speak, she said quickly, "I'm going to bed." She needed to get this out while she had the strength.

"I don't know when I'll be up." With a grimace, he waved the phone in his hand.

"I think I'd better sleep in my room tonight," she said. "I'm really tired."

His face went blank, then hardened, and he stared at her for a long moment. "That's up to you," he said with a soft, low, expressionless tone.

"Good night."

He nodded and spoke into the phone. "Hello, Aunt Faye. I suppose you've heard the news." He turned his chair toward the windows.

She fled upstairs. An air of disconsolate exhaustion hung about the room as she prepared for bed.

Once between the sheets, she concentrated on relaxing her muscles while she tried to entice sleep, but when she thought about Davis, she moved restlessly across the mattress. She finally decided she must be searching for him.

Oh, God. Nine days—or rather, nights—and she'd become so used to having him next to her that she missed him when he wasn't there. She turned resolutely on her side "away from him" and recited the names of the presidents of the United States until she fell asleep.

———◆———

Davis finished his phone calls about ten-thirty and set the answering machine to pick up immediately. He didn't want any more phone calls tonight from Louisiana or anywhere else. He laid the list of names and addresses for the journal copies on top of the stack and turned out the lights. Stretching as he walked, he left the offices and climbed the stairs. At the top, he stopped, looked toward the front of the house. Nothing moved in the silent darkness.

Anger didn't hit him until he walked into his bedroom. His *empty* bedroom. Barrett hadn't changed her mind. Had he been hoping she would?

Damn right he had. Damn right she should be right there, all curled up, smelling good, waiting for him to spoon himself around her.

What was she doing? Telling him in no uncertain terms she wouldn't share his bed unless he agreed to publishing Mary Maude's story?

What was the matter with her? Couldn't she let him inform the family and make a decision—a decision he realized he'd actually made about the time Lloyd was yelling at him. Look at the trouble the tale was already causing. The truth had to come out in public. What was the old adage: Two people can keep a secret if one of them is dead?

Concealing the facts was impossible. Too many people knew the story. In fact, he'd bet the phone lines in Louisiana were already humming with the news. Trying to cover up Mary Maude's act would only lead to more family arguments and destroy the famous Jamison solidarity.

Besides, the tale was good history. If he had learned anything from Dr. Barrett Browning, it was that.

So why wasn't she where she was supposed to be? Didn't she trust him? Fuming, he went to bed.

Two hours later, he was still awake. When he turned over to see what time it was, he couldn't see the clock until he sat up. He was on her side of the bed.

Damn.

Grumbling about stubborn women under his breath, he got up, stalked out of his bedroom, down the hall, and into hers. The security landscape lighting illuminated the room only faintly through the curtains, but he could make out the bed and the lump under the sheet.

He walked around to his side, lifted the sheet, and slid in beside her.

When he touched her, she mumbled, "What? Davis?"

"Hush," he ordered and pulled her into his arms. "I just need to get some sleep."

She didn't say anything, but her body went rigid for a moment. Then she sighed and relaxed.

He inhaled deeply her unique spice-and-female scent and felt all the tension flow out of his muscles. This was the way it was supposed to be.

———————◆◆◆———————

Lloyd looked at the clock on his desk. One in the morning. Damn Davis! And damn that professor of his! What was he going to do now?

He looked at the spreadsheet displayed on his computer. Glanced again at his notes with several versions of columns of numbers adding and subtracting and all coming to the same conclusion. He was in deep shit.

And his cousin had just dealt him a death blow. Not only was he going broke and would be forced to sell all his properties, maybe even the house, but, after the news about Mary Maude came out, he'd be shunned in the community. No longer would people look up to him, ask him to be on charitable committees, speak of him for a position on city council—his long-held secret ambition.

Grace, the only good thing in his entire life and whom he didn't deserve, would leave him. How could she stay with such a pitiful man, with a descendant of a murderess?

He ought to get some sleep. God knew, he'd had precious little of it lately as his financial worries kept him awake half the night. Despite his efforts to hide his insomnia, Grace had noticed and suggested he go to the doctor for a physical. He'd muttered, "Yeah, yeah," but hadn't told her the real reason, of course. He wasn't the kind of man to burden his wife with such problems.

No, instead he was just like his father who had run the finances single-handedly until the day he died. His mother had been more than willing to let him do so. Even today, she looked to her son to take his father's place in financial decisions. Thank God he had never used any of the money she had offered in his businesses. No matter what happened to him, she would be all right.

She'd practically fainted when he told her about Mary Maude. Then she'd pitched a fit about how he had to do something, make Davis understand, stop any gossip or publication.

What a contrast his mother was with Grace, who'd simply given him a hug and said, "If Mary Maude could live through a philandering husband and the Yankees, the present generations of Jamisons can handle a little publicity. Don't worry so much, dear, everything will be all right. Davis is a good man. He'll take care of the family."

Hellfire and damnation. Even Grace thought more of his "perfect" cousin than she did of her husband. She'd leave him for sure.

He had to get hold of himself. Surely there was a way out of this quagmire.

He looked at the numbers again. Started another column on the spreadsheet. Maybe if he moved this money from here to here, sold that set of apartments, got rid of this other house and the vacant lot next door, and wrestled this amount out of his fool client, he could hold on financially.

The only thing left then was the murder scandal. He had to regain Grace's confidence in him, had to make her realize he could protect the family as well as Davis. He had to destroy the journals. From what Davis said, without them, nobody could prove Mary Maude did anything to Edgar Sr.

But how would he get inside the house? How could he force the professor and Davis to give him the journals?

He pushed back from his desk, leaned down, and opened the bottom right-hand drawer. There it was. It would certainly help.

———◆◆◆———

Where was she? It took Barrett a minute to realize she was in her room, not Davis's. The alarm clock had not buzzed, but the sun was shining brightly, so she must have slept late.

She was lying on her back. Davis was next to her, but on his stomach with an arm flung out across her abdomen. What was he doing here? He'd come in after she'd fallen asleep . . .

And then what?

She remembered waking up when he joined her. He'd muttered something about needing to get some sleep and pulled her into his arms and cuddled.

No kiss, nothing else.

She'd gone right back to sleep. She wasn't sure she'd really woken up. But the event wasn't a dream, because here he lay. She remembered searching for him in the bed before she slept. He must have been having some problems too. Only his must have been worse to bring him all the way to her.

She tilted her head and looked down at his arm. Usually they were not so close together when they woke—they might be touching, but not this . . . what? The way his arm lay across her with his hand on her hip looked like he was reassuring himself of her presence. Or was he keeping her there?

So much for her idea to put some physical distance between them. She still didn't know if he had made a decision or what it would be. She looked at the light filtering through the sheer curtains. Did she really want to face those questions the first thing in the morning? Before she'd had a cup of coffee? No way. She needed her wits about her when negotiating with the man beside her.

Neither did she want to make love—the way they had on past mornings—without knowing what her future held. With regard to the Windswept papers at least. The question of his trust in her would resolve itself when she knew his decision. Wouldn't it? Or was it the other way around?

She turned her head to look at him. He was facing her, but appeared to be deeply asleep. With his morning beard growth and mustache, he really did look like a pirate—and she was the booty he'd captured from a merchant ship.

A pang of longing ran through her, and she had to fight to stay still, not to snuggle closer. Oh, God, how she loved this man. But here she was again, right where she started, yearning for him and having no clue—well, leaving the sex out of it—as to what he really thought of her, if he really trusted her, if he loved her back.

She had to get out of bed. Thinking those thoughts led to madness.

Carefully, smoothly, she slid out from under his arm. He grunted, grabbed her pillow and pulled it to him, took a deep breath and subsided. She tiptoed to the closet, gathered something to wear, and headed for the bathroom. He was still asleep when she carefully closed the door behind her. Despite her efforts, the door made a sharp snap when it shut.

Davis opened his eyes. What had woken him? Some sort of click.

Where was Barrett? He was clutching a pillow

smelling like her, but it was a poor substitute for a warm woman.

He sat up, tossed the pillow to the head of the bed, and stretched. At least he'd gotten a good night's sleep, and he felt ready to face more phone calls from his family. And to discuss the ramifications with Barrett. As he ran through the situation between them in his mind, he grinned. His head was functioning again, his path was straight and true. He knew exactly what the problem was with Barrett. And how to solve it.

He got out of bed, looked around. No robe. He'd been so pissed about not being able to get to sleep last night, he'd come here stark naked. Well, no matter.

He walked out to the balcony, leaned over, and listened. The dining room door was open and he could hear Eva and Barrett talking in the kitchen. Good. Now he knew where she was. They had to talk this morning. But first he needed to shower and shave—and to let Peggy know he wouldn't be in today. Then he needed some coffee. He wanted to be wide awake when he made it crystal clear to Barrett how things were going to be between them.

Chapter THIRTY

*B*arrett sat at the kitchen table finishing her second cup of coffee and reading the paper when Davis walked in and took a seat across from her. She flashed a glance at him. Dressed in jeans and a knit shirt, he was evidently not going to the office today.

He wore his negotiating face, but he didn't say anything. Neither did she.

Eva bustled to bring him his juice. "The usual, Mr. Jamison?" she asked.

"Fine," Davis said, drank the juice, and looked at the *Chronicle's* front page.

Gonzales came in from the dining room, looked from Barrett to Davis and back, and raised his eyebrows. "Good morning, Mr. Jamison," he said, then turned to Eva and asked, "Do you have the grocery list ready?"

The Gonzaleses knew something was up, Barrett thought, but they had the good sense to ignore it. Too bad she couldn't do the same. She'd wait until they left on their shopping trip before asking about Davis's decision. She felt alert and rested, ready to take on the eagle across the table. Good or bad, she needed to know where she stood with him.

Eva served Davis, and the Gonzaleses left. Davis didn't say anything, only picked up the business section and read it while he ate.

Barrett finished the comics and started on the first section—or let herself appear to be reading as she ran through scenarios about where to begin the discussion. She made herself keep calm, but she couldn't help clasping her hands tightly together in her lap below the table top while she read. When she turned a page, she watched him out of the corner of her eye.

He sat there reading and eating. Didn't look up, didn't give her a clue as to his thoughts.

Finally he put down the paper, finished off his coffee, and sat back.

And looked straight at her. With that granite hazel gaze of his. She met it with, she hoped, just as much determination in hers.

"Davis," she said at the same time he said, "Barrett."

She shut her mouth. He waved a hand and said, "Go ahead."

"I'd like to talk about trust first," she said. If it was the core problem, as she had come to think, they needed to start there.

"Good. So would I," he said, bending forward with his elbows on the table. "Why don't you trust me?"

"What?" She sat straight up. In all her plans for their discussion, she hadn't expected that question. "I don't trust you? No, it's the other way around."

He shook his head. "Not the way I see it."

"I can't imagine how you could come to such a conclusion. You'd better explain it to me then," she said.

He leaned back and ticked off his points on his fingers. "First you tell me the matriarch of my family is a murderess. Then, before I can absorb the facts, properly inform my family, and decide how to manage the situation so the family won't get hurt in the coming media brawl, you accuse me of going back on my word and ignoring my grandfather's wishes. You don't trust me enough to give me the time to come to terms with this mess before you leave my bed without so much as a discussion."

His bed? This wasn't about sleeping with him. Or was it? No, she couldn't let him sidetrack her, and she countered, "You asked me to leave out the murder! You don't trust me enough to write a story sensitive to your family and its concerns. You don't know me well enough to trust my integrity and honesty and know I wouldn't do anything to intentionally hurt you or your family. But I can't and won't lie, even by omission, about what happened in the past."

"I didn't ask you to leave out the murder, only to give me some time to think."

True, he'd asked her what she'd do if he *did* ask. Had she jumped to another conclusion? No, because underneath, the question had not been hypothetical, and the result was the same. "I'm giving you the time. But Davis, I didn't know where I stood with you last night—if you'd abide by our agreement or kick me out of your house, if you trusted me as a historian and a person or thought I was good for sex and nothing else. How could I share your bed under those circumstances?"

Before he could answer, a loud noise outside drew the attention of both of them. A big dirty Cadillac screeched to a halt on the driveway by the back door.

"God damn it," Davis muttered and stood, but didn't move from his place by the table.

Barrett felt her eyes widen when Lloyd got out and stalked around the car to the kitchen door. It must have been left unlocked because he just barged in and slammed it behind him.

She rose when he entered. She had been sitting on the side of the table closest to the door and she turned around to face him.

Lloyd looked pale and gaunt, with bloodshot eyes

behind his crooked glasses, beard stubble on his chin, and a rumpled suit on his body. She was close enough to smell him, a sour odor reeking of anger and fear. She took a step backward toward Davis several feet behind her.

"What do you want?" Davis asked in a deadly calm voice.

Lloyd drew himself up and glared past her at his cousin. "I am not going to let you ruin the family. I'm here to burn those journals."

"I'm not going to hurt the family, and I'm not going to let you destroy anything. You're being irrational and you know it. Come sit down and we'll talk about it."

"Irrational? I'll show you irrational." Lloyd opened his jacket and pulled out a gun.

Barrett froze. She was used to seeing her policeman brother Greg with a gun, but Lloyd held a huge, old, black six-shooter with a bullet probably big enough to take down an elephant. She couldn't see Davis, but she heard him shift his position.

"Back up, Barrett," Davis said, speaking in a low, soothing tone. "Give me the gun, Lloyd. You're not helping your case."

Lloyd waved the pistol back and forth, then aimed it at her. "You stay still, professor. You're going to show

me those writings. Then we're going to burn them."
He moved to her, grabbed her arm and spun her around
to face Davis, who took a step in her direction.

"Uh uh, Davis," Lloyd said. "I'm in charge here.
Back up." After Davis did what he ordered, Lloyd held
on to Barrett's right arm with his left hand and pulled
her closer. He kept the gun pointed at his cousin.

"If you're in charge," Davis said, "do you expect
me to sit here and do nothing while you take Barrett
to the office?"

Lloyd was silent for a moment, and Barrett turned
her head enough to see his face. He was sweating and
looked confused. Then he scowled and said, "No. I
expect you to come with us. I want you where I can
keep an eye on you. And remember, I've got hold of
the little bitch."

Tightening his grip, he gave Barrett a shake, but
she refused to wince. She was too angry and frustrated. Just as she and Davis were getting to the crux of
the matter between them, here came his cousin.

"All I care about is getting rid of those papers,"
Lloyd snarled. "I'm going to be the one who protects
the family this time. You think you're so high and
mighty. I'm—"

Barrett tuned out his ravings. What could she
do? Davis was too far away to rush him without get-

ting shot, and Lloyd sounded like he was about to explode. Well, she wasn't about to stand there and let him. As if she were interrupting a normal conversation, she said, "Lloyd."

He paid no attention and kept ranting, his voice rising in pitch and volume. "—the one they're all going to look up to now. I don't care what Granddaddy thought. I'm—"

"Lloyd," she repeated, a little louder.

"—taking over now and there's nothing you can do—"

"Lloyd!"

"What?" He didn't look down at her, but shook her again. His movement caused the gun to wobble in his hand.

"Do you have any sisters?" she asked in a sweet voice as though speaking to a child.

"What? No. Hellfire and damnation, woman! What's that got to do with anything?" He kept his eyes on Davis, and she felt his grip on her arm loosen.

"This." She reached out with her left hand, thrust the gun away to the right toward the windows, and smashed her right fist up against the bottom of his nose.

"Oowwww!" Lloyd yelled as Davis snatched the gun with one hand and punched him in the jaw with the other. He staggered backward, hit the door, and slid to the floor. Holding his nose with both hands, he sagged to the side and started crying.

Davis put the gun on the table, grabbed Barrett by the shoulders and shook her. "What do you think you're doing? He could have shot you!"

"I didn't want him to shoot *you*!" she answered and for emphasis poked him in the chest.

"Oh, hell, Barrett!" An expression of complete exasperation on his face, he pulled her into his arms and held her tight. She held on right back as an enormous sense of relief struck her. She could feel his heart beating as rapidly as hers.

After several seconds, Davis let her go and she turned around to look at Lloyd.

He sat, still on the floor, still crying. "Oh, God," he blubbered, "I'm ruined. I've lost everything."

Davis gazed down at his cousin and sighed. As much as he'd like to leave Lloyd to solve his own problems, he couldn't do it—the man needed help if he was willing to go to these lengths. But how to give it and convince him to leave the papers alone? Back to negotiating.

He gave Barrett a quick squeeze and released her. They'd discuss her conduct and the matter of trust later. First, he had to take care of his cousin. "C'mon," he said as he hauled Lloyd up and plopped him in the chair Barrett had vacated.

She handed Lloyd a dish towel and he dabbed it at his nose. Davis picked up the gun and opened the cylinder. "It's not loaded," he told Barrett as he put it in a drawer on the other side of the room.

"Damnation, I can't do anything right," Lloyd mumbled into the cloth, but he stopped crying and seemed to have some control.

Davis poured a cup of coffee and set it before his cousin. Barrett moved to his original chair, and Davis sat down between them. "Are you still bleeding?" he asked.

Lloyd dabbed at his nose. "I don't think so," he said in a scratchy voice. He sighed and blew his nose, then took a sip of his coffee. He didn't look at anyone.

Davis waited until Lloyd had taken a few more swallows. All the negotiating techniques he knew said to get the other side talking, so he kept his tone matter-of-fact and asked, "What's really going on? For you to act like this, it has to be more than Aunt Cecilia giving you grief."

"I'm running out of money. I'm going to lose everything, all my properties, my house, probably even Grace." Lloyd shivered, and his hand trembled when he put the cup down.

Davis said nothing, although the statement came

as a shock. He thought his cousin was doing well financially. He shot a glance at Barrett who sat utterly still, her hands clasped on the tabletop and no expression on her face. Her attention was focused on the other man.

Before anyone said anything else, Eva and Gonzales returned. Davis rose and went to the door. "Eva, will you come in right away and fix my cousin some breakfast? I think we need some more coffee too."

While Eva scrambled eggs, Gonzales unloaded groceries. Davis said nothing, only watched Lloyd drink his coffee.

When Eva put the eggs and warm tortillas in front of him, Lloyd dug in like he hadn't seen food in a month, so Davis waited until he slowed down. He told himself to be sympathetic, no matter what. "Why are you going to lose everything?" he asked.

"I made some bad money decisions," Lloyd finally said, "and got caught in the last market downturn. Then my accountant died and the books were in a mess. Then I had a cash-flow problem. One thing led to another . . ." He went on to explain his financial predicament, his mother's pressure, and his fear of the Windswept revelations.

"Why didn't you come to the family for help?" Davis asked. "If not me, then one of the Louisiana cousins?"

Before Lloyd could answer, another car drove up and stopped behind the Cadillac. "Oh, no," he groaned as one man and two women emerged.

"Who are they?" Barrett asked as she watched the visitors come to the door. The woman in the lead was about her size, with short wavy brown hair and an anxious expression. The other two were tall and looked equally worried. The man was about Davis's height but heavier in build, and the Jamison family resemblance showed around his eyes. The woman, a slim strawberry blonde, had probably been a beauty queen in college.

"It's Grace, Lloyd's wife, with Taylor and his wife Corinne," Davis told.

When Davis opened the door, Grace shot by him without even a hello. She went straight to her husband and put her arms around him. Lloyd sagged against her, mumbling, "I'm sorry."

Taylor and Corinne came in, and Davis introduced Barrett. Then he moved the six of them into the family room next to the kitchen. Its two large couches and three easy chairs would be a more comfortable place to talk. When it came out the threesome had had no breakfast either, Eva set to work again, and Gonzales put on another pot of coffee.

Davis pulled Barrett aside as the group settled

themselves and whispered in her ear, "Don't mention the gun."

She looked back at him and nodded. She agreed— no need to bring that up unless Lloyd forced the issue.

She thought about excusing herself from what would clearly be a private family discussion, but Davis took her hand and seated her in the chair next to him, so she settled back to watch. She did have a vested interest in the outcome, she reminded herself, and maybe she'd learn some answers to her questions.

"Why don't you tell everybody what you told me, Lloyd," Davis said. "Then we'll all know what's going on."

Lloyd told his story for the second time and ended it with, "All I could think of was destroying the journals, so I got in the car and came here."

"Grace called us in the middle of the night," Taylor said, taking up the narrative. "She'd woken up and couldn't find Lloyd. Ever since you told him about Mary Maude, he'd been cursing you and making wild claims about destroying the papers, so we figured he'd come over here, and we followed. We tried calling, but all we got was the answering machine."

Grace looked at her husband sitting next to her and tightened her hand on his. "Lloyd, I love you. I have no intention of leaving you for any reason. I know your father never talked about finances with your mother, and he never would accept help from anybody, but you are not your father and I am not your mother, and it's clear we could use some help. If you won't ask your family, then I will."

"But . . ." Lloyd stammered.

"Lloyd," Davis said, "we're all family here. We may not always like or agree with each other, but none of us is going to let any of us fail. The family, especially our Granddaddy and Taylor's, taught us that. No real harm has been done."

"Right," Taylor added. "All of us have a cash-flow problem from time to time. I'll have my accountant take a look at your books."

"And I'll send over one of mine," Davis offered.

"I've already thought about selling the bottom land Granddaddy left me," Lloyd ventured.

"Let's not sell any family property until it's necessary," Davis said.

"I agree," Taylor concurred, then brightened. "You know, the apartment complex on the highway might be a good candidate for liquidation or redevelopment."

Grace mentioned another possibility and they discussed properties while Barrett watched. She couldn't help but think of the long-held Southern penchant for holding onto the land, keeping it in the family, no matter what. She'd read about it and now, here it was, alive and well in front of her. She was musing over the phenomenon when the talk turned to the old plantation and she heard a question that brought her back to the present with a thump.

"What about Mary Maude and the journals?" Corinne asked. "Could we see them?"

"Yeah," Taylor put in, "what are you going to do about the prospective scandal?"

Barrett looked at Davis who gazed back with a smile she couldn't interpret, but it sparked a little flame of hope in her.

"First," he said, "let our historian tell you the whole story, not the half-assed version I gave you."

Feeling vastly encouraged, but not letting herself take anything for granted, she started at the beginning. "When Mary Maude married Edgar, she was certain she had found her 'perfect love,' and it wasn't until a few years after the birth of her fourth child that she discovered Edgar's unfaithfulness." She repeated the tale to what she quickly realized was an enthralled audience. Even Lloyd looked caught up in the long-ago events.

When she finished, however, he was the first to speak. "This business is going to ruin us," he muttered.

"Honey, it's going to make us the toast of the town," Grace rebutted.

"What?" her husband drew back as if she'd just

taken a bite out of him.

"I love your mother dearly, but she still lives in the nineteen-fifties and -sixties, when society was ruled by the much older generation who swept everything remotely scandalous under the rug. They believed a transgression against the social order tarred a whole family with shame. Maybe you haven't noticed, but we don't live like that anymore. People don't care about what your ancestors did—except when it makes good dinner conversation. Everybody, and I mean every man and woman in the parish, is going to invite us to dinner to hear about Mary Maude and Edgar. You mark my words," Grace said with a sharp nod for emphasis, "your law practice is going to be increasing."

"I agree," Corinne said. "Look at the Marlows. They've been living on the reputations of their ancestors for years, and the whole lot was nothing but a bunch of carpetbaggers. Besides, good for Mary Maude. I'd have killed the philandering son of a gun too."

Everyone looked at Taylor, who quickly said, "Don't worry, I'm going to live a long, happy life."

"There are some other considerations," Davis said.

Barrett held her breath.

"The family knows now," he continued, "and the story is going to come out. Some Jamisons are incapable of keeping a secret, and we know who they are.

The truth would be told under any circumstances because Barrett and I have a deal, just like the one she had with Granddaddy. She can use anything in the papers to write her books and articles. Scholarly or otherwise. Neither Granddaddy nor I made any restrictions previously and I don't intend to impose any now. But she and I will be in charge of the telling."

He looked at his cousin. "What did you think she was going to do, Lloyd, run to the tabloids? Sure, they'll pick up on the more lurid aspects of the story, and there'll be other publicity, but we can weather it."

"Damn right," Taylor put in.

"Of course," Corinne concurred.

Davis turned to Barrett, reached out and took her hand, looked straight into her eyes. "I don't condone what Mary Maude did, but I can understand it. I've learned a lot about history in the past weeks, just listening to and watching you. We have a story here that ought to be told. You're the one to do it."

She let out her breath in a whoosh of relief. "Thank you," was all she could say. Davis was smiling, a wide grin under his mustache, and she returned it as exultation flooded her senses. He did trust her, he did have faith in her abilities, and she loved him.

Taylor asked another question of Davis, but Barrett didn't hear it. All sorts of ideas and possible plans for the book and articles were running through her head. Then they were all rising. Taylor, Grace, and Lloyd went upstairs to take naps before driving home. Davis headed back to his office to return the fourteen calls Gonzales reported were waiting on the answering machine. And she found herself showing Corinne the journals and the Herbarium.

In late afternoon Eva whipped together an early dinner. Barrett looked around the table and thought the dining room held a definite warmth for once, the cold driven out by the family within its confines.

At the end, Lloyd cleared his throat and announced, "I have something to say." When he had everyone's attention, he hesitated, grimaced like he was having a difficult time forming the words, but finally continued, "I just wanted to apologize for putting you all through this mess and for helping me and Grace clean it up. I'll have a talk with Mother and make her see the light."

"No, *we'll* have a talk with her," Grace interjected and put her hand in his.

"Right," Lloyd agreed.

"And I'll handle my mother," Taylor put in.

"Anyway," Lloyd said, looking somewhat irritated at being interrupted, "I apologize—especially to Barrett and Davis."

"Apology accepted," Davis said and Barrett nodded.

"Amen," Taylor said, "and now we'd better get on the road. Thanks for your hospitality, Davis."

The others echoed his thanks, and within minutes Barrett and Davis stood arm in arm and watched the two cars drive over the bridge.

"They're nice people," she said. "Even Lloyd has some good points."

"Yeah, he's not too bad when he stops trying to take over or to impress everybody. He was just pushed to his limit. I'll bet Grace talked him into making the apology. I've never heard him apologize for anything ever before."

Davis turned her to face him. "And speaking of ever before and ever again, I almost had a heart attack when you shoved the gun away and hit Lloyd. I don't ever want you to take a chance like that again. What did you think you were doing, fighting with him? He could have turned the gun on you, and it could have been loaded." He had his hands on her hips and used them to give her a little shake.

She rolled her eyes. She should have known he'd bring up the subject. "Do you remember me asking him if he had any sisters?"

"Yeah, so what?"

"First, he didn't have me in any kind of threatening

hold. Second, once he said he didn't have any sisters, I knew he wouldn't be expecting anything from me. Third, I grew up fighting with three brothers. Fourth, Greg showed me a bunch of self-defense moves. Fifth, I knew once I had deflected the gun, you'd be right there. Sixth . . ."

He put his hand over her mouth to stop her from talking, but it was okay, because she couldn't think of a sixth.

"Promise me you won't take a chance like that ever again."

"Bmmh Mm dmmt xmmmt . . ."

He squinted at her. "I know neither of us expect to be in such a situation again. I don't care, I still want your promise. Just nod yes or no."

"Hmmmph." She glared at him, then nodded.

"Okay." He took his hand away and replaced it with his lips in a light kiss. "Thank you for putting up with my family."

She grinned up at him. "You're welcome."

"Now come with me. We still have something to settle." He put his arm around her shoulder and marched her through the house to his office.

Barrett didn't protest. She wanted privacy also.

Once there, he drew her down on the couch while he sat on the coffee table across from her. His legs straddled hers, and he put his hands on his knees, elbows out. He looked her straight in the eye and said, "I believe we were in the middle of an argument when Lloyd showed up. You had backed down from claiming I asked you to leave out the murder, but said you didn't know where you stood with me and couldn't share my bed under those circumstances. Is that correct?"

Barrett sat up straight and stared back at him. She ignored the physical trap he'd placed her in. That sort of domination didn't work on her, as her brothers could attest. She wouldn't, however, let him surprise her into saying the first thing popping into her mind. The man was really a killer negotiator; despite all the brouhaha with Lloyd, he hadn't forgotten a word they'd said before his cousin's arrival.

She mentally reviewed their statements before the interruption. She didn't agree with the "backed down" interpretation, but she'd concede the point for the moment. She wouldn't give in on the real question, though. "As I recall, the major subject in our discussion concerned the issue of trust."

"Yes," he said with the damn straight face she still couldn't read.

"I didn't think you trusted me."

"And I thought you weren't trusting me."

She took a deep breath. He was correct: she hadn't

been. Better to get it over with so they could move on. "Looking back, I see that you are correct. I apologize, Davis. I shouldn't have jumped to the conclusion you were going to deny me the use of the journals. All I could see were my plans for tenure and promotion slipping through my fingers. I should have been more sensitive to the situation with your family, more understanding of the shock Mary Maude's confession caused. I should have had more faith in you."

"No, don't apologize. You were right to worry," he said with a rueful smile. "I honestly didn't know what I was going to do until I talked to Lloyd about your discovery. As I was explaining to him, I told him we could handle the resulting publicity and had time to prepare good responses. I knew then I trusted you to tell the story, but the family kept hounding me, and the next thing I knew you were telling me you were going to bed alone."

"You were so tied up with the phone, and I was trying to keep some distance between us just in case . . ."

"In case . . . ?" he said with raised eyebrows.

She couldn't tell him the truth about guarding her heart. She wasn't ready to make such an admission without knowing how he felt about her, so she answered in a small voice, "In case you tossed me out."

"Barrett," he said, taking her hands in his, "I am

not going to throw you out. I want you here together with me, forever."

"Forever? Here?" He did want her. His answer thrilled her but at the same time shocked all rules for proper negotiating tactics right out of her head. "Here? In Houston?" she repeated and spoke the first thoughts that made their way through her mind. "But what about tenure? My career?"

He smiled, a little quirk of his mustache. "What about it? I want you to have a career and tenure, if that's what you want. I'm not asking you to give up anything. On the contrary, I asking you to add something to your life—*me*."

What he was asking was wonderful, but . . . "Davis, how can we be together if I'm up there and you're down here? I can't be here and teach my classes or work on committees or do all I have to do to gain tenure."

"We'll work something out." He squeezed her hands, leaned in, and gave her a light kiss.

"It's easy to say, but difficult to bring off," she answered. One portion of her brain registered the golden glints in his hazel eyes while the other, larger part whirled around in her skull trying to analyze the ramifications of what he was saying. "I've thought about this, and a long-distance relationship is so difficult, so taxing, and we both work so hard . . ."

"You've thought about it already?" He grinned, a full-fledged "Ah ha!" upturn of mouth and mustache. His grandfather's roguish glint was back in his eyes too. "Then your answer's yes?"

"No! Yes! I don't know." She shut her eyes and took a deep breath. "Wait," she said on the exhale. She opened her eyes and looked at him. She spoke slowly, feeling her way through her earlier introspection. "Yes, I thought about it and you, but I couldn't come to a conclusion about how to make it all work."

She jiggled their clasped hands for emphasis. "You have to understand my situation. If I want to get anywhere in my profession, I need tenure and the title Associate Professor. Once those are granted to me, they give me a legitimacy, they're proof I'm a historian of substance, not someone hanging on to the fringes or incapable of doing the work. Without them, I may not be rehired the next year or be able to do a number of things connected with the History Department and the university. With them, if I change schools, I'll be able to bargain for a tenured place as a condition of my contract.

"But to get any of it, I need to be there, at my school, working with my department, with my college. I'm under a deadline for publications. I need to spend long hours writing, researching, and grading. Travel

will eat drastically into that time, and driving or flying back and forth every week is exhausting, no matter
who's doing it. Your work requires travel too. Our
schedules could keep us apart for a month or more.
When would we have time for us?"

"Trust me," he answered. "We'll work it out."

"You're not listening to me, Davis," she said. He
was so damn smug, as though they had nothing to
worry about. "Look, this time I'm the one who needs
details, information. I'm the one who needs a plan.
It's your turn to let me think the situation through."

He frowned, and the smug look slid off his face.
"All right," he said, "but no more of this separate bedroom shit."

"Fine." She'd go to his bed, but she didn't know if
she'd gotten through to him. They still had so much
to discuss about logistics and timing. When would
she find time to write? Did he really understand her?
At least he wasn't saying things like, "You don't need
a career when you've got me." But would he become
jealous of the demands on her time?

Before she could put any of her thoughts into
words, Gonzales appeared at the doorway. "Excuse
me," he said, "but Mrs. Cecilia Walker is on the phone,
and she sounds frantic."

Davis groaned. "She's probably looking for Lloyd.

Thank you, I'll take the call."

While he attempted to calm Lloyd's mother, Barrett went into her office and began to tidy up, moving Mary Maude's journals from where she'd been showing them to their visitors to a small side table. When she picked up the volume she knew was the final one, she didn't get a good grip and the back cover swung open. An envelope fell out.

She turned it over and read the names on it. *"Davis Jamison and Barrett Browning"* were clearly written in Edgar Jamison's hand.

Chapter
THIRTY-ONE

"Oh, my God." She spun around and rushed to Davis's office. He took one look at her waving the letter and said into the phone, "Lloyd and Grace are on their way back home, Aunt Cecilia. They'll explain everything. I have to go now. Good-bye." He hung up over her sputterings. "What's the matter? You're pale."

Barrett held up the envelope in front of him so he could read their names.

"Where did this come from?" he asked, rising as he took it from her. He walked around the desk.

"It fell out of the last journal."

"Granddaddy was playing tricks with us, the old rascal." He tore open the envelope, took out the contents and held the letter so they could read it together. It was dated a month before the old man's death.

Dear Barrett and Davis,
If you have found this letter, then you have discovered how Edgar Sr. died by Mary

Maude's hand. I read her journals in the
1960s, but wasn't sure what to do with
the information. At that time of social
upheaval, the ensuing scandal could have
affected the livelihoods of several members of the family, mostly because of
the self-righteous old biddies (both male
and female) who ran the parish. Note I
said livelihoods. You know I've never given
a good God-damn about what people have
merely said about us, but I wasn't going
to be the cause of difficulties costing
our relatives their jobs or businesses.

Times have changed. It's time to tell
the story.

It took me a long time to find you,
Barrett, a smart, able historian, one who
would care about the characters and
could do justice to them.

I wish to hell I could have been there
to see the look on your face, Barrett,
when you opened the trunk. And when you
read the journal. And when you told Davis
about his great-great-great grandparents.

I particularly wanted to be present when
you told the family, Davis. I know you

can handle them, but I planned on being the one to take the brunt of their anger.

I'm not there, but, Davis, you are.

Don't go all overprotective. The family is strong, you know that. Oh, Cecilia and Phyllis will give you some static, but they'll get over it. Don't let Cecilia make Lloyd crazy either. He's had enough to do, getting over those two parents of his. Thank the Good Lord for Grace.

Davis, make sure Barrett publishes our story. It's a doozy and will help her with her career.

Barrett, you use every bit of those papers you can in your history.

You both have my love.

Take care of each other.

　　　　　　With much love,
　　　　　　　　Edgar

P.S. If you don't, I'll come back to haunt you.

"Oh, Davis," Barrett said as she blinked to hold back her tears.

"Yeah," he said, sounding a little hoarse also. He cleared his throat before continuing. "Now we know what he wanted to do. And what he wanted you to do: Write the Windswept story."

"I do miss him. I wish he could have been here."

"Me too." He laughed. "It certainly would have saved us some wear and tear." He laid the letter on the desk and took her into his arms. "Speaking of wear and tear?"

She raised her eyebrows at him. "Yes?"

"Did you really think I'd go back on my word?"

She thought over the past day for a minute. "No, not really," she said. "Although you scared me badly. I was more upset because I thought you didn't trust me to do a good job."

"Why would you think that?"

"First, because when people ask for time 'to think things over,' it usually means they're looking for a way out. Second, because I didn't know how protective you would be about your family, or how much influence they had over you. I am an outsider, after all."

A funny look passed over his face for a second and a gleam came to his eye, but then he seemed to shift gear. "I know how you can make it up to me."

"Make up what to you?"

"Your lack of trust in me."

"Wait a minute. What about your lack of trust in me?"

"I never mistrusted you."

She knew she wasn't that far off, so she gave him one of her "teacher" looks.

"Not really," he said.

"Okay, how can I make it, whatever it is, up to you?"

"Let's go upstairs, and I'll show you." He waggled his eyebrows and rubbed against her.

She started laughing. He truly was such a rogue.

Then he leaned down and kissed her and she stopped laughing.

The next morning Barrett lay on her back and watched Davis's bedroom grow slowly lighter until she could make out a few colors and details. She'd lain awake for over an hour, trying to reconcile her ambition with her love for Davis. What was at stake here? His love for her and subsequent happiness versus success in her chosen field.

She'd been focused on her career for so long. She'd gone through undergraduate and graduate school in a blaze of work, had subordinated everything to get her Ph.D. as fast as she could. She hadn't dated, had barely taken time to come home to visit. Then she'd accepted the offer from Texas at Grand Prairie with the goals first of tenure and then of making a name for herself. She'd worked like a fiend for several years. True, she'd made the mistake of dating Wendell Truman, rising star in economics, but he'd turned out to be a dismal scientist indeed and jealous of her successes to boot.

Davis would not be dismal. Would he be jealous of her career? No, she really didn't think so; he seemed so proud to introduce her to his friends and clients at the party. He'd be protective, probably overly so, but, after her experience with her brothers, she knew how to handle him. Would he understand her need to do research and write, both basically solitary endeavors? Probably, because he'd seen her work habits since she arrived and he seldom interrupted her. In fact, he worked as hard as she did.

What was she so afraid of? Why couldn't she throw caution to the wind, stop worrying, and tell him yes, she wanted to be with him forever too? All her life she'd jumped to conclusions on very little evidence, or so her family told her, and now that she'd taught herself not to—well, almost—here she was dithering.

It had to come down to her feeling a loss of control. She had everything to do with her career all lined up in a nice little order, her life planned out, and here came Davis into it.

And she loved him. A rush of warmth ran through her as the thought, the reality of loving him settled into her brain and her body. She'd be a fool to push him away. No, worse than a fool, a complete idiot.

He'd said, "Trust me, we'll work it out."

She'd take him at his word and tell him yes when he woke up. Together they'd manage the distance and the time.

She grinned to herself as she turned over on her side away from Davis.

The sky was just turning pink with dawn when Davis woke up. He reached for Barrett and drew her into his body spoon fashion. His bottom arm was under her head and his top curved around so his hand could find her breast. The feel of her in his arms was so right, so complete. He knew she felt the same way.

All that business about their being separated had shaken him at first. Would she say no because of a few miles and a little time? He'd surprised her when he'd said forever, but that's exactly what he meant. He'd showed her last night how much he loved her.

The words of his sister came back to him. "I know this will be hard for you to comprehend," she'd said more than once, "but women cannot read men's minds. Tell me what you want, and we'll negotiate." Good advice, Martha.

He kissed Barrett's shoulder as he tweaked her nipple.

"Mmmmph!" was all she said, but she captured his hand and held it with both of hers. She snuggled closer.

"Barrett," he whispered.

"Mmmmph?" came the reply and another wiggle.

"I love you," he murmured in her ear, rising up just enough to see her profile.

"Good. Thank you. I love you too," she said in a sleep-laden voice, but she smiled.

He pulled himself back and propped up on an elbow, turned her over to face him. He slid his top leg between hers and put his hand on her breast. She opened her big blue eyes and gave him another smile.

"I need you to rescue me, from ex-wives, wastrel brothers, and crazy cousins," he said.

"I need you to rescue me from unscrupulous historians, overprotective brothers, and my tendency to jump to conclusions," she answered.

"I want you to be successful. I want you to be happy."

"I want the same for you."

"We'll be together. I'll open a Dallas office."

"I'll look for a position down here as soon as I can."

"I trust you with my family's secrets, I trust you

with my heart. Marry me, Barrett."

"I trust you with mine. Yes, I'll marry you."

"When?"

"Not right this minute." She stretched her leg up over his and snuggled closer. His erection fit perfectly between her thighs. She pulled him down into a hug and whispered into his ear, "Right this minute, I have something else in mind." She slid her dampening core along his thoroughly aroused sex.

The movement took his breath away. "What?" he managed to croak.

"Celebrating our engage—" was all she managed to get out before his lips found hers.

Epilogue

Three Years Later
Saturday, July 1

Barrett sat by the pool on a typically sweltering summer afternoon drinking iced tea and watching Davis swim laps. Watching her husband. Three years of marriage and she still was thrilled when she spoke or thought the words, "her husband." She reminded herself of Mary Maude in that regard, but she knew she would not come to the same ending.

It had been a momentous three years. They married as soon as her parents could return to Houston. After a short honeymoon, Barrett returned to the Windswept papers, but university classes began all too quickly. They spent the school year flying back and forth on the weekends, which worked out pretty well as she needed the records, especially the journals, for her articles.

In the fall, she presented a paper on Mary Maude,

her journal, and her life—including Edgar's demise—
at a history conference.

A firestorm of media inquiry and public interest en-
sued, with everyone from the National Organization for
Women to the National Association for the Advancement of Colored People putting in their two cents. She
and Davis tried to be careful about granting interviews,
but it was impossible to resist *60 Minutes*. Several pub-
lishers announced interest in her planned book, and she
quickly found an agent to handle the negotiations.

Somehow in all the hoopla, and as Grace predicted, Lloyd found himself much sought after in his
businesses and his law practice. Grace kept a firm hand
on him, however, and did not allow him to make any
public statements. The rest of the family kept a low
profile. Several African-American families claimed
descent from Edgar's children. Windswept itself became a favored destination for tourists, a reunion of
descendants of former slaves from it and neighboring
plantations took place on its grounds, and St. Gregoryville prospered as a result.

The second year of their marriage, Barrett wrote
Mary Maude's story and published it in the third to
good academic and popular reviews—and excellent
sales. Her university granted her tenure.

All the publicity, the book, and several articles

resulted in the offer of a tenured position from a university in Houston whose history department wanted to build a woman's studies program. Barrett accepted the offer, of course, and was ecstatic to be home with Davis again. The first thing she did after getting settled was redecorate the living and dining rooms and hang the seascape of the Texas coast, Davis's wedding present to her, in their bedroom.

Barrett quit her reflections to admire her husband as he climbed out of the pool. The man had a great body, and it was all hers. He dropped down on the lounger beside her.

"Have you given any more thought to those movie or TV miniseries offers?" he asked, reaching for a towel.

"No, I still think it's a Jamison decision as to whether they want their family name to become a household word, especially after the story is 'Hollywoodized.'"

"Okay, I'll call around and see what they think, but I have the feeling they'll go for it, especially after they hear our plans to establish a scholarship fund with the proceeds." He took a drink from her tea glass. "Did I mention, Bill called today?"

"No, you didn't. How's he doing?"

"I don't know what you told him that rainy day, but he must have listened, because the fundraising for his charity is going great guns, and he loves it. He seems to be quite good at it." He grinned in reminiscence.

"How much did you give him?" she asked.

"Nothing gets by you, does it?" He named a number. Then he looked at her closely. "Okay?"

"Fine." She gave him a hug. "We have something else to discuss." She tried to be serious, but she didn't quite make it.

"I know. What to name our firstborn." He grinned at her and kissed her quickly.

"Davis! How did you know? I didn't find out for sure until this morning."

"You forget I know your body too well not to have noticed changes over the past few weeks." He cupped her ever so slightly swollen breasts, then took her tenderly in his arms. "Oh, honey, you've given me a great gift. I love you so much."

"I love you too, Davis. . . . If it's a girl, what if we name her Mary Maude?"

Don't miss the next novel by Ann Macela:

YOUR MAGIC OR MINE?

A battle over the "correct" way to cast spells is brewing in the magic practitioner community. Theoretical mathematician Marcus Forscher has created an equation, a formula to bring the science of casting into the twenty-first century. Botanist Gloriana Morgan, however, maintains spell casting is an art, as individual as each caster, and warns against throwing out old casting methods and forcing use of the new. A series of heated debates across the country ensues.

Enter the soulmate phenomenon, an ancient compulsion that brings practitioners together and has persuasive techniques and powers—the soulmate imperative—to convince the selected couple they belong together. Marcus and Gloriana, prospective soulmates, want nothing to do with each other, however. To make matters worse, their factions have turned to violence. One adherent in particular, blaming Marcus and Gloriana for the mess, wants to destroy the soulmates.

Something's got to give, or there will be dire consequences. The magic will work for them . . . or against them. But with two powerful practitioners bent on having their own way, which will it be—Your Magic Or Mine?—and if they don't unite, will either survive?

ISBN#1933836326
ISBN#9781933836324
US $7.95 / CDN $9.95
Paranormal Romance
OCTOBER 2008
www.annmacela.com

ANN MACELA
THE OLDEST KIND OF MAGIC

Daria Morgan is a magic practitioner, one of a group of people who uses magic and spells to do their everyday jobs. Her job: A management consultant.

John "Bent" Benthausen is a CEO who, despite every improvement in product and production, can't get his bottom line out of the Red Sea. He needs a management consultant.

With her special gifts, Daria gets right to the heart of her employer's problem—crooked employees. Crooked, vicious, employees who are now out to get Daria. Those are just Problems One and Two.

Problem Three: There is an ancient force, an irresistible compulsion, called the soul-mate imperative. It's known throughout the practitioner ranks for bringing together magic-users and their mates in a lifelong bond. And it won't be happy until the participants surrender to the inevitable . . . the Oldest Kind of Magic . . .

ISBN#1932815430
ISBN#9781932815436
US $6.99 / CDN $9.99
Paranormal Romance
Available Now
www.annmacela.com

ANN MACELA

DO YOU BELIEVE IN MAGIC?

According to lore, an ancient force called the soulmate imperative brings together magic practitioners and their mates. They always nearly fall into each other's arms at first sight. Always . . . or so the story goes.

But what happens if they don't? What happens when one mate rejects the other—in fact won't have anything to do with him? Who doesn't even believe in magic to begin with?

Computer wizard Clay Morgan is in just such a position. Francie Stevens has been badly hurt by a charming and good looking man and has decided to avoid any further involvements. Although the hacker plaguing her company's system forces her into an investigation led by the handsome practitioner, she vows to keep her distance from Clay.

The imperative has other ideas, however, and so does Clay. He must convince Francie that magic exists and he can wield it. It's a prickly problem. Especially when Francie uses the imperative itself against him in ways neither it, nor Clay, ever anticipated.

ISBN#933836164
ISBN#9781933836164
US $7.95 / CDN $9.95
Paranormal Romance
Available Now
www.annmacela.com

Christine Carroll

Children of Dynasty

Eight years after her breakup with Rory Campbell, Mariah Grant, sole heir of her father's construction company, returns to San Francisco from self-imposed exile. Her father is ailing, the business is floundering and in danger of being devoured by an arch rival; Mariah's expertise is desperately needed.

Rory Campbell, also the sole heir to his father's construction giant, realizes that in spite of the intervening years, Mariah still heats his blood to boiling. Trouble is, their fathers—men once as close as brothers—are now, mysteriously, sworn enemies. Their businesses are battling, and fraternizing with the competition is considered consorting with the enemy.

Then there is a deadly, and suspicious, accident on a Grant skyscraper, killing Mariah's oldest friend. But was he the target? Will the elder Campbell stop at absolutely nothing to bring Grant down and keep his son from rekindling forbidden fires?

The war is on. Empires are at stake . . . lives hang in the balance . . . and the time has come for . . .

The Children of Dynasty

ISBN# 9781932815429
US $6.99 / CDN $9.99
Contemporary Romance
Available Now
www.readchristinecarroll.com

Christine Carroll

The Senator's Daughter

Sylvia Chatsworth, flamboyant daughter of a U.S. Senator, and Lyle Thomas, rising star in the San Francisco D.A.'s office, are the city's latest item. Until the tabloid news paints Sylvia as a party girl too naughty for Lyle, and her parents suggest they'd be happier if she disappeared. So she does just that.

For a hefty fee, the Senator sends Lyle off to find his daughter. When Lyle locates Sylvia in the Napa Valley and finds she's changed her image, he's intrigued enough to delay turning her in. Attraction growing, they hide out at a romantic Victorian Inn.

Lyle isn't idle, however. He's hot on the trail of some questionable real estate trades—schemes that connect a missing developer and his vintner brother, the D.A., and the Senator's "blind" trust. When a local spring in wine country turns up with mercury pollution, Lyle and Sylvia wonder how far someone would go to crash land prices and pull off a real estate coup. And is her father hip deep in Mafia activity?

With their growing love threatened by arson and attempted murder, there's also the question of trusting Lyle . . . when Sylvia discovers he's on her father's payroll . . .

ISBN# 9781933836300
US $7.95 / CDN $9.95
Contemporary Romance
Available Now
www.readchristinecarroll.com

THE SHADOW

SHELLEY MUNRO

Occupations often run in families, and mine is no exception. I'm Lady Katherine Fawkner, cat burglar in training. Under duress, I might add, but someone has to keep the family safe. Father's gambling has escalated into debts, and with that debt comes outrageous interest charges and goons threatening bodily harm if overdue money isn't paid. So, here I am, attending a society ball, researching the rich and their jewels for my first heist.

Wouldn't you know it? I'm looking for rubies and find a man instead. Not just any man, but a cop. A cat burglar and a cop? No future there. But I can't stop thinking about Inspector Kahu Williams.

To make matters worse, now there's been a murder. And if that's not bad enough, my past has returned to haunt me. I've stumbled across a photo of a child who is the mirror image of my precious daughter. In my hands I hold a clue to reveal the identity of my child's father — the man who drugged me six years ago. So I'm hot on the trail of my revenge for date rape while Inspector Williams searches for a killer. But we keep running into each other and . . . no, this is not going to work . . .

ISBN# 1932815503
ISBN# 9781932815504
US $6.99 / CDN $9.99
Contemporary Romance
Available Now
www.shelleymunro.com

HOT FLASH

KATHY CARMICHAEL

Calm, Cool and Premenopausal.

Single mom and chef, Jill Morgan Storm's frenzied life is about to become even more chaotic and filled with night sweats as she sets out on a scheme to find, and wed, a traveling salesman. In return she's hoping for for one week of marital bliss, three weeks off and a monthly paycheck.

Enter Davin Wesley, the opposite of the type of man Jill is searching for. He's an elementary school teacher who refuses to skedaddle out of town like a good little potential husband.

Jill isn't sure if she can keep up the protests because his kiss is pure fire and he won't be discouraged. With hot flash after hot flash, can she say no while her temperature rises and her libido screams *Yes?*

ISBN# 1934755036
ISBN# 9781934755037
US $7.95 / CDN $8.95
Mass Market Paperback
Contemporary Romance
FEBRUARY 2009

For more information
about other great titles from
Medallion Press, visit

www.medallionpress.com